SURRENDERING TO THE
SEA LORD

LORDS OF ATLANTIS

USA TODAY BESTSELLING AUTHOR

STARLA NIGHT

Cover by Earthly Charms

For inquiries:

Starla Night
starla@starlanight.com
https://starlanight.com

SPECIAL THANKS

TBR Publishing and Sophie Wallace Proofreading. Thanks so much!

————

And special thanks to my newsletter subscribers! They enjoy bonus stories plus a steamy prequel novella, *Sea Lord's Castaway*. It takes place twenty years before the entire series, so there are no spoilers. It's just fun!

Get it free at http://smarturl.it/StarlaNewsletter.

ONE

Milly balanced at the top of the dramatic beachside cliff and trained her antique spyglass on the lockbox a quarter mile away.

She'd gotten permission from the Azores equivalent of the Parks & Rec Department to install the silver box in the long sea grass above the red volcanic sand. It was the size and shape of a US mailbox.

And like a US mailbox, someone had been driving by and bashing it.

The first time, the cell phone inside had survived. The second time, vandals used a cherry bomb. A ragged chunk of wood post remained.

She had to stop it.

The mermen were counting on her.

Black flies and fuzzy honeybees buzzed across her bare shoulders in the overcast summer heat. Milly waved them toward the clumps of blue wildflowers cushioning her hiding spot.

She switched the heavy brass spyglass to her other eye.

Her elbows ached on the folded fleece jacket she used as a cushion. Her contacts stuck to her eyeballs; she'd had her eyes open too long. Her throat was scratchy and her tongue was a dry lump in her mouth.

How did detectives endure stakeouts? Cross that occupation off her "possible future" list.

Milly trained her spyglass on the lockbox again.

As she well knew, a couple thousand years ago humans and mer had lived in harmony. Atlantis had been the mer-human ancient metropolis. A great catastrophe had sunk Atlantis and driven the mer into hiding on the ocean bottom. Humans forgot they existed except in legends.

Two years ago, mermen were rediscovered.

Blame the GoPro.

Secretive, tattooed, heavily muscled mer warriors could shift between normal feet and scuba-like fins at will. Females had died out after the catastrophe and so they were now all male. They surfaced only to woo "sacred brides" on isolated islands sworn to secrecy. They carried their sacred brides to the bottom of the ocean, their brides produced a child — always male — and then the brides were returned to the surface to live out their lives as if the oceanic interlude had never happened.

A generation ago, the sacred islands had emptied. Modernized. Climate change had swept them away. Or the lure of TV, washing machines, and fast food had.

The mer population had crashed. They risked dying out.

Rebel warriors wanted to woo modern brides. Traditionalists enforced their ancient, secret covenant.

Then, the GoPro incident forced the issue.

Two years ago, a rebel mer warlord had pursued and

married a modern treasure hunter named Lucy. Their courtship — and the ensuing mer battles — were recorded on her cell phone and posted to Facebook.

The warlord was exiled. Traditionalists would kill him on sight.

But Lucy discovered oceanic super powers after transforming. Powers thought to belong only to the mer "queens" of legend. Together, she and her husband survived all assassination attempts and escaped to the new rebel city "Atlantis" reborn in the shadow of the old mecca. It was a beacon for mer who wished to flee their traditionalist rulers — and, someday, meet a modern woman bride.

Someday.

Few rebels made it to the surface. Traditionalists still ruled the oceans and enforced their covenant of secrecy.

Milly knew all this in great detail because her older sister, Zara, had been one of the last sacred brides. She'd lived in a mer city known as Dragao Azul in a deep trench below the Azores Islands. During the height of the controversy — and just before the mer were exposed to humans — Zara gave birth.

She and her husband, Elan, had sided with the rebels.

They lost.

Zara was forced to the surface. She nearly died. Her husband and child were held hostage within the city. All hope for being a family faded.

A year later, rebellion engulfed Dragao Azul and the ruling All-Council laid siege. Zara learned about her queen powers. She braved her old captors to rescue her husband and child. While doing so, she drove off the army and saved the city.

The new rulers had begged her to stay.

Now she was their queen.

Talk about a dream job!

Zara didn't see it that way. She was less interested in ruling and more interested in seeking other "lost brides," women like her torn from their mer families and forced to the surface. Her mission was to bring justice — reunions or restitution — to these women.

But the lost brides weren't coming forward, so Zara was going to them. Seeking them out, taking statements, offering counseling. Right now she was in California.

Her absence left the city vulnerable to more All-Council attacks.

So, when the emergency came, a warrior would surface and call Zara. She would fly back to the Azores, dive beneath the waves, and once more save them.

Milly had to protect the emergency cell phone in that lockbox.

She trailed her spyglass across the few visitors on this isolated beach.

Elderly historians argued over the jagged cliffs of the former caldera. A family of young naturalists collected red volcanic rocks, seashells, and drift wood in buckets. Tourists moseyed away from the parking lot and down the beach.

All showed no interest in her lockbox.

Good.

Milly had rigged a trap.

Any vandal who dared to plant another bomb right now would get a major surprise.

The only problem would be if a warrior surfaced instead.

But that wasn't likely. After Zara had broken the siege and dispersed the All-Council army, large-scale violence

The merman didn't stop.

She shut her car door. "Don't step on the grass!"

His head whipped to her direction.

In person, his skin appeared a dark olive tinted with actual green. The tattoos she'd identified were a shimmery, iridescent purple. Strange and beautiful.

How did they create their incredible colors and intricate designs? No one knew.

Between the long, wet tendrils of black hair, his mesmerizing green eyes pierced hers.

She stumbled on the even parking lot cement.

He jerked his gaze away and waded into the long sea grass.

She ran. Her tennis shoes crunched the volcanic gravel. "Watch your step! We set a—!"

BWWWWAAAAAAAAAA.

Her air horn deafened the beach.

She slammed her hands over her ears.

The warrior stumbled back. His toes lifted off her artfully-concealed, grass-covered pressure plate. The air horn stopped.

Her ears rang.

She dropped her hands. Silence stuffed her ears like cotton.

Everyone on the beach stared.

So much for secrecy.

The merman was stunned.

"I'm sorry!" She hurried to him. "Sorry. I can explain."

The warrior pressed his fists to his chest.

Had she given him a heart attack?

He staggered. The lockbox key dropped from his lax fingers.

She ran. "Hey! Are you okay?"

He fell to one knee.

"Hey!"

The warrior collapsed.

Had she just killed the merman she was supposed to protect?

TWO

Uvim floated on a black sea of pain.

Something stroked his forehead. Long and cool. Tender seaweed? Kindness. Her soft touch soothed and comforted. Healed.

The pain receded.

A sweet voice was speaking. What? Unusual tones.

"...and I'm so, so sorry. I wanted to stop the vandals by myself. Please don't be dead."

The blackness faded.

His body floated...

A concerned face hovered over his. Light obscured her features, shining from behind her, blinding.

...and then he whumped onto the gritty rock. He shuddered. Everything ached. But he lived.

Her hand stilled. "Are you okay?"

The light eased and he saw her.

Dark tendrils of flowing hair. Narrow pink lips, a slender nose, an oval face, and brown eyes shimmering with tender concern.

A clear, bright light glowed in her chest. *Resonance*. She had a strong soul.

Her fingertips stroked his cheek.

His skin tingled.

She smiled. "Hi."

Warmth glowed in his chest.

"You're alive. Thank goodness."

Words. Familiar words. His least-proficient human language. English.

English?

His stomach dropped.

He was exposed. To humans!

Uvim grunted and tried to rise. *Escape*.

The horizon rotated. A giant fist pressed his chest to the ground.

"Whoah." The human female hovered. "Take it easy. You had a shock."

Someone called out to the female.

"He's fine!" She turned and waved at someone over her shoulder. "Just surprised. Huh? Oh, no, he's a tourist."

Panic squeezed his chest.

"Exotic tattoos," a voice said.

"You can get ink done in Horta. Just off the main street."

"Ooh, so cool," another voice chimed in.

More humans! Approaching!

"Yep. Okay, have a great night." His female's voice lowered to a gentle murmur. "Don't worry. I'll hold back the crowds."

Crowds!

He opened his mouth. No sound emerged. Only a hiss.

"Don't speak. Er, unless you want to."

He had to escape.

Uvim tightened his abdomen and rolled upright.

The horizon tilted. Sky plunged into surf. He reeled.

"Oh! Sitting up." She slid her slim arm around his back, steadying him. "Next time, warn me."

But he couldn't.

He mustn't touch. He mustn't speak. He mustn't be here.

Uvim had to return to the ocean. Crawl or slither. Now. Before another moment passed and another human saw him.

She tightened her arm. "Relax."

No. He mustn't. He—

Her touch disabled him like a potent toxin. He had no choice but to obey.

He sagged.

She stroked his shoulder with her long fingers. "Good."

Her soft breasts pressed his shoulder. The twin points of her nipples hardened into small pearls. Hardness and softness tantalized his over-worked senses.

Heat flooded his cock.

Strange.

"I'm so sorry." She lowered her healing fingers to rub his flexed shoulder blades. Her hands splayed across his bone in a soothing, enticing pattern. "I set the trap this afternoon. You must be extra sensitive to noise."

Yes. Noise.

Earlier today he had hidden his trident and daggers in a shallow sea cave, camouflaged himself with an orange waist-thigh covering the humans called "swim shorts," and watched the beach empty.

Then, he'd emerged.

He'd crossed to dry rocks and nearly reached the lockbox when this female had called out to him. His foot had depressed a flat plate. A loud pain had blared in his ears.

Then, a whale had crushed his chest. Colors had faded and the sky had plunged into the sea.

He rubbed his chest with a flat palm.

Humans had developed terrifying weapons. No wonder the tyrannical All-Council ordered the mer away from the surface.

"I was trying to protect the lockbox." His human lowered her eyes. "You must be so mad."

He was not angry.

"I'll make it up to you. Will you let me?"

Uvim opened his mouth. No words rolled across his leaden tongue.

He must reach her. He must communicate.

Uvim shook his head.

Her soul light darkened. "You won't let me?"

No! That was not what he meant. He shook his head harder.

"Oh, you mean, you're not mad?"

He nodded.

Her soul light brightened. "Thank you. That's generous. You're nice."

Nice?

Heat pooled in his chest and in his strangely hard cock.

She sighed. Her soul light dimmed again. "I feel like an idiot."

Curse his silence!

Uvim forced the foreign English words. "You ... are ... kind."

There. He had done it! He had spoken to a female. In her own language. With his tongue.

"Sitting with you is the least I can do." She lifted her

head. "The Sea Festival starts next week. I wanted to stop the vandals before someone got hurt. Oh, the irony! If Vaw Vaw's sons had set the trap, it would've worked."

Vaw Vaw. An affectionate name for a grandmother in Portuguese.

But this female predominantly spoke English.

He rehearsed his sentences.

"Your bravery ... is honorable. Your trap ... is effective."

"Effective. Yeah." Her soul light brightened.

He had comforted her.

Success!

"I'll pick up the trap before anyone else gets hurt." She released him and jumped to her feet.

Cold unease seeped into his skin.

Without her distracting touch, his reasons for surfacing slammed into him: His city was under attack.

He rocked to his knees.

The horizon rotated.

"Oh! You stay here." She eased him onto his knees. "You're trying to call Zara, right? I'll get the cell phone."

See? Kindness.

He closed his eyes. A headache pressed on the back of his skull.

Around him, Milly — for if she was protecting the lockbox, she must be Queen Zara's sister Milly — waded into the long grass. She unearthed heavy-looking planks and dragged them away. She scooped up the lockbox key from where he'd dropped it and returned with the cell phone.

The "cell phone" was a smooth silver rectangle. It was heavier and smaller than the carved stone he'd practiced with in the city.

He pressed the side button. A "screen" flickered. Once it steadied, he traced the "triangle" pattern.

Nothing happened.

"Oh, did I set up the replacement wrong?" She leaned over his shoulder and drew a square. The cell phone flashed the expected colors. "I didn't know how Zara set up the first cell phone."

He pressed the pattern to contact Queen Zara. The cell phone emitted a strident ring.

Milly knelt facing him.

Zara's voice emerged. "I'm not answering the phone right now so please leave a message."

Silence.

He stated the message his elders had composed. "A Newas hunting party camps at the edge of our territory."

Perfect. Every syllable enunciated. He had practiced endlessly on his long journey to the surface.

He waited.

Milly whispered, "Why does Zara care?"

Why? Because it was an invasion.

Milly frowned. "How big is this hunting party?"

He splayed his hand. Five.

She wrinkled her brows. "Five warriors are a threat to your city?"

He nodded.

"Okay... Well, hang up. Zara will call you back. Oh, you know what? Tell her to call me back," Milly said. "Go ahead. Say, 'call your sister.'"

"C-call your sister," he repeated, stumbling over the unpracticed words.

She leaned over and swished the screen. The light turned to black. Then she took the cell phone and fixed the operations to match his training.

"Zara will call back soon. It's morning in California."

Milly locked away the cell phone and brought him the key. "She must be driving or interviewing someone."

His fingers closed around the toothed metal.

Delay cost lives. His warriors needed the answer now. The defense of the city rested on his shoulders. He must give his elders an answer.

Milly chewed her lip. "Is a little hunting party *really* an emergency?"

He nodded.

"I don't get it."

He measured his words. "Raiders..."

"Raiders? I thought you said it was a hunting party."

The foreign warriors appeared to be hunting. But they might scout for an All-Council army or be terrorists intent on maiming lone patrols.

He shrugged.

"So why don't you force these potential raiders out?"

A hunting party must be treated with respect. The laws of honor required it.

She sighed. "I guess assigning a patrol to them is not an option. You have a vast territory and a shrinking population."

Milly understood. If even this human understood, then Queen Zara would rule wisely.

He willed Queen Zara to call now.

"So ... I thought your king normally decides stuff like this. Why ask Zara?"

Because Queen Zara had said the king could no longer rule unopposed. Elders and warriors must agree with his ruling. She called it a special name. What was it?

He remembered. "Democracy."

"In a democracy, everybody votes."

Yes. Everybody had "voted." But they could not agree.

And since their king was no longer allowed to issue the final decree, Queen Zara must do so.

Milly blew air, pushing her lower lip so short tendrils of dark hair at her crown danced. "Well, Zara's going to *love* that."

Would she? Good. Queen Zara clung to much anger. And she had a strong reason to hate Uvim.

If she loved this question, her feelings would soften. She might forgive the elders — and forgive him.

"Mermen don't get sarcasm." Milly's lips pulled to one side. "Sorry. I was kidding. She's going to be pissed."

Pissed?

"Angry."

His stomach dropped. *Another* reason for her anger. Did she not have enough reasons already?

A family of humans carried sand buckets past. They gawked.

Queen Zara had also ordered the mer to avoid humans.

Uvim rose to his knees.

The horizon rotated.

He bent over, braced, and pushed up.

The world whirled.

He fought nausea and staggered to his feet.

"Hey!" Milly wrapped her arms around his torso and braced him upright. "I said to give me some warning."

Sweat broke out on his chilled body. "The ocean..."

"Hold on to me."

Milly was a small woman. Her soft breasts cushioned his hard torso. One curvy thigh braced his damp waist. Her dark hair slid across his fingers like ribbons of sea-silk.

Uvim sucked in a breath and tried to straighten.

She squeezed him. "I've got you."

Her voice teased his ear and her soft breath tickled his lobe.

His cock strained.

Why? Her chest glowed. Brighter than sunlight, brighter than stars, and brighter than any soul on this beach. Why did her light affect him so?

Knowledge teased his unsettled mind, probing for a way in.

But he could not think. He leaned too heavily on her small frame.

"I will ... crush ... you..."

"Nah. I've been power-lifting Snuba gear all summer." Her fingertips traced his hard vertebrae. The tender strokes deeply comforted. "Anyway, I'm lucky you don't want me fired."

"Fired?"

"Relieved of duties. Voted off the island. Exiled to a dreary fate."

Exile?

His throat tightened.

Even in this injured state, he would fight to the death to protect a bright-souled female like her — a bride — from exile.

"Never a bride," he vowed.

Never again.

"That's a relief. But I'm not anyone's bride."

Of course she was. A soul this bright belonged in the sea.

Milly pulled back. "Did you hit your head?" She stroked his forehead. "Let's go to my place and rest."

Desire warred with duty. Her warm soul light bathed him with soothing radiance.

He resisted. "Humans cannot see..."

"You've already revealed yourself to me." She eased a step forward. Her soft hip grazed his hard cock. "Nobody's at my house. I promise."

"I must ... report."

"Report what? That you left a message? You can barely stand. How can you swim?"

"My duty…"

"I'd feel terrible if you got hurt worse."

"I must not…"

"Right? So rest."

She eased him toward a slab of smooth, black stone covered in rows of metal-glass boxes. She angled him to the maroon metal-glass box she had called out to him from. The heavy plates were stacked beside its thick wheels.

"If you're not better by the time Zara calls, I'll grab my scuba gear and try to help."

This small human was offering to help him go to the echo point? Underwater?

The echo point was far. Surrounded by predators. Deep.

He shook his head violently.

She laughed. "I said I'd *try*. Not that I'd actually do you any good."

"Too dangerous."

"Oh yeah? If it's too dangerous for me at full health, it's definitely too dangerous for you now."

Curse it. His duty…

"Don't stress out. Zara will call tonight. Rest at my place until you've got something to report."

He set his feet, resisting her movement. "Here."

"You can't rest here. See that sign? No camping."

He shook his head.

"Vandals are trying to blow up the lockbox."

Then he would remain to protect it.

She eyed him sideways. "You'd rather stay here and expose yourself to the *human* vandals? In this state? All alone?"

"You…"

"I 'faced them' from that cliff." She pointed at a distant, grassy headland. "With a spyglass. And a half-baked idea about reporting their license plate to the *policía*."

Human justice.

Hmm. He did not wish to interfere with human patrols.

They staggered to the slab and he collapsed against the sun-warm maroon metal. She stowed the heavy plates in the rear and fitted a toothed key into its body.

Going to Milly's private castle was improper. Wrong. Only partly because he wanted it so much.

"Your husband…"

"Huh? I told you I'm not married."

"Future."

"Future husband?" She cocked an amused brow. "Let me tell you. My future husband, whoever he is, will understand. I got you into this mess. I'm going to get you out."

"Milly—"

"And if you won't come to my cozy, safe house, I'll stay here. Then I risk getting in trouble with vandals or the law or both *and* I spend an uncomfortable night on the beach with rocks jabbing into my back."

He shook his head. She must not remain here.

"I have to." She smiled with an edge. "You're my responsibility now."

He ground his teeth.

She swung the door open and took his elbow to help him enter.

He stopped her.

"In the past ... they cut off..." He wiggled the fingers of his hand. "For touching ... another male's bride."

"Well, that was the past." She wedged her shoulder under his arm again. "Zara doesn't remove body parts."

Fine.

He had violated her future husband's rights many times on this beach. Leaned his full body against Milly. Savored her curves.

And he wished to caress the swell of her breasts beneath her lavender covering. Touch her more.

Strange.

What was the meaning?

He pined over this attractive female and her bright soul light.

But his fascination was impossible.

It was not his turn to pursue a bride.

THREE

Milly folded the weakened warrior into her passenger seat.

He dwarfed the space. His broad shoulders and powerful thighs sucked out the oxygen. Intricate amethyst tattoos crinkled across his tantalizing dark olive skin.

She stretched across his lithe, muscular torso to fasten the seatbelt.

It took all her will not to slide her sensitive palm across his unyielding pectorals.

An addictive scent of musk, tempered by earthiness and sea salt, teased her nostrils.

How would he taste under her tongue?

Delicious heat filled her belly.

Danger.

Milly breathed through her mouth to cut off the scent. She clicked the belt and pulled back.

His intense sea-green eyes followed hers. Threads of amethyst hid within the sea-green like flecks of gemstones buried within secret depths.

His face rotated, decisive jaw inches from her parted lips.

Temptation.

Her pussy throbbed.

She avoided his gaze, closed his door, and stepped away. Milly sucked in a deep breath, flushing the addictive scent from her mouth. She turned to the rugged volcanic beach, heavy sea grass, and crashing waves.

This warrior did *not* affect Milly.

Threatening clouds tightened around the island. She tasted the low buzz of rain.

Still breathing through her mouth, she got in on the driver's side, started the engine, and drove onto the island highway.

Her heart pounded.

She was strangely excited about driving this merman to her house.

Calm down.

He wasn't the first merman at her house. He wasn't even the first merman in her car. Her sister's husband, Elan, held that honor.

She obeyed all traffic laws while curving around small Faial Island.

Across the cloud-shrouded strait, Pico's dramatic cone-shaped caldera silhouette darkened the sky. The archipelago, of which only nine islands were occupied, was filled with tiny fishing villages and vineyards. Four hours' flight from Boston and two hours from Lisbon, the aban-doned island group had been settled by Europeans in the 1400s. Today it belonged to the Portuguese.

Atlantic sea birds trilled to escape the swelling winds. This far north and outside of the Gulf Stream, temperatures rarely exceeded the 80s in summer and never froze in winter. But that mildness came with a price.

In the Azores, the weather changed in a heartbeat.

The late July pressure meant a storm, if it was coming, would whip the ocean into a tourist-excursion-wrecking frenzy.

"Oh, I'm Milly," she said, realizing they'd never exchanged names. "I'm Zara's sister."

He nodded and gazed out the window.

Not the most talkative.

She slowed for a stop sign. "What's your name?"

"Uvim."

"Oooo-vim."

He chuckled.

She tried his name with different inflections, but that only made him laugh harder.

She would never be a translator. Or an interpreter.

Above Faial's main city, medieval Horta, she turned inland. Blue hydrangeas muffled the road as they drove deeper into the rugged, sparsely populated, dense green volcanic terrain.

"I appreciate you coming to my house."

"Because." He gestured in the direction of the beach. *She would have remained with him in the open.*

"Right. So I appreciate your flexibility. You don't speak much, do you?"

He frowned.

He did not speak much, but when he did, his voice was quiet yet compelling. The kind to murmur hot promises into her ear and then bite the lobe.

She shivered.

Even his accent was calm.

Calm. Controlled.

Seductive.

"It's okay," she continued. "Better to stay quiet than to chat people up with lies."

His frown deepened.

"Really." She lifted her hand off the steering wheel to...

Wait.

What was she doing? Had she intended to reach over and rub his olive-amethyst knee? To reassure him ... and enjoy his solid muscle?

Luxuriate in his power. Trace the intricate tattoos. Feel the heart-thumping desire once more filling her core with liquid heat.

Um, no.

She returned her hand to the steering wheel.

He stared at her chest. Grass blades stuck to her loose lavender T-shirt. She brushed them away.

His gaze focused.

Her breasts tingled.

Calm down.

He wasn't savoring her curves. He was doing the merman thing: Invading her privacy and sensing emotions she didn't wish to share.

She called him on it. "Is my 'soul light' interesting?"

His gaze flicked to her face and then away. Out the window. "Humans fluctuate too much."

"We lack biofeedback."

He looked her direction again. *Biofeedback?*

"It means we'd have better control if we could see our own lights."

He grunted.

Milly turned in to her driveway.

Her house was a comfy two-story, two-bedroom in white adobo and a red terracotta roof nestled into the lush side hill. Very Azores. She'd gotten it after selling Zara's Sea Opal engagement gift. The precious gemstone — with rare healing properties — had paid for her tuition, car, house, and this transitional period after university where she decided what to do with her life.

As queen, Zara possessed an entire Life Tree full of rare Sea Opals now. She didn't need the first Sea Opal or its bitter memories from her year as a sacred bride.

A red Volvo parked in Milly's spot.

Her stomach dipped.

Milly parked next to the Volvo and tapped her hands on the steering wheel.

No one was supposed to be here.

Uvim leaned forward. "Problem?"

Brody sauntered out of her fenced patio and closed the gate behind him.

Anger surged. *Trespass.*

Milly shut off the engine with a vicious jerk. "Stay in the car." She exited and closed the door.

Brody was her coworker at the dive shop. He'd been her classmate at the university. And once, she'd almost let him kiss her.

Almost.

"Hi, Milly." His blond dreadlocks bounced on his lanky, tanned shoulders.

"What are you doing here?"

His smile arrested. "I wanted to check on you."

She folded her arms.

"How did your stakeout go?"

"Fine."

"The pressure plates worked?"

"Yes."

"Ty assured me they would."

She pivoted to her trunk. "You want them back?"

"You caught the vandals?"

"No."

"Later is fine."

He lingered by the front door, friendly blankness on his easy-going face like he was waiting to be invited in.

Milly jerked her chin at her patio. "Were you waiting long?"

"Half an hour. I figured you'd be home soon."

"My cell phone accepts texts."

"I didn't want to disturb your 'operation.'"

"So you disturbed my home."

He twitched. "Why are you so touchy about visitors? You're normal at work. But nobody's ever been to your house. You never let anyone in."

"It's complicated."

He stepped closer.

She stepped back. "Sorry to bother you."

He stopped. "I want to help you, Milly."

"I don't need help."

Wind shivered through the green foliage above her house. A low rumble of thunder echoed across the hillside.

The passenger door opened. Uvim stepped out of the car, his bare feet flat and human on the sparse dirt. He gripped the door.

Uvim had sensed her emotional distress. Despite his fear of exposure, he revealed himself to help.

Her chest warmed.

She rubbed her chest. No tender feelings for the attractive male. He was far too dangerous.

Brody gaped. "What's that?"

"He's my guest," she said, drawing the line in her heart.

"Is he safe?" Brody echoed her own thoughts.

Anger surged again.

No one got in her head. Not again.

Milly struggled to keep her tone light. "Go home, Brody."

"And leave you?"

"I can take care of myself."

Uvim eased around the car door, closed it, and lurched.

Brody dropped into a defensive pose. "Stay back."

She hurried to Uvim's side. "I thought you were staying in the car."

Uvim grimaced. "That male ... he dims your light."

Brody raised his voice. "Milly, what are you doing?"

"*Go home*, Brody." She wedged her shoulder under Uvim's thick bicep. Together, they staggered to her door. His intimidating muscle snuggled her like a security blanket crossed with a loyal pit bull.

Brody backed away. "Don't let *this guy* in."

"Don't you come to my house."

"Are you kidding? Jeez. Sorry." Brody edged around them and scuttled, hurt, to his car. "I'll see you at work. Maybe."

"Bye."

Brody's Volvo backed out of her driveway. He drove off. Infuriating.

She braced Uvim against the white adobo, fitted her key in the deadbolt, and let them into the kitchen. Milly eased the hulking warrior into one of her kitchen chairs.

It creaked but held his weight.

She strode through the house, opening windows and airing rooms, then returned to the kitchen and inspected the contents of her avocado green refrigerator. Not all her appliances dated from the seventies but most shared the color scheme.

It gave her a much-needed chance to breathe.

Calm.

"Are leftovers okay?" She pulled out the Tupperware of pecan-dijon halibut and rosemary potatoes, divided the portions in two, and heated hers in the microwave. Milly set the chilled plate in front of Uvim. "Elan eats everything cold."

Uvim dipped his head in thanks. "You will not hunger?"

"Hunger? Oh. No." She handed him a fork and poured half a cup of chilled café au lait. "I keep making too much."

The microwave beeped.

She carried her steaming plate to the small kitchen table, just large enough to fit both their plates and coffees, and sat in the other chair.

Milly clinked his cup. "Cheers."

He sipped the coffee, rolled it across his tongue, and drank the rest in one gulp.

Approval.

Maybe her warrior didn't talk much, but she knew what he meant to say.

Er, *her* warrior?

She lit into her food. Crisp, creamy potatoes and thick savory fish steak with a delightful crunch.

He watched her eat. Then, he stabbed his fish and conveyed a too-large forkful to his mouth with trembling care. Her sister's toddler had more confidence with his dinner playset. Had Uvim never used a fork before?

Maybe not.

Elan had used a fork. Zara had made him practice when she'd told him about her modern life.

Uvim ate silently.

Her brother-in-law had also been quiet. He'd kept Milly at a polite, welcome, distance.

Uvim was different. Injured but not soul-sick. Controlled but not on the brink of losing his mind.

Calm.

That's what Uvim was. *Calm.* His presence stilled her swirling thoughts.

And his hard body evoked forbidden desires.

She focused on her food.

He finished his meal and rested the fork on the side of his plate, mirroring her.

"Done? I'll show you where to sleep." She rose.

"I ... patrol." He made a fist. "Defend against ... your enemies."

How honorable. But Uvim would not defend her against a cockroach right now.

She sat. "Brody's appearance tonight was a misunderstanding."

He lifted a brow. *Disbelief.*

"We almost dated."

His questioning expression remained.

"Tried to start a relationship."

Surprise and then a dark shadow crossed his face.

"It didn't work out," she assured him.

Wait. Why did she have to assure Uvim?

Her chest burned hot and cold, which meant her soul light was probably setting off fireworks.

Uvim struggled for words. "You ... did not ... touch."

"Stop looking." She covered her traitorous chest. But Uvim was right. It was hard to date a guy if she couldn't bring herself to touch him. "How did you know?"

"You are ... not ... his bride."

Mermen and their brides. She dropped her hands. "I may be no one's bride."

"You *are* a bride."

She smiled. It was easier than arguing.

"You ... allow no males ... near your home."

"I allow no one near my home. Male, female. Nobody."

But you brought me.

He didn't say it aloud. She heard the statement in her mind.

Uvim was special.

So was this house.

"I love my house. It's *mine,*" she defended herself. "No one can make stupid rules or threaten to kick me out. I can live my life as I like. And it's where I retreat when I get overwhelmed."

Overwhelmed?

"With life. It's tough after you graduate. I have a degree and I'm still trying to find my place."

"Your place ... is the sea."

"I wish."

His brows lifted.

She held up her palms. "But not enough to pay your price."

His frown returned. He didn't like her calling the mer marriage ceremony a transaction. Even though it was.

Here's how it worked:

A bride accepted a merman's offering – aka, Sea Opal – and he "claimed" her with his kiss.

She drank the nectar from a blossom of his city's Life Tree. If her soul truly resonated with his, then she transformed into a mermaid.

Transforming took stages. First, she saw and heard and breathed underwater – passive traits. Second, she could speak and shift her feet into fins. Third, and only if she truly embraced her new identity, she could wield their mystical soul-connecting resonance into a super power.

The super powers only worked underwater. But they were still pretty amazing.

Zara and the first bride, Lucy, could project a shield. Another bride, Aya, could push others away. Aya's cousin Elyssa could lay her hands on any mer and heal.

Milly wanted to join their ranks. She wanted to heal or shield or push. Save cities? Sign her up.

But there was the hitch.

Despite her dreamy fantasies, she'd never kiss Uvim.

Kisses led to more kisses. Nakedness. Yielding control while desire swept her away.

She liked her feet under her, thank you very much.

"I can't have a normal life," she finished. "I'm going to be an awesome aunt to baby Zain. I've got no interest in getting close to a guy or making my own children. None. Zero. Zip."

She was *not* imagining how Uvim would taste. If his mouth was as addictive as his scent. Or tracing the crinkly amethyst tattoos under Uvim's orange waistband — with her tongue.

His smooth, curved olive skin. The weight and shape of his male member. Hard or soft? How it would plunge into her throbbing feminine—

"None," she said firmly.

His gaze dropped to her chest. He sensed her truths and her lies.

She splayed her fingers across her breastbone. "If you weren't a merman, your attention to my breasts would be flattering."

He lifted his gaze as if to ask, *I am not flattering?*

"I don't share my feelings with strangers."

"I am Uvim." *Not a stranger.*

And he thought she had shared many feelings.

"Mostly anger." Milly picked up her empty coffee cup. "And my commitment to lifelong celibacy."

"Your husband ... will change you."

"I don't think so."

He looked smug.

"I hate to blow your mind, but I'm probably the only college graduate in this archipelago who didn't hook up with at least three, four other coeds."

He frowned. *Hook up? Hit on?*

"'Hook up' means sex."

Uvim flinched.

"Sorry. I know mermen only get one shot at finding their brides."

He blinked suddenly as though smacked by an unwelcome realization. His forehead creased with unhappiness.

"What?" she asked.

"A warrior cannot..."

"Hook up," she supplied.

"...embrace any female."

"You said that. He could get his hand cut off just for touching."

He shook his head. "Only his bride makes him react."

"React?"

He gestured to his damp swim shorts.

The bulging crotch.

His bulging ...

Oh.

Ohhhh.

She'd seen a few multi-colored merman cocks in her day. Loud and proud, they'd swung loose. Relaxed. Because she wasn't their bride?

Huh.

"You only get hard for one woman? Ever?"

He nodded.

She leaned back in her chair. "If humans were the same, it would solve a ton of problems."

"You are a bride."

That again.

"I'd love to be a mermaid. I'm not going to lie." She popped out of her chair and carried their dishes to the sink. "Live underwater. Develop mystical super powers. No one would ever trap me again."

"Trap?"

She scrubbed the dishes. "Just as an example."

"Milly."

She shivered and increased the water, loud, to drown out her own heartbeat. "Uh huh?"

Silence.

She shut off the water and turned.

He'd slid out of his seat and knelt in front of her.

Her stomach flip-flopped.

This male attracted her. Bad. She would melt in his arms.

He stared up at her as though he could read the secrets in her heart. In her soul.

She should have knocked out a less tempting warrior.

But that was okay. She'd be rid of him by morning. As soon as he came to his senses, she'd—

"Milly." He took her hand. Enveloped her in warmth. "You are my bride."

Uvim observed Milly.

His pronouncement — *You are my bride* — led to nothing. No reaction.

Then, heat bloomed in her chest.

Bold. Fierce. Brilliant.

She accepted his claim.

Relief filled his heart.

He rose.

Her gaze followed. Clear brown eyes flecked with gold and copper. She reflected awe and hope. "Me?"

"Save our race."

Her soul light burned even brighter. The light wrapped around his heart and drew him in.

He leaned down.

Her lips parted.

He tilted to seal their promise with his kiss.

She blinked and jerked back. Her soul light flared, darkened, flared. "I — no, I can't."

Milly couldn't become his bride?

Uvim's stomach dipped.

"I mean!" Her voice rose with panic. She ripped her hand free and backed against the ledge. "I told you. I can't touch or kiss."

Yes, but the compulsion to kiss her had come from *her* soul.

He wished to seal their promise. Unite their lips and join their bodies. *Her* soul had reached out and *his* had responded.

Now she repelled him. Her arms crossed. Panic shrilled her voice.

Yet her soul pulsed with hunger. Desire. Need.

Confusing.

And bitter. The pain of her rejection was sharp as a poisoned blade stabbing into his unguarded side.

His balance wavered. He rested a palm on the ledge beside her elbow. "You do not desire me ... for your husband."

Her soul flared.

She desired him.

His tension eased.

Hers increased. She tightened her arms, denying the hot pulse of longing even now reaching out to him. "I can't desire. Sorry."

The pain stabbed deeper.

How could she say one thing while her soul denied her words?

A new realization eased the bitter tang poisoning his heart.

Perhaps she could not feel her soul's wish. Perhaps she was ill or injured. Perhaps she could not sense her hunger.

Then, the transformation elixir would heal her. It healed all wounds. It would heal hers.

He knelt once more. Careful not to touch her. Holding the formal position of supplication. "Become mine."

The tangle of needs tore at her inner light. "I'll never touch you. Never kiss. I won't bear your son."

He understood her conditions.

Her brows wrinkled. "Why doesn't that push you away?"

"You are my bride."

Her expression cleared. She looked down at his hard cock straining the orange fabric. "You react."

He could not lie to his bride. "Only you."

Her soul flared. She liked thinking about his hard cock. Her soul wished to use it to bring herself pleasure. Her lips parted, exposing a delicate, pink tongue.

His cock pulsed.

She jerked her gaze away. "Uh ... well, I'm the first woman you've ever seen, right?"

He shook his head.

"So maybe you'd 'react' to other women too. You don't know." Then, she blinked. "Wait. You have seen other women?"

He nodded.

"When?"

He had seen Queen Zara before she became a queen. He'd seen females today on the beach. And he had seen females on the road, and inside other metallic boxes, while they traversed the island.

His connection to Milly had snapped into effect.

He hadn't understood his body's reaction. Her comments just now had forced him to face the truth.

It was a problem. He was not allowed to claim a bride.

But Milly *was* his bride. He could no more turn away from her than he could turn aside the incoming tide.

"You are my bride," he repeated.

"But I can't be." She rubbed her glowing chest with one palm like she wanted to contain the light or hide it away from him. "You need a woman who will treasure you. Or, at least, your body."

He shook his head.

A new fear flashed across her face. "You can't accept me like this."

He accepted her.

"You can't. I will never give you, uh, satisfaction."

He understood.

Panic raised her voice again. "You don't understand."

"Milly."

She caught her breath. Her hands clasped in the echo of an ancient prayer. "Don't say it. You *don't* understand."

He had said nothing aloud. She understood his intention with no words passing between them.

They connected.

And her fear for him was evidence of her kindness. Perhaps the Life Tree elixir would not cure her illness. Perhaps she would never heal. Perhaps she would endure as two people, body severed from soul. That horrible thought made a hard lump in his throat.

He could not accept that fate.

No, he *must* try to heal her. She deserved to know her own radiance. To experience wholeness.

Only the Life Tree could heal.

Uvim would take her as his bride even if she never in her whole life shared his body's desire. Even if someday her soul turned against him and she darkened with hatred.

The elixir was her only chance.

"Accept my claim. Become my bride."

She closed her eyes and mashed her fingers against her forehead. "You can't live a life without intimacy."

"Your kindness—"

"It's not kindness. I'm trying to stop you from being victimized."

"I am no victim."

Her eyes snapped open. She fixed on him. Her gaze trailed across his bare torso, focused on his ready cock, and continued its perusal while her soul glowed with desire, need, acceptance.

But her voice was flinty. "You will be."

She had explained her conditions. "I accept."

"I'll use you!" She slammed her hand to her chest. "I want mermaid powers more than anything. If you tell me I can have them scot-free, with no strings attached, it's not going to be my fault if I take you up on it."

He nodded.

She huffed with irritation. "Don't you get it? We will never have sex. You'll never have a 'young fry.' You'll be one more merman who's not contributing to your dwindling gene pool. The whole race will end and it will be my fault." She wiggled her hand at him. "Save yourself for an undamaged woman."

So even she recognized her soul's injury.

He had to heal her.

"I will not touch," he promised.

"Don't."

"Have your powers. 'Scot-free.'"

She held up her hand. "No."

"I accept, Milly."

"Stop!" She clamped her hands over her ears. "I'll use you to get those super powers and leave you with nothing."

"Our souls—"

"You have to stop tempting me!" She pleaded. "You don't know how much I want those powers."

He stepped closer. "Accept."

"You can't sacrifice yourself. I won't let you."

"Binding my life to my love is no sacrifice." He hooked her hand and meshed their fingers. Hers were soft and slender. "Our souls already entwine."

She tore her worried gaze to their interlocked fingers. Her voice trembled. "You don't deserve this. What crime did you commit?"

The knife twisted.

He sucked in a breath. See? Their souls *were* synced. She asked about his crimes. The shame that tortured him. Drove his blind obedience. Forced his strict observance of duty.

No longer.

Claiming a bride violated Dragao Azul's law.

The stones he had placed around his heart would tumble and reveal the monster within.

His bride shunned his kiss? He risked an eternity unable to embrace the one he most desired?

Yes.

He deserved this.

Milly lifted their entwined hands. "You want me to become your bride even knowing I might never get closer to you than this?"

He nodded.

"All right." She hardened. Square shoulders. Icy tone. "Where's your Sea Opal?"

His heart leaped in his chest.

She accepted.

But there were new problems. "The mating gem is in my city."

"Days' journey away." Her soul light brightened, and a relieved smile curved her lips. "Why are we talking about this now? You'll recover, swim to your city, come to your senses, and by the time you get back, I'll be long gone. Uh, I mean, we'll both think things over and make the smart decision."

She pulled her hand free and stretched her fingers.

Cold seeped into his empty hand.

And her soul light faltered. She did not enjoy this solution. She felt scared.

If separation scared her soul, he must keep her close. "There is another option."

"What?"

"The sacred island."

"Ilha Sagrada?" Her soul light fluctuated dangerously. She hugged an elbow. "There's nothing left. Just a lonely island and an empty cave."

"Beneath. There is a pool of elixir."

"You're serious."

He nodded.

"God, I'll regret this." She pulled out her cell phone.

Her hand trembled.

"I will go to the island," he vowed. "When I am recovered."

"Why wait?" She clicked a button. Tinny ringing sounded in her phone. A harsh light shone in her eye. "Let's go tonight."

FIVE

Uvim wanted Milly for his bride. Even knowing they would share no intimacy.

He must have screwed up in a past life.

Milly waited for the call to connect.

"Tonight?" His gaze smoldered. Keeping his distance made his green eyes snap and his hard jaw clench. "I cannot swim."

"We're not swimming."

And her haste wasn't eagerness.

His heat crossed the too-small kitchen. Her heart cartwheeled in her chest.

This was a dangerous plan.

Her warrior consented to keep his hands off her. How long would that last?

It took all her will not to tease him. Rub up against his body. Accidentally stumble into his arms and see his control crumble.

Allowing herself anywhere near this gorgeous male, who unleashed her suppressed hunger, was like pouring gasoline next to an open flame.

His addictive fumes filled the warm kitchen. She suffocated in need. Her lips begged for a taste of his mouth.

She *must not* give in.

"You know Ilha Sagrada?" His gaze smoldered. "It is secret."

Her stomach panged. "Not—"

The phone connected.

"You better not call off." Her boss Nicolette's Australian accent twanged, making her threat sound cheerful. "Tomorrow's the big meeting of the Sea Festival committee and I promised you'd pitch your 'Snuba Like A Merman' experience."

Milly took a deep breath. "I'm calling off."

"Milly!"

"And I need to charter your yacht."

"This experience was *your* idea!"

"I know and I'm sorry."

"You can't make it up. We need this experience to promote the desperate plight of those sexy, tattooed mermen."

"Want to meet a merman?"

Uvim stilled.

Yes, she offered him up on a plate for her boss. That's what dating Milly would cost him. He asked for this torture.

Maybe he'd wise up and reconsider.

Nicolette paused for a long beat. "At the Sea Festival?"

"As soon as you get to the harbor."

"I'm still at the office and I can see the harbor out my window."

"Okay, then as soon as *we* get to the harbor."

She tsked. "Roberto's expecting me for dinner."

"I have leftover pecan-dijon crusted halibut with rosemary potatoes."

Her boss laughed. "You have an answer for everything."

"Only when I'm asking for a favor."

"Okay. I'll help." Her boss worked out the conditions of the charter and hung up.

Uvim's low voice carried a note of protest. "No humans."

"You're only exposing yourself to one human." She dumped the rest of the dishes in the sink. "And it's the price of our passage."

His expression resisted, but he did not protest.

She gathered an overnight bag and closed up the house again. They drove to the harbor in silence. She fought the flutters in her stomach.

This was crazy. Utterly crazy.

She parked in her usual spot. The dive shop was dark; her boss's yacht at its slip in the public marina was lit. The sun had long dipped beneath the horizon, the clouds had magically cleared, and stars glittered on the pale night sky.

Couples, mostly tourists, strolled the quiet cobblestone walks beneath the moth-spattered street lights.

Milly unbuckled her seatbelt and opened the door.

Uvim remained in his seat unmoving.

Silent protest.

She paused. "Now or never."

"No humans."

"Walking past a few people is the only way to go through with this terrible mistake. If you've changed your mind, great."

His eyes narrowed.

"You have ten seconds before good sense reasserts itself and I call the whole thing off."

He rested his fists on his knees. His knuckles turned white.

"Look. I asked my boss for help. I hate asking for help." She pulled her leg back into the car and shut the door. The dome light went off, returning them to darkness. "What matters to you more? Duty or me?"

His silence was his answer.

Duty.

Disappointment captured the flutters in a "reality" net and dragged her down.

It was his fault she'd started to dream.

Not just for the offer of mermaid super powers.

Like her reactions to him meant she was ready to heal. Her past could stay there. Like, if she asked Uvim for help, he'd give it without strings attached, and he wouldn't come after her later saying he'd made a mistake or she was wrong to have asked.

Like she could finally be free.

And that possibility was why she'd planned this sudden departure. Why she would terrify herself by returning to Ilha Sagrada. Why she was about to dredge the darkest hours of her past into her present.

It was why she pushed him now. Even though good sense said she should drive right back to her house and acknowledge it was the merman concussion talking.

"You can stay in the car. I'm going to chat with my boss. This is your last chance."

She exited, pulled her bag from the back seat, and ambled to the darkened dive shop.

Her passenger door clicked. Uvim emerged.

The tension in her chest eased. Whew. She'd almost felt small and helpless.

Never again.

Once she transformed, she would always take charge.

He closed the door and followed her down the docks to her boss's yacht, the *Sunny Adelaide*.

SIX

Uvim trailed his bride across the narrow, bobbing slats of wood constructed over the still ocean.

Other humans strolled past.

Their gazes flayed his skin.

Many humans walked here. His orange covering did not disguise him well.

He padded barefoot. His torso was bare. His skin and tattoos, his bearing and his broad height, set him apart like a flounder in a school of herring.

Every muscle in his body tightened in protest.

Milly stopped beside a large white boat. "Here we are. Get ready to pay the price."

He had not already paid it? Uvim braced.

A petite woman crossed a plank to their dock. "G'day, how ya going mate? I'm Milly's boss Nicolette." Her short, gray-streaked hair bobbed as she smiled. "Will you do the foot there?"

Foot there?

Milly nudged him. "Change your foot. You know." She flexed one foot up and down.

Shifting.

His gut clenched.

Yes, the modern world knew of mermen. Yes, Dragao Azul no longer followed the ancient covenant restricting mermen to secrecy.

But little had changed. Even Queen Zara, the ultimate rebel, had ordered them to remain hidden.

Milly would not accept his claim unless he paid this price.

His heart thudded. Sharp air scratched his throat.

He lifted his right foot and flexed. His toes elongated and spread. The skin between his toes stretched tight, transforming his stubby human toes into a large mer fin.

"Ta. That's convenient." She aimed her cell phone on his fin. "Now, stand next to my ship and smile."

She darted to touch his side.

He stumbled sideways away from the woman.

She hesitated. Her smile died. "Huhhh."

He had offended her.

But she must understand — she must know — he must not touch—

"He can't touch another man's wife," Milly told Nicolette. "It's a warrior thing."

"Why? I won't shrivel."

"He'd expect your husband to cut his hand off."

She rocked back onto her flat foot coverings. "Ew. He's touching you."

"I'm not married."

"Bugger! I'll stand on your unmarried side." The petite woman cozied up to Milly and lifted her cell phone. It reflected their faces. "Cheers!"

The image froze.

She reviewed it, froze a few more images, and then touched many buttons.

"That's going on the blog," Milly said under her breath.

"Blog?"

"Er, never mind." She led Uvim across the plank onto the bobbing boat.

Milly's boss picked up the plank. She and Milly untied ropes. The boat rumbled and moved backward, cutting across the quiet harbor. She twisted a wheel. The boat pointed toward the opening in the sea wall to the more violent surf.

"How about doing a meet-and-greet at the Sea Festival?" the petite woman called to him. "You'd be the highlight of the show. Offer a selfie station. Thousands would take your picture. You'd be famous."

Nausea roiled in his belly.

He pursued a bride out of turn and exposed himself to many humans. Exposure to thousands? Nightmare.

Milly touched his forehead. Concern filled her eyes. "You're unwell. Why don't you lie down?"

Nausea welled higher.

Milly did not know of his shame. She had agreed to become his bride. He was not worthy.

When she knew, she would not be so kind.

The boat rocked.

He gripped the rail.

"Are you all right?" The petite woman looked over at him. Her face was lit from below. "Is a merman going to be seasick?"

He shook his head.

"Is this your first time on a boat?"

He nodded.

"What?"

"Yes," Milly translated. "It's his first time."

"Take it easy!"

"Come on," Milly insisted. She put her arms around his shoulders.

The boat dipped, rolling him into her.

She led him down steps inside the body of the boat to a small chamber. The growl of the boat vibrated in his bones and the air tasted strange. She eased him onto a bunk — soft — and helped him lie down, then rested a thin fabric over his body.

"Feel better soon." She pinched his big toe. Her lips curved into a teasing smile. "Your fame awaits."

"Queen Zara..."

"I'm working on Zara now."

He shook his head.

Queen Zara said the undersea world was too deadly for new brides. War endangered them. The mer must safeguard their city and avoid exposure.

She focused on the brides of the past. Brides who understood their world and their risks. Brides who possessed untapped powers.

After the old brides returned, the mer could forge new relationships on the surface.

Even though it had been a year and the city had not seen any brides, old or new, join them.

Milly spoke with the authority of her sisterhood with Queen Zara. "The Sea Festival celebrates the relationship of the Azores islanders with the sea. They want to honor our new friendship."

"Our ancient covenant ... connected us to Ilha Sagrada."

"In the past." She rested both hands on his ankles. A bright fire burned in her soul. The energy matched her clear brown eyes. "Make a new connection."

He shook his head again.

She shrugged and withdrew her hand. "If you won't show yourself, then when I'm a bride, I will."

"Do not expose yourself."

"I'll wear clothes."

"That ... is not—"

"I know, I know. I'm teasing." Her amusement changed to firmness. "You're fighting an underwater war with a dwindling population. You need all the friends you can get."

He understood her point.

She leaned back. "A hands-off bride like me won't do you any good."

"Milly." He rested his big hand on her small one. "You do much good."

Her soul light flared.

He enfolded her cool fingers in his warmth.

Her lips trembled. "I wish I could believe you."

"The Life Tree will heal ... your illness."

"What illness?"

"Doubt."

She blinked. "Wait. My doubts are an 'illness'?" Her soul light darkened. She jerked her hand back. "I'm not sick."

She *was* sick, but he did not mean to hurt her. Uvim rose.

"Stay down." She stood and backed away, her gaze focused on anything but him. "Rest. We'll talk in the morning."

No.

How could he explain himself? What words would make her calm and bright?

Her soul light fluctuated.

It reflected the panic in his heart. "Milly—"

"Go to sleep." She exited, closing the door behind her. "Goodnight, Uvim."

She would not become his bride.

His soul contracted with her rejection.

Her footsteps echoed in the dark hall.

Like the hollow in his chest where he was supposed to have a heart.

Because his words would never reach her.

SEVEN

Milly's blood boiled.

She stormed up to the deck. "Turn the boat around."

"That was fast." Her boss peered into the darkness, sailing on instruments. "Is your warrior going off?"

"Yeah," she lied.

He'd called her ill. And yes, she was irritated. Taking offense was an excuse.

In the close quarters, his addictive scent had curled around her nose. Heat had flushed her cheeks and desire had throbbed between her legs. She'd fallen toward him like being sucked into the growing wave of a tsunami. His wave would sweep her away and she would never come up for breath.

She'd had to run away.

He'd called her ill. She was ill. A sick, desperate control freak.

If the Life Tree cured her of being able to control herself, then she wanted nothing to do with it. Not even mermaid powers were worth losing her will.

"He's impossible." She waved her fingers.

Her boss lifted one brow. "You didn't convince him to become the new Sea Festival ambassador?"

"I'll go to your committee meeting tomorrow and pitch the Snuba experience like you wanted."

"Milly."

"What? You were fine with the 'Snuba experience' before."

"Before you dangled a live, muscular, gorgeous merman in my face."

"I'm not. Not really."

"Second thoughts about the island?"

"No."

Her boss quieted for a beat. "Your therapist was a real ding bat."

"There were no others. And I wasn't flying to the States."

She tapped her ceramic mug. "Care for a cuppa?"

"Turn the boat around and it's a deal."

"Look in the Esky there."

Milly opened the portable cooler. Inside was a bag of plastic tubes the width and length of her index finger. Black marker labeled the bag *Merman Repellent.*

Merman Repellent?

"What's the story?" she asked.

"Roberto took those off a guest during this morning's whale watching tour. The guest asked if it would repel whales."

"Would it?"

"Yes. It's a stick of dynamite."

"Dynamite!"

"He bought it, he said, off somebody in the harbor last

night. I stayed late to check. They're selling at a few stalls. I don't think the vendors have any idea what it is."

"You called the police?"

"As soon as Roberto confirmed the contents. Pull the fuse. You can deactivate it."

Milly tugged out the white string. Her boss pointed out the chemical coating that made it burn underwater.

The strange texture felt gritty between her fingertips.

"The powder's inside. It's inert until it catches fire. Then, don't be in the water unless you want your insides on your outsides. *Kaboom*."

Oh. *Merman Repellent*.

Her stomach lurched.

Dynamite fishing was illegal in the Azores. The only time she'd seen it was on TV. *Crocodile Dundee II*. It was illegal in the New York Harbor, too. Throw a stick in, watch the fish float belly-up on the surface.

The scene didn't show the fish smashed to bits on the inside. Punctured air bladders, shattered bones.

Explosions underwater didn't look as serious because the mushroom cloud was invisible. In fact, they were a factor of magnitude more deadly.

She twisted the bag of candles closed.

A piece of paper crinkled beneath the dynamite.

On the paper, a triangle surrounded a fish head with stick legs. X's showed the fish head was dead. Next to it a meat cleaver dripped.

Right.

"Why would someone do this?" she asked.

"What have the mer got to hide? Secrecy makes people nervous."

"The mer hid for a thousand years so we wouldn't hunt

them." She stowed the dynamite. "Apparently they were right."

"The key is the Sea Festival," her boss said. "We show them mermen are nothing to fear. They're only seeking love and a good life and children. Convince your friends."

"You can't erase millennia of secrecy overnight."

"It's been two years."

She dropped silent.

"How about that cuppa?" her boss asked.

Milly descended to the galley and brewed a strong pot of coffee. She banged around the small space until she'd made up a tray of sliced tomatoes, soft farmer's cheese with pimento, and thick bread and carried the whole set up to her boss.

"Ta." Her boss touched the small hydrangea petals Milly had pinched from a disintegrating bough in a vase and had sprinkled next to the farmer's cheese. "There's a nice touch, Martha Stewart."

"Three month hospitality internship," she reminded her boss. One of the many careers she'd tried after losing her way.

She sipped the coffee. "Is your warrior our new Sea Festival ambassador?"

"I didn't wake him."

"Go on."

"He needs his rest. I accidentally knocked him out today."

"He was clear-headed enough to refuse my first offer. You should have hit him harder."

She snorted.

"The mer need this, Milly."

She didn't fight. Her boss was right.

They had to do something.

The yacht reached Ilha Sagrada. They anchored the boat at a safe distance and sacked out on the deck for the night.

Milly awoke with the sun.

Tiredness scratched at her dry eyes and nerves buzzed in her guts. She skipped her contacts for glasses, fixed a quick breakfast in her boss's galley — more coffee, canned ham, buttery sourdough toast and macerated strawberry jam — and ate with Nicolette on the deck.

Ilha Sagrada appeared at the edges of the morning mist. Sharp white cliffs. Dense, leafy green concealed the dark interior.

Her stomach knotted.

Uvim climbed the stairs to the deck.

He nodded to her and followed her gaze to the island.

A shaft of sunlight burned through the morning clouds and caught his hard jaw. The tattoos shimmered, iridescent, like gemstones beneath his dark olive skin.

The toast stuck in her dry throat.

She washed it down with coffee.

He padded to the table and sat across from her. Studying her, he constructed a similar breakfast although he used the jam knife to serve everything.

"You're looking better," she said, not commenting on his table etiquette.

He nodded.

"Glad I didn't kill you." She said it under her breath but he still glanced over.

Pressure to apologize about her shortness the previous night expanded her tongue.

She took another bite of toast.

Her boss joined them. While Milly cleaned up breakfast in the galley below, Uvim transferred Milly's scuba equipment to the island. She finished and joined him on the deck.

His orange swim shorts hung on the deck.

He stood on the island.

Her boss grinned. She'd enjoyed an eyeful.

Milly stripped, including her glasses, and dove in. Warm summer water splashed across her body, saturating her tight black swimsuit and dive shirt. She put on her prescription mask and carried the rest of the gear to the steep, undercut shore.

She climbed out and waved. "See you in an hour."

Nicolette waved back. "I'll be waiting!" She lay out on the deck with a book.

Milly turned to face the greenery. The edges fuzzed. Uvim climbed out next to her.

Now they were alone.

She swallowed.

This island starred in her nightmares.

But facing her nightmares — and her past — was necessary to become a mermaid.

The powerful warrior at her back filled her with calm.

She glanced back to talk to him and soothe her nerves. A flash of amethyst below his shorts line drew her eyes to his massive, erect—

She jolted away.

Licks of arousal fire coursed through her body. Her pussy throbbed. She tightened the muscles in her thighs, squeezing them together. *Stop.*

All that rippled, corded muscle was a reason to stand proud.

Don't drink in his masculine contours. Control. She needed control.

"I will find the church." He bent his knees to dive into

the water.

She lifted her vest and tank. "This way."

After a slight delay, he followed her through the foliage. She parted it and skidded down a slick path into a familiar cavern.

Weather-smoothed columns held up a ceiling cracked by age. She strode to the back. The cavern widened into a rounded chamber with a central pool.

Acid burned the back of her tongue.

She swallowed.

Ghostly voices echoed in her skull.

You owe us. We helped you. Don't be so ungrateful.

Milly dropped her scuba equipment, ripped off her mask, and fought to control her nausea. Uvim would not understand if she threw up.

Even now, he was eying her. "Milly."

"I'm fine." She tried to manufacture a smile.

He frowned. "Your illness?"

Mermaid powers. Focus on the mermaid powers.

"Fine."

"You are not fine."

A sob bubbled in her throat.

She gritted her teeth. "Ignore it."

He stood a respectful distance from her. But he would not leave. Not until she explained.

"Four years ago I stood here when Elan emerged from that pool and selected my sister, Zara, for his bride." She swallowed again. "It was supposed to be me."

He frowned in surprise. "You desired First Lieutenant Elan?"

"Desired? No, I was terrified."

"Terrified?" His frown deepened. "Your mother ... prepared you."

"Uh, no."

"Grandmother? Elders?"

"My parents had heard about a mysterious 'Sea Lord' giving out Sea Opals and decided I would be his next bride. So they forced me here. I assumed it was human trafficking."

He tilted his head. *Human trafficking?*

"Traffickers buy and sell slaves."

Slaves?

"People who have no choice."

He growled.

"I know decades ago sacred brides competed for the honor. Zara's still researching. But the most recent former brides were in her position. Taken by accident or escaping a prior abduction."

He growled with horror. "Accident or abduction!"

"That's why none of them have returned with her. I think some — maybe all of them— want to, but it means returning to the darkest places in their lives. And it's not easy to do that."

She was living proof.

He still looked shocked.

"Anyway, since I was expecting a human trafficker, I was even more terrified when a merman actually emerged from the pool. Then, he stole my sister."

"Queen Zara resisted!"

"No."

"But — Elan stole—"

"I misspoke." Milly had been terrified of the strange male but even more afraid of her parents. "Zara fought our parents and lost. My dad nearly killed her. Elan saved us. Then, he proposed. She had to decide right here," Milly pointed with her toe to the spot on the chalky ground, "whether to go with Elan. If she refused, he would descend alone and that would be the end. She gave me his Sea Opal and together they left."

Uvim clenched his fists. "Corrupted. The sacred ceremony."

"Elan was also furious."

"Furious?" He shook his head, so angry he could barely speak. "Sacred brides are honored. The highest... Many snuck. Hid. In our church. To increase the mating. They want to unite. Many times. Warriors come many times every year."

"This island has been empty for decades."

"Yes, *this* sacred island," he agreed. "Sank. Generations ago. There are — were — others."

"The Azores had natural disasters. Eruptions. Migrations. Traditions were lost."

Uvim's jaw clenched. "Your parents faced punishment?"

"Elan avenged your honor."

He did not look reassured. "Where are they?"

"My parents? Jail. Unrelated charges."

"Human justice." Uvim's fists flexed. "If they walk free, they will answer to me."

It was funny but his protective rage made her feel a little better.

"Thanks." She unwrapped her BCU and attached its hoses to the oxygen tank. "You know, I came back. Sacred brides return after a year. Zara was early."

Uvim said nothing.

"I guess you know." Milly focused on her equipment to keep her hands from shaking.

To expunge the memories of blood and tears.

She'd be fine once she got under the water. Everything would be different. New. Unfamiliar.

She'd be a whole new woman and these nightmares would no longer plague her.

Uvim toed the edge of the pool. "I will return."

"Return?"

He folded over and disappeared.

Now she was alone in the cave of nightmares.

Distant wind shivered through the island foliage. The fuzzy walls closed in. Just like—

No. She was fine. An adult.

Milly backed into the wall and slid down it, wrapped her arms around her knees, and stared at the fuzzy outline of the stilled pool for the third time in her life. Like all the other times, willing someone to come out of it and rescue her.

This time was different.

"I'm fine. Totally fine."

EIGHT

Milly was clearly not fine. Her illness grew with every passing moment.

You know, I came back. Sacred brides return after a year. Zara was early.

Shame tightened his throat.

Yes, Queen Zara had returned early. Against her will. Ruined in body and in mind.

Milly must not learn his role in her return or she would change her mind and refuse to be his bride.

Uvim dropped into the narrow hole to the ocean beneath the island.

As the salty liquid embraced his body, he shifted from human form into mer.

Darkness fled, exposing the rock and sea creatures in brilliant light. Their melodious songs vibrated in his chest, painting an audible picture of the surroundings. His lungs vented air through gills in his back. And his feet transformed at the ankles, unfurling into fins.

He bent his right knee, then his left. Shifting thickened his skin to rubber. The humans had a mythical image of mer with their legs fused together but that was a strange mistake. His legs remained separate, same as in human form. The balls of each foot elongated into fins.

He kicked, descending.

The path split into two. One descended to the open ocean. The other ended in the lair of a scratchy, off-tone cave guardian.

Promising.

He kicked toward the jarring squawks and squeaks.

The path split again. Off to his right, the noise became horrendous.

Giant cave guardian.

Uvim had no wish to be crushed to death. He kicked to the left. An air pocket appeared.

He rose from the pool and measured his steps up stairs to the inner pool of mating gems. They had lain here, undisturbed, since the sea levels had risen and storms had closed off the old entrances.

The cave guardian was dangerous.

But he craved to make Milly his. Now.

Before she knew the full truth.

Before her illness grew any worse.

He had seen no person, mer or human, so severed from their soul. She insisted she was fine when her soul light darkened to black. She could not live this way. She would collapse.

He returned to Milly in the upper chamber.

She was sitting cross-legged, hugging her arms around her knees, glaring at her cell phone.

His movement drew her eye.

She shoved the phone into a plastic bag and left it on the ground. "Well? Did you find the elixir?"

"This way."

Her light flared. "Let's go."

Already she felt better.

Good.

She shouldered her vest and tank, cinched on a belt threaded with stones, and staggered to the pool. She strapped a glass mask around her eyes. Two plastic fins dangled from her fingers.

"I wish you'd put on shorts," she muttered.

"No."

She removed the hose she'd been biting. "No?"

"Shorts restrict movement." He must protect her and maneuver well. "Follow me."

He dove to the first junction.

She hovered at the surface.

He ascended with a fin-flick. Even when he was right in front of her face, she looked past him.

He touched her face.

She jolted and oriented on him.

Human vision was bad under the water. That was how the mer had avoided detection for so long.

She fumbled with a small black cylinder. A weak light flattened the narrow walls. She accepted the touch of his hand guiding her, and she shone the flashing light over the walls and bounced from one to the other. Her big silver tank scraped outcroppings with a hollow metallic twang.

Her soul light darkened.

The flicker of her confidence sliced into him like a knife.

Soon the water would be the most pleasurable experience. He swore it.

He kicked at the pace of a sea slug.

Despite her light cylinder *and* him drawing her the

correct way by the hand, she veered toward the cave guardian.

He waved her toward him.

She didn't notice. Her heart thudded loud and fast. Her hands trembled. Her soul light blackened.

Had she lost him? Human vision truly *was* bad. Did she not hear the noises of the cave guardian?

He hooked her elbow and drew her to him.

She startled, wide-eyed.

But her soul light brightened. Her heart rate dropped. She kept both hands on him for the rest of the journey.

He flipped over, led her into the larger cavern, and ascended. Her bubbles tickled him with feathery promises.

Her soul light fluctuated. Fear, danger, anxiety.

"Almost there," he coaxed.

"*Grghl.*"

In their two states, he couldn't understand her and she couldn't understand him.

He lifted her into the air bubble.

She removed her glass mask and spit her air hose. Shudders wracked her body. She hugged herself.

He rubbed her clammy arms. The slick fabric bunched. "You are cold?"

"Nightmares." She shook her head. "Cave diving is the stuff of nightmares. It was much worse than I imagined. If you hadn't been there..."

How brave she was to swim deep into the darkness. How had he not realized she felt scared and alone? He had seen but not understood. Curse his blindness.

She splayed the light cylinder around the space. "These are stairs. At the top is that ... is that a bowl of Sea Opals?"

"Yes."

Her soul light flared to the pinnacle of happiness.

"Woohoo." She wiped more water off her face and then struggled with her garments.

He helped her unsnap and remove her puffy black vest and tank. They rested her equipment on the lowest, widest steps.

She was almost his bride. She would drink the elixir and heal her illness. He would claim her.

No one would stop him.

He led her up the narrowing steps to the dish at the top of the small dais.

She stared into the water.

Generations' worth of mating jewels filled the deep dish. When they had steeped long enough, their powers leached into the water.

She squinted at the undisturbed stones as though trying to make out their shapes. "This is it? This will transform me?"

"Yes."

She rested her fingers on the edge of the curved stone. Her other hand positioned the slender light.

"Drink," he said.

As though his command broke her spell, a deep sadness darkened her soul light.

His belly dropped.

"If you hadn't been there..." she repeated softly. "I wouldn't have survived."

Her soul dipped into darkness.

"Drink," he insisted.

The elixir would fix her. It would fix everything.

Her shoulders drooped. She stared at the mating gems as though facing reality for the first time and realizing she didn't want to mate a silent, un-expressive, not-dutiful warrior like him.

No. She wanted this. Their souls synced.

"Drink."

"I'm so sorry." She retreated to a lower step. "I just can't."

NINE

Uvim was silent.

The silence and darkness of the pitch-black cavern, barely illuminated by her weak diving flashlight and then hard to see with her fuzzy vision, pressed like a boulder on her chest.

Milly waited for his anger.

The recriminations.

How could you? We were counting on you. All we asked is one little thing. You can't even do that right.

He said nothing.

She babbled. Explained. Justified.

"I want to do something important with my life. Something useful. *I got a second chance. It has to mean* something."

He listened.

"After Elan — and Zara — saved me from my parents, I decided to become a marine biologist. She was taken and returned before mermen were revealed, so nobody believed my story — or, later, hers. So, I would prove mermen existed. Except then some kid with a GoPro captured them on video. And there was the incident with Lucy. Dragao Azul rebelled, Zara reconciled with Elan, and nobody needed a marine biologist anymore. I lost my purpose."

"You have purpose."

"As what? Of the fields I've tried — hospitality, translation, marine science — I realized that I have nothing special to offer. Other people are much more qualified."

"A queen will defend our city."

"Zara's ten times stronger than I am. She's been rescuing people since we were children. I've only been a victim."

The hard truths cut, but that's why they were hard truths. And now, at the moment she prepared to smash Uvim's life, she had to handle those sharp corners before they both got hurt.

"So, I can't trap you. I just can't."

"You do not trap me."

"I'm not sick."

His head jerked. In the dark, it was difficult to tell his expression, but he looked surprised. He had expected her to say something else.

"You are."

"There's not a thing wrong with me. I promise you."

He seemed to choose his words. "Your soul is bright. Strong. You are capable of great love."

Her chest tingled.

"Heal your rift. Embrace your power. Live without doubt. Surrounded by love."

She wanted that. But it was too late.

"Drink the elixir. Heal."

"I don't want to."

His mouth opened and closed. She'd stunned him.

She explained again. "I thought I could use you to get mermaid powers."

"You can."

"I'm sorry, but I can't be around you anymore. As soon as we return to the surface, I'll never see you again."

He remained silent.

But it wasn't a "judgy" silence. There was a difference, and even though she could barely make out the fuzzy shadows on his hard face, Uvim was trying to understand a foreign concept.

Then, he moved.

His powerful thumb stroked her cheek. Gentle. Kind.

She closed her eyes and drew strength from his kindness. "You can't do this."

"Your soul craves wholeness, Milly."

"Well, too bad." But she didn't move. She wanted the sensual stroke of his thumb. The rough shape of callouses from gripping a deadly trident. The trim edge of his clean nail. "I realized I can't afford it."

Not if it makes me crave you.

His even breathing calmed her. The ocean was still and the air stuffy in the flashlight-lit dimness.

"Why?" he asked.

Maybe it would be easiest to explain.

She opened her eyes. "Because you're here and I'm not afraid."

He tilted his head.

"This cave is dark. Almost as dark as the engine room my parents locked me in for several weeks."

He was silent. Respectful. Not put off. He wanted to make her fears stop. Release her from the horrors she'd endured.

Even though it was dangerous, she liked him. Against her will, she liked him.

And that was why she told him things she told nobody. Not even Brody.

"My aunt raised me too strictly. In my last year of high school, I reached out to my rich biological parents. They invited me to join them in the Azores. But, they didn't see me as their long-lost daughter. Or even as a person. And their invitation wasn't from a place of kindness."

She stared into the pool of glittering Sea Opals. Ones that her parents and other greedy narcissists would do anything to possess.

"It's embarrassing, but I didn't realize what my parents were trying to do." She gripped the flashlight. "I wanted to finish high school. They kept delaying my registration. Every night, they'd have these wild parties on their yacht. They'd tell me which of their creepy friends to talk to because 'he would help with my college tuition' in the next year. And, they always pushed pills and wine.

"But I was seventeen. A ridiculously sheltered seventeen. *Staying awake until nine* was exciting.

"I never realized they were trying to drug me to have sex."

She'd talked to a psychiatrist after Zara had gone undersea and before mermen had been revealed. Big mistake. Mermen stole her sister? Crazy talk. The psychiatrist had pushed antipsychotic drugs. She'd refused. He'd threatened to commit her.

Everyone had thought she was unhinged. She'd started to fear they were right.

Uvim frowned. "A drug cannot increase resonance."

"Oh, those creeps didn't care about resonance."

"Resonance produces young fry."

"Most of them don't care about 'young fry'."

"It is the purpose of joining," he insisted.

How sweet.

Naive. Honest. And sweet.

"If all guys had your priorities — and honor — the world would be a better place," she said.

He flinched.

Huh? But she was agreeing with him. "What?"

"No." He shook himself. "You escaped?"

"I'll skip ahead." She took a deep breath and continued in her memory. "Once I figured out my parents' intentions, the 'nice' mask slipped off. They took me prisoner."

Sticky-sweet moisture beaded up on her clammy skin. Her swimsuit squeezed her like a snake. Her throat closed.

She swallowed.

"They took my passport." Swallow. "Money. Phone. Clothes."

Swallow again, acid burning the back of her throat.

"Everything. They locked me in a bare room in their yacht. Pitch dark. No electricity, no food, no windows. They would take me out every few days if I promised to 'be good' at their next wild party, which meant to tell no one what they were doing.

"But who would I have told? Their drunken friends wouldn't have believed me."

"You survived."

She swerved away from the final memory. Her deepest shame. He didn't need to know. She didn't need to remember it.

"I mailed a letter to Zara. A week later my parents took me here. To Ilha Sagrada." She smiled but her cheek muscles twitched. "You know what happened then."

He darkened. "Milly. You survived."

"Not all of me." Her self-respect, her belief in herself, and her trust were damaged beyond repair. "Just now, the cave returned me to my nightmare."

"You survived it."

She glared at the powerful warrior. "It's your fault."

He blinked. "My?"

"I handled it because you were here."

He took one of her fists and loosened it, threading his fingers with hers. "I will be. Always. By your side."

"That's the problem." She tugged her hand free before she got too comfortable with his strength. "I hate asking for help."

"You do not have to ask."

"You say that now. Later, when helping me is inconvenient, you'll regret your offer."

He tilted his head the opposite direction from before. "No."

"You will. You'll be busy and then I'll ask and—"

"No. Do not ask." He placed his hand in the center of her chest. "I sense desire. You do not ask. Our resonance grows and I will know. Near or far. You will not ask."

"But..." She swallowed. "I'll never get stronger if I have to rely on you for my sanity."

He moved her palm to the center of his chest. "Your soul dims. Fear. The elixir gives strength. Then, no fear will darken you again."

Her resistance faded. She couldn't help it. She didn't want to be irrational and jumping at shadows for the rest of her life. She wanted to be whole.

Reliable.

Strong.

She wanted to have faith in humanity. And she wanted humanity to have faith in her.

"What if I'm never healed?" she pushed. "What if I'm always afraid?"

"I will never father a young fry." *I would rather spend eternity beside you, never touching, than any other fate.*

He broke her heart.

But maybe, just maybe, there was a way out of this darkness. For them both.

"That would be a terrible fate," she whispered.

"I would endure any torture. Any exile. To remain with you."

Her warrior — yes, she was thinking of him as hers, just because she'd knocked him out and then, while he was woozy, lured him to this sacred island — was sexy when he turned serious.

She set the flashlight on the small lip beside the pool and linked their hands. "Fine. I'm willing to try."

"Try?"

"You'll never make me ask for help? Prove it." She looked up into his shadowed eyes. Terror and hope fluttered in her stomach at the same time. "What do I want from you right now?"

TEN

K iss me.

Milly's wish filled his chest. No words passed between them.

Flutters brushed Uvim's stomach.

If he satisfied her, then she would accept his claim and become his bride.

Uvim leaned to claim her lips in a—

She jolted a step back and put a hand over his mouth. "Wait!"

Fear sliced into him.

He was wrong. She did not want him. Not a male with his dishonor.

He rocked back on his heels.

"You weren't wrong. I *do* want to kiss you. But it's my first one. I don't want to scare myself. That would be the worst." She laughed shakily. "Just give me a minute."

He waited.

She splayed her fingers across his lips, stroking his jaw and cheeks. Soothing yet teasing. She spoke as though trying to calm herself. "You know my past. I could never tell anyone else. Not even Brody."

He dipped his head. Keeping her fingers on him. This contact was important.

"Brody's nice. He's undemanding. You are less, uh, comfortable."

Fear. Again, fear.

"You want to say something." She slid her fingers along his jaw, releasing his mouth to speak.

"I will only make you comfortable."

Her lips quirked. "I believe you, which is crazy because I didn't believe anyone else. I thought I'd go my whole life as an aunt to Zain and I was okay with that, you know? Well, not okay, but resigned."

"Our souls resonate."

She touched his cheeks, strengthening their connection. Of all the humans, her light remained bright even as it fluctuated with her thoughts. She did not give way easily to sadness or depression.

He nuzzled her hand and nibbled her fingertips.

She rubbed her thighs together. "So, um, let me think. How to make sure I won't feel trapped even for an instant..."

She felt trapped?

Uvim knelt on the step below hers and held out his hands, palms facing up.

She squinted.

Ah, the darkness of the chamber. So strange. He could see so well. He lifted his hands until his fingertips brushed hers.

She rested hers on his large palms.

Heat flared.

He closed around her, sealing in the heat. "Accept my claim and become my bride."

Her soul light shone with brilliance.

She sat on the steps above him, placing herself at his eye level. "I'm willing to try."

She accepted his claim.

Milly accepted his claim.

Even though she had survived a brutal imprisonment. Even though she had been betrayed.

And still she accepted.

Now, he must claim her.

She watched him, eyes wide and pupils dilated.

Kiss me.

"Let me." She trailed her fingers along his neck to his shoulders. His muscles fascinated her. Or maybe it was his tattoos.

Her soul light reached for his. Desire twined around his cock.

He hardened.

Her lips quirked again in her smile. "I just remembered. You've been naked this whole conversation."

Was that funny?

She sucked in a nervous breath.

He remained still on his knees. He would not rush her. He promised with his posture, his gaze, his everything.

She rested her palms on his shoulders. Sucked in a breath. And leaned forward.

Soft hair brushed his chest.

His skin tingled.

Her lips brushed his. Warm, soft. Precious.

His destiny changed with her touch.

Their mouths met, touched, played. Exploring. Discovering. Learning each other. There was no rush. Even though his heart thundered and his cock demanded to possess her so none other could make a claim.

Calm.

She nibbled his lips.

He caught hers and slid the soft flesh between his gentle teeth.

She deepened the kiss, opening to taste.

The inner heat and wetness of her mouth teased him. Her flavor was sweet as jam and slick as honey. Hinting at secrets within.

He trembled to take her deeper.

Uvim clenched his hands into fists and pressed them into his thighs. His duty was to his bride. She led the kiss. He would not wrest that control away.

She broke the contact. A thrill of wonder warmed her tone. "You know? Actually, I'm okay."

Okay? She was very okay. She was shining.

So why was she pulling away? Had he disappointed her?

"I never got this far with Brody." She wiped her mouth as though swiping him away. "I — oh, no! You were wonderful. So, you don't have to hold yourself back."

Relief eased his heart.

He cupped her cheeks. Her skin was soft and warm beneath his thumb.

She rested her cheek against his hand.

He slid his thumb along her damp lips.

She teased his thumb with her small white teeth.

His cock filled with undeniable heat.

She was his destiny.

He drew her forward. Treasuring her. Loving her.

She watched him until the last moment and then she tilted her chin up, presenting her lush mouth, and closed her eyes.

They fit together. Nose to nose. Mouth to mouth.

Hot need swept aside his natural caution. He delved into her dark crevices, claiming her wet mouth for his own.

She stroked his tongue, accepting his intrusion and tangling. Her light shone.

He wanted her. All of her.

Her hands clenched his shoulders.

Too hard. A warning? He released her.

She panted. Her eyes unfocused. Stunned and mesmerized.

He felt the same way.

She rested her forehead against his. "Maybe this can work. With a little more practice, it'll even become natural."

More practice?

He claimed her mouth a third time. Plunging between her liquid lips, he drove his hunger into her with hot, even, deep thrusts. Each thrust was a promise. She was his duty. His purpose. His ultimate devotion.

She slipped her arms around his broad shoulders. "Mmm."

Her soft breasts caressed his pectorals. Pearly nipples traced hot lines of desire. Her knees jutted on both sides of his torso. She slid off her step and into his lap.

He took her.

One arm locked around her flared hips, pressing her to him. The other hand slid up her back, along the curve of her neck, to her damp brown hair.

Her feminine heat ground against his hard cock.

She released her moan. "I want to sleep with you."

He did not want sleeping. His cock throbbed hot and ready for her slick center. He savored her gently rounded derriere.

She giggled and buried her face in his shoulders. "There's hope! I *want* to sleep with you. No hesitation."

"You are not afraid," he acknowledged.

"I was never afraid of sex. Only of losing control. But, maybe, I can get swept away and keep my head above water." She stood and helped him rise. "Let's finish the ceremony."

He led her to the top of the steps, scooped a palm full of the shimmery elixir, and held it to her lips. She sipped.

"Tastes salty." She tilted his palm for another swallow. "How do you know if it's working? Whoah. Did someone turn on the lights?"

He shook his head.

"I can see." Milly twirled, taking in the chamber with new eyes, and descended the steps, inspecting the worked stone.

But he would conduct more tests before risking the fright of submerging—

"Cannonball!" She leaped, arms looped over her knees, and smashed into the pool.

He slid down the steps. Waves splashed the steps and smacked the walls. Silence returned.

Interfere? Assist? Wait?

She burst above the surface, coughing and gasping.

He dragged her onto the stairs.

She hacked. "Ugh. I couldn't breathe. Everyone says the water pours in like drowning the first time — well, the first twenty times — but not like being suffocated in a plastic bag. My lungs never transformed into gills!"

She rubbed her neck.

He stroked her lower back. "Gills."

She lowered her hand to his location and pinched the tight fabric of her human "swimsuit" and "swim shirt" coverings.

"Oh!" She laughed with relief. "How silly. I knew that!"

And then she peeled off her tight coverings, set them atop her pile of equipment, and rolled backward into the water.

He ducked his head beneath the surface.

She kicked her bare human feet until she was beneath a ledge and then she released her air bubbles and opened her mouth.

So fearless.

Milly seemed cautious. But she could also leap into danger with both arms open.

She thrashed.

He eased beneath the surface, his own shift seamless. For him, entering the water was as easy as opening himself to the weight of the water deep within his body. Shifting to walk on land emptied him, left him ragged and vulnerable.

Milly spasmed, mouth and eyes opened. She rotated backward. Her soul light darkened.

He sped to her. Panic? He touched her leg to pull her back and ensure she was safe.

Milly's soul darkened.

She wasn't transforming.

ELEVEN

Pitch dark black drowning...

Uvim's hand gripped her ankle.

How did she know it was Uvim's hand? Well, it had his calm feelings. *Calm feelings? What the heck? How was she thinking at all?*

She must not be drowning.

Milly opened her eyes.

Before her, the rock wall crinkled inward. A small, white nudibranch wiggled its bright orange and purple feelers at her. The neon slug sang like a deep-throated crooner. "Boop boop?"

Behind it, another slug responded. Neon red, patriotic blue, and a deeper bass. "Bop bop!"

And another, even closer to her face, glowed like sunshine and sang in baritone. "Bop boop bop."

Nudibranchs did not sing.

She had transformed.

Uvim tugged her. As she rotated to face him, the lights and sounds of the ocean lit up like an instrument panel. Even in this small, barren area the darting flutes of curious fish and the woodwinds of tiny micro-fauna trilled above the bass line of nudibranchs, sponges, starfish, and other dark cave-dwelling creatures.

Her vivid warrior, broad and strong, suspended in front of her like safety.

Even though the kisses they'd shared moments ago were the opposite of safe.

Desire heated her.

He waited.

"Their lights and colors are so vibrant," she said. Underwater, her words vibrated in her chest. "What's that noise?"

"Their souls."

Oh. Wow. "I can hear their souls?"

"Underwater, resonance is music."

Like his chest vibrations weren't real words but she still "heard" his voice. Just in her chest cavity instead of in her ears.

The plants and animals — even the rocks — made a symphony.

Greeeeech.

One instrument needed a tune-up. Like bagpipes with a wheezing hole.

GREEEEEECH.

The sound grew louder as she focused on it. "One's scratchy."

"That is a giant cave guardian."

Cave guardian? Zara had never talked about a cave guardian. "What's that?"

"Many arms."

"An octopus?"

He nodded. "Giant."

She stretched her arms and paddled her stubby, human feet. Even though she didn't have fins like Uvim, it was so fun to flip and somersault, twist through the water and zoom. She could swim by sound.

Or sight.

Entering this pitch-black cave had triggered her worst fears. Exiting it with new eyes revealed the beauty and possibilities hidden just out of sight.

She was free.

Uvim floated after her. He almost seemed ... proud?

"What is it?" she asked.

"You are brave," he said.

Milly had been many things since her abduction. "Brave" wasn't one of them.

"Other brides were fearful." He darted around her, surrounding her at once and flickering away like a match. "Your destiny *is* the sea."

She swelled with hope.

Perhaps he was right. Perhaps this was her place.

Could she trust? Could she dare to hope?

Uvim drew her into his arms. "Come with me."

Her feet tangled with his smooth fins. "Where?"

"Dragao Azul."

He wanted to make their marriage permanent.

No escape.

His arm tightened around her waist, pressing her belly to his. His lashes fluttered and he looked at her. His gaze warmed and his serious mien eased.

He offered himself to her. She could have him if she dared.

Her feminine core ached with hunger.

"First, I will convey Queen Zara's message at the echo point," he said. "And convey the message to my — our — city. And then we descend."

Right, he still needed to convey a message to his city.

She relaxed in his arms. It was easier in the water. "Let's take my stuff back to the boat. I'll check my messages one last time."

He released her, leaped out of the pool, and pushed in her tank and BCU. She deflated the vest for easy carrying. Its bubbles tickled her like a burst of tiny fish. She pushed it through the narrow cave corridors, now well-lit with her mermaid super senses, through the submerged interior of the tiny island.

He trailed with her plastic scuba fins and prescription mask.

The tank was so unwieldy. She banged it against the walls and laughed. "If the ocean was my destiny then why aren't I more graceful?"

He grabbed the tank, arresting her progress, and traded for the smaller items. "You smile."

"That proves my destiny?"

They passed a side-passage. The wheezy bagpipes grew louder. An alarmed squeal mixed in. High-pitched, crying for help.

"Is she okay?" Milly asked.

"She?"

"The 'cave guardian.' She sounds hurt."

"They all sound distressed."

Really? Huh. He was the expert.

She tried to shrug off her discomfort. The return trip went a lot faster now she could see. At the secret pool inside the sacred island church, she flopped onto land. Water drained out of her like a sieve. She coughed and took a deep breath. *Air—*

Gravel pierced the back of her throat.

She threw up the water and gasped like she'd just survived drowning.

Which, technically, she had.

It took forever to cough out the extra mucus and grossness.

Uvim padded past her on his human feet. He dumped her BCU and tank next to her plastic bagged cell phone and then returned for her mask and fins.

She dragged herself over to her cell phone. The fuzziness of her vision seemed different. Despite not wearing her glasses or her prescription mask, her peripheral vision seemed improved.

In the daylight, her lumpy nude body shamed her. Sure, if she had Uvim's muscled form, she'd parade around naked. There was her swim shirt. Where was her swimsuit?

Did she forget it where she'd stripped it off in the cave? Bother.

She tugged on her swim shirt grabbed for her phone. The fuzzy phone icon blinked. Voice message!

"Zara called," she announced.

Uvim dropped to her side. His knee rested next to her thigh displaying a heady view of his thick, tattooed, aroused cock. He looked her in the eye, unselfconscious. "Her message?"

She tried not to drool at his hard abdomen and below. He was the perfect specimen of male and he got hard only for her.

Milly clicked the speakerphone to play.

"Milly, this is disturbing." Her older, protective sister sounded exhausted. "You're not acting as a go-between for the mermen, are you? You don't belong in their world and you never will."

Queen Zara's pronouncement — *You don't belong in their world and you never will* — immediately influenced his beautiful Milly.

Her soul light darkened as though her flame had been doused with a bucket of seawater.

Sudden cold chilled his skin. And next came panic.

"You're too sweet," Queen Zara continued. "The undersea world is dark and dangerous. It'll rip you apart."

Her soul light brightened, then dimmed again. She clenched the cell phone so her knuckles whitened.

"In answer to the question about the hunting party, I could care less. Tell the mermen to do whatever makes them happy."

He rested his hand on her curved calf.

She startled as if she had forgotten he was sitting beside her.

"And make them promise they'll never come near you again."

His heart shuddered with chill.

"Only contact me if the All-Council shows up," Queen

Zara said. "Or a bride. I want to talk to all brides before they descend to the city. Or else!"

Queen Zara's message ended.

"Well, now you know what to tell your elders." Milly clicked buttons on her phone. "Are you going back to Faial or can you make your report from here?"

"Here."

"I'll call Zara back, but it's after midnight her time so we'll have to wait on a response."

Milly left a message acknowledging her message and promised to call again.

Queen Zara wished to keep Milly away from the warriors. She would be angry once Milly explained. And even angrier once she realized the warrior closest to Milly was him.

The longer Milly remained in this temporary transformation, the more vulnerable she would become to meeting a worthier warrior — and joining to him, instead of Uvim.

Anxiety rubbed his chest like an ill-tied dagger, sharp and cutting.

She rubbed his ankle. "Hey. It'll be okay. Zara won't stop us from being together unless we let her."

As always, Milly understood him even without words.

"But I have to admit, I felt a lot clearer under the water."

Resonance. It shone brighter under the water. No interference from the air.

And she was not fully healed. She still spoke words that did not match her soul's wish. The elixir needed more time.

The ocean *was* her destiny.

Could he accept if her destiny did not include him?

She wore his human covering "swim shorts," hugging

them to her waist with one hand, and dragged her equipment to the lip of the island.

Her boss was sunning on the deck.

Milly waved.

Her boss shouted back. "Welcome!"

They swam the equipment to the boat. He ducked below to detect surface predators — warning sirens of sharks, distant growl of a cave guardian, hissed warnings of poisonous jellyfish. She kept her head above the rolling waves.

Did she fear to shift?

Had she reconsidered his claim?

After transferring their equipment, she climbed the rungs until she almost reached the deck. She pulled off her shirt, tossed it across the deck, and rested her forearms on the smooth wood.

She squinted at her boss. "Uvim's taking a field trip. I'm not sure when I'll be back."

Her boss raised a brow. "You've got work tomorrow."

"Maybe you can put in a good word with my boss."

Nicolette snorted.

Milly pushed her cell phone in the plastic bag up with the other equipment. "Don't answer if it rings. It's probably Zara."

"I'll talk her ear off," her boss said.

"She's very anti-exposure right now."

"I'll talk her into exposing herself." Her boss grinned. "The Sea Festival is counting on exposure. Lots and lots of exposure."

"See you soon." Milly released the ladder and fell back into the ocean.

Nicolette waved at Uvim and clicked a button. The yacht rumbled. A thick chain raised the anchor.

Milly submerged.

He ducked his head.

She kicked away from the surface.

He flew after her. She spasmed. He trapped her arms and legs, completed his own shift, and rumbled. "Yield to the change."

She sucked in water. Her eyes stared, wide and panicked. Her light dipped and soared. She shook.

Her resistance terrified him.

"Be strong, Milly."

"God, I hate that." She focused on him. "Tell me we can reach the cave from out here."

Yes, it was open to the ocean. "Why?"

"I left my swimsuit and my flashlight."

He kicked down, senses attuned to the dangers of the open ocean. The boat chugged away from the island.

"Your boss is leaving."

"I told her to."

How would Milly return to Faial Island?

He kicked into the narrow entrance warriors used to enter the sacred island.

They separated to navigate the tight turns.

Their progress slowed. And he missed her skin on his, soothing and enticing.

"Hey." She turned her head at the division in the tunnels. The angry growl of the deadly cave guardian rasped. "Are you sure nothing's bothering her?"

"Who?"

"The cave guardian. She sounds hurt."

He was sure.

They reached the pool. She groped a hand out of the water and dragged in her swimsuit and flashlight. She looped the flashlight around one wrist and tied the swimsuit to her bicep. "Let's go."

"Go?"

"You have to send the message, right? To the echo point."

"No." She was vulnerable.

"I'll protect you. I'm a mermaid now."

Except she didn't have powers.

Wild currents, huge denizens, and other warriors infested these waters. His own warriors, or another city's. Or, in the worst case, the All-Council's.

The minimum escort for safe travel was five warriors. Five *armed* warriors.

Or, one fully-empowered queen.

Uvim pointed out one problem. "Your fins..."

She clasped her stubby human feet. "I'll practice while we travel."

He knew how to fight bare-handed. But not if his hands were full with a vulnerable bride.

She huffed. "I know what you're saying."

"I am not—"

"You're not-saying I'm dead weight."

"Milly..."

"I'm too useless to protect myself so why imagine I can protect you?" Her soul light darkened. "I get it. Those mermaid queen super powers don't arrive instantly."

"That is not—"

"Sorry for asking something impossible."

She had become a mermaid to be useful and his halting words caused her pain.

What could he say so she would brighten and understand?

Grrrhawk!

A raucous growl overhead made them both jump.

A black shadow swirled on the ceiling of their narrow cavern.

His stomach dropped.

The giant black cave guardian heard their soul songs as they heard hers. She had squeezed into the crevices overhead and crept too close.

One tentacle wrapped around Milly's shoulders, squishing her arms to her sides.

He grabbed Milly's ankle.

She yanked Milly through the passage.

"Eep!" Milly squeaked.

He held on.

The giant cave guardian dragged them through the twisting tunnels into her lair.

And he had no trident. No daggers. Nothing to defend them from a creature able to crush a mer with one arm or bite him in half with the powerful beak.

He would sacrifice his life to save Milly.

They emerged into an open cavern. The giant cave guardian whirled. A thick tentacle flew at his face.

Wham.

Black dulled his vision. He flew across the cavern and scraped the ceiling.

The cave guardian had thumped him with a tentacle.

Milly's voice rose in protest. "Don't do that! You hurt him."

The giant cave guardian growled. Unrepentant.

He shook his head to clear the fog.

He must not threaten the giant cave guardian. They were moody and prone to violence.

The giant cave guardian drew Milly toward one eye, clacked her beak, and stared at Milly with her other eye.

Her tentacles caressed Milly like a parent examining a new child.

Or like a predator tasting its new prey.

"Hello," Milly told the giant cave guardian.

"Do not move," Uvim entreated.

Milly nodded tightly.

One tentacle curled around Milly's flashlight. She removed it from Milly's wrist and eyed the cylinder.

"Oh, you like my flashlight? You can have that."

She warbled an off-tune reply and the tentacle with the flashlight disappeared into a deep crevasse in the lair.

Milly struggled. "Oh, look!"

The giant cave guardian growled.

"Milly," he warned.

Milly wiggled an arm free and pointed. One tentacle was shorter and torn on a ragged edge. "I was right. She's missing an arm. How did that happen?"

The giant cave guardian quieted and offered its stub at different angles. Milly petted the injury, cooing a reassurance. The stub glimmered.

Glimmer?

Milly's hands emitted a glow?

Impossible. Queen powers did not appear until after she had mastered her fins. The warriors from Atlantis, who first discovered modern brides could wield the powers of legendary queens, had shared this truth.

"Take it easy now," Milly told the giant cave guardian. "I'm so sorry. Feel better soon."

She disentangled herself.

The giant cave guardian allowed her to go.

She paddled to Uvim.

He wrapped her in his arms, holding her tight, his senses still tuned to the unpredictable denizen before them.

"Are you okay?" She examined his forehead and stroked where the giant cave guardian had struck him.

His forehead grew warm.

Was it his imagination? Her power must be a healing touch. Queens had such powers. But how could she wield these powers without the final ritual uniting them in marriage — and binding her soul to Dragao Azul's Life Tree?

"You warned me that the ocean was dangerous." Her soul glowed. "The giant cave guardian took us both by surprise. I'm sorry I didn't believe you."

Her apology was unnecessary. He was the failure. But her words were kind.

He flew through the tunnel back to the open ocean. The giant cave guardian's noises grew faint.

Her soul light flickered and she snuggled, warming him. "Around me you keep getting knocked out. You'll be sorry you laid eyes on me."

"Never."

"You say that now..." She dimmed.

He wanted to explain to her. Tell her the words she needed to convince her.

His heart beat for her. She was his world, his future, his hope, his soul.

But instead, he circled back to the same statement. "You are my bride."

"For now."

He shook his head, still upset.

"Sorry. This is me, not you." She stroked a lock of his hair. "I'll be useful. Someday."

They broke into the open ocean. The seafloor fell away. Currents swirled around his body. He passed the current for the echo point and the current that would lead him down to Dragao Azul.

Schools of pelagic fish combed the surface currents pursuing their favorite larvae and plankton. They fled their own predators — marlin, barracuda, whitetip and tiger sharks — who took note of the new prey entering their sphere: a lone merman and his bride.

The surface was denser and deadlier than any other region of the ocean.

He kicked for a current to chase her boss's boat.

Two tiger sharks peeled away from their unsuccessful pursuits and oriented on him. Sirens sounded a warning.

Milly looked around. "What's that?"

"Sharks."

"They sound like police sirens."

Hungry? Territorial? Either could give him trouble with hands full and no weapons.

The sirens grew louder.

Loud screeching announced the re-appearance of the giant cave guardian. She exploded from the narrow cave entrance and filled the ocean, looming monstrous in the open ocean. Huge and black, her mass dwarfed even human boats.

Milly lifted her head from his shoulder. Her soul beamed and she laughed. "What are you doing, you big black girl?"

The giant cave guardian jetted toward her. The screech changed to a happy squawk.

All predators — including territorial sharks — scattered.

"Are you following me?" She giggled. "Should I call you 'Clifford the big red dog'? You're black though."

The giant cave guardian accepted her name. A huge

black tentacle wrapped around Milly trying to force him off.

"Whoah! Okay, be nice to Uvim. I'm swimming with him now. You'll get your turn."

Clifford released Milly, accepting her promise.

He kept on the same path after the boat. The current tasted old. He would have trouble catching up to it. No problem tracking it, but more difficulty reaching it before the harbor.

Or, he could risk and dive for the echo point.

He changed direction and dove.

Milly tightened her grip. "Whee!"

Clifford descended as well heeling them. Her song sawed the water with happiness.

"Where are we going?" Milly wriggled, excited. "You're taking me to the echo point?"

"Yes."

"I promise to listen. If we're in danger, I don't know if I can do anything, but I'll try."

"I made a mistake."

"Hmm?"

"You are not useless."

"Well, to be fair, you never actually said I was."

But he had dismissed her. That had been his mistake.

He forced himself to find the words. "A cave guardian is formidable. A *giant* cave guardian is unstoppable."

"I know. You got hurt because I couldn't protect you."

"You protect me now."

She lifted her head from his shoulder again.

"You befriended a giant cave guardian. No warrior has done this."

"What are you saying?"

"Clifford drives away predators. She makes our path safe. Because of you."

Her soul light brightened. "I've done something useful."

He nodded.

She snuggled him. "I don't know if I believe you but you sure know the right things to say."

He relaxed. For a moment.

Because soon they would reach the echo point. He must convey his message.

Queen Zara was not the only one who wanted to prevent their union.

If his elders discovered that Uvim had taken Milly for his bride, they would cast him from the city with dishonor.

He had done it anyway.

Because she was his bride.

Uvim carried her deeper into the deadly world of the mer with a giant cave guardian on his fins and prayed to the Life Tree that he could protect Milly.

Milly snuggled against her hard warrior — in every sense of the word hard — and studied him in the strange underwater light. This close, she could enjoy his appearance even without her glasses, contacts, or prescription-strength mask.

A straight, dominant nose. Low cheekbones. Thick, expressive lips pursed as he kicked.

Lips she had tasted.

Her nipples tingled.

Contrasting amethyst crinkled across his green skin like veins of precious gems. How did they tattoo? She wanted to know about it.

She wanted to know about him.

"I'm so excited you're taking me with you," she said, snuggling closer.

His lids lowered with calm. "I could not leave you."

"Will you show me everything? The danger and the beauty. I want to know this world."

He complied.

They crossed the vast ocean.

A brilliant light shone in all directions, even down. Before her change, the ocean had thickened with a blue color when she'd looked down. Now, bright light stretched to infinity. If she squinted, she could pick out animals — life — miles down.

The squawking of the giant octopus grew fainter as Uvim kicked hard.

Long crackling electrical wires trailed from Portuguese man-o-wars. Deadly to humans, but according to Uvim, they only gave mer a painful sting. He skirted the buzzing filaments. Normally invisible, she would never miss the electric blue threads again.

This was a marine biologist's dream

They skirted siren-warnings of blue sharks, bull sharks, and even a bullhorn of a basking shark with its gaping, plankton-eating mouth.

An entire pod of blue whales swam by. Their multi-harmonic whale song filled the ocean with thoughtful hums. A shimmering school of mackerel sang.

Rush hour in downtown Los Angeles had nothing to this. There, every car played its own radio; here, every fish sang its own song.

If he could see her soul light now, he must know she was shining with excitement.

Milly splayed her hand across his broad pectoral. So much taut muscle contained under the patterned skin. She circled his darker aureole with her thumb. He let out a pleased rumble.

Hers.

She jolted. Not thinking about *that* right now.

She moved her hands to safer territory — around the delicious bone of his shoulder — and rested her head in the hollow. "I can't wait to visit my old scuba spots and really see the world."

A note of caution entered his tone. "The elixir is temporary."

"It won't wear off right away."

His jaw flexed.

"I thought it had to last until I reached Dragao Azul and drank the permanent nectar," she said. "That takes a few days."

"A warrior never leaves his bride."

"Wait, so separating might make it wear off faster? Separating was your idea."

He did not argue. He left his point for her to understand.

She didn't want the elixir to wear off. This was amazing. She had her own giant cave guardian friend. Her hesitation before had been fear. She could never go back to an ordinary life.

"Maybe we should descend to the city after all," she said.

His gaze flicked up to their surroundings and a rumble of disapproval sounded in his chest. "Queen Zara judges the unworthy."

"Maybe she just wants to warn the brides not to expect roses and hearts."

"She is my queen."

"And she's my sister."

"I must obey."

"And I don't have to."

His duty-bound heart disliked it.

Okay, new plan. "Can someone else bring the blossom?"

He was silent for a long time. "There is another problem."

"You're the only one who can touch the blossom?"

"No."

"Then...?"

"We pursue our brides in order. The most honorable first."

Okay. "What number are you?"

"Twenty-eighth."

Oh.

Ohhhh.

"That's kind of far down the list," she said.

"There will be consequences."

"Consequences? You've already transformed me."

He swallowed hard.

"You won't get in serious trouble, will you?" she asked. "Your people wouldn't exile you."

He did not reply.

Ominous? Hard to say since a squawking, squeaking, honking giant black octopus bounced along in the water behind them. She frolicked in a wonderful mood. It was like being tailed by a giant puppy.

Yeah. A huge, cheerful dog. Like Clifford the big red dog, only black.

So, he couldn't ask for a blossom because then they would know he had broken the rules.

"Then what was your plan when we got to Dragao Azul?"

"Queen Zara must approve."

"There is no way Zara cares about 'what order' warriors get married. People fall in love all the time."

"People," he agreed. "Not mer."

"Well, you have fewer opportunities. But when you

have more opportunities, then it won't be such a big deal, I promise you."

He thrummed as though she had said something deeply comforting.

Well, maybe she had. Uvim's entire city had been unsuccessful in getting sacred brides for years. Elan's luck finding Zara was an outlier. How often did cities send warriors to receive a bride? It might have been decades. Generations.

And she blithely promised the mer would have "more opportunities." Like bride candidates would just fall in their laps. On the bottom of the sea.

Magically.

Well, when Milly was queen, she would make those opportunities.

"Did you ever go to the surface?" she asked.

He looked at her sharply.

"To search for a bride," she clarified.

He shook his head once. *No.*

Why so stiff?

She tried to reassure him. "If they punish you for going out of turn, then when I get my queen powers, I'll un-punish you."

He blinked. "You?"

"As soon as I show off my super powers, your people recognize me as a ruler. That's what happened with Zara. Right?"

He looked blank.

She nudged him with her elbow. Teasing. "Did you forget?"

But he *had* forgotten. Forgotten that she could make decisions and be respected.

His doubts sank onto her shoulders. "You don't think I

can do it, do you? Even if I get super powers, you don't think your people will ever respect me."

"Queen Zara is forceful."

Her heart lurched.

She had plenty of doubts inside. But she'd put her faith in his. He'd been so sure her destiny was the ocean.

Now that was a mistake?

"You are saddened," he said.

"I know I'm kind of dumb." She tried to keep the hurt out of her tone but that was impossible. "I put my trust in the wrong people and I don't learn from my mistakes. But I am going to be a reliable, responsible queen who revitalizes your city and attracts lots of new brides. I am."

"Yes, Milly."

Yes? *Yes?*

"Then if you believe in me, why are you doubtful?"

"I am not doubtful."

"But you said Queen Zara is forceful."

"When she fights," he agreed. "You must not fight."

She snorted. "Well, I'm sorry, but we're not saints. A fight *will* happen."

He did not answer.

The elixir was supposed to solve everything. She'd get the mermaid super powers she wanted and be in charge of her own destiny.

But instead, now Uvim was in trouble. The super-dutiful warrior had violated his code of honor to claim her as a bride. He wouldn't take her to his city until she got permission from her older sister — of all people — and even there he didn't think she had the poise to issue commands.

She swallowed back her pain and tried to ease it with a joke. "If they don't listen, then I'll sic Clifford on them."

His jaw flexed again. The words vibrated from his

chest; his mouth remained closed. "You wish to protect me?"

"Yes."

"Be silent now."

Uvim swam into still water.

The echo point.

All around, currents pulled hard and fish, plants, debris swirled like a tornado. But inside this still water, she watched them go by like looking out a glass window.

Faint words and phrases echoed. Different languages — some English — warbled on the water along with unidentifiable sounds. He floated forward, up, down. Like tuning a radio dial, different messages sounded.

Raiders on the ridge, one male voice echoed. *Prepare for war.*

... large migration on Sol Sud.

... fire! Send warriors ...

... in ... all are welcome ...

... flavor. "Car." *A metal box that conveys humans across the surface.* "Dog." *A furred, toothed, four-legged animal kept for defense and companionship.* "I love you." *No meaning is ...*

They floated away from the loudest, clearest broadcast — teaching English? — and she strained to hear the teacher's answer.

"Wait. I—"

Uvim held her tight and shook his head, panic in his gaze.

Her heart thudded.

If she had just revealed her existence then she would feel seriously dumb.

... rior Uvim, report.

This was it. A direct current to Dragao Azul.

He threw back his shoulders and expanded his rib cage.

She released him.

He tightened his grip as though afraid to lose her. He pressed her against his chest.

"Queen Zara issues orders about the All-Council and brides!"

His chest vibrated.

His shout echoed in her chest.

He frowned, startled.

Queen Zara issues orders about the All-Council and brides! QUEEN ZARA issues orders about the ALL-COUNCIL AND BRIDES! QUEEN ZARA ISSUES ORDERS ABOUT THE ALL-COUNCIL AND BRIDES!

His shout amplified, growing louder and louder.

His eyes widened.

This wasn't good. She pressed her hands over her chest.

The vibrations quieted.

His shoulders relaxed. He'd been holding them taut in concern.

Well, hopefully, nobody would notice the weird amplification. Maybe it wouldn't be audible by the time the vibrations reached the city where another warrior was listening in.

"Send warriors!" he shouted.

Send warriors! Send warriors! Send warriors!

The amplification was normal for the second part of his message.

Thank goodness.

Clifford caught up with them. She flew outside the echo point growling and shrieking and spreading her legs in the "happy parasol" twirl.

Okay, ordinary octopi made a parasol. Clifford was

more like a parachute. Even with one tentacle missing and a second one cut half off, she was magnificent.

She danced around, sneaking her tentacles into currents and chasing off everything. A school of fish erupted from one current in a shocked mass. A swordfish in a crossing current veered off. A pod of dolphins swooped close, curious, and then darted away.

The echo point wobbled as the cross currents tangled. The vortex pressed against the still water bubble.

Uvim tightened his hold on her. *Time to go.*

He kicked.

As they left the direct current to Dragao Azul, two final words flew back at them: *Guerreiros vem.*

She translated Portuguese. *Warriors come.*

Ominous.

They exited the echo point.

"We're not waiting?"

"Warriors will swim to the beach." His jaw set. "I will meet them there."

On familiar territory. Where he had the advantage.

Hmm.

Uvim kicked free of the currents, navigating the creatures disrupted by the antics of the huge cave guardian, and set a different direction. Still in explanation mode, he pointed out the different tastes.

"Taste?" she repeated. "You 'taste' currents?"

He nodded.

They followed the new 'taste' of the current on a twisting, turning path over deep water until it reached land. Faial Island. The volcanic beach.

The waves grew shallow. They crashed onto land.

Gravity dragged her down, a million times heavier.

Milly let go of Uvim and fell on her hands and knees in

the evening surf. Water drained out of her lungs like she'd swallowed a pool. It burned. Everything hurt. Her lungs spasmed and she choked.

Uvim stroked her back. "Do not fight the shift."

Milly gasped, tears running off her nose.

She would get through this. She would.

They had met on this beach days ago. Days? As far as she could tell, it had only been one day, but Zara had warned her not to trust time underseas.

Uvim stood watch over her. His outline was ... not fuzzy. Oh, no.

He was naked.

She pulled on her swimsuit. Now, at least, she was decent.

She groaned to her feet. The slightest waves at her ankles threatened.

Uvim steadied her.

"I'm dangerous," she warned.

He pulled her to his powerful chest. "I will protect you."

She rested her forehead on his rippling shoulder. "Thank you."

And when she was queen, she would protect him.

He stroked her hair. Silky and wet. Her body thrummed with sudden awareness. His proud member pressed against her fabric-covered hip. Her pussy throbbed.

She wanted him.

If she was brave.

Milly straightened.

She was different now. Everything was different. She was a mermaid! Soon to be a powerful queen.

Probably.

Unless something went wrong.

Rough volcanic gravel scraped her bare feet. She picked her way across the overcast beach, heading to the cell phone. She'd call her boss and ask for a pickup. And everything would be fine.

Half way across the beach, fuzziness returned to her vision, and she stumbled more.

Uh oh. The lockbox hung off-kilter from the base.

"Oh, now what?" she groaned.

Tiny puncture holes — hundreds of them — had assaulted the metal, bending and ripping it into Swiss cheese.

"Well, my trap with the pressure plates wouldn't have stopped this," she said.

Uvim cupped his masculinity in one hand for modesty. With his free hand, he touched the punctured metal. "What weapon makes this kind of damage?"

"A gun." She let out a long sigh. "Which is illegal."

This problem she'd hoped to solve herself could no longer be just hers. She had to involve Vaw Vaw's family. And maybe the *policía*.

Ugh. Her stomach squeezed. Did she have to ask for help?

Yes. Yes, she had to. She was a queen now. Or, she would be soon. Her personal feelings had to die. The mer deserved her total commitment.

He traced the holes. "What is the meaning of this symbol?"

"Symbol?"

He drew it. The bullet holes carved an image into the lockbox. She squinted harder. A triangle. Inside was a sort of ... what Greek symbol was the upside-down y? A lambda? With an apostrophe.

She shook her head. "I don't... Oh, wait. I do know."

The same marking had accompanied the Merman Repellent. A triangle around a fish head with stick legs. The apostrophe must be the cleaver.

A slow breeze shook the grasses in warning.

Goosebumps stood up on her damp skin.

She wasn't cold. She just didn't want to deal with this.

But vandals had broken the cell phone inside. Again.

"Your warriors won't need to use this tonight, right?"

He nodded.

She turned away. "Come on. We've got to hitch a ride and make phone calls."

FOURTEEN

"Hitching a ride" meant walking along the beach and exposing themselves to humans. Most agreed to take Milly to town, and then saw him, and their souls darkened in fear. They changed their minds.

"Why do they fear?" he asked. "They have the advantage on land. I have no weapons and only one free hand."

"It's your size. Try looking less intimidating."

He did not know how to accommodate her request.

She found someone she knew, and they rode in a wheeled metal box — car — to the town, collected Milly's cell phone, scuba equipment, and the purple wire-rimmed disks she'd been wearing in front of her face the day they'd gone to the island, which she seemed to don with relief. He got his covering from her boss. The females exchanged many shocked words because three days had passed under the water.

They drove to Milly's house. No foreign cars blocked the entrance. And, Uvim walked under his own power. This was good.

Milly sagged. Dark circles shadowed her eyes.

He felt strong. Revitalized.

They were together. She had transformed and swum to the echo point and returned, with a giant cave guardian in tow, and they had faced no incidents.

The Life Tree smiled on them.

Soon, she would be his.

"Are you hungry?" she asked, setting her scuba equipment inside the kitchen and walking through the house to open the windows and air it out.

He could not eat when she was so exhausted. "No."

"Me neither." She took a deep breath and stretched. "I want to sleep."

His chest warmed.

Their bodies had pressed close during the trip. Hers had fitted to his perfectly as though mer were designed to travel the ocean in pairs rather than the solitary trips he'd made his entire life until now.

He wanted to remain close on land. And sleeping with her would let him touch, stroke, explore, devour her.

"Not sex," she blurted.

She hadn't requested sex. She'd requested sleep.

He nodded.

She washed her scuba equipment on the patio and hung it to dry, and then came inside and washed dishes in the sink. She showed him how to dry, and then she took him to her bathing room and showed him how to bathe his teeth and face before bedtime.

These little rituals made her normal life. Not sailing with strangers. He wanted her quiet moments, always.

"I take it you don't do this underseas," she said, around a frothy mouthful of a cream she called toothpaste. "No brushing your teeth?"

He shook his head.

"You probably don't eat as much chocolate."

"What is chocolate?"

She choked.

His heart stopped. He hovered. She was choking? Should he rip the tooth stick out of her mouth?

She spat and turned the toothbrush on him in vehemence. "You don't have — no, wait." She held up one palm and turned away, rinsing her toothbrush and washing out her mouth. "I don't want to know."

Ah. She was not ill. He relaxed, his own tooth stick — brush — in hand. She had gotten alarmed when wondering about chocolate.

He could answer that question. "We do not have—"

"Stop!" She put a hand to his mouth again. With him towering over her, she had to lift onto her tip toes to pretend to be intimidating. "I told you, I don't want to know. Let me worry about how to feed my chocolate addiction later."

He dipped his head and spoke beneath her fingers. "I apologize."

Her chest flared. She lowered her fingers to his chest and traced the tattoo swirling over his broad collarbone. "You're so hot when you apologize."

When she did that, additional heat flooded his cock.

He would apologize more.

"And when you do anything else," she amended and sought his mouth for her kiss.

Heat flared between them with the brightness of her soul light.

He opened his mouth and she slipped her tongue in, brave and daring. Darting, sparring, meshing, desiring. They had spent the flight in close contact and yet it had not been sexual. Now, it was.

She pulled her mouth away and lowered to flat feet

with a decisive, triumphant thump. She faced her fears on land just as she had overcome them in the cave. Their kiss reaffirmed her healing.

Practice. She needed practice to become closer. Grow their resonance. Become one.

He relished this practice.

They finished in the bathroom. She found him a yellow covering she called a "T-shirt" and showed him to the couch. "Make yourself comfortable."

He rested against the flat, deep beige cushions.

She put one foot behind the other and tucked her hair. "I'll be right back."

She pattered upstairs and returned later in a soft lavender covering with buttons up the front. It bared her legs below the knee and her arms below the elbow. Her nipples peaked against the soft fabric. Her hair hung in two braids.

He leaned forward.

She showed her braids. "I didn't want you to eat my hair. I hope you don't mind."

He didn't mind.

She grabbed a colorful fabric from the opposite couch and stepped closer. "May I?"

He would always allow her whatever she wished.

She pushed him into a lying position against the couch. She seated herself, spread the fabric over his legs, folded the glass-frames on the table and lay beside him so her derriere cozied against his hard cock.

"Sorry," she murmured, snuggling in closer.

He would accept this torture. "You are very warm when you apologize."

She laughed. "Thank you."

Hmm. He had gotten the phrase incorrect.

Speaking had never been his strength. That's why his actions must be his voice. Strict obedience so others knew he was an honorable, responsible warrior whose devotion to duty was unquestionable.

Now, they would question.

Milly rested her head against his bicep and wrapped his other arm around her waist, cinching their bodies together. The couch was wide, but she intended not to roll off while sleeping and he promised to ensure her safety. He would not close his eyes for the whole night.

He could use this time to decide how to approach the coming warriors.

How many came? For what purpose?

"I will leave tomorrow," he murmured.

She blinked awake. "Leave? I thought you had to stay with me. To keep the elixir working."

"Remain on land."

Where it was safe.

She partially turned. "I have work. We're taking out a snorkeling and Snuba tour. The first stop is less than a nautical mile from the beach."

"Remain human."

"Yeah." She sighed. Her soul light dimmed. "You know, it's a long way back to Ilha Sagrada if I need a refill."

Uvim must greet the warriors. If they intended to separate him from Milly, then he would know how to proceed. But he must at least hear their orders to know how he was in violation.

"If you become unable to shift, I will retrieve a mating gem and blossom for you myself."

"Even if you get in trouble?"

He nodded.

"Just to be clear, I don't need another Sea Opal. Not if it makes you go away."

She rejected his mating jewel?

"Accept."

"I don't want you to risk." Her soul light darkened. "I feel so powerless. How can I be a mermaid already and yet feel even worse than before I had changed?"

"You are sad."

"No ... yes." She tried to laugh. "I should take comfort. You committed even though we haven't slept together."

"We are sleeping together now."

She laughed and her soul light brightened. "Yes. Sorry. We haven't had sex."

His cock pulsed. "I am committed."

"I know, but... Even if we tried to, and I got scared and changed my mind?"

"Yes."

"Even if I never conquered my fears?"

"Even if an entire year passed, and you left the sea behind."

"A year, huh?"

Some matches were not instant. Resonance could grow.

"After a year, if the warrior and his bride still do not resonate, he must return his bride to the surface."

"She had to hold out for a year if she never loved the warrior, huh?" Milly traced a tattoo.

"I am prepared."

"Yeah, you're prepared to wait for a year and I'm stressed out because it's been ... what? Four days?" She laughed again. Such a bright, cheerful, resilient woman. Praise the Life Tree she was his bride.

But the risks remained.

Their union was not sacred until they performed it in

front of the Life Tree. Other warriors could woo her. And who would not? A bright, shining woman like Milly? She was the most desirable bride on this island.

Possibly on the surface world.

He mustn't leave his station at the echo point nearest the Azores beach. His heart urged him to drag her to the city against his queen's orders.

His heart thudded.

No.

Dark thoughts poisoned his mind. He sucked in a deep breath and released it.

Soft strands of her hair tickled his forearm. Dangerous tendrils of possessiveness curled around his heart.

The mer would not accept his bride. Would they punish him? Or her?

Milly wiggled her rump against his cock, brightening his darker thoughts. "When we're snuggled like this, I feel like I can trust you. Like you have my back."

"Have your back?"

"It means you'll support me."

She had such faith in him.

"Always," he murmured.

He would fail all others — his city, his fellow warriors, even his queen — but he would not fail Milly.

No matter the cost.

FIFTEEN

Milly had so much to do before work.

That was why she dragged herself awake with a horrified gasp. What time was it? She scrambled for the alarm she hadn't set. Oh, no. The tour!

She flailed. The couch was empty.

Uvim sat in the kitchen cupping a glass of water.

"I'm sorry I don't have time to drop you at the beach!" She pounded up the stairs. "Did you need breakfast? Grab anything in the fridge!"

She put in her contacts and was selecting clothes when, of course, Zara called.

"You're calling so late!" Milly tugged a dive shop T-shirt on over her bikini and cinched the belt on her capris. "It must be after midnight?"

"I just finished the last interview. We've hunted down another bride. Right here in California!"

"Congrats." Milly jammed on her water socks and ran down the stairs.

"This one's going to join us. I know I said that about the last three but the next one is different. I can feel it."

She grabbed her scuba equipment — she kept the phone jammed to her ear — and hauled it outside.

Uvim helped her.

She didn't want the elixir to expire while she was leading a tour underwater. She didn't want to wake up on a boat to Brody administering CPR. Those lips were not the ones she wanted sucking her face. Yuck.

They dumped the equipment in her trunk.

She stretched with a groan. "So what's up?"

"I wanted to check on you," Zara said. "Ilha Sagrada is a gateway for ordinary women to turn into mermaids."

Milly laughed hysterically.

Uvim cut to her.

"Elan says I'm being overprotective again. I'm just glad to hear you're okay."

"I'm great. Everything's fine here. Um, how did you know I was at Ilha Sagrada?"

"Your boss answered the phone."

Uh oh.

"That woman needs to give up," Zara said. "Because some criminals are passing off dynamite, our warriors need to stand up and paint targets on their chests? How crazy can you get?"

"She'd keep them safe," Milly said, trying to keep the note of defensiveness out of her voice. "People should know the mer aren't scary. They're just like you and me. It would help them find brides."

"Find brides? That's what I'm doing. Finding the brides the mer rejected and giving them a chance to come home."

"Good. I meant find *new* brides."

"New? No, Milly."

"But there's a line of twenty-eight warriors waiting to—"

"How do you know?"

Double uh oh.

She hemmed. "Ah ... lucky guess?"

"That warrior told you. What's his name?" She pondered for a moment. "It doesn't matter. Look, just stay away. Do you understand? I don't want you getting involved with the mer."

Uvim stiffened.

She tightened on the cell phone. "Zara—"

"They're in the middle of a war! Undersea armies are trying to *kill* each other. Asking you to check on the cell phone lockbox was a mistake. You could run into one."

Milly let out a long breath. "It's too late. I'm already involved."

Zara's voice dropped low in horror. "What?"

"A merman and I are close."

Uvim stood ramrod stiff, as though perfect posture would impress Zara, he raised his chin and braced.

Zara sputtered. "What could you possibly mean? Do not tell me you are already together with one of those finned, tattooed freaks!"

Uvim flinched.

"Zara—"

"They're thoughtless, awful, violent creatures. Elan's the only reasonable one and even he can be nuts! You will not be enslaved by a mer who treats you like you're a possession to be claimed!"

Uvim endured Zara's verbal lashes with stony-eyed flinches.

Milly couldn't allow this to continue. "Zara."

"God, I will not live with myself if you—"

"Zara!"

"What?"

"A merman is already my *brother-in-law*."

Zara dropped silent.

Milly rubbed Uvim's hand.

He looked away.

Zara let out a huge sigh. "Oh my god, Milly. You had me. You really had me."

"I'm a laugh riot." She squeezed Uvim's hand. "But listen to yourself. Are you Dragao Azul's queen? Or are you one of our mysterious enemies?"

Zara was silent for a long moment. "Our?"

"Your attitude causes fear. Me being involved with a merman wouldn't be so bad. I'd get magical powers."

"Those 'magical powers' did me no good when I needed them."

"You liberated Dragao Azul."

"After. You don't know what it's like to have your life — your husband and your son — ripped away from you while you're begging them to stop. The bastards never even looked sorry."

Uvim flinched.

Could he still hear? Milly switched the phone to her other ear.

"And I hope you never do," Zara said darkly.

"Maybe they were just doing their duty."

"They'll be doing their duty when they stab you in the back. And I won't have that happen, Milly. Not to you."

Uvim's shoulders tightened like she'd hurt him even deeper.

She gritted her teeth. "I'm not as useless as you think."

"You're not useless. Just inexperienced. I won't let you make a mistake."

"Maybe it's not a mistake."

"It is. Believe me. I know."

Her chest heated like the sun had broken through the

clouds. But what could she say besides, *Oh yeah? I know too*. And then Zara would freak out.

Milly focused on breathing.

"You always look to the 'bright side,'" Zara said into her silence. "Pretend everything will turn out all right. But everything doesn't turn out all right. And sometimes things go worse than you can imagine."

"Keep trying," she insisted.

"Or take a step back. For your own safety. And for everyone else, too."

Milly had been through a lot. Zara had been through more.

Exiled from the city on the day of Zain's birth, torn from her husband and newborn, forced to the surface still bleeding, Zara had collapsed all alone. Milly had found and rushed her to the hospital. She'd barely survived.

Physically, she'd recovered, but jagged pain fractured her heart and mind. Her strong, fearless, just sister had hidden in their house, burrowed into a shell of her former self.

Milly had cared for Zara as best she could for that year. But it had taken the return of Elan — and Zain — for Zara to finally heal.

Now another year had passed. Milly needed to respect Zara's past while still making Zara aware of how wrong she was.

The future of the mer depended on it.

Zara cleared her throat. "I've got to get to bed and you're late for work."

Crud. She was.

"This conversation is so not over," Milly said.

"Bye bye," Zara said and hung up.

Ooooh.

She would strangle Zara. Milly would board a plane, fly to California, and choke sense into her older sister.

"Bye," she snapped at her already-darkened phone, shoved it in her capris pocket, locked up, and raced to the sedan.

Uvim did not join.

She engaged him over the roof of the car. "Get in."

"Queen Zara ordered me to stay away."

"No, she ordered *me* to stay away."

His jaw flexed. "She is not wrong."

"Actually, she is."

His brows furrowed.

The amethyst and green depths mirrored his worries. Hurt mixed with betrayal.

She wasn't the only one who'd tried to keep secrets.

"Get in the car." She opened her door and got in. "I'll explain on the way."

He did so.

Thank you for having faith in me.

She checked his seatbelt. Snug. She drove into the bright sunshine on the winding road to the harbor.

"I love my sister," Milly said, "and I know she's only trying to protect me. But I'm an adult."

"She is my queen."

"But she's not *my* queen."

He blinked. As though he had forgotten. Just because he was subject to Zara's rules — and Milly was dating him — didn't mean *Milly* was subject to Zara's rules.

"Zara ordered me not to involve myself. But I already have. Obeying her order isn't possible even if I wanted to. Which I don't. I want to see where this goes. Where 'we' go." She took one hand off the steering wheel to gesture between them. "With you."

He didn't respond.

Uh oh. Had her confession come too late?

She stopped at a stop sign and gripped his knee. "Will you go away?"

He looked down at her hand. "I will remain."

Whew. She let go to pull onto the main road. "Well, good. Then we'll figure this out together."

"You did not tell her you were a bride."

"True."

He looked at her face.

She didn't take her eyes off the empty road. "Zara wasn't in a place to listen."

"We cannot descend to Dragao Azul until—"

"I know."

"Milly, do you not wish—"

"Of course I want to be your bride!"

"Then—"

"Look, there's no point in scaring Zara. She might abandon her search. And for what? Just so we can upset her in person?"

He closed his mouth.

She sighed. "Sorry. I will tell her. I have to figure out how to explain so she understands."

He looked away.

Hiding his disbelief?

Ugh.

When would she stop worrying people? She made Zara worry. She made everyone worry, and all because she wasn't capable enough to resolve her problems on her own.

One of these days, when she found her place, she'd know it because she'd tell people she was fine and they'd believe her. That was how she'd know.

"I'll ask Vaw Vaw and my boss," she said.

He remained silent.

The harbor buzzed and the small streets lined with tourists arriving early for the Sea Festival.

They passed the dive shop. Tourists lined up inside for Brody's safety talk and life vest fitting.

Milly parked under the shade.

She was in so much trouble.

"We've got to run." She jumped out of the sedan and tapped the roof. "Let's go!"

Uvim exited to the building's shadow. "I cannot expose myself to so many humans."

"The rules are different now. You're no longer required to stay hidden by the All-Council or the ancient covenant."

He shook his head.

Okay. Fine. She didn't have time for this argument. "I'll meet you here tonight?"

"Milly..."

Her cell phone rang. It was her boss.

Good thing she didn't need this job to survive. Because her boss was going to fire her.

She hit the button to deny the call.

Uvim struggled to express himself.

Milly shifted her scuba gear up her shoulder. "Can it wait?"

"Our warriors deeply injured Queen Zara."

"Yeah. I know."

"You could also be injured. Because of us." Deep shame twisted Uvim's expressive lips. "You do not know about that night."

"You ordered Zara to the surface?"

He frowned.

"No, someone higher up must have given that order. Oh. I get it. You 'escorted' Zara to the surface?"

His jaw dropped slack. "Queen Zara told you?"

"No. You did. Just now."

His brows wrinkled. "You are formidable, Milly."

She hugged him with one arm. "Thanks. I like you too."

"But I injured your sister."

"That was wrong and you owe her an apology." She stroked his locks. "You've regretted it for a long time, haven't you?"

"Even at the moment." His chin trembled. "I did not speak out. No one listens. I do not use the correct words. I cannot convince them." He shook his head, avoiding her sympathy. "I hate this about myself."

Okay. She was going to be super late.

She dropped her gear on the cobblestone and leaned in.

He waited a long moment, and then he gave in and dipped his head. Their mouths touched, enmeshed, became one. His lips opened and wet heat mingled. His tongue entangled hers, sizzling electric. His hot kiss stole her breath, swirling delicious longing and passionate aches in her belly.

If she let him, he would do what she most feared. Sweep her reason away. Enchant her so she belonged only to him. Drop her to her knees and make her beg.

And she would thank him for it.

Milly stroked his firm, male cheek. "You didn't speak out in a dictatorship. Protest meant death. Or 'exile', which is worse. Silent devotion to duty was the only way you could survive."

"Many others were not silent."

"And what happened to them?"

He frowned.

Exactly.

She stroked his wrinkled forehead. "Everything is in

upheaval. Humans are struggling to accept the mer exist. In the mer world, only Atlantis and Dragao Azul have dared to honor queens, and in your city, it was only because they had to. Things don't change overnight — usually — but they are changing. So now is the time to speak your mind."

"I ... I cannot."

"Now is the time to try again."

"Milly, you..." He trailed off without finishing his thoughts.

"I'm listening. Even to the words you don't say. I still hear them." She lifted onto tip toe, pressed a kiss to his trembling lips, and dropped to her tennis shoes. "So try again, okay?"

His brows lifted. His expression lightened like she'd lifted a weight off his shoulders he'd been carrying for a long time.

Well, good.

She shouldered her heavy dive bag. "Sure you don't want to join me on the tour? My boss would love a merman guide."

"That change may be too fast." He stepped back, his expression stern with duty. "Watch for me."

"I will."

He studied traffic, lowered his head and trotted across the street to the harbor.

She paused at the shop door.

He was meeting the warriors from his city today. And although he didn't say he expected any problems, his anxiety hummed.

Zara had lost everything in a single moment.

Was this her last view of Uvim?

He crossed the dock, dove off the slats — to the shock of

the tourists moseying the opposite direction — and disappeared beneath the gentle swell with no splash.

Her heart squeezed.

This separation was not forever. He would return.

Hopefully, her mermaid powers would still be functioning.

SIXTEEN

illy understood him!

Uvim dove beneath the bobbing boats. So many so close together formed a strange ceiling on the water's surface.

He had not spent long on the surface or near humans. In this harbor, a thick layer of muck suffocated the coral. The oily taste of the harbor did not deter the hardier urchins and anemones and nudibranchs.

Or one other unexpected resident.

Growls echoed over the harbor, muffling the friendly noises of the other creatures.

Somewhere nearby lived a large cave guardian.

Strange.

Uvim found Milly's tour boat. He would follow it to the first location, near the beach, and await the warriors.

A large, black shadow moved beneath his fins.

He startled.

The tentacle snuck between the wooden poles.

He followed it back to...

A boiling mass!

Breathing black mud smooshed to the shallow harbor floor. Familiar... It was missing one tentacle ... half of another...

The giant cave guardian of Ilha Sagrada!

"Why are you here?" he demanded, taking up Milly's habit of speaking aloud to her friend Clifford. "Do you know what humans do to cave guardians? Their corpses hang from poles beside their 'barbecue' cooking fires. You would make a feast."

She warbled.

The sound grated on his chest.

He continued his lecture. "The boat propellers will cut your skin. Another injury would make Milly sad."

Her warble changed to a melancholy growl.

"Go back to Ilha Sagrada. That is your place. This small harbor is not safe for you."

She drew in her tentacles, squeezing herself into a small mass.

It was still at least twice the size of the largest human boat.

"Come." He kicked for the mouth of the harbor. "This way."

She did not follow.

He paddled slowly, explaining why she must not remain. She uncurled from her tight hole and dodged ships on the way out of the harbor.

Outside the wall, wild currents puffed her funnel. She stretched, uncoiling her tentacles with a satisfied growl.

Satisfied? Perhaps he, too, could sense her feelings as Milly did. If he took the time to listen.

"There is a good cave that way," he pointed toward the distant beach. "Another lies across this island."

Clifford squeezed into the lee of a boulder and snacked on a surprised crab.

Apex predators such as her were a "shadow of death" to lesser creatures.

But not to humans. Not right outside their own harbor.

"Will you not go?"

She upended rocks and snacked on wiggling creatures underneath.

Perhaps she was lonely.

A few boats motored overhead. Some entered the harbor; others left. She scanned them.

"Follow one to safety," he encouraged her.

After some thought — or a large enough snack — she pushed off the floor and followed.

He led her toward the beach.

On his way, the familiar motor sound of Milly's tour boat chugged out of the harbor. It curved in his direction and then angled out to sea.

Curse it.

He told Clifford, "Follow this land and you will see the good cave."

She veered toward the boat.

"Do you understand?" He pointed. "There. Go there."

She eyed him first with one eye and then with her other eye.

He sensed amusement. As if she knew what he was saying and wondered how long it would take *him* to figure out she wasn't interested.

Very well. He had done his best to show Milly's friend shelter.

He turned and kicked.

Not as fast as when he'd held Milly in his arms.

The so-called "bride effect." Everything felt better with a bride, whether swimming or eating or breathing.

Now he'd experienced it. The bride effect was true.

No wonder so many males suffered from "newborn sickness" — the refusal of an otherwise-honorable warrior to give up his bride after she had produced the requisite young fry.

Most warriors swore they would not waver from the ancient covenant. But when they had to bid farewell to their brides, most did not do so happily.

Elan was the first to go crazy and battle his own warriors. He was also the first warrior to claim a sacred bride during the rebellion. And Queen Zara — Bride Zara then — was the first bride who had ever fought to remain.

That night was seared in his memory.

Elders had summoned him from the barracks to First Lieutenant Elan's castle.

First Lieutenant Elan had floated unconscious. Bruises had blackened his broken body. His newborn young fry had cried in an elder's arms. Bride Zara had struggled helplessly in her bonds.

Touching a bride was a violation. Who had bound her? How without touching?

Long ropes had dangled from her immobilized limbs.

He had been ordered to take one end and convey her to the surface.

He had balked.

Why this brutal action? Why so suddenly? Brides always waited for a short recovery period before crossing open ocean. It was dangerous. And on this dark, bloody night, the elders could not even find five healthy warriors to be an escort. But they were desperate to be rid of her loud, rebellious voice. So, they ordered the last trio of warriors to convey her, weakened and bloodied, to the surface.

His superior, Warrior Soren, had taken one rope. His friend Dosan had taken another. So, Uvim had taken the last rope.

They'd obeyed orders.

Queen Zara had screamed at them on the long, dangerous journey. Her screams had broken his soul.

He had *known* it was wrong.

Violating the ancient covenant and keeping a bride was anathema. But when Uvim saw Bride Zara stumble onto the beach that night, he had understood her curses. The rebel voices were right.

The ancient covenant was wrong. Separating a mother from her husband and newborn was wrong. His obedience had been wrong.

And it was too late.

That horrifying night had changed many lives.

Elan had been the most honorable First Lieutenant ever to serve Dragao Azul. After losing his bride, he became a hostage in his own city.

Soren had refused promotion. He chose exile — and helped King Kadir found the rebel city of Atlantis.

Dosan had also been damaged. A darker, angrier world view cracked his obedient facade.

Only Uvim had not changed. Silent then. Silent now.

Milly said he had a choice. That he had been silent for self-preservation.

Was that true? Could he speak without fear? Had their city changed so much?

His father had never been a loud warrior. But the elders had respected his words.

Uvim would never be loud.

Could he claim respect?

"Uvim!"

He turned toward the shout.

Two warriors swam inland from the open ocean. Tridents gleamed at their sides and daggers were tied to their powerful biceps and thighs.

His stomach lurched.

Two warriors? The minimum number to imprison him?

Or take his place?

SEVENTEEN

Milly watched Uvim disappear beneath the waves of the harbor and then she turned and raced into the dive shop.

She was so late.

Brody had already fitted the day's tourists with swim masks and weight belts.

"Good morning, Brody," she called as she passed him finishing the safety spiel for their tour group.

He turned away. Cold shoulder. "Everyone, this way for the boat."

Right. He was still mad.

Today would be a long tour.

Their boss sat at the reception desk and eyed Milly over the rim of her reading glasses. "Having a lie in? What about our Sea Festival strategy?"

Erk. "You could come on the tour with us."

She waved it away. "I've been there."

"We might see mermen."

"Get your beefy merman to pose with a tourist and I'll forgive your lateness. We'll post the photos on our blog and become the only tour agency with real mermen guides."

Milly rested her palm on her chest. "Technically you already have one."

"Where are your tattoos?"

"In a place I can't show you."

Her boss's brows lifted in mock shock.

They both laughed.

Milly strode into the back room, exchanging her empty scuba tanks for filled ones. She shouted to the main office. "Today's a great day for snorkeling. Why else do you own a dive shop?"

Her boss grimaced at her computer screen. "You might imagine this is a dream. But the dream comes with big mobs of taxes and receipts."

"Look at the clear weather!" She set her filled tanks next to the door. "I bet we have a hundred feet visibility."

"I also have another Sea Festival committee meeting today." Her boss followed Milly into the kitchen where Milly checked and repacked her lunch supplies. "I pushed with all my might for a 'merman kissing booth.'"

"We are not doing a kissing booth."

"Five dollars to squeeze his biceps. Ten dollars to slip him the tongue."

"I'll tell Roberto!"

"I'm just mucking around." Her boss sighed. "Your sister is a tough cookie. The committee's already agreed to a merman 'ambassador' giving the welcome speech for the boat parade. Your sister won't even let one stand next to the podium."

"That's a huge responsibility," Milly noted. She tried to be neutral. Even though Zara and she were fighting, she wouldn't be disloyal.

Her boss tipped the dregs of her pot into her grungy coffee cup. "But a wonderful chance for non-threatening visibility for their plight."

"You know." Milly counted and recounted her fresh-baked bread loaves. "I *could* do it. I am a mermaid now."

"You don't look it."

That was a problem. She didn't even have fins. And everyone knew fins took forever to control. Milly flexed inside her tennis shoes. Her feet remained stubbornly human.

Her boss poured in a packet of raw sugar. "Our ambassador needs to be tall, muscled, and show off those mouth-watering tattoos for all to have a gander." She posed, her steaming mug tipping. She leaned against the counter and blew steam from the mug. "The women will find it bonza."

"Their husbands won't get a good impression," Milly observed.

"Their husbands need to be more confident."

"And confidence is how they'll compete with warriors who subsist on a seafood diet and wrestle sharks?"

"Do the mer really wrestle sharks?"

"No," Milly said. "At least, I don't think so. Those things are so loud. Not as loud as a giant octopus, but you can hear them coming."

"Loud?" Her gaze sparkled in fascination. "What do you mean, loud?"

Brody broke in with a knock and an odd expression on his face. "Boss? Got a minute?"

She glanced over. "Yes?"

He set a plastic bag of small white birthday candles on the table.

"I took these off one of our tourists just now." He moved the bag to show the paper labeled *Merman Repellent*.

Their boss sighed. "And this is the reason we need an ambassador. Search the tourists."

He nodded and departed.

Her boss set aside the baggie of dynamite. "I'll call the police. Again. Oh, speaking of bad news, that man stopped by again."

That man.

Milly's heart thumped.

Run.

No, no. She could be wrong. Right? Deep breaths. This was her job, and she wasn't getting driven away by a jerk.

Milly stood her ground. "Vernon?"

"He said 'you'd know him if you thought about it.' I had the idea he did you a favor."

Her stomach rolled. "Yep, Vernon."

"I told him if he wanted to talk to you he could do it right here during business hours with myself and everyone else present, and he took off right quick." She shook her head. "He had a fancy diving watch but doesn't use it for diving. You know?"

Yes. She knew.

Vernon had helped her when she'd most needed help.

And now he wanted her to pay.

Milly carried the last box of supplies to the tour boat. Every person she passed made her heart thump. She hated these feelings. *Hunted and vulnerable.* This must be how Uvim's warriors felt when they patrolled alone near the Newas hunting party. Their skin must crawl and their eyes must dart to every face as they braced for attack.

Milly's parents still languished in jail. Their trial was in another few months. They'd had a lot of friends in the Azores. Good people who couldn't believe the evil they'd concealed under their affable facade.

Quite a few of those good people had attacked Milly. She wasn't immune to the hurt, but she'd gotten good at sniffing out the former friends who would chase her on the street and call her an ungrateful liar.

Thank goodness Uvim was still here. Even out of sight in the water.

EIGHTEEN

Uvim wheeled to face the coming warriors.

He had no weapons. Nothing to defend himself.

The warriors kicked in a relaxed formation. They were not here to capture a dangerous prisoner.

One warrior — Xalu — swam eagerly. He gave Uvim a short nod of respect and continued inland, toward the beach.

Good. That was not the act of a male intent on warfare.

The other warrior was Second Lieutenant Dosan.

"Uvim!" Dosan shouted again.

Uvim nodded to Dosan but did not slow or alter his course. Milly's boat made fast, steady progress. He could not delay.

Dosan seemed surprised. He kicked long, hard strokes and fell into his swimming pace. "What are you doing in this place?"

A simple question with a complicated answer.

"You cannot say?" Dosan's smile twisted with irony. "Your silences are missed."

He did not mean to be silent. "What are you doing in this place?"

"I am to take your position," Dosan said.

Hollow unease filled his bones. Like he was tumbling straight into the mouth of a shark.

He shook himself. "No."

"Yes," Dosan chortled. "I will listen at the echo point and convey orders from Queen Zara to our elders. You will descend to the city and rule over the warriors there."

"You are Second Lieutenant." And during Elan's absence with Queen Zara, Dosan was the acting First Lieutenant.

"Congratulations," Dosan said. "Now, you are."

It was a promotion.

No.

Dosan anticipated his excited acceptance.

But he did not feel excitement nor acceptance. Not at all.

"Me?" he choked. "Impossible."

Dosan's mouth twisted into a rueful smile. "Do not regret my demotion."

He shook his head. Dosan's demotion was unfortunate but his own situation filled him with horror.

"I told First Lieutenant Elan I was not a popular choice for his Second. He is absent and Queen Zara does not wish to rule over the warrior's hierarchy."

"No?"

"She only rules on the All-Council and brides. You conveyed that message."

"But you are already here."

"Yes, Xalu and I had started. My demotion awaited us at the echo point." His smile sharpened. "The elders happily offer the Second Lieutenant position to a warrior who will not blare his opinions. You must leave. Now."

No. Uvim refused.

"Xalu carries his offering to engage his bride."

Uvim jerked up short. "He does?"

"His flower blossomed."

His flower!

"There was much celebration. We began on our way. And then your message arrived."

This could not be. Surely the flower had blossomed for Milly. Now Xalu carried it.

He would give the flower to Milly. The honorable warrior would dazzle her — the *most* honorable warrior in Dragao Azul — and she would accept Xalu's mating jewel and drink his flower's nectar because he could give her all she desired.

Power. Respect. Pride.

"Xalu stows the flower for safety and then he will come to you. You have been here longer. You must have seen his bride."

Uvim kicked harder to outrun this horrible fate.

Promoted. Separated from Milly. Leaving her to the most honorable warrior of Dragao Azul with an offering she would not refuse.

No!

Dosan coasted along beside him. "Why are you chasing this human boat?"

"Milly."

"Milly, Queen Zara's sister?"

He nodded.

He would capture Milly and carry her away to a place of safety. A place where she would never meet Xalu or accept his offering.

"And did you know a giant cave guardian chases you?"

"Clifford. She and Milly are friends."

"A human has made friends with a giant cave guardian? Extraordinary. Humans eat cave guardians. How did they meet?"

He gritted his teeth. "Under water."

"Where?"

"Ilha Sagrada."

"Ilha..." Dosan kicked hard and placed himself in front of Uvim. "Stop."

Uvim darted over the top of him.

Dosan redoubled and blocked him with his trident.

Uvim darted beneath.

"Do not fight me, Uvim."

He kicked hard. Dosan was a stronger warrior but Uvim was faster. And, truly, neither wanted to fight.

Dosan thrust his trident at Uvim, forcing him off-rhythm to avoid the blade. "Do not fight!"

Uvim wheeled so his head was upside-down and glared at Dosan.

Dosan's sapphire gaze accused him. "You are twenty-eighth in line."

"She is my bride."

"You may not take a bride! Twenty-seven others come before you."

"She is mine."

"Do you not understand?" Dosan shook his trident. "We have too few warriors. The city territory is undefended. Raiders from distant cities like Newas plunder our hunting grounds. If you surface and find a bride — if even *you* do this, a silent warrior twenty-eighth in line — how can the second through twenty-sixth remain at their posts?"

Dosan himself was twenty-seven.

Uvim understood this.

But he could not give up Milly. The fire in his heart would not allow it. "Give me the blossom."

"Xalu will fight you. I will, too." Dosan grimaced, furious and helpless at the same time. "You should understand. This is impossible."

Clifford crept up behind Dosan. The giant cave guardian made a gentle sawing noise that faded into the background ocean. Dosan didn't notice.

But Xalu, approaching from a far distance, noticed. He eased forward. Although within sight, he could not hear their words.

Most likely.

Dosan squared off against Uvim, unaware of those gathering behind him. "You must introduce Xalu to Milly."

Uvim growled. "Never."

"I order this as your friend."

"Any male who threatens my bride is my enemy."

Dosan's brows drew together. "When did you learn to speak? I dislike it. My silent friend, who understood his duty to the city, was much better." His hand tightened on the trident.

Clifford shrieked.

Dosan whirled, startled and then horrified.

Clifford puffed her funnel and gathered her tentacles underneath her like a massive undersea ink cloud. She dwarfed the stunned warrior.

She jetted toward Dosan.

He darted to the side.

She chased him away from Uvim with all tentacles.

Xalu pulled up as Clifford herded Dosan to him. Easier to chase them off together.

Thank you, Clifford, for your fine service. Your loyalty to Milly is exemplary.

The two warriors swam in opposite directions, kicking hard to outswim the giant cave guardian.

She jetted between them, jubilant, like a crackling electrical storm. She was having great fun.

Dosan and Xalu both hugged their tridents to their sides. Against her, such weapons were useless.

Uvim kicked right-side up and chased Milly's distant boat.

He had to get to her. He had to sweep her away before it was too late.

NINETEEN

The journey out to the first snorkeling site passed quickly.

Milly stowed the gear and prepped the morning snack — strong coffee and crusty, flaky pastries with custards and chocolates — and arranged them on silver trays she had brought over from her short-lived restaurant internship.

As she was serving it, Brody oriented their passengers on today's tour. "Stay together in the buddy system and watch out for wildlife. Our resident oceanographer and naturalist, Milly, will point out the native life she sees."

He made eye contact as he introduced her.

No more cold shoulder. Whew.

Across the medium-sized, two-deck touring boat their boss's husband Roberto, an islander, called for attention in accented English. His salt-and-pepper hair waved in the breeze and his still-impressive sailing biceps flexed as he held up a package of dynamite.

"This is forbidden. You turn it in to us now and you are

okay. We find it later and you will report to the *policía*. Understand?"

Brody crossed his arms, watching Roberto.

No wonder her boss wasn't worried. With a husband built like a sea captain, she could cozy up to all the muscle she wanted. Anytime.

The tour — full with couples, a few families, and college kids on vacation — only partially paid attention. Some outright ignored him, posing for selfies. Others lined up to help themselves to her coffee and pastries.

After a minute, Roberto carried the bag with him back to the steering wheel.

"Ugh," Milly said, under her breath. "Not *more* dynamite."

"More every day." Brody glanced at her sideways. "Be careful."

Visions of pulverized fish guts sloshed in her head. She shuddered. "You too."

One father — a middle-aged man with thinning gray hair and a large paunch — loaded his plate up with chocolate phyllo pockets. He elbowed Brody. "Does it give you the heebie jeebies? Knowing a half-human monster is in the water watching you?"

"They're not half-human," Milly asserted, striving to stay light. "They're totally human. They shift."

Their paying customer ignored her. "Watching your girlfriend? With his beady, fish eyes?"

Brody smiled tightly.

"You know how to keep them in line? A hook!" He hooked his fat mouth with his crooked index finger.

"That's offensive," she snapped, dropping the pretense. "My in-laws are mermen, you know."

He guffawed. "So are mine. Cold fish! Ha ha."

It was on the tip of her tongue to say *she* was a mer.

But this jerk wasn't the kind of person to apologize or learn. And she didn't want to announce her change to the rest of the tour. Not when she still concealed it from her family and her sister.

She glared at Brody for backup.

Brody smiled and shrugged, *not* backing her up, and furthermore, trying to shut her up. He silently reminded her they had a job.

So frustrating!

Her boss was right. Secrecy hadn't done the mer any good. It empowered jerks to make offensive comments.

Milly would talk to Zara again. The mer needed a calm, well-spoken ambassador representing them at the international Sea Festival.

They arrived at the snorkeling cove. Brody showed how to clear masks and snorkels. Milly helped the tourists roll backward off the ledge of the tour boat into the calm waves. Her group kicked around on the surface. Half opted for life jackets.

Milly had been to this shallow reef, on a slope thirty feet deep, many times. She monitored her group and pointed out curious Mediterranean rainbow wrasse, wide-eyed flounders, speckled parrotfish, and little porgies. And she held her breath to kick, pointing out the coral-lined ledges where species of moray eels hid, eyes wide and mouths gaping.

As she descended, the mask suctioned to her face and pressure made her eardrums squeak. She had to exhale to equalize.

Snorkeling on the surface was calming, soothing, and centering. Descending into the water's embrace was better.

The tourists were typical. Some gushed, thrilled with

everything she showed them. Others whined about jet-lag, sunburn, hangovers, and returning to the hotel room. They returned to the boat early.

She kept an eye on the enthusiastic tourists who took up the whole time.

Uvim must be nearby. Right? Even though she couldn't see him, his presence heated the water. Hot and prickly.

If only she took off her mask and snorkel, she'd be able to see much farther.

Tempting.

But she kept her mask on. So long as air surrounded her eyes, she could see like normal. And so long as she held her breath to dive, the air stayed in her lungs like she was ordinary.

Although she'd worn a bikini beneath her dive shirt today just in case.

If she didn't get that blossom, then someday she would be an ordinary person. Again. Forever. This vast undersea world would close.

Leading marine tours was fun, but she stayed because her boss said she was making an impact, connecting people to nature, and advocating for a better world.

Before, she'd tried and gotten bored with being a chef. She could never open a bed-and-breakfast — one of her discarded life plans. And she would not become a translator, another early goal. Her Portuguese wasn't that great and everyone else's English was extraordinary.

Where was her place?

Under the water like Uvim said?

On the surface, someone screamed.

TWENTY

Uvim approached Milly underwater.

She dove beneath the surface, holding her breath as she appreciated shallows fish.

His flight disturbed wildlife. Dogfish cut the water ahead of him, their camouflage revealing their shark shape.

On the surface, a human screamed.

Milly looked up. Splashing marked a grand exodus to the boat and everyone retreated, creating a clear spot around Milly.

Perfect.

She tilted her body and kicked for the surface.

He grabbed her plastic fin.

She jolted in surprise.

He tugged her down.

She panicked and kicked, fighting him.

He ripped off the rubber mask.

She struggled and then blinked, seeing him, and relaxed. Her mouth opened and bubbles drained out. "*Wob-wob.*"

Good. She calmed.

He kicked hard, swimming away from the coming warriors.

She coughed and choked, gripped onto him as her body spasmed, shifting. Her nails gouged his shoulders.

He endured.

"Ugh." Her words vibrated in her chest. "Shifting sucks."

His nerves twinged. "It gets better."

"Thank goodness." She inspected his shoulder scratches. "Oh, no. I'm so sorry."

"I am unhurt."

"Are you sure? These look awful. I need to trim my—hey, where are we going?"

"We must escape."

She grabbed him. Her plastic fins tangled in his legs. "What's going on?"

"Warriors are coming."

Her soul light darkened. "You're in trouble?"

"For you."

"Warriors are coming for me?" She considered this for a long moment while the reef flashed by. "But they can't touch me, right? It's not allowed?"

"They will not cause injury. They have come to claim you."

"What?"

"The first warrior. The most honorable. He has come."

"Another warrior has come to propose?" Her tone changed. "Does he have the blossom?"

His heart squeezed. "Yes."

"Hmm." She tapped his shoulder. "Stop."

Inside, his heart screamed in agony.

But his bride gave an order.

He slowed.

"A new guy has shown up," she mused. "He has a blossom. If I drink, I become a queen."

Clifford's screeching grew louder. Her black form emerged like a dark cloud.

He kicked again. Unable to stop himself.

She tapped his shoulder. "So if I drink the nectar in his blossom, do I become his?"

"His," he confirmed grimly.

"Hmm."

He swallowed. Her soul flared for him. The elixir had started to heal the breach between her soul and her body. But now she considered leaving him.

His greatest fear.

Uvim's throat closed. An ache spread over his chest. He swallowed. His throat muscles convulsed.

He had to ask. "Do you wish to become his?"

"I'm just considering my options."

If she wished to become Xalu's bride... No. Uvim could not contemplate this. There must be words he could use. His silent devotion was not enough. He must communicate his feelings to her.

"Oh, who am I kidding?" Milly rolled her eyes and wiggled to be free of his embrace. "This is stupid. I know what I want. Let go."

His arms twitched. Refusal pumped his blood hot and cold.

Duty first.

He forced himself to let Milly go.

She kicked toward the surface.

No.

His fingers closed around her fin. Arresting her.

She glanced at him. Questioning.

Release her. Uvim, where is your honor? Release her!

His fingers trembled.

Was he such a monster? He refused his own bride?

She wiggled. "I'm in the middle of work. They will do a head count and realize I'm missing. If I don't surface soon, they will be very frightened. And when I do surface, they're going to know I'm not entirely human."

His fingers spasmed. His hand opened.

She smiled, sweet, and kicked to the surface.

His heart broke.

She bobbed above the waves. The boat was some distance away now.

The humans on the boat shouted something to her.

She bumped a fist on her forehead.

They shouted again.

She bumped her fist. Not answering.

Their shouts cut off.

She dropped her head beneath the waves and lifted one arm, holding the tip of her pink breathing tube — snorkel — above the surface.

"Well, this is awkward." She glanced up at her raised arm. "I didn't want to shift just to tell them I was okay — and then shift back to finish this discussion — and then shift back again to finish work. Ugh. So I gave them the silent 'all-clear' signal. But we have to resolve this now. Any delay and they'll come and fish me out."

There would be no delay.

The black shadow loomed.

She squinted. "Is that Clifford?"

"Yes."

In the shallower water, the giant cave guardian flattened herself. She reached him and Milly and shrieked with goodwill.

Milly laughed and, with her one free hand, patted Clifford's outstretched tentacles. "I think my eardrums just ruptured. Except I don't hear you in my ears, I hear you in my chest."

Clifford rolled, her large eyes swirling around her funnel.

"I like you too. If you stick around, you'll make my coworker Brody's day."

Clifford meandered after a darting dogfish.

"What a nice octopus. I thought she'd return to her cave."

"Normally they do."

"Then I feel extra special." Her chest lightened.

Her sweet, compelling light would soon not be his. His heart squeezed.

The warriors approached. They stayed well beneath the waves, skirted the frolicking cave guardian, and focused on Milly and Uvim floating high above them.

Uvim flexed for his trident.

Dosan was well-armed. Xalu glared at Uvim. Both looked hurt and angry as though he had corrupted a sacred ceremony.

Uvim would feel the same if their positions were reversed. That his bride had been snatched from him.

He darted in front of Milly.

She rested a hand on his shoulder. "One of these warriors wants to marry me?"

"Yes."

"Which one?"

"The most honorable."

"Bride Milly!" Dosan bowed; Xalu did as well. Their tridents gleamed with deadly authority. "Uvim has taken a bride out of turn."

"It's not his fault," she said. "I knocked him out and then seduced him."

Dosan blinked. "How is this possible?"

"I wanted to be a queen, so—"

"No." Uvim pressed her back, keeping himself between her and the startled warriors. "She did nothing. I sensed her resonance and acted."

"I did knock you out," she said.

"An accident."

"Yeah, but I—"

"Bride Milly." Dosan bowed again. "Will you not come away from the surface and meet your true husband?"

Uvim tightened. His soul refused. He would not—

"No," she said.

His heart stuttered. She refused?

Dosan's mouth dropped open. He looked at Xalu.

The honorable warrior stiffened. Rejected, for the second time, on seeking his bride.

Uvim would pity Xalu if he did not involve Milly.

"I can't descend," she clarified, shocking everyone again. "I'm pretending to be human so I have to keep the snorkel clear of the water. You two come up here."

Both warriors squirmed.

"Approach the surface?" Dosan sliced his trident through the water. "We could become exposed to humans."

"Maybe even your brides," she agreed.

"Our brides?"

"I've got a boat load of tourists over there." She jerked a

thumb over her shoulder. "They're partnered but they might have single friends."

Dosan and Xalu regarded each other as if they did not comprehend her words.

"Approach the surface," Uvim suggested.

They kicked closer. But only so Dosan could protest. "No, Bride Milly. Do not confuse us by talking about other brides. Your husband is here."

"Oh yeah?" She lifted a brow. "You know what? You're right. He is."

"Come join with him."

She paddled forward.

No.

Uvim kicked in front of her.

"It's okay." She looked straight into Uvim's eyes. "This will only take a second."

Disbelief filled him with cold fear. He could not let her go. She must not go away.

She turned from him.

Every paddle of her plastic fins made him want to dart forward, grab her, and drag her away.

But he was a dutiful warrior.

An obedient, dutiful warrior.

She paddled toward Xalu.

He lifted his chest and threw back his shoulders.

She passed him.

Huh?

Her arm extended to the surface to keep the tip of her snorkel out. She ducked beneath to stop in front of Dosan.

"It's nice to meet you. But I don't think it would work out between us. I like Uvim quite a lot. Thanks anyway."

What?

Dosan's giant frown nearly split his face in half. "I am not your intended husband."

"You're not?"

"He is." Dosan pointed to Xalu.

Was it not obvious? Xalu had twice as many honor markings and carried himself with the dignity of a warrior without equal. How had Milly mistaken Dosan?

"Oh. Sorry." Milly paddled back to Xalu, popping her snorkel above the surface once more. "He had the big trident, so I thought he was the important one."

Dragao Azul's most honorable warrior regarded Milly with wordless consternation.

"Uh, right." She tried to give him a better inspection. "You, uh, do look very, uh, honorable."

Xalu replied. "You shine very bright."

"Thank you."

"You are welcome, Bride Milly."

She smiled. "So you're here seeking your bride. You have the blossom?"

"And the mating jewel."

"Of course."

They fell into silence.

Uvim's tension ratcheted higher and higher.

At any moment she would realize Xalu was the most honorable husband and she would choose him.

All he could do was watch.

If he could only speak — if he only could convince her—

"Well, I'm sure you'll find your bride soon," she said firmly. "Good luck."

Milly turned away and paddled back to Uvim.

What was this?

She'd stared upon the most honorable warrior and

turned away? She *rejected* the most honorable warrior of Dragao Azul? She returned to Uvim?

Xalu frowned.

"Wh—what has happened?" Dosan kicked forward, placing himself before Uvim. "Your husband is Xalu."

She pulled up short. "Um, no."

"He is the most honorable warrior. He is the next warrior in line!"

"I'm sorry," she said. "He's not my husband."

"He has the flower!"

"I know, and I want that." She paddled around Dosan. "But I'm with Uvim."

Her cheerful smile, matched by the warm flaring in her soul light, made him reel.

Her smile faltered.

His heart clenched and his chest squeezed.

She poked Uvim's abdomen. "Why do you look so shocked? You know we're together, right? I don't sleep with just anyone."

He nodded, jerky.

She sighed and nestled in his startled arms. "This was fun but I need to get back to work now."

Truly?

Milly was his?

Dosan darted forward. His trident rose as though to strike an enemy, but he was uncertain where to strike. "You cannot unite with Uvim."

Xalu kicked toward the boat, eying the underside as though trying to see the souls above. He agreed that Milly was not his bride.

Praise the Life Tree.

Delicious liquid heat hardened Uvim's cock. She chose him. *She chose him.*

Dosan shook his head. "No, you *must* be with Xalu."

"Why are you so upset?" Milly eyed him. "Who are you?"

He straightened. "Dosan, of—"

"Second Lieutenant," she said.

He faltered. "Former. Uvim is Second Lieutenant now."

She hugged Uvim closer. "Congratulations."

He tightened his arm around her midsection, cinching her close.

Dosan frowned. "Uvim, do not pursue a bride out of turn. Release your claim and return to Dragao Azul."

He refused.

Dosan growled. "Do not force me to bring you to justice."

"Don't force yourself," Milly retorted. "Problem solved."

"I have no choice."

"You think you have no choice," Milly mused. "I don't have time for this. Look. When does Uvim take over for you? Officially?"

"As soon as he receives this message."

"Oh, so he's already your superior?"

Milly's words were true. Uvim *was* Dosan's superior.

Dosan's mouth opened and closed, even though he was speaking with his chest. Some surface habits were ingrained.

"Then, as your superior, he's not leaving," Milly said.

"But..." Dosan eyed his trident as if he were no longer certain why he was carrying it. "But *he* is needed in the city."

"Uvim's definitely needed here. The single most important thing warriors can do, right now, is to make a positive impression as the Sea Festival's welcome ambassador."

Her soul light brightened. She truly believed in her words.

But despite her warming confidence, unease seeped into Uvim's chest. He was no speaker.

Dosan also reacted. "I will not allow Uvim to throw away your honor or break the basic tenets of the mer."

"You have it easy." Milly tapped Uvim's chest. "Uvim stays here. If you force him back to your city, then you're disobeying Uvim — your superior — and his orders. So, the only way to maintain your honor is to obey him. Which means to let him stay here. Right?"

Dosan stuttered. "Uvim?"

Uvim stroked Milly's curved back. His bride was compelling. "Remain with me now. We assist Xalu with finding his bride. You will escort Xalu's bride back to the city."

Milly pressed her lips to Uvim's. "Stay out of sight."

"Always."

"We're kind of having a situation here. Someone is selling stupid 'Merman Repellent' as actual sticks of dynamite. We confiscated everything but who knows what jokers might throw from another ship? Stay out of sight."

"We prefer secrecy."

"Right. I'll be seeing you."

She kicked to the surface and gasped, choking and flailing, as she shifted. A white ring landed in the water. She threw herself over it. Humans towed her back to the boat.

Dosan held his trident in one hand and then the other. Torn.

Uvim regarded his old friend.

Without Milly, the dynamic changed. He and Dosan

had fought together on many assignments. Such as that night, long ago, when they had both carried a bride against her will to the surface and led to their city's rift — and near destruction.

Dosan rubbed his wrinkled forehead. "Our elders will spit us like hunted longfin."

"They already disliked you."

He laughed.

Unexpected.

Familiar sarcasm twisted Dosan's lips, as though he were swimming free of an ink cloud and could finally see. "Yes, that is right. My complaints were loud, but I still obeyed. Perhaps our elders will learn to appreciate me in my absence."

Uvim nodded.

"But," Dosan twirled his trident, "I never believed the dissenter would be you."

True.

"Perhaps your silence masked the real danger all along." Dosan fixed his trident to his side. "Your orders, Second Lieutenant Uvim?"

How strange to hear such a title. Dosan awaited his orders.

Uvim lifted his chin. He would strive for wise decisions.

Xalu drifted on the tides, lost. His bride was not Milly. His bride was not on the boat. The sacred islands were empty. Where must he look?

A good question.

Uvim too had impossible tasks. He must still gain a blossom to secure Milly. And he must decide how to handle her ongoing requests to expose the mer at the Sea Festival.

This festival was important to her.

"We will discuss," he said. "Remain with the tour boat today. Out of sight."

"One question." Dosan kicked under the boat's shadow. "What is this object your bride warned us about?"

"What object?"

"I believe she called it, 'dynamite'?"

He shook his head. It was a foreign word. He had studied much of English but his Portuguese — the most recent language of the sacred islands — was stronger.

"No?" Dosan's lips curled with the irony. "We will know when it attacks."

TWENTY-ONE

illy chucked seawater, heaving and coughing, while the strong arms of her coworkers dragged her on board.

"Jesus, Milly!" Brody glared at her in panic. "What the hell happened?"

"Down the wrong pipe," she choked.

He wrinkled his brows in disbelief. "Where were you?"

Milly gasped. Her heart jumped. She made it look as real as possible. "Thought I was going to die."

"Die?!" A panicked woman shrieked at a looming shadow in the water. "Shark! Shark! I saw a shark!"

Brody wheeled on the woman. "Calm down. We already established it was a dogfish."

Dogfish had the shape of a shark but the pattern and coloration of a muddy brown to protect itself from larger predators.

Such as a giant octopus.

The woman gasped. "But I saw—"

"Something like this?" He showed her the picture of the dogfish on his phone and she calmed.

"Before. But just now I saw something different! It was large and black."

"Shadow." Milly's voice rasped in her throat. She coughed, face hot. "A cloud."

"A cloud?" The woman evaluated the cumulonimbus rolling in. "Oh. Maybe..."

Whew. They had escaped.

Brody gave Milly a long, searching look and then tended to his guests. The tourists Milly was supposed to tend as well.

Milly escaped to the galley to prepare lunch. Grilled ham and cheese paninis, cut pineapple and melon, prosciutto and potato chips, her favorite crusty bread, farm cheese with spicy pimento, snackable yellow lupini beans, and cookies.

Half way through preparations, the condiments got fuzzy, and she remembered to put her glasses back on.

Huh.

So, now it was official. She was with Uvim.

Xalu — the beefy warrior broader than he was tall, with smoky black tattoos and a righteous lilt to his chin — was not her type.

Would he forgive an accidental air horn injury? Doubtful. But she couldn't get a read on him. They didn't resonate.

Being presented with another husband had cleared her feelings. She didn't want to be a queen just for the special abilities. She wanted to be with Uvim.

Uvim's surprise she preferred him had been comical — and a little sad.

Why had he been so surprised? Couldn't he see the "fire" in her soul? Didn't he know she was changing? Yielding? Falling for him?

Surrendering to the tide of her feelings?

Milly carried out her trays. The tourists devoured them with enthusiasm. Maybe her chef's training hadn't been useless.

Everyone gorged and napped while Roberto piloted to their next destination.

Confiscated dynamite hung from his steering column. Good thing the sunlight couldn't set it off. This much dynamite would blow him — and the boat — to bits.

This sea was too beautiful to be dynamited.

Roberto anchored at their destination: a sea cave on a secret seamount between Faial and Ilha Sagrada.

She pushed the thoughts from her mind to focus on her job: Fitting the tourists with Snuba regulators and harnesses.

Brody gave another safety talk. He ended it with, "Aside from the fantastic coral, you'll see 'Octopus Hollow,' a series of caves where an entire colony of octopi lives in harmony."

How close was Clifford? Maybe they'd see a lot more.

Milly double-checked tanks and then she and Brody pushed in the Snuba rafts. She snapped each tourist's harness to the raft via a twenty-foot rope, then secured the regulators.

Snuba was neat because it united the freedom of snorkeling with the depth of scuba diving. While their air tanks floated on the surface, the tourists could paddle to the limit of their ropes and examine sea life. It was the closest any human could get to the freedom of the mer — and freedom stopped at the length of the hose.

People were naturally buoyant, so they had to wear weight belts to descend. Otherwise, they'd pop to the surface.

Funny how she didn't need a weight belt after she transformed.

Brody led the first group for their twenty-minute tour.

Milly monitored the rafts and bubbles with Roberto. Some second group members, waiting for their turns, strapped on their snorkels and paddled around the surface.

Brody climbed out at the twenty-minute mark.

He said nothing about seeing a ginormous black octopus. But he stared at Milly again as though he had a lot of unanswered questions.

After he got back, Milly prepared the second group. One woman with a voluptuous purple swim dress and crinkly black hair remained behind. Her husband slept on her thigh and she shaded him.

"He's not feeling well." Her tone sounded resigned. "I have to stay behind."

"Are you sure? This is the best part," Milly said. "You'll be back in twenty minutes. I could find him a pillow."

"It's fine, hon. Thanks."

How unlucky! Well, she would not force anyone into the water. Milly double-checked weight belts and cleared regulators.

Her tourists held onto their rafts, bobbing in the gentle waves.

"Visibility's so good - almost a hundred feet. The octopi are out," Brody called to her.

He loved the octopus colony.

She waved an acknowledgment, checked in with her group, and dipped below the surface.

Exotic coral tangled on a pointed seamount that housed vast marine life. They fringed a deeper drop-off. But the highlight was the colony of octopi living in the cave-pocked rock.

The octopi popped out of their caves like curious residents of a multi-story apartment building.

Their big bulbous heads and plus-sign eyes were so cute. Easy to see why Brody liked them. A few batted colorful stones. Others stood up on their arms like apes resting on fists. Others twirled, multi-color parasols.

She continued to glance outward. Her humanity limited her vision but Brody was right. Unprecedented visibility let her see much farther into the dark depths than usual. With her prescription mask, they veered sharply into focus.

Something flickered on the edge of her vision.

She turned.

A male with long fins swam along the underside of the boat.

Who was that? Dark tattoos ... Sapphire?

Unease slipped into Milly.

Their bubbles obscured a great deal. Maybe no one else would notice...

The tourist next to her turned and jolted. She tapped her husband and pointed.

Uh oh.

Soon everyone on her tour gestured excitedly and nodded. They saw Dosan. Several ascended to the rafts and called out to the others on the boat.

And she'd just told the warriors to stay out of sight!

Oh well.

Their twenty minutes of air finished. Milly helped everyone ascend and disconnect the Snuba equipment. Roberto sounded the chime to recall the snorkelers to the boat. She ascended the ladder with the first Snuba raft. Her tourists chatted about their sighting.

"I swear I saw a merman," one woman was saying.

"I did too!" her husband said. "I swear I saw two."

"Three!" said another woman.

Her husband agreed. "I thought someone was swimming without their regulator or mask and then it hit me. Hello! It must be a merman."

"So cool!" the first husband enthused. "They'll never believe this back home."

"I'll never forget it my entire life," the other said, while their wives grinned.

These couples were as thrilled with seeing mermen as they had been with seeing the other marine life. So, there was hope for humanity. And the family with the jokester husband was quiet. Ah, the brash father snored on the deck.

"Look, Jen." The husband who'd been ill nudged his wife and pointed at the returning Snuba divers. "You missed the best part. I swear you're the only woman in the world who would work through her own honeymoon."

Jen sighed, resigned. Although her husband had the dark creases under his eyes, she looked like she had a deeper tiredness in her soul.

Milly dove in for the last Snuba raft. She unhooked the tanks and handed them up to Brody one at a time.

Brody said nothing but something weighed on his mind.

A dark stone slid across the raft.

"Weight belt," Brody noted. Someone had just dumped theirs on top – unfastened – and the square metal weights slid off. He hauled the rest of the belt onto the deck.

Two loose weights plopped in the water.

She sighed and fixed her mask. "I'll see where they go."

"Wait—"

She dove.

The weights dropped like stones.

She kicked a few feet and oriented herself against the

closest landmarks. Gorgeous coral. Close to the octopus colony. Really, really far from the bottom.

This was pristine.

And impossible to collect the distant, tumbling weights without revealing her transformation.

Oh well. She'd be back.

Milly kicked for the surface. Time to return to the harbor, report to her boss, and figure out what to do with three warriors instead of—

Something buzzed near her face.

It was a long, white, plastic candle. The string was lit; it fizzed.

How could it burn underwater? It must have a water-proof coating—

Dynamite!

TWENTY-TWO

Dynamite.

The realization slammed into Milly like a fist. Her heart thundered in her throat. This slender white plastic stick could kill her right now.

No, the fuse was long. She had a few precious seconds.

A few precious seconds...

She kicked after it, snatched the tube, and pulled out the fuse.

The fuse hissed in her shaking fingers. The white coating disintegrated leaving only a dull black thread.

The dynamite — the actual powder — was in her other hand. So it was safe.

She had de-activated—

White-hot pain gnawed on her fingers.

Ow!

Her hand spasmed. She jerked back, releasing the burning fuse.

"*Wob,*" she burbled in pain. Her voice disappeared in the air bubble. She closed her mouth to the water.

The fuse hissed to the tip and fizzled out. It became an inert black thread.

Her fingers throbbed.

She was so dumb.

Uvim appeared before her. He gripped her wrist and examined her burned fingers.

She tried to tell him. "Dynam-*wob*."

Crud. Did he get it? She lofted the white cylinder. *This was dynamite.*

Another dynamite struck the water and hissed.

No!

She thrashed.

He released her, darted to it, and captured the hissing dynamite.

And then he held it. Hissing. In his hand. While the spark chewed up the fuse closer and closer to the explosive body.

She lunged for him and yanked out the fuse. This time, she released it. The fuse hissed and dissipated.

She stared at him. *Did he understand?*

He stared back at her. Blank.

Crud. Crud. Crud.

She kicked for the surface.

He launched her to the surface.

Milly flew out of the water. "Brody!"

The boat bobbed. Guest chatter muffled her cry.

She smashed into the water. Under the surface. She coughed liquid — *Do not shift!* — and forced herself out. Waved and shrieked.

No breath. No voice.

She gagged. "Brrgh!" There, her voice came back. "Brody! Roberto! Brody!"

Brody's head popped over the tourists. He approached the railing and his searching gaze lit on her. "Milly?"

Further toward the bow, another stick of dynamite dropped over the side of the boat.

It would shatter the hull.

She threshed her plastic fins toward the bow. "Someone's throwing dynamite!"

"What?"

She lofted the plastic dynamite she'd disarmed. "They're throwing dynamite! Now!"

His face blanked in horror.

He turned, scanned the guests, and an unrecognizable expression crossed his easy-going face. He shoved through the guests. "Roberto!"

A stick of dynamite arced high over her head and plopped the water behind her.

One close to the hull. One far behind her.

She couldn't get both.

Milly focused on the one closest to the boat.

"Milly!" Brody shouted, muffled. "Get out of the water!"

She kicked hard.

"Get out!"

She ripped off her mask and dove.

The dynamite closest to the boat descended. It stood out in stark relief. Her scuba fins sped her forward. She grabbed the plastic tube and separated the fuse.

It hissed and went inert

Deactivated.

Safe.

She gulped water.

Her stomach rebelled.

She coughed and sucked in more seawater.

Her body fought the shift. Her will crumpled. It couldn't stand against biological need.

She kicked the wrong direction, drowning herself. She thunked the seamount and passed the panic.

Songs tangled in the surrounding water.

In the colony, each octopus squawked like a seagull fighting over French fries in an ugly yet so adorable song. Nudibranchs, parrotfish, wrasse. Rock crabs. Tiny sea horses.

Dynamite would destroy them.

Human dynamite.

Her and Uvim too.

The warriors appeared in stark relief. Startled by her appearance. Unsure of what to do.

"Bride Milly!" Dosan kicked for her. He held out the hissing stick of dynamite like a torch. "The dynam! You chased it."

"Destroy it! It's a bomb. Pull out the—"

Uvim grabbed the dynamite and crushed the white cylinder in his hands.

"—fuse."

The powder floated away. The plastic peels dropped. The fuse floated on another current, away from the dissipating powder, until it went out.

Well, apparently crushing it worked too. "Okay. Sorry for the scare. But if any of that powder had ignited, we'd be fish food."

He and Xalu both looked surprised.

"A dangerous accident," Dosan said.

"No."

They turned to Milly.

Their naïve confusion was so heartbreaking. She wished she could lie and say it was a mistake. But Brody had searched bags. Roberto had made an announcement. And no one had thrown dynamite until they spotted mermen.

"I'm sorry," she said.

Uvim was grim. He understood.

The others did not.

"What is the meaning?" Xalu asked.

She tried again to explain. "There are always a few jerks who make life harder for everyone else."

"Humans attack us now?" Xalu looked at the surface. "Do they not understand? We mean them no harm."

"Yes. They should." She had no easy answers. "Brody and Roberto must be taking care of the culprits right now."

"We are so few," Dosan mumbled.

"Secrecy is our only safeguard," Xalu said. A harsh note made him bitter.

"But why?" Dosan gripped his trident. "We triumphed over the All-Council. We came so far."

Her heart squeezed. She reached for Uvim's hand. He took hers, already moving toward her with unspoken understanding.

"This will stop," she promised. "You speak at the Sea Festival. Everyone will see you are good people who've endured tyranny and atrocities and survived. And until the Sea Festival, I'll take responsibility for you. You're under my protection. Nobody's getting hurt on my watch."

The warriors relaxed. Believing in her.

"You're safe," she said.

Slender cylinders spattered the water. Like someone on the boat had dumped over a bucket of fish. Except these fish were hissing dynamite.

Oh, no.

"Destroy!" Uvim shouted.

The warriors scattered, attacking the dynamite. She dove, capturing and yanking fuses.

One white dynamite hissed past her face.

How many more?

Uvim chased a stick of dynamite floating above the octopus colony.

The small octopi came out on their ledges and watched the falling, hissing sticks — and the desperate warriors — with friendly curiosity. An empty dynamite body landed on a rocky ledge right in front of one of their caves. A brave red octopus batted it off like an irate neighbor sweeping off garbage.

They'd be pulverized. Smashed by the shock wave into jelly. Their caves would shatter. The playful, adorable octopi.

She kicked harder to reach the barrage of falling explosives. Yank, yank, yank. So many hissing fuses. No way she could stop all in time. No way.

There. She deactivated the ones closest to her. Xalu and Uvim had destroyed theirs. Only a few sank out of their reach ... the warriors got them ... and they were almost done...

The last dynamite twisted on a current. It dropped into the colony. The fuse hissed to the lip of the plastic.

No!

She braced.

Dosan cut in front of her like a shadow across the sky. A flash of a long rod — a trident — glinted in the sunlight.

The spark disappeared inside the dynamite body.

He slashed.

His movement made a choppy current. The dynamite bounced.

The tip of the dynamite "candle" separated from the

body. Broken in two, the fuse pulled free. In the opposite direction, the caustic explosive powders dissipated.

But not fast enough.

The burning fuse ignited the specks of powder.

A flash.

Boom.

The coral cracked and shrieked in agony. The rocky caves shuddered. Octopi scattered. The red one flopped on his ledge, limp.

The shock wave punched her in the sternum. "Ungh."

It stung but she would be okay.

Uvim, behind her, rubbed his chest and his head. His cheek bled from a slender cut. Xalu was even farther back. He rubbed his head and grimaced.

She was closest to Dosan — who had nearly been on top of the dynamite.

His trident slipped through his hands. It spiraled into the abyss.

His eyes rolled back into his head. He curled into a fetal position and sank.

Oh, no!

She chased after Dosan. Xalu and Uvim arrested his fall. She tried to check his pulse.

Xalu edged her away with his beefy, black-swirled shoulder. "You must not touch a male who is not your husband."

"Then stop touching me," she snapped.

He frowned at Uvim.

"Collect his trident," Uvim ordered.

Xalu dove.

She felt his neck. No carotid pulse. She pressed her ear to Dosan's sapphire-swirled chest.

Lub-dub. Lub-dub.

Whew. A heartbeat.

"He's still alive." She lifted her head. "We have to get him to a hospital."

Uvim shook his head. "No time."

Dosan moaned in pain.

Was it her imagination? Were his iridescent tattoos losing their color and fading?

Uvim's intense fear was not her imagination.

She tried another tack. "What do you normally do?"

"Take him to the Life Tree."

"For first aid?"

"What is this, 'first aid'?"

"I mean if he's hurt a long distance away. What if there's no time?"

Uvim's grim expression said they had no alternative. "The Life Tree essence provides healing."

"Life Tree essence..."

Xalu returned with Dosan's trident.

She wheeled to Xalu. "Give me the blossom."

He stiffened. "You are not my bride."

"Not for me. For Dosan!"

"He is already a mer."

"Gah! Uvim, explain."

Uvim blinked and then said, "Is the blossom safely stored?"

"Yes, in our cave."

"The mating gem too?"

"I have that." Xalu reached into the woven seaweed bag strapped to his bulging thigh and removed a Sea Opal the size of her fist. A darker , smoke-swirled color, it was otherwise very similar to the one Elan had given to Zara.

She reached for it.

Xalu jerked it away.

"I'll give it back," she said. "I promise."

Uvim gestured for Xalu to obey.

He grimaced, then released the gem.

It fell into her palm. Smooth and warm. She'd forgotten how beautiful and pearlescent they were. She'd told Uvim she didn't need his Sea Opal, but now she kind of wanted it. Just to have. For herself.

She placed Xalu's Sea Opal on Dosan's bare sternum. "Now what?"

Uvim and Xalu had no idea.

She had no idea either. She willed the Sea Opal to work. "Feel better soon, Dosan. Please."

The gemstone shimmered.

And so did his chest.

Hey! Was that his soul light? Had she achieved a new mer power?

But no. The glow faded. And she couldn't see any glow in Uvim or Xalu. She had to guess their feelings — taut, anxious — the old-fashioned way.

Dosan's lashes fluttered. He uncurled and lay flat.

Xalu and Uvim both relaxed but their worried frowns remained.

She pinched Dosan's fin.

"Ngh." He rolled, pulling his fin away.

The Sea Opal rolled off his chest.

Xalu dove and caught it, replacing it in his woven pouch.

Probably it had done all it could do. She turned to Uvim. "Can Dosan shift?"

Uvim didn't know.

They had to do something. A hospital was their best bet. "Let's get him to the boat."

Xalu and Uvim carried Dosan to the surface.

Milly glanced back.

Octopi gathered around the motionless red octopus. Clifford hovered over the far side of the outcropping, peering down. Her sad wheeze stirred Milly's heart. Like punctured bagpipes playing a dirge.

Oh.

Milly wheeled to the mourning creatures. The octopi parted for her. She gathered up the limp red octopus and held it to her chest.

It hung lifeless in her arms.

Tears pricked her eyes. A current swept them away. The whole ocean tasted like her sadness.

"I'm so, so sorry," she whispered.

Small tentacles curled around her wrists.

The red octopus was alive! But barely.

The other octopi swarmed her in a group hug, sharing in her sorrow. They carried the feeble, injured red octopus out of her arms and into a cave to finish their mourning.

Milly turned and kicked hard. She got ahead of the warriors and led them to the tour boat.

She had taken responsibility for them. She had promised they would be safe. And her people — a tourist on *her* boat — had hurt them. They had hurt Dosan. They had hurt the octopi. They had hurt her reef.

Never again.

TWENTY-THREE

Uvim levered Dosan's limp arm over his shoulder and hauled him onto the tour boat, exposing their existence to their enemy.

He clambered onto the deck with a loud thud.

The humans stepped back.

Milly shifted badly once more, coughing and choking. She bent over the railing and gasped.

His shift was more graceful. The seawater drained out his gills and they sealed to form air-breathing lungs. He'd already flexed his fins back to human feet to climb the ladder.

Xalu climbed up behind him, coughing the water out of his lungs. He gripped Dosan's trident along with his own. Both he and Dosan still wore daggers strapped to biceps and thighs.

Xalu leaned closer to Uvim. "Why are they frightened? They are expert at land combat."

"Weapons violate human laws."

Xalu's grip tightened on the tridents. "But they wish us harm."

"Not all."

Milly spat to clear her vocal cords. "Roberto!"

An older male approached. He eyed the warriors and addressed Milly. "Are you all right?"

"I'm fine. Dosan needs the cot."

He returned with a bundle of metal and fabric. Milly directed it beneath the shade of a tent. Roberto and another male pushed and pulled it, unfolding it into a taut canvas sheet stretched across a metal frame.

She motioned over Uvim.

He laid Dosan on the worn canvas.

Dosan grimaced in pain. He coughed hard, curling in on himself, and then collapsed. A large red mark covered his chest. Black bruises radiated from the center.

"Take us home," Milly ordered. "As fast as possible."

Roberto moved to the steering controls. The boat vibrated and they moved.

The human male known as Brody handed Uvim long rectangles of fabric. "Put these beach towels on."

Ah, their nakedness.

He accepted the body-sized, flat rectangle. How to wear it? There were no fastenings. He pinched it with one hand.

Milly folded one edge against the other, tucking the soft fabric against his waist. It fit snugly.

Xalu watched her action. He tucked his own "beach towel" without help.

As expected of the most honorable warrior.

Milly spread the final towel over Dosan.

His injured chest rose and fell.

Brody glared at Milly. "What were you thinking?"

"It's my fault." She rested her healing hands over Dosan's chest. Worry and regret shamed her. "I told them to stay near. I didn't consider the visibility."

Brody rubbed his forehead. "Obviously that's not what I meant."

"What did you mean?"

"You dove back into the water, Milly. You could've been the one on this cot."

"I should have been."

"No way."

"I asked for help," she said bitterly. "Dosan got hurt because of me."

"You're allowed to ask for help."

"I promised no harm would come to him."

"So?" Brody let out an exasperated sigh. "Since when are you the all-powerful Queen of the Ocean?"

Her eyes widened. Her soul light darkened. She hugged her fists to her chest.

No.

Uvim pulled her to stand and then enfolded her trembling, small form into his arms. She *would* become an all-powerful queen. She must not darken her light.

"You are not a queen yet," Uvim murmured.

Milly relaxed into Uvim, tipping her head back and resting on his chest. "I should have done more."

"Well, what are you doing now, dragging him out of the water?" Brody demanded.

"We owe him," Milly said.

A female wearing a deep purple covering that flowed over her curves crept close to their group. She knelt beside the cot and stared at Dosan, fascinated.

Xalu glanced at Uvim. He also noted her presence.

Her soul light shone with gentle brightness. She was no threat to Dosan.

Uvim lifted his chin, signaling for Xalu to ignore her encroachment.

His subordinate — a male who should by any right be above him — stood steadfast.

"Dosan slashed the last stick of dynamite so most of the powder dispersed," Milly explained to Brody and now the second female. "Only a small amount ignited."

Brody's brows lifted. "A small amount caused that giant geyser?" He blew out a sigh. "At least no one was hurt."

"An octopus may have died."

His soul light darkened. "May have?"

"He looked dead. When I picked him up, I felt a small movement. So..." She hugged Uvim tighter. "I hope he didn't die."

Brody dropped his head into his hand.

Milly scrubbed her own red eyes. Moisture shone on her palms.

Uvim pressed a comforting kiss to her crown.

Her soul light flared.

Yes, she accepted his comfort. In the midst of this tragedy, she accepted him.

Milly finished her explanation. "Without Dosan the blast would have killed us. The whole colony. Me. The boat. He saved us. He saved all of us."

Brody lifted his head, pinched the bridge of his nose, and sniffed. "They'll answer to the police."

"They?"

Brody pointed.

At the stern, several males stood guard over an older female and her son. Her dim soul light revealed her fears. Her son crossed his arms over his thin chest. His soul fluctuated. Unsettled, trying to look fierce, but scared.

His father, a heavyset male, strode in front of the guards. His exasperation reached the back of the boat. "It was a joke. I want my lawyer."

Milly flared, bright and hot. She shouted, "You're going to need one!"

The father thrust out his chest. "Hey! They didn't know, all right?"

"No, it's not all right! They destroyed precious marine life and almost killed someone!"

"I didn't see anything."

"Because!" Milly strained against Uvim's arms. "We stopped you! Almost."

He stepped toward them, mean and aggressive. "You don't know anything."

Her frustration and anger made her tremble.

Uvim held her. "Xalu."

Xalu stepped forward clenching both tridents. His deep voice vibrated with deadly intent. "Do you challenge the mer of Dragao Azul?"

The aggressive male swallowed and stepped back. "Nobody meant nothing. It's a misunderstanding. You'll see."

"Sit down," Milly snapped.

He curled back his lip in fury.

Xalu inclined his head toward the man and pinned him with a fierce warning.

The aggressive male sat.

Xalu straightened and rested the tridents in the crook of his elbow.

He was calmer than Uvim. This was Uvim's first time leading on his own. Dosan had always been his voice. His encouragement. His friend.

By his side.

And now he lay dying.

The concerned female in purple rested her palm on Dosan's forehead. "Is he going to be okay?"

Milly looked up at Uvim.

He had never faced such surface weapons. "I do not know."

The humans gathered closer to hear.

The female stroked Dosan's forehead.

"He will pull through." Milly's voice rang with determination.

Everyone looked at her.

Her chest glowed.

She pulled free — strong now — and knelt beside the woman. She touched Dosan's chest.

His soul light glowed. Steady and even.

"With our help," Milly added, her fingers grazing his bruise. "And a hospital."

"No hospital," Uvim said.

"But he has blunt force trauma."

Uvim shook his head.

"Actually," Brody looked up from his silent introspection, "any hospital will probably turn him away."

"What?"

"I saw it on the news. One of these ... people ... got shredded by a boat in Florida. He collapsed on a beach and vacationers rushed him to the hospital. The hospital refused to treat him out of fear of making him worse. Their biology is unknown."

"No chest X-rays..." Milly stared at Dosan. "We have to do something."

"He must rest," Uvim said. "Rest and quiet."

"Rest and quiet will not happen. Not at our place."

"Your castle is quiet."

"My house is too small. And Vaw Vaw has rooms but her house is loud and always full of people." She bit her lip. "What are we going to do?"

The female paused mid-stroke. "We have a quiet place."

Behind her, a male spat his water.

"It's a rental," she said, ignoring the male. Others handed him papers to dry his mouth and wet coverings. "We have extra rooms. It's close to the harbor."

"Would you?" Milly asked, grateful.

"Jen," the male hissed.

Milly looked back at the male. "If your husband doesn't mind?"

"Husband?" She jerked up and looked around, her soul light doing a rapid fluctuation. She lit on the male behind her. "Ian?"

"You're Mr. and Mrs. Isaacs, right?"

"Oh, ew!" Ian laughed. "We have the same last name because she's my sister."

Milly grimaced. "Sorry."

Jen mirrored her expression. "My ex—"

"The lying, cheating, dickless jerk."

"—is out of the picture. This isn't a honeymoon."

"It's a honeymoon from him," Ian said.

"I have a non-refundable deposit on a big rental for just me and Ian. And my maid of honor. Former. But she won't mind if we bring anybody home."

Milly looked to Uvim. Consulting him — as the leader — about his warriors.

He considered Dosan's safety and delivered his order. "You must also shelter Xalu."

Xalu straightened. Doubts vanished from his now blank face. The most honorable warrior would obey.

"We can," Jen promised.

Milly leaned over Dosan one more time, wished him to feel better, and squinted as though trying to see his soul light.

It remained steady.

She sighed and stood. "I have to call Zara. She'll be mad but she has to know."

Milly disappeared through the crowd inside the boat house.

Strangely, the glow in Dosan's chest remained strong. Had he already healed so well? The black-red bruise was daunting. But with Jen kneeling at his head, stroking his forehead — just like a human, so careless with her touch — he glowed as if he were still near a future queen.

But Milly was inside the boat now...

"Hey." Brody met Uvim's eye. "Thanks for saving the octopus colony."

Uvim nodded.

"They're the highlight of my trip." Brody looked away and rubbed his nose in embarrassment. "I know it's kind of dumb, but they always come out to say hi. Like they know me, you know."

"They do."

"Huh?"

"Know you."

He made a dismissive pshaw. "Me and everybody else with a face mask."

Uvim considered the words needed to show Brody the truth.

The male was angry and hurt. Milly had once made an overture to become his mate. She said Brody did not care. Perhaps she was correct. Perhaps Brody only coveted Uvim's closeness with a female while his heart still searched, alone.

Brody's soul was bright. He was a human male of the ocean, an ally of the mer. If female warriors existed, one would select him for her husband.

Uvim must reach him before he changed his allegiance to this new enemy.

And so, he forced himself to speak.

"You have a bright soul," Uvim stated. His words sounded awkward on his tongue. "It resonates with the ocean. That is why the cave guardian 'octopus' emerge for you. They recognize you as a friend."

Brody's soul brightened. He rubbed his chest and looked away again. "If you say so."

But this time, his embarrassment vibrated with pleasure.

These were the words humans must hear.

Enemies hated the mer.

Those like Brody who wished to become friends must hear kind words.

Uvim finally understood.

This was why Milly wished for a warrior to speak at the Sea Festival. To share his words. To touch the souls of any humans who would be a friend.

Very well.

He would dedicate his new mission, as Second Lieutenant, to select the best warrior to speak.

For as long as he was a Second Lieutenant.

TWENTY-FOUR

Uvim studied Xalu. He was a very honorable warrior. But his soul was troubled. Could he give the speech?

Xalu stiffened. His tridents gave silent warning.

So far, he was not very welcoming.

The other humans Milly had called "tourists" gaped.

One older female braved approaching Xalu. "Can I ask a question?"

He looked to Uvim for permission.

Uvim nodded.

She brightened. "What's your name?"

"Xalu."

"Zay-looo?" She licked her lips. "And, uh, how do you see without goggles?"

"Goggles?" he repeated. His voice was deep and resonant even on the surface.

Her husband hung on her arm. "To see sharks, she means."

"I hear them."

The couple blinked and laughed in surprise.

"You hear them?" the woman repeated.

"Yes."

"It's like you have another sense."

"They *do* have another sense," their trainee-aged youth said from a seat behind them. The youth swiped his cell phone.

"Another sense," she repeated. "Wow."

"How did you know that?" the husband asked the son.

"It's all over Snapchat."

Xalu lapsed silent.

The couple moved to the railing. No others dared approach.

Perhaps, once Dosan healed, he would give the speech. His words flowed.

The boat returned to its dock in the harbor.

Milly changed into new coverings and her glasses, so he dove over the side, collected his orange swim shorts from the cave where he had stashed it, and clambered up onto the dock to return to Milly's side.

Police apprehended the mother and son. Dosan was moved to the rental for his own health. The police detained and interviewed the passengers, including Milly and Uvim.

One police inspector with smooth black hair and a crisp, dark uniform — even in the hot sun — asked multiple times whether Uvim desired a "visa" for traveling to "America."

"I remain with Milly," he stated.

The inspector looked at Milly.

She looped her arm with Uvim's, soaking her thin T-shirt sleeve on the salty moisture. "He's not going anywhere."

The inspector clicked his writing implement. "You still intend to testify at your parents' trial?"

"Yes. My sister will too."

He made a note.

"There's one more thing." She pointed at the fish-man symbol on the paper included with the dynamite. "Someone shot a similar design into the side of the lockbox a few days ago."

"You did not report this crime."

"I'm sorry. I was so busy. And I didn't think it was very serious."

"You were mistaken."

Her soul light darkened.

Uvim intervened. "She reports it now."

The interviewer placed the writing implements in his covering pocket. "Where is the lockbox?"

"It might still be standing. Otherwise, Vaw Vaw's family will have it. Do you know who's behind the vandalism?"

"You may go."

She frowned.

Uvim pushed. "The criminal is known?"

"No." The inspector sighed. "This drawing was found in a seized yacht. It is crude but different. Perhaps the organizer is trying out logos."

"Organizer? So you think it's bigger than a couple vandals?"

The inspector grimaced as though he had already said too much.

He allowed Milly and Uvim to leave. As they crossed the busy street to her car, she did a double-take at a passing car and darkened.

"What bothers you?" he asked.

"I thought I saw someone I knew." She shook herself. "Bad memories."

They crossed in front of the dive shop.

He would ask more questions but Milly's boss hurried out to greet them.

She handed a covering — T-shirt with the dive shop logo on one breast — to Uvim. "You're both alive."

He pulled the T-shirt on. It strained across his torso.

Milly turned to her boss. "I'm sorry we scared you."

"Too right." She squeezed Milly's hands. "The Sea Festival *will* go on. These acts of violence will not deter us."

Milly dropped her hands and hugged her boss. "Thank you."

She patted Milly's shoulder. "Thousands will see your welcome speech, Uvim. And on the internet, hundreds of thousands. You'll address them all."

Milly waited for him to protest.

But he did not.

Her boss released her and made two fists. "We'll fight!"

Uvim stiffened.

Undersea, a raised fist was the universal gesture for a challenge. Two meant a dangerous fight with no rules, no mercy, no survivors. When lofted this long, it showed contempt for the other male.

"Good on you," she said, oblivious to her insult. "Mermen and humans are the same. Nothing to fear."

He forced himself to echo her words. "Nothing to fear."

Milly studied him strangely.

"And you, Uvim, will show that to the world," her boss finished.

Milly's eyes stayed on him but her mouth questioned her boss. "What do we need to do?"

Police opened the dive shop door and waved for her boss.

"I'll mail you the details. Rehearsal when they complete

the stage," her boss said, skipping back. "I can't believe the festival starts this week!"

She dropped her fists.

His shoulders released and his racing heart slowed.

Milly opened the car doors. Heat billowed out. She rummaged in her trunk, folded a towel across his seat, and checked his buckle. They left the hot street behind. Milly drove to Jen and Ian's quiet home.

Uvim entered his second human dwelling.

The layout was similar to Milly's. White walls, tile floors, and a variety of resting objects — low couches, large stuffed chairs, and tables. A flat black panel displayed pictures and sound.

These things, along with unsecured openings called windows and secured openings called doors, matched Milly's.

The brother, Ian, gave the tour of the rental. In one quiet room, Dosan slept. Jen nursed him.

Xalu had escaped with both his and Dosan's tridents. Now, he patrolled their private, fenced pool.

With Xalu and Ian, Uvim shared the mystery organization's logo: a triangle around a fish head with stick legs being stabbed by a weapon known as a meat cleaver.

"Milly believes this is a rude depiction of a merman being killed," he explained.

Xalu gripped his trident. "This is war. Someone must tell the elders."

Yes. Someone must

"Milly reported to Queen Zara," Uvim said.

Xalu's eyes narrowed. "The *elders* must be told."

"They will be."

But Dosan was injured. Xalu must protect him from further attack. And Uvim could not leave Milly.

Doubts remained in Xalu's eyes.

Would he refuse Uvim's leadership?

The honorable warrior stepped back. His face blanked. Neutral.

Uvim released his fears in a long breath. Xalu would not challenge him today.

Truly, he longed to return to the ocean. Now. And stay there.

He could see vast distances under the water. Track predators darting miles away.

But he could not spot his enemy in this air world. And that meant he could not protect Milly.

The problem rattled him during the drive away from the rental. Milly drove to the harbor lockbox — a shiny, new metal box rested on the pedestal — and then she drove on to Vaw Vaw's house for the evening meal.

The ride was silent. Her mind was occupied. But it was an easy silence. She seemed much calmer than when she had stormed away to report to Queen Zara.

"You agreed to the welcome speech," she said, breaking into his thoughts. "Even though you refused before."

He nodded.

"Why?"

"We must make an overture of friendship to those humans who would become our friends."

She sat taller. "You understand."

Yes. He finally understood.

"Great." Milly slowed and turned onto a bumpy gravel driveway in front of a large white adobo house with a red tile roof. "Um, Vaw Vaw really likes mermen."

Tension eased from his shoulders. He welcomed a peaceful meal with a Portuguese grandmother.

"So, it's likely she'll ask you to give a speech."

"Another will give the Sea Festival speech."

"Another? Who?"

He shook his head. Not him. Dosan or Xalu must. Not him.

Milly parked. Her lips curved wryly. "Sure? Now's your time to practice."

Humans spilled out of the house, raced across the yard, and swarmed the car.

He braced himself. "What is this?"

"A human family."

"One family!"

"Welcome to Vaw Vaw's." Milly unsnapped her seatbelt, tossed him a careless grin, and got out.

"*Bem-vinda!*" they shouted to her. The car door closed on the noise. She was engulfed in cheerful young fry.

Welcome.

Small hands tapped on the glass.

Young fry. So many young fries.

He eased the door open and exited into the enthusiastic, young crowd.

More young fry than he had ever seen in his life surrounded Uvim. Hands touched him, poked his tattoos, thunked him. Small females and small males. They poked his bare feet. "*Barbatanas!*"

He obliged, flexing his feet. The toes unfolded, surprising some, and his fins emerged.

They shrieked in appreciation.

"Vaw Vaw." Milly hugged a diminutive female. "*Este é meu namorado. Uvim.*"

The female, Vaw Vaw, finished Milly's hug and then strode to him. The crowd parted around her like waves flowing around a powerful rock. Her arms opened wide. She wore glass eye coverings, like Milly, but on the end of a pink necklace hanging from her neck. Streaks of gray in her brown hair denoted age and dignity.

He tried to step out of her way.

She swerved and wrapped her arms around his midsection, chatting away. *"Vem-bindo à nossa casa! Você fala português? Você é tão corajoso e forte. Pode nos falar um pouco sobre tua pessoa?"*

Welcome to our home! You speak Portuguese? You are so brave and strong. Will you tell us a few things about yourself?

He tensed. This diminutive female touched him all over. He was with Milly. Such touching was not allowed.

But Milly, a gentle bride, was unbothered. She smiled sympathetically at his discomfort and told the elder, "He isn't used to touch from 'another woman.'"

"Pshaw," Vaw Vaw said, switching to flawless English. "He will learn."

But she also released him.

He breathed a sigh of relief.

"I love meeting the new members of my family." Vaw Vaw thumped Uvim on the back. "Milly, very nice job bringing another warrior here. Warrior Uvim, welcome to my home."

He dipped his head. Milly's family was used to warriors. They knew First Lieutenant Elan.

"Please say something."

His heart clenched.

Already? Now? In front of these people?

"Shush," she told the children and chattering adults. "He will speak."

They stared.

He stilled like he'd drifted into the maw of a megalodon.

His mouth dried. His tongue felt heavy as a stone. Old fears whirled in his head.

Humans are dangerous. They do not understand. Obey the ancient covenant. Escape!

Vaw Vaw's extended family waited for his speech.

No words came.

Milly wove through the crowd to his side. Her bright light glowed sweet and warm. She took his damp hand. "These are already your friends."

He nodded. Stiff.

Her low voice encouraged. "Say what's in your heart."

He focused. What was in his heart?

Terror. Speaking to humans was exposure. Exposure was fatal. To a warrior's health and, more importantly, to his honor.

Or his words would offend, expose his unworthiness, and turn these friendly people into an enemy of the mer.

Beneath that?

Confusion. How could he reach out to humans when he could barely communicate with his closest friends?

Beneath that?

Hope.

Under the fear and confusion, he still clung to hope.

Milly rested one soothing hand on his taut shoulder, rubbing his tension. She turned to her relatives. "He's very pleased to meet you."

Small smiles flickered over faces. Reaching out to him.

He needed to reach back.

"Thank you." He forced the words over his heavy, dry tongue. "This home. Your kindness."

They smiled as if he'd communicated more than sentence fragments.

That was because of Milly.

Milly always understood him. Even when he was silent. With her in his arms, he might finally express his feelings. Because of her encouragement.

He would try. Someday.

"Come." Vaw Vaw linked arms with him. "Welcome to my family."

He moved through the crowd and into the human's dwelling.

This was his second dwelling today. Milly's house and the rental both had few furnishings. Vaw Vaw's house was larger but held so many objects it felt much smaller. Dark wood, large and small images nailed to the walls, a tiled room bubbling with foods called "seafood stew" and "braised vegetables" and "fried chicken sausage," and a room crowded with a long wooden table and objects called chairs where they ate the evening meal.

They ladled steaming foods onto his plate searing hot.

Milly had left him and returned blinking and watering at the eyes, her eye-glasses stowed away. Now, sitting beside him, she pointed out the cooled, fresh-baked herb bread, chilled creamy cheese, olives, and other edibles while he waited for the hot foods to reach a palatable temperature.

"Warrior!" the young fries shouted from their sections of the long, bent table. "Warrior, do you like *futebol*? Do you like *arroz doce*? Do you like *bacalhau*?"

He did not know *futbol* or *arroz doce*. *Bacalhau* was cod. He nodded.

The young fries cheered. Their parents' heart-warming smiles extended to him.

Between questions, he overheard Milly defending herself to one of the older relatives.

"Police came by the harbor," one of older relatives told

her, in Portuguese. *"We are watching now for the symbol. It's tourists, yeah? Young college kids."*

"Foreigners," another agreed.

"We don't know for sure," Milly protested.

The others waved away her objection.

A third noticed Uvim listening. *"We have no problems with your kind."*

He inclined his head.

The trio of older males returned the gesture with respect.

The second male reported. *"Kids are watching the lockbox."*

She frowned. *"Tell them to be careful. And I'm sorry for this hardship."*

He laughed. *"What hardship? 'Go play at the beach. OK, paizinho!' It is no hardship."*

Milly looked away to spread a creamy butter on her bread. Her soul light dimmed.

The first one tapped Milly's shoulder, forcing her attention on him. *"Don't struggle alone, yeah? We are your family. My little niece, ask for our help."*

Milly forced a smile. *"Yes. Thank you."*

Uvim caught her eye.

She softened and rubbed his thigh under the table.

They finished the meal, Milly bade farewell to her relatives, and they returned to the car.

He slid into his seat and closed the door. "You do not wish to ask your family for help."

"Technically they're not my family." She checked his seatbelt, started the engine and waved to the relatives, and pulled onto the main road. "Vaw Vaw was my neighbor when I was too young to remember, before my aunt took me and Zara to America. Vaw Vaw kind of adopted me. Not officially, but she's the grandmother I never had. Do you have that?"

"Yes."

"Adoption?"

"When a father cannot parent, his king adopts his young fry."

"I should be grateful for all she's done. But the others chastise and evict me from my own projects. It's so frustrating!"

"They do not respect."

"Yes! Yes, that's it exactly. I'm a child to them. They still call me 'little.' I graduated from college!" She sighed and stopped, looking both directions at the empty cross road, and continued. "I will never be an adult in their eyes. But ... well, maybe they're right."

Her light dimmed.

This was her greatest fear. That she was useless. That she could not contribute. That she would waste her second chance and bother others all her life.

"You are an adult," he stated.

"I didn't report the vandalism. If reporting it would have stopped this mysterious organization, then the one who almost got us killed wasn't the kid and his mom throwing dynamite. It was me."

She pulled into her parking location at her house and stopped the engine.

A harsh silence fell over the car.

She rested her hands on the steering column and her head on her hands. Her voice emerged smaller than ever before. "I'm not responsible enough and I never will be."

But she *was* responsible.

She cared about the warriors. She'd risked her own life. She'd saved Dosan.

An irresponsible person would run away from her problems. Milly faced hers head-on. The problems arrayed before her were as large and vicious as a school of deadly megalodons. It was not her fault her problems could swallow up whole cities in their monstrous maws.

"I know." She sighed and lifted her head off the steering wheel. "But if my problems were that mammoth, you'd think I'd get better at hiding, or wielding an elephant gun, or something."

He tilted his head. "I said no words."

"Huh? Oh!" She laughed. "Sorry. Sometimes I feel you disagreeing with me. I can almost hear you in my head. Not real words, but ... well, anyway. I can't let the bigness of my problems stop me from dealing with them. I need to grow bigger. Or smarter. I need to work twice as hard and solve them."

Her soul light strengthened.

Optimism. Resilience. Even in the face of crushing rejection — even facing shame and loss of honor — she gathered her strength and spread hope through all around her.

She tapped the steering wheel and got out of the car.

He followed.

The hot evening sun drove them through the house, opening windows and savoring the ocean breezes. He enjoyed the simple routine of settling for the night.

She returned to the kitchen table, dropped her shoes and purse on a chair, and checked her mail. "Oh, there's an article about you guys." She paged through papers filled with news and read him a story about the ongoing debate in a location called "the United Nations" about whether or how to assign citizenship to the mer.

"Today, some leaders refused to vote because they claim the mer have not yet proved they are human. You cannot

give citizenship to monsters,' one outspoken representative claimed. What the heck? Monsters?" She dropped the newspaper. "Why are people so heartless?"

He studied her.

"It's just, maybe your All-Council is right." She shook her head. "Maybe humans are too dangerous and the only way to keep you safe is to run away and hide."

He offered his hand. "Milly."

"I know," she said, again, even though he had said nothing. "My soul light. Sorry. I'll get over it."

Sadness dampened her voice and her soul light.

She passed him, crossed the doorway, entered the living room.

His arms looped around her middle, stopping her. "You work hard."

"Yeah?" She sniffed and scrubbed at her cheeks. "Not hard enough."

"You asked for help. Many times. This is not easy."

"Many times?" She leaned against his chest, surrendering to his embrace. "I guess I did. And look how that turned out."

He supported her silently.

Dosan had helped — and gotten injured. Vaw Vaw's family had helped — and chastised her for not seeking their help sooner.

"I suppose handling the consequences with grace is what I need to work on now." She sighed. "Adulting is hard."

"You are doing this 'adulting' well."

"I assumed the vandalism was a harmless prank. Bashing mailboxes is such a cliché in the States. If I hadn't been so determined to solve the whole problem myself then Vaw Vaw's relatives might have caught the vandals in the beginning. Dosan and the little red octopus would have been spared."

"You speak out now."

She tilted her head to look up at him, sad and chagrined. "Thank you."

Her soft derriere pressed against his hardening cock. Her slim shoulder blades slid against his pectorals as she fit her curves into his hollows.

Her curved neck invited his teeth.

His cock throbbed.

Milly was his destiny. His bride. His queen.

But he would not move. He would not slide his hands up her sweet curves, cup her tender breasts, or taste the salt on her neck. He would maintain his control—

"Hey, Uvim?"

He cleared his dry throat. "Yes."

"I need you."

"I am here, Milly."

"You have my back."

"Yes."

She arched her back. Her soft derriere pressed against his hard cock. She rolled her shoulders. Her feminine curves rubbed across his hard-strung abdomen.

His cock strained.

He sucked in a breath through his teeth. "Always."

"Sweep me away. Give me the strength you promised. Help me stand on my two feet."

"I will do this."

"Do it now." She arched against him once more, filling his cock with taut heat. "Chase away these doubts. Make me believe I can someday be a queen."

Yes. He would do this. A thousand times yes.

"Fill me with your passion."

He sucked in a breath. Had he understood her?

She tilted her head to catch his eye over her shoulder. "I'm asking for help. Will you help me?"

In answer, he gripped her hips and ground her soft curves against his bulging hard cock.

TWENTY-FIVE

Milly wanted Uvim to sweep her away.

Sweep away her doubts. Sweep away her fears. Fill her with hope.

So she could give in to the passion she'd been running from and prove losing control wouldn't destroy her.

In answer, Uvim gripped her hips and ground her against his hard cock. Her cleft straddled every delicious inch.

Magnificent.

But she couldn't lose control. It wasn't responsible. She couldn't—

Uvim rumbled, deep in his broad chest. His pylon-thick warrior's biceps tightened. The demanding ridge of his cock stroked her dampening feminine core. She was so wet. Milly clenched her thighs together. But that only made her slick lips rub, setting off delicious fireworks in her pussy.

Dangerous. Too dangerous.

"Trust in me." He slid one hand up her trembling side and down again to grip her hip. "I will not betray you."

"I don't worry about *you* betraying me," she said.

"Give in to pleasure."

His large palm slid up her belly and cupped her breast. Desire ached in her center.

"Give in to desire."

His thumb brushed the hardened nipple.

Pleasure made her shudder.

"Give in to your wish."

He pinched and teased the pearl.

Delicious agony swelled.

"Give in to you."

His other hand slid across her belly and teased the edge of her trembling mons.

She gasped.

Give in to you.

What if her worst fear — being out of control — was okay?

What if *fear* was okay?

Fear was okay. Okay. Her fear was okay.

She could feel the fear without panic. Feel the fear and accept it. Feel the fear and forgive herself for it.

She'd never healed. So what? She'd never "gotten over" her imprisonment. Who got over that? Her fear was her situational awareness. It was her early warning. Her safety alarm.

Now it was okay to let go. Forgive herself. Accept her new reality.

And yield to her desires.

She grabbed his hand.

He stilled. Hungry yet respectful.

Uvim had the control to love her on her terms.

Milly needed to trust in that. Trust in him. And, most importantly, trust in herself.

She pulled his hand away from her mons and curled his fingers around the door jamb. "Hold here."

His knuckles whitened.

She placed his other hand on the opposite door jamb, pinning him to the doorway.

His green gaze smoldered. He was a male willingly trapped. Unable to go forward. Unwilling to go back.

All he had was his hope. His trust. And his desire.

His desire strained the orange swim shorts.

"Thank you for trusting in me." Milly rose on her tip toes to kiss his cheek.

He swerved to capture her lips.

She brushed his lips and swerved away, placing her kisses on his rough jaw.

Her control. Her conditions. Her desire.

She would make his entrapment pleasurable.

Promise.

He rumbled approval deep in his chest.

Her pussy throbbed.

Perhaps she could do this.

Milly forced his shirt up and off, then kissed the gorgeous corded muscle at his shoulder and traced the crinkly amethyst tattoos across his broad collar bone, over his unflinching pectorals. He closed his eyes.

His obvious pleasure made her wet and tingly.

She lowered her head once more, and swirled her tongue over his olive nipple.

It contracted. He growled low. Primal.

Her own nipples contracted.

She moaned and kissed across his powerful ribcage, lower, over mounds of abdominal muscle. He was magnificent — and at her mercy.

Milly knelt.

He looked down at her, desire soaking his intense expression, his teeth gritted in anticipation.

She curled her fingers over his waistband and tugged the swim shorts down. His dominant cock pinioned the dense fabric. She peeled back the canvas to reveal the muscles across his waist standing in sharp relief, a nestle of dark hair, and finally his long, thick cock.

Her female sex tingled.

She forced the shorts off and tossed them in a corner, then slid delicate fingers up his prominent thighs to the thatch of dark hair.

His cock bobbed. The amethyst tattoos crinkled across his member like a fractal.

Uvim's was the first cock she'd ever unveiled. The first cock she'd ever wanted to see. And it captivated her in an aphrodisiac spell.

She wanted him inside her.

His breathing labored. He was reading her mind again. Her wicked, hungry thoughts.

Was this a good idea? Could she maintain control? Or was she skimming along a path to losing herself once and for all?

Milly no longer cared.

She just wanted to touch Uvim. Possess his cock. Make it hers. Make *him* hers.

Have him and release herself from her self-imposed cage.

She cupped Uvim's thick cock. He was hot and heavy and silk-smooth.

His breath hissed between his teeth.

Her touch gave Uvim pleasure.

Power surged within her.

She stroked his skin.

He groaned.

Holding his cock was like containing desire. If desire had a weight and shape, it would be this amethyst and olive cock.

She nuzzled the head.

His breath hitched. A drop of pre-cum beaded up on the tip.

How did it taste? She darted her tongue to the slit. Salty. Masculine.

Hers.

Uvim trembled. "You..."

She looked up.

His hungry gaze warred with a troubled emotion. "I must pleasure you."

"I'm enjoying myself," she reassured him. "Pleasuring you gives me pleasure."

"To produce a young fry, you must experience the ultimate pleasure. Not I."

She ran her tongue over the amethyst tattoos.

Uvim growled. "This pleasure is ... not something ... I have trained for."

She laughed. "You trained for this, huh?"

"No, I—"

"For making babies. Er, young fry."

"Only when I pleasure you five times will we produce a young fry."

"Five times? You mean, have sex five times?"

He shook his head. "Five pleasures in one joining."

Five orgasms each time. Heh.

"I applaud your dedication." She wrapped her damp

fingers around his trembling cock. "But we're not producing 'young fry' right now."

"No?"

"We're increasing our resonance."

She sucked his head into her mouth. He tasted of salt and ocean and he smelled of male musk.

Her feminine slit grew slippery.

He groaned.

His heat filled her mouth.

Her tongue stroked his cock.

He groaned more desperately. "Milly."

Her sex throbbed.

His desperation made her so hot. She wanted to touch herself but she also wanted to finish him. The two desires warred. She sucked harder, taking him deep and swirling his length, tasting him as if he were plunging into her.

And then she lost control.

Gripping his cock with both hands, she bucked, releasing her limits, riding the wave of desire to its utter peak and flirting with the crashing edge of wildness—

He jerked back, ripping his cock from her mouth, and wrapped his hands around his throbbing member.

His body convulsed. Hot liquid shot out, striping her T-shirt and capris.

She touched the liquid. His heat lingered on her tongue.

Success.

She had done it. With no experience. She had brought a man — male — Uvim — to a climax. She'd lost control, and he'd lost control. They'd lost control together and yet both made it home.

He let out his breath in a hard burst.

Her pussy throbbed with unmet desires.

She'd taken control of his desire. Could she control her own?

Milly lowered her capris, dipped her hand beneath her soft cotton panties, slid her fingers over her mound and gently gripped her throbbing, wet pussy. The ache intensified.

Oh, yes. She could finish herself off.

Uvim focused on her buried, stroking hand. His gaze, smoldering with heat before, burned red hot. "May I?"

Her pussy clenched with new excitement. Terror fought with desire.

She respected her fears without letting them control her. "Not sex."

"Only pleasure," he agreed.

Her hand stilled.

She knew how to get herself off. Fast, painless, efficient.

He'd trained to give her five orgasms...

The temptation to know, to have these five orgasms — or any orgasms by another person, much less a delicious warrior with iridescent tattoos — won. She took his offered hand.

He helped her rise to her feet. She rested on her tennis shoes. He turned her to face away and planted his feet behind her. One masculine forearm arm tightened around her midsection and cupped her aching breast over her soft T-shirt.

She sucked in a breath. *Calm. Accept. Give in.*

He thumbed the nipple.

Spicy heat twisted her sex, squeezing out liquid desire.

She whimpered.

His other hand slid over hers and cupped her mons.

Her hot thrill twinged with worry. "Don't touch under my clothes."

"Milly." His deep voice rumbled in her ear. "You are my queen."

He would only do what she wanted. He would stop right now if she wished. She was his queen. He wanted to worship her the way she had just worshiped him.

She wanted him. Now. Forever.

Milly spread her feet, opening for him.

His chest rumbled approval.

While one hand thumbed her throbbing breasts, his fingers slid over her cotton briefs. He respected her request to keep his hands off her skin. Through the soaked fabric, he traced the shape of her sex. Explored her plump sex lips. Captured her pleasure.

And owned her.

Uvim gripped her sex, teased her bud, and massaged her feminine lips.

Delicious tingles poured into her body, healing her with sweet promises.

She needed him. Her body throbbed on fire. She wanted his cock in her slick channel, his fingers plunging in and out of her wet heat, bringing her to the peak.

Milly canted her hips and ground against the wall of male at her backside.

He kissed her neck and sucked.

She exploded. Pleasure erupted in her center. Her chest filled with bubbles of satisfaction.

Milly sagged in Uvim's arms. Spent, she craved his security and kindness.

He held her close.

She rubbed his loving forearm. How did he always know what she needed before she did? This must be their resonance. Their connection.

Uvim kissed her slender neck.

His hand massaged her mons.

Desire twinged.

His cock hardened against her back, ready to pleasure her again.

And again. Times five.

Her control against this kind of pleasure was unpracticed and weak.

"Maybe touch just a little under my clothes," she gasped.

Uvim peeled off her panties, baring her slippery feminine rose to his commanding touch. He teased his fingers between her lips, learning her channel and spreading slick hunger.

She parted her legs, opening to him.

He circled around and knelt in front of her. "Milly?"

He wished to worship.

She gave in to his wish. "Yes."

He nuzzled her feminine sex. His tongue sought her sensitive bud. He stroked. Singular, steady, focused.

Pleasure exploded.

She gasped and held onto his powerful shoulders. The wild waves crashed over her again.

He was not familiar with receiving a blow job but he was a master at pleasuring her.

She bent over on top of him, resting her cheek on his shoulder blade.

She wanted more.

She wanted everything.

But...

If she asked, he would thrust his cock into her, fill her with more pleasure, and become her first — and only.

But committing was her final move. It meant she gave up on other paths in life and chose Uvim forever.

She couldn't make that decision now. Not while she was swept away. She needed her feet under her. Her head clear. And her heart strong.

Right now she was the opposite of strong. She was sated. Oozing with yumminess. Lazy from pleasure.

This had to stop.

Her thighs trembled to hold the awkward position.

He pulled back and stood, supporting her. "We will sleep together now?"

Well, maybe not quite yet. She leaned against the immovable warrior. "Let me show you how much fun it can be to use a shower. But don't get water in my eyes. I'm wearing contacts."

"Contacts?"

"Thin slips of plastic. Shaped to help me see farther."

They washed each other. She spread her foamy body wash over his hard mountains and valleys, learning his shape on the micro level. The exact pattern of one sharp amethyst fractal, the tiny scars that nicked his abdomen, thighs, buttocks. He lived a warfare-filled life. His story lay exposed on his skin. She learned it as a lover, treasuring every memory.

He studied her with the same intensity. Curious about the birth mark beneath her left breast, the scar from tripping and whacking her head on an elementary school desk, and the way her littlest toe jutted funny from breaking it in a bike accident when she was nine.

"This marking." He brushed his fingertip across her small blue butterfly. "It is a decoration?"

"A tattoo. Our version." She canted her hip to make the ink more visible. It adorned her pubic bone, hidden beneath her smallest bikini. Secret. "A butterfly symbolizes trans-formation."

"Butterfly," he repeated and knelt. The shower bounced off his head in a refreshing spray. He pressed a kiss to the small drawing.

They had been naked before, pressed up against each other swimming through the ocean, but this was different. More intimate.

Couldn't she commit to this man?

Some truths she knew immediately. The first time she'd stepped off the plane in the Azores she'd known she was home.

The first time she'd belted Uvim into the sedan, she'd known. She'd imagined tasting his kiss. She'd fantasized about losing control.

Why was she still hesitating?

Today he had walked into Vaw Vaw's crowd, handled her hug with more aplomb than her brother-in-law Elan, and even challenged his deepest fears to give a speech. Because he knew it was important to Milly.

She had always wanted to become a proud matriarch like Vaw Vaw. In her dreams, her isolated childhood trio — herself, Zara, and her aunt — would change into a huge family. She'd be surrounded with happy, loving children, in-laws, grandchildren. And they would look to her for an encouraging word, a gentle hug, and Milly's fierce, unconditional love.

For a long time that dream had seemed out of reach.

Now, Milly could almost see it. Herself, a proud matriarch with a huge, loving family. A man at her side, just as proud.

Uvim.

They just had to survive Zara's wrath, his elders' punishment, and the mysterious new dynamite-throwing enemy. Oh, and help Dosan heal and improve human-mer relations at the Sea Festival.

Just.

This time, she would be useful.

She would work hard and find her place to belong.

TWENTY-SIX

Uvim sensed Milly's fears.

Faint, like the distant warning siren of a territorial bull shark, those fears nipped at the corners of her smiles and dragged her soul light down.

He had to convince Milly to focus on her faith. Faith in him. Faith in her. He must find the words to reach her.

After the shower, she removed her plastic "contacts" and wore her glasses until sleep. They spent the first night together on her couch, snuggled until his arm went to sleep and then she did. The next day Milly ran errands — shopping, checking the state of the lockbox, swimming in the ocean.

Above water, his soft words and his intimate touches only drove the fears a little distance. In the quiet, they returned with a crash. Frightening her. Frightening him.

Underwater, the fears quieted.

He introduced her to the small cave guardian patrolling where the mer stashed their tridents and daggers.

She held out her hand. The fierce yellow octopus

wrapped one tentacle around her fingers, pinching like a human handshake. She giggled. "Nice to meet you."

He released her hand, puffed his funnel, and strutted across the cave entrance, displaying his importance to the mer.

She giggled again.

If only Uvim could leave this land now, take her to the city, and claim her. Her doubts melted away beneath the waves because she lived her destiny. Her soul knew this was where she belonged.

She had so much love.

But he could not compromise Dosan's recovery.

They exited the water and ended her errands by driving to the rental.

Dosan convalesced on a long white "lounge" chair beside the shimmery blue pool. Beside him rested the remains of a sandwich and blended ice drink. His physical recovery proceeded. The black center of his red bruise had faded to greenish purple.

But he was strangely quiet. Solemn. Not friendly nor sarcastic. "When will you dispatch a message to the elders?"

"When you recover."

Dosan frowned.

"Dosan. What are your hopes for friendship between human and mer?"

He jolted. His shoulders dropped to a defensive position. "Why do you ask this?"

"Someone must give the welcome speech at the Sea Festival."

Dosan eyed him for a long moment. Then, he studied his bruised chest. "Do not order me."

"You speak well."

The sapphire warrior looked away. "I have been angry for too long. Now, my feelings are confused."

"Confusion is acceptable."

He shook his head. "This confusion will not win allies. I lose my thoughts. Ramble."

"You will heal."

"It is not because of an injury." He focused on Uvim. "You must speak."

"I am no speaker."

"You do not speak often. But your words focus. The humans will understand. You will gain their sympathy."

Uvim shook his head. "I cannot convince anyone."

"You have softened Queen Zara's sister to our cause."

"She does not carry Queen Zara's anger."

A smile cracked Dosan's lips. "For you, perhaps. Xalu and I find Bride Milly's anger frightening."

"She had never been angry with you."

Dosan's brows rose. "Never? Then I hope I will never see her angry with me."

Milly's soul light was strong. She glowed with gentleness and deep humanitarian love. Did Dosan and Xalu not see this?

"She will be a strong queen." Dosan changed the topic and fixed on Uvim. "You must soften the humans."

Uvim shook his head again. "I cannot."

"You are our leader."

"I practice Queen Zara's 'democracy' and give you this power."

"Then I also practice Queen Zara's 'democracy' and refuse."

They reached an impasse.

He left the warriors and finished the evening with Vaw Vaw's family. No news of the mystery organization, despite police confiscating their dynamite throughout the harbor. How was it smuggled into the island? Was it being smuggled? The relatives shared many theories.

They passed another sweet night.

The world seemed to be holding its breath. This time could not last. Milly frowned at her phone. When would Queen Zara listen to her message?

"It's unusual," Milly said. "She must be buried in research right now."

This long neglect seemed strange.

What if the city fell under attack and she was needed?

Was Queen Zara imprisoned somewhere in need of rescue?

"I'm sure it's fine. While we're waiting, I'll show you my favorite places on the island." She looped her arm in his. "It's a date."

This "date" excited her.

It excited him too.

First, they stopped by the rental to check on his warriors. No one answered their summons so Milly called Ian. No answer.

"I'm sure it's fine," she said again, less confident.

Milly drove deep into the winding back roads up to the green-fringed caldera. As she parked, her cell phone rang. Ian! Everything was fine. The women had been shopping while the men slept.

The warriors reported to Uvim. He listened in the parking lot. Turbulent clouds and trilling birds swooped over the rugged pit of the island's old volcano.

"I am stronger but not prepared to travel," Dosan said. "I will remain here, resting."

"I, too, will remain here," Xalu said. "For security."

Milly finished tying her tennis shoes and asked for the phone. "I want to speak to the women."

He handed back her cell phone.

"How are things?" She bounced from one foot to the other. "Is everything going okay? No cultural misunderstandings I can help clear up?"

She was silent for a long moment.

Her soul light flared. She winked at Uvim and walked around the car, gazing over the caldera with a barely suppressed grin. "Mmhm? Oh, that can happen. Yep, that sounds normal. Ha ha! Well, you have to make your own decisions, so, good luck."

After a few more minutes, she returned the phone to her pocket and led him to the start of the hiking path. "Things are exciting over there."

"Exciting?"

"I think hosting two warriors would be pretty exciting." She wrapped his arms over her shoulders, curling him protectively around her. "We are past the 'excitement' phase and are in the 'wonderful' phase."

Yes, he found his arms around her, touching her shoulders — and other places — to be very wonderful.

He could continue these soft days filled with Milly's intoxicating presence for the rest of his life.

The following day she had work. In the morning, she led a scuba tour group. They frisked everyone and opened bags so no weapons boarded the boat. Uvim journeyed with her, his presence drawing many furtive glances. At Milly's urging, he accepted questions.

The humans' many questions touched on his oceanic life and then centered on a variation of two: Did he like surface things? What did he think of the surface?

Was this knowledge useful? Could he incorporate this human curiosity into his welcome speech?

His welcome speech.

Uvim's belly squeezed.

He must convince Xalu or Dosan.

The mer's future depended on reaching out in friendship.

In the afternoon, Milly drove him to the interior of the island and swam in a cold fresh-water lake. That night, at home, he helped her create the dinner. Humans ate much less raw material and much more cooked items. They ended the night watching the picture-sound screen called "TV" snuggled up on the same couch where they slept.

Her boss called in the middle of their viewing to schedule the Sea Festival Committee Meeting.

"Tomorrow. Got it." Milly ended the call and stretched. Her back arched over Uvim's lap. "Real life is about to intrude. I can just feel it."

He felt her shoulder blades in his thighs. "This is not real?"

"This is a beautiful dream." She sighed, wistful. "I want to do so many more things with you. Take you to a restaurant. Watch a soccer match. Picnic on the beach."

That future sounded beautiful, too.

"We'll see how much we can fit in before the Sea Festival." She rolled over on his lap and clicked the remote. "Then we'll go to your city. After the marriage ceremony in front of the Life Tree, you must show me around."

His heart stuttered.

She watched the "TV show" about friends living together in a human city.

He cleared his throat. "I show you?"

"Your favorite places. Where you grew up, and your daily life, and whatnot."

Even though she talked about becoming a queen, she rarely spoke of marrying him. And sometimes her self-doubt made it sound as if she would still change her mind.

To know these contented days might continue ... that she *chose* him and would continue to do so forever despite his silences, his doubts, his shame ... his heart pushed up into his throat and he couldn't breathe.

She sensed his silence held deeper feelings and rested her head on his chest. "You do still want to marry me, right?"

"More ... than I can say."

She wove her fingers with his. "Great."

Her soft breast brushed his hard pectoral. His cock heated, rising to attention. He tried to ignore his reaction and focus on the show. It was important to learn about human relations. Even if the tightness of his swim shorts made his cock ache.

She turned. Her hand rested on his hard thigh and drifted over his cock.

Hunger warred with control.

She nuzzled his ear. "Are you watching the show?"

Was this a test?

"Yes. Are you?"

"No."

He turned.

Her lips caught his. Their mouths meshed in a sweet, hot kiss.

Without breaking contact, she pointed the remote and shut off the TV. And then they kissed each other in their other favorite places.

And then she removed her clothing and straddled him

nude, her gorgeous pussy stroking the fabric where his cock strained and shuddered with wave after wave of pleasure.

After, he held her close as her even breathing sent her into a deep, satisfied sleep.

Milly was right. These days were a beautiful dream.

He could not bear to wake up.

But he must.

TWENTY-SEVEN

The following day, they drove to Milly's work to meet her boss about the Sea Festival Planning Committee.

Nicolette ushered them out of the dive shop. "The committee chair will meet us at the stage."

Brody raced behind them. "Milly! I have to get those pressure plates off of you. Ty needs them back."

"Sure." Milly glanced around. She'd had to park farther away today because of traffic. "They're in my trunk still. Where's your car?"

"Way up the street."

"Ohhh. I'm the other way."

Her boss tapped her wristwatch. "The committee's waiting and so's today's private tour, Brody."

He bounced on his laced footwear.

"I'll look for you when we get back from the meeting," Milly promised.

"Cool." He waved and headed to the dock.

Her boss wove through the small streets and crammed-full shops. White buildings with red tile roofs, a lumpy road

Milly called cobblestone, and green trees shimmered in the hot morning breeze off the midsummer day.

While they walked, Milly's boss pointed out the pre-festival activities had begun.

"The festival takes place across two weeks," she told Uvim. "There are always boat races, an inter-island swim across the channel, a music festival, shopping tents, and extravaganzas."

Her boss reached Faial's main road and followed the curve of the harbor. A long human-filled bus parked at their side. Waves of humans jumped out. Some noticed him. They marched past.

"As you can see, the tourists have arrived." They walked around banging and strident construction. "Boats are crammed into the harbors around the island while the rest anchor off-shore."

They waited their turn to cross a busy street and enter the marina.

"The festival starts in two days," Milly told him.

"Yes, and in between the first and second week, there's always an official welcome ceremony." The walk sign changed. A huge school of humans crossed the street. Her boss paused and focused on Uvim. "That's when you come in."

They crossed the busy road.

On the oceanic side, humans posed with cell phones in front of the colorful harbor wall. Paintings stretched along the rock wall and the walkway in front of the calm ocean.

Although they had driven past this sight many times, it was his first time seeing it in person.

"Legend says sailors must paint a mural to bring good luck to their voyage," Milly said.

Many human boats of different sizes bobbed in the

marina. Beyond them, across the channel stood Pico Island's large, black volcanic cone.

They climbed the steps to the top of a newly constructed platform facing the ocean. Wide enough for an entire delegation of warriors, the barren stage elevated and exposed him to all humans within view.

On the platform, Milly's boss introduced the committee chairman of the Sea Festival: a short, chubby male with a balding head. He sweated in a dark suit.

"The centerpiece this year is the mid-festival parade," he said. "Boats are being decorated with garlands and colors. This," the committee chair pointed to a lopsided, old boat being towed across the harbor, "will be the Friendship Float."

Milly's brows wrinkled. "That's it?"

"I know what it looks like," her boss rushed to assure them. "But don't freak out. It's seaworthy."

"It looks a little, uh, worn."

"Local artists constructed the decorations," the committee chair said. "After the Friendship Float makes its tour of the harbor, its final rest will be on land right there." He pointed at a low, concrete pedestal off to the side of the marina. "And that's where it will stay as a monument to our friendship."

"It's pretty fab," her boss said.

"So, you — Warrior Uvim? — will stand here."

The committee chair led them across the flat stage to a wooden shield block.

Cover. He gripped it.

"Ignore the podium," the committee chair said. "We'll remove it for your remarks."

No.

"The public wants to see you. You're not wearing these ugly swim shorts, are you?"

Ugly? The orange swim coverings were ugly?

Milly suppressed her smile.

"Perhaps you could wear your native dress?" the committee chair suggested.

Her boss laughed. "That would be revealing."

"His 'native dress' is naked," Milly explained.

"Yes, then, something less revealing." The chair cleared his throat again. "You, Warrior Uvim, will make the welcome remarks. After you finish, the float will erupt with flowers, showering us in petals."

"Shower us with flowers!" Milly made an "o" of surprise. "Like out of a cannon?"

"No, the artist has created a bag attached to springs. It will launch the delicate petals into the sky. On Warrior Uvim's signal, they will flutter on boats and guests like a million butterflies."

"Sounds cool."

Uvim faced his doubts squarely. "What must I say?"

"Anything," the committee chair said. "Traditionally, we welcome guests and express our hope to enjoy the festival together."

"It's our first year with mermen," the boss said.

"Yes, so, any friendly words will be well-received."

The committee chair and Milly's boss descended the steps chatting.

Uvim counted the empty, semi-constructed tiers.

The sun peeked out between clouds. Its light burned a hot, focused ray on the busy street, empty stage, him.

Tourists stopped and looked up at him. They raised their cell phones.

He fought the urge to dart off the back of the stage, clamber over the rock wall, and dive into the ocean.

On the day of the ceremony, many more humans would fill this region. Watching. Staring. Waiting for words that might never come.

Milly took his arm. Accepting and soothing. "You've got over a week until the ceremony. You'll figure it out. You're a Second Lieutenant now."

He shook his head.

"If you really can't do it, then maybe I can talk Elan into it."

A new fear clenched his stomach. First Lieutenant Elan was here?

Queen Zara was here?

No. He would know.

"Asking Elan was my original plan." She nuzzled his lips. "Before I met you and everything changed."

He closed his eyes and lived in her kiss.

Everything had changed for his Milly. Why had it not yet changed for him?

He accepted her comfort and, hand linked with hers, descended the steps into the crowd.

Milly smirked at his inappropriate shorts. "We'll find you new clothes after lunch."

Her boss purchased "lunch" from a local restaurant. Milly ordered cold dishes: Chilled seafood stew, brined limpets, and a tasty bowl of frozen mammal milk "ice cream."

After eating, Nicolette returned to the dive shop. Milly took Uvim "clothes shopping."

She held up one large, white shirt decorated with blue slashes. "This one is appropriate. It says, 'I love the Azores.' Ooh, here's another one. 'Faial' - heart - 'Love'."

He relied upon her experienced eye, pulling on the T-shirts at her request. Each one strained across his pectorals. She touched the fabric with an approving hum.

His cock hardened.

"Maybe I can find a shirt that better shows off your biceps." She turned to browse another aisle.

A shady male stood in her way.

She recoiled into Uvim's chest. "Vernon."

"Milly. I've finally caught you." The male snarled. Milly's soul light darkened. "Leave me alone!"

"Your parents took you in. The way you've repaid them is shameful."

Uvim growled low in his chest.

Vernon stopped and looked for the source of the warning.

Milly's soul light stabilized. She rested a hand on his forearm. "You don't know what you're talking about."

"Ha! How quickly you forget..." His gaze traveled up to Uvim and his accusation trailed off. "What are you?"

Uvim answered. "Hers."

"What?"

Milly curled Uvim's arm around her belly. "He's my future husband. And, right now, my body guard. I asked you to leave me alone."

He jerked back. Indignant. "How dare you intimidate me?"

"Well, how dare you harass me?"

"I'm not harassing you." He puffed his chest like a spiked fish. "I felt sorry for you. Your parents gave you too much freedom. You abused their trust."

Her soul darkened again. "They tried to pass me around to their friends!"

"*You* came on to *me*."

She huffed, frustrated and impotent, a big mass of fear and anger and shame. "Because — because — Just go away!"

"Stop testifying against your parents."

"They kidnapped—"

"*You* called *them* for help. And now they're suffering for your lies."

Milly's light dimmed.

No.

Uvim pulled her behind him and squared to the male. "Go."

"Hey, back off." Vernon leaned away from Uvim. "You can't loom over me like this. Are you threatening me? I'll call the police."

"Call."

"You think I won't?"

"I hope you will," Milly said, shaky.

"I will!"

"Ask for Inspector Periera. Tell him how you've been coming to my work, approaching my boss, and now following me into a store. He'll be interested in how you're trying to influence my witness testimony for the kidnapping of my nephew."

His anger wavered. "Nephew?"

"They imprisoned him. Just like me."

"But you—"

"I tried to escape by any means possible. But you said I was there voluntarily."

"You were!"

"So they got off," she said. "They were never punished. My obvious 'delusion' that my sister was abducted by a huge, tattooed merman was proof I was crazy and my testimony couldn't stand."

She hung on Uvim. The huge, tattooed merman. "I'm clearly crazy. And a liar."

Vernon shook himself. "But you weren't kidnapped."

"Because that would mean you failed to see a 'cry for help' right in your face," she sneered. "My case is long over. My dad resisted arrest. I wasn't a 'credible' victim so nothing went to trial. Why are you here?"

"Because ... your parents said..."

"My parents asked you to intimidate me? Get rid of me?" She poked the man in the center of his dark chest. "You tell them I'm not going anywhere."

"This is another lie." Vernon stumbled back, palms out, defensive. "I helped you. You should just ... be ashamed."

He ducked out of the shop. A bell attached to the door jangled.

"Wish granted," Milly murmured. "I am ashamed."

He pulled her into his arms. "No, Milly."

"It's okay." She melted in his embrace. "Thank you."

They stood silently in the middle of the shop giving and receiving comfort.

Finally, she stepped back. Her smile did not reach its usual strength. "All done here? Those look good."

"You are sad."

"Yeah. It's fine. Well, not fine, but I'll explain in the car."

She carried his new shirts and shorts to the front of the shop, gave the attendant colored papers, and they walked back to her sedan. Her silence was watchful as though expecting an enemy around every corner.

Her attitude had been guarded at her house the first day during her meeting with Brody. She had relaxed around Uvim. This morning, at the Sea Festival stage, she had smiled at strangers and cameras.

Now, she looked at everyone with mistrust.

Uvim wished to find the man Vernon and drag him to the police station by the throat. He should face human justice for his criminal actions.

They reached the dive shop. She opened her trunk to store the bag of purchases. The pressure plates filled her trunk full.

She sighed. "These have cursed me since the beginning! I'm sorry I ever asked for them." Then, she darkened and, as she drew out her cell phone and typed, muttered, "I'm sorry I ever asked for anything."

He rubbed her back.

"Brody's still out with the tour." She stretched with a big yawn. "He knows where to find me. Let's go home."

Uvim entered her hot car and buckled his own belt. As she backed onto the crowded street, he spoke. "Explain."

"I keep asking the wrong people for help," Milly said. "You'd think I'd learn my lesson but I don't."

"Your lesson?"

"I asked my parents for help to escape my strict aunt. I walked into their prison. Later, Zara couldn't get travel visas for Elan and Zain to escape your city's undersea war, so I reached out to my parents. They'd skipped the country to escape my father's brief 'resisting arrest' sentence. They manipulated me again. Baby Zain paid the price."

"Human justice did not prevail."

"The police couldn't prove I'd been imprisoned. And friends like Vernon swore I'd been a happy guest." She snorted. "Because all my parents' 'happy guests' don't brush their teeth or shower for weeks."

He had brushed teeth and showered daily. He'd enjoyed those activities almost as much as he enjoyed pleasuring Milly.

"Anyway, Vernon was the last person they pushed me on. After they'd locked me in the dark all those weeks, I broke. I could not survive another day in the darkness. Every second I thought I'd suffocate. Starve to death. Commit suicide. I thought I was going to die."

Uvim's chest squeezed. His hands opened and closed. His heart burned. He could not travel in time and rescue her. No wonder she was still so injured by the shock waves from her past.

"He's right that I came on to him. I did. I would have done anything to escape the engine room."

He said the only thing he could. "You survived."

"Yeah." She shook her head. "I don't know why my parents pushed me on a guy like Vernon. He's not into underage girls. Maybe they owed him money. He has a vested interest in them not going to jail. He'll probably never see a payment.

"After Vernon refused my 'offer,' he let me use his hotel stationary to write a letter, and he even mailed it. Zara got the letter, rescued me. Then, she got involved with Elan and caught up the undersea war. Let's just say that both Vernon and probably Zara believed, at least at one time, that helping me was the worst thing they ever did."

Her soul light darkened.

He repeated his words to reach her. "You survived, Milly."

"I broke," she contracted. "And now, I know my limit. If I don't get in trouble, then I don't have to ask for help."

"You needed help," he insisted. "You could not free yourself."

"Couldn't I?" She sighed. "I don't know. I thought I couldn't. You have a lot of feelings at seventeen that are different when you're twenty. That's why I refused to commit my heart to you for so long. But ... you are the reason I could face him today. I backed into you."

"I will always 'have your back.'"

She laughed. "Good. I meant more generally though. You've given me more confidence. Belief in myself. Not only can I survive, but I can also reach for my dreams and create the life I've always wanted."

He understood.

And he also realized the root of her refusal to ask for help. "You believe asking for help injures."

"Well, everyone says I should have dealt with my parents myself. Like an adult." She stopped at a sign and waited for the slow, endless traffic clogging the small roads. "Although, Zara confronted them 'like an adult' and they tried to kill her. Twice."

"Why were you not also in danger? Had you confronted them, would they not also have tried to kill you?"

"Um, well, I don't know." She dropped silent as she drove past the lockbox. Youths played in the grass and sand. "I never thought of that."

He reflected on what she had told him about his silence. That perhaps his silence had been a strength.

"Asking for help is not weakness, Milly."

"I know..." But her tone disagreed.

"When danger threatens, you must ask for help. Perhaps you will not receive it. But a responsible adult asks."

"Thanks. That means a lot from you." She drove up her road and turned into the driveway.

"Me?"

"Yeah. You're the most dutiful, responsible guy I've ever..."

She stopped the car in front of her house.

The door hung open.

He unbuckled his seatbelt and exited the car. There was someone at her house. He would protect Milly. Uvim strode to the door.

Her car door slammed behind him. "Wait, Uvim!"

A shadow figure exited the house and stepped into the light.

Queen Zara.

He stumbled to a stop.

Her powerful soul light burned in her commanding chest. Her brown gaze crackled with fury. She held up a crumpled piece of paper like an accusation.

His stomach lurched.

"You," she accused, uncoiling her rage like a weapon, and shook the crumpled paper at Uvim. "I ordered you to stay away."

He snapped to attention.

"How dare you disobey? How dare you endanger my little sister?"

The queen was right. He had disobeyed her and endangered Milly.

"Go back to your city this instant."

Milly walked up behind him and wrapped her fingers around his numb forearm. "I'm his bride."

Queen Zara shook her head. "Never."

"Zara—"

"No." Queen Zara ignored Milly and focused her fury on Uvim. "You betrayed me. You nearly killed me. You, of all the mer, should feel ashamed for daring to come to the surface."

"Zara, you're making a mistake."

"No, I'm saving you from making one."

"But—"

"Never surface again. If you do, I will exile you for all eternity."

Bitter blackness squeezed his chest. He couldn't breathe. Couldn't speak.

"You're misunderstanding," Milly insisted, trying to step between them. "Let him explain."

Queen Zara flushed.

Milly prodded Uvim. "Explain."

He opened his mouth.

No words came.

"There's nothing to explain. I will never forgive you." Queen Zara damned him. "You will never, ever have a bride."

TWENTY-EIGHT

Uvim's spine straightened as if it were made of rulers. Milly couldn't see soul lights but Zara's accusations destroyed him inside. Her duty-bound warrior was being ripped apart by the person he respected more than anyone else in the world.

Her sister.

"Leave now," Zara ordered, so angry that she was shaking. "Slink back to your city and die."

He turned on his heels.

Milly rested her palm in the center of his chest. "Wait."

He jolted to a stop. Not daring to look at her, he kept his gaze over her shoulder, on the sea in the far distance.

If Milly had a healing power, please let it heal his shattered heart.

She understood Zara's anger. They'd only had each other. Zara remembered their traumatic early childhood. Failing to protect Milly from their parents had kicked her in the heart. Now, she went a little crazy over Milly's safety.

But Milly was an adult now.

"Get out!" Zara shouted.

"What the heck, Zara?" Milly tried her old tricks to reel her sister back from the brink. "Do you expect him to walk to the beach?"

"I don't care!" She brandished a crumpled paper. "Every instant he's here you're in danger."

"What are you talking about?"

Zara thrust the paper at her.

Milly smoothed the computer printout, keeping one hand still on Uvim to ensure he didn't obey Zara's order and leave. She read the warning message. "*We're watching. Monster, go back to hell. Ignore us and we'll blow you out of the water. The Sea Festival is only the beginning.*"

Uvim rested on his heels. A new watchfulness animated his taut gaze. He was still hurting from Zara's accusations but could not turn off his protective instincts.

"It's a ploy to scare us away," Milly protested. "An empty threat."

"Oh, they're watching." Zara stabbed the paper. "This got shoved under the door *after* I got home."

"Then the police can catch them. We're not giving in to their terror."

"Yes, we are."

"This has to go to the police." Milly pinched the edge between her fingertips. "It could have fingerprints. Especially given how crumpled it is."

Zara's mouth opened and closed. She looked chagrined. "I crumpled it."

Uvim spoke low to Milly. "We must warn the other warriors."

"Good plan." And what a relief. He would put aside his hurt and work with her to protect the Sea Festival. "Summoning more warriors will guarantee we discover any hidden bombs."

"Dosan," he clarified, "and Xalu."

"Oh. Well, sure, they should be on their guard—"

"Wait a minute." Zara whirled on Uvim with new fury. "What are you still doing here? Collect your warriors — the ones who nearly got Milly killed — and get out."

He stiffened.

She faced off against Zara again. "You can't order him away. This is my choice." She lifted her chin. "I say he's staying."

"You drank temporary elixir," Zara snapped. "It will wear off."

"I won't let it."

"You are going to stay on this land until that stupid elixir wears off and then you'll be a human. Ordinary. Normal. And safe."

"I love him."

Zara sucked in a breath.

Uvim searched her face. Not happy at her confession. Panicked.

Panicked?

Panicked or not, Uvim was her warrior. She had trusted him. Now, she would fight for him.

"No," Zara thundered.

"You don't get to decide."

Why was Uvim panicked by her confession? He'd told her over and over he wanted her for his queen. Did he *still* think she wasn't ready? He obeyed Zara, Queen of Dragao Azul, over Milly, queen of his heart?

"You have *no idea* what you're talking about." Zara gestured at Uvim. "Don't you know this warrior dragged me to the surface? I nearly died."

"I know, but—"

"You're confused. But I'm not. There's no relationship here. I forbid it."

"Zara." Milly took a deep breath. "Uvim's not going anywhere. We're together."

"Phone," Uvim said. "I need it."

What the heck?

Milly turned on him. "Uvim?"

Zara snapped in irritation, "Quiet. We're fighting."

"Cell phone."

"Uvim—"

"*Now.*" His tone was flinty. Uncompromising.

Zara's eyes narrowed. "Don't order my sister around."

He flinched but remained resolute.

Milly took his hands. They were so big. Tremors shook them like earthquakes.

Her anger died.

He *did* love her. But he was so battered by Zara's attack he crumpled.

She handed him her cell phone.

He operated it expertly. In moments, it was ringing. He held it to his ear. "Ian? Operate your car to Milly's castle. House. Yes." He ended the call and handed the phone back to Milly without meeting her or Zara's eye.

She fumbled the phone. "You called Ian?"

"He comes now."

"You can't leave."

Uvim turned on his heel and strode to the road.

Milly stormed after him. "I need you to convince Zara."

He tapped his throat. *He had no words.*

"You don't need words. Now's the time to stand together. Prove that we love each other and believe in the Sea Festival."

He shook his head.

"Stay."

He reached the road. His gaze flickered over her shoulder to Zara. Panic flushed his features again. He returned to Milly, even more determined. "I must go."

"No."

"It is an order."

"So? I'm ordering you to stay!"

His jaw flexed. She put him in a hard place. Yes, Zara was his queen.

But Milly was a queen too. Maybe not officially, but she would be soon.

In his heart, she should be his queen already.

Ian's rental Ford Fiesta pulled into the driveway. Ian parked and got out with a friendly wave, picked up on the fight, and ducked into the car again.

Uvim started for his blue Fiesta.

No.

She grabbed his hands. "Don't go. Zara might be your queen but I'm your — I'm your bride. I need you."

He softened and threaded his fingers through hers. "You do not need me."

She huffed. "Yes, I do! That's why I'm ordering you to stay."

He kissed her fingers and released her.

Her stomach lurched like a wild eddy spun her away. She thumped on her heels.

He opened the car door.

She forced down the sickness and shouted, hoarse. "Do not get in that car."

He got in the car.

"Do not drive off!"

The blue car drove off.

"Come back!"

She clenched her fists and stamped her feet and bit her shriek.

Uvim chose duty over her. Pain screamed in her chest just like the one she was

trying to hold in. This was the pain she'd been trying to protect herself from all this time.

He'd made her fall in love with him.

She gave in to passion and surrendered. She'd let him sweep her off her feet and now he dragged her under.

The sky closed in like a giant blue box. Even though she was outside, the sunshine suffocated her like the darkest yacht. All alone, her heart begged for his love.

Her desperation made her weak.

Her love held her hostage.

Just like she'd always feared.

...

No.

No, she wasn't weak.

Tears burned in her eyes. But not helpless tears.

Angry tears.

He drove away without a backward glance but Milly wasn't shell-shocked. She wasn't broken. She would not latch on to the next man who passed by because Uvim had shown her how to love a man and accept his love in return.

She was whole. She was powerful.

She was furious.

"I'm sorry." Zara lowered her arms. "Warriors like that only want one thing."

"Honor?" Milly asked, sarcastic raw.

"A baby." Zara gestured at the empty road. "He didn't love you as a person. You were just a vessel to him."

What. The. Heck.

"You don't know him. You don't know anything about him or me."

"I know enough."

"Has interviewing lost brides affected your brain? Or were you always this bitter?"

Zara jerked her head back. "I didn't save you from our parents so you could shackle yourself to the first abusive brute—"

"No, you saved me because you love me. And I'll never forget that. But Uvim is different."

"He is the worst of all!"

"He regrets what happened. Everyone regrets it. It ripped the city apart."

"It ripped me apart! He didn't show remorse."

"Because—"

"Like just now. I shoved his crimes in his face. He didn't say anything!"

Her sister was so, so wrong.

"Don't waste your love on him," Zara continued. "He just left."

"Because you ordered him. Like his elders in the past. He's a dutiful warrior. He performed his duty."

Zara blinked. "But ... he didn't protest."

"Because he couldn't."

Skepticism twisted Zara's features.

"You're his queen, Zara. Don't forget. You'll turn into a bully." Milly stalked to her sedan. She still pinched the crumpled computer printout between her index finger and thumb.

"Where are you going?" Zara demanded, following.

"I have to report this warning to the police. Then, I have to catch Uvim before he obeys your stupid order and leaves."

"The police can't do anything. Look. Our enemy is going to 'blow us out of the water.' They've planted a bomb."

"Then we have to defuse it."

Zara rolled her eyes. "Are you nuts? The harbor's huge."

"We have a week."

"Enemies could plant it the night before."

"If three warriors aren't enough to secure a harbor, what about the army?"

Zara whipped her head back and forth. "Mixing mer and humans is the last thing we need right now."

"Mixing is exactly what we need right now. People have to see–"

"This warning is serious."

"Mermen scare people, Zara. Even though there's a lineup thirty long to meet brides."

"Because mermen are hardheaded idiots who cling to traditions that kill them."

"Like humanity never clings to stupid traditions."

"You know this is different."

"The Sea Festival is important. We need to save it. We have to. We're the only ones who can."

"It's too dangerous."

"Zara, these warriors need a leader. You're not even there! You ran away. You're not trying to help them find the brides that will give them a future."

"I'm trying to find the brides they already threw away!"

"They forced the other brides to the surface because they were doing their duty. And that duty was toxic, but they were brainwashed for generations — for centuries — that it was necessary to be safe. Now, when the mer are finally opening their cities and holding out their hands, you're not around to lift them to the surface. You're not around to introduce them to brides. You're not around to coach them on how to live on the surface."

"Because—"

"You're not around and so the 'welcome' they receive is fear. A stick of dynamite. Bomb threats. If that goes on, the mer will retreat. Traditionalists will regain their power."

"This is not my fault."

"No, but abandoning them is."

"And a little welcome speech at an island festival will make everything better?"

"It's a start. And that's all they need. All *we* need. A start."

Zara frowned.

Milly pressed. "Call the army. Dragao Azul's warriors will safeguard the sea and the police will safeguard the air."

"This is crazy."

"These 'bad guys' run us off and everything Elan fought for — everything *you* fought for — is washed away."

Zara remained silent for a long moment.

In the house behind Zara, Zain squealed. "Maaaa!"

Elan's deep voice soothed him.

Milly had bought this house for herself and Zara. Zain and Elan were welcome. This family made her house a home. And the rest of the world needed to know such a life was possible.

"We will not run away," Milly promised. "We're going to show up. In force."

Zara shook her head.

Milly insisted. "I'll take my chances."

"But I won't." Zara flashed at her. Brave and fierce. "I failed you once. I'm not letting you get hurt again."

Zain squealed again. "Maaaa!"

Elan's voice raised as he soothed Zain.

"It's okay," Zara called over her shoulder. "We're done here."

Milly's brother-in-law, Elan, appeared at the open dining room window. Large, well-muscled, and imposing, the aquamarine warrior looked much better rested than he had when Milly had seen him last. Being with Zara, his soul mate, had smoothed the dark hollows under his eyes and filled out his gaunt features so he again resembled a powerful, just law-giver — a First Lieutenant to be reckoned with.

Even if he currently wore a T-shirt scrawled with #1 *Dad*.

He balanced toddler Zain's bare feet on the window ledge so the two-year-old could bounce, arms out, and appeal to his mom. His squeal turned into a giggle. "Maaa!" And another giggle with multiple bounces. "Maaa. Up!"

His onesie read, #1 *Son*.

Zara scooped up Zain and rested him on her hip. The toddler wiggled.

Her little nephew was so friendly, so fearless, so resilient. He had not seen his mother for the first year of his life, but now he called for her whenever she disappeared from his sight for too long.

Elan nodded to Milly. "You are well."

"Nice shirt," she replied.

A smile gentled his fierce features. "You can buy these. 'Family shirts.' They celebrate a family connection."

"That's nice. I know what to get you for Christmas next year."

"Yes, they are my and Zain's wardrobe. Zara does not wear hers."

Milly lifted one brow.

"It feels like bragging if I wear it in front of the other lost brides," Zara mumbled. "I'll, uh, go put it on."

"Good." Milly sucked in a breath and straightened. "And then, let's go. Talk to Uvim. Really listen to him. And then we'll go call the army."

Zara shifted her weight onto her back foot, hugging Zain tighter. "I can't do that."

Her anger flared. "You won't help me protect your own people?"

"You're more important."

"I'm not, Zara. And I'm not the only one counting on you. You're a queen. Take responsibility." Milly got into the sedan, buckled up, and reversed.

Her chest clenched. A sob stuck in her throat.

Uvim had told her it was not wrong to ask for help. Others chose whether to give it. Milly reacted. To never give up, to seek help elsewhere, to defend herself from a person who had turned around and tried to hurt her for asking.

Everyone needed help sometimes. Asking did not make her a child.

Solving the problem made her the woman.

Uvim had better prepare himself.

Because after Milly solved the Sea Festival bombing, she would go after him.

TWENTY-NINE

Uvim remained silent during the ride to the rental where his warriors awaited his command.

Milly's furious, heartbroken face filled his mind.

Pain tightened his chest. He clenched his hands to fight off the agony.

Ian cleared his throat. "That was awkward."

He did not feel awkward. He felt relief. A bitter, anxious relief.

Leaving had been necessary.

Queen Zara had ruled.

He'd known she would sever their connection. For a time, Milly's love had made him hope to avoid Queen Zara's rage. He had almost convinced himself Milly was right and Queen Zara would forgive his greatest shame.

But inside, he'd always known this judgment was coming.

He had taken a bride out of turn. He had committed great violence against Queen Zara. Milly would never be his.

Now the judgment was here. The fear was over.

His chest squeezed.

No matter his pain, he could not let Milly and Queen Zara fight. Queen Zara was too powerful. Milly had dismissed his concerns many times. She had never seen Queen Zara's powers.

What if his presence caused Queen Zara to lose control? Her rage was deadly. An accident — Milly hurt — Uvim shuddered. He couldn't stand by and allow it to happen.

With his absence, Queen Zara would calm.

Milly was angry at him for leaving. But at least she would be safe.

"She'll get over it," Ian continued, rolling through a stop sign without pausing. His seat belt dangled, unbuckled, next to the window. "Whatever it was. Women always do."

Milly would get over her anger.

Queen Zara would show her the truth. Uvim was unworthy. Her desire for him would fade.

And after Queen Zara understood Milly's destiny to be a queen, she would introduce Milly to a worthier warrior. Twenty-seven worthier warriors existed. She would soon forget Uvim and lead the happy life her kind, generous soul deserved.

He would never recover.

Wanting Milly for his own had been wrong. His selfishness had nearly caused her injury many times. He should never have turned his back on his duty.

All he'd ever had was duty.

"Your warriors have been great." Ian stopped the car in front of his dwelling. "I had my doubts but my sister's like a new person."

Uvim followed the human into the familiar rental while

Ian recounted the differences in his sister. She was no longer depressed about her ex. She had taken time to appreciate herself.

"And then," Ian strolled through the kitchen, "when my sister and Sydney got kidnapped, your warriors jumped right into the fight to—"

He stopped. "Kidnapped?"

"You didn't hear? Things have been so chaotic. We just got back from the police station, actually. Giving statements."

"You must inform Queen Zara."

"Okay, sure. I think Milly gave me that number. I'll call right now." Ian held the phone to his ear, waiting for Queen Zara to answer, and gestured for Uvim to exit. "We're okay. You can see for yourself."

He strode outside.

The human women lounged on the long chairs on the tile. His warriors wrestled in the pool. Xalu stood in the center, fists raised in victory, a rare smile creasing his lips. The clear water lapped at his chest. Dosan's shadow flitted the length of the pool. Xalu's smile fled, and he fell with a splash. Dosan jumped up in his place and raised his fists in victory.

The women cheered.

Xalu re-emerged from beneath Dosan and they grappled. Training exercises turned into spectacle while they frolicked, oblivious to duty or honor.

"Dosan." His voice snapped with cold. "Xalu."

Dosan and Xalu stopped splashing and straightened.

The laughter of the females faded.

Uvim forced his words. "You are well?"

Dosan rubbed his chest. "Yes. Even a doctor would not discover I had jumped on a grenade."

"A what?"

"Dynamite common in human warfare."

Ah. Of course.

Dosan had learned much from the humans in his few days of rest and recovery.

"Xalu?"

The most honorable warrior straightened. His large hands were empty; he had stowed Dosan's trident and daggers. "I am well."

"You were attacked."

Xalu nodded. "We reported the attackers to the police. They face human justice now. As Dosan's attackers faced human justice."

"You did not report to me."

Both warriors stiffened.

His guts burned.

Because he had been lax on order. Duty. He had claimed Milly out of turn and he had neglected his duty to the elders. He had allowed their insubordination.

No longer.

"We return to the city."

Their expressions changed to shock and anger.

He ignored their rebellion. He was the Second Lieutenant. They must obey. "Come."

Great splashes sounded behind him. Protests by the women. Uvim strode through the kitchen, passing Ian chatting with Queen Zara on his cell phone. The women's protests grew louder and cut off.

Sad partings were not Uvim's business. They should have known this separation was coming.

His warriors' footsteps sounded behind him.

Dosan broke the silence first. "Now? You want to leave now? What of your bride's important Sea Festival?"

"She is not my bride."

Their movement behind him stopped.

He turned.

Both Xalu and Dosan regarded him with disbelief.

Xalu spoke. "You dare to abandon a bride *you* took out of turn?"

Pain lanced his chest.

Uvim gritted his teeth. "We never completed the ceremony."

"Because you did not travel to Dragao Azul," Dosan said.

He shook his head. "She did not wish for me."

Xalu growled. "Her wish for you was clear to any male with eyes."

"Milly *is* your bride," Dosan said, agreeing with Xalu. "And you must honor her devotion."

"Queen Zara has issued her order. Bride Milly is not mine."

They both looked shocked.

His chest squeezed. "We return to the city."

Xalu straightened. "No."

No?

Insubordination. Because of his weakness. Because of his failures.

Uvim squared to the males. Xalu had spoken and Dosan united behind the most honorable warrior.

"Obedience is your first duty."

"My first duty is to my bride."

What? *Xalu's* bride?

"You have found her?"

"I have."

"She drank the nectar and accepted your offering?"

"She will."

"Queen Zara must know about brides."

"I will tell her." Xalu threw back his shoulders, baring his chest to Queen Zara's judgment. "And she will never separate me from my bride. Not even if I must exile myself from Dragao Azul and live as a human."

The most honorable male of Dragao Azul would exile himself, the worst punishment, and live as a human? For his bride?

Only two years ago such a statement would have been unthinkable.

But now Xalu spoke it. Aloud.

The world had changed.

No one, not even a queen, could stand in the way of a warrior claiming his bride.

"You do this?" Uvim breathed.

"My bride has already promised me a room in her castle."

"Home," Dosan corrected. "Human home. And I will remain with my bride as well."

What? Dosan had also found his bride? Uvim forced his lax jaw to move. "But you are number twenty-seven."

His friend's lips twisted. "Spoken by number twenty-eight."

"You have no offering. No flower."

"My bride Jen does not care." He glared at Uvim. "And I honor my bride. Her wish is to be with me no matter what. I will not refuse her."

Duty warred with Uvim's deep shame. "Queen Zara is queen."

"On her orders, would you force an injured Bride Milly to the surface?"

He flinched. Their roles in harming Queen Zara had

caused splinters of rebellion to grow in their minds. All bore the scars.

"I would not," he said.

"Neither would I," Dosan replied. "I would not take Bride Milly or Bride Jen or Bride Sid-o-ney."

"Sydney," Xalu corrected.

"Sid ... doney."

"Sydney."

"Bride Syd-nee," Dosan stated. "I will stand by them. All of them. And you must as well."

Could Dosan be correct? They had a higher duty to brides than to their queen. A higher duty than to their elders.

Xalu growled. "Do you dare—"

Dosan placed a quelling hand on the taut warrior's smoke-black forearm. "He will see reason."

Xalu subsided.

There was one other major problem.

"The Sea Festival is at risk," he shared. "Because of the mer. We endanger all. Queen Zara wishes us to leave so we carry away the danger."

Both warriors puffed up with pride.

Xalu spoke. "We have already defended our brides from attack. We will collect your bride and protect her."

"Milly is with Queen Zara and First Lieutenant Elan."

The warriors relaxed.

Queen Zara and First Lieutenant Elan were both, together, the most powerful warriors in Dragao Azul. And Queen Zara, being human, could see enemies on the land.

His unease remained. "You will not depart before the Sea Festival?"

"We wish for acceptance," Dosan said, and Xalu nodded. "Welcome in the city of our brides. Human cities are vast. Brides Jen and Syd-nee have explained it is impossible to greet the citizens of 'Atlanta' in one location."

"Recording the Sea Festival and transmitting our welcome over the 'internet' echo point is best to greet all," Xalu decreed.

And it was important to Milly.

Now, important to the mer.

Very well.

Then, he would support his warriors. "Show me the place where you defended your brides from attack."

"It was not here. It was at a warehouse."

"Show me."

They walked through the house and exited to the car.

The two women were waiting. Both of their soul lights flared with a warrior's challenge.

As the warriors crossed the warm stone, the women straightened. The first, Sydney, put her hands on her hips.

Uvim stopped.

His warriors passed in front of him, continuing toward Ian's car.

Sydney waggled her finger at Xalu. Her brown-black hair were pinned. Soft, gold-colored fabric pants and shirt caressed her full curves. "Where do you think you're going?"

He halted. "The attack site."

"Not without me." She lifted her chin. "I'm your bride and I say you're not going anywhere without me."

He swept her into his arms and lowered his voice. "Yes, my Sydney."

"That's right." She snuggled into his embrace.

The woman from the tour boat, Jen, blocked Dosan with crossed arms. "And you're not going anywhere without me."

Dosan eased onto his heels. "But I must find another grenade to jump upon so you will find me a heroic and handsome warrior."

She eased into a smile, her tense shoulders relaxing, and slipped into his sheltering arms. "I already think you're heroic. Don't get hurt."

He stroked her cheeks with his thumb. "You must stop me."

"I need you, Dosan." Her thick lashes fluttered, and she melted into his kiss.

Their soul lights glowed in unity.

Uvim's chest squeezed. A happy, heartfelt pain that celebrated their unions and worried for how best to protect them from the dangers of the unkind world.

No, he could not order these warriors away from their brides.

Milly had hesitated to become his.

These brides did not hesitate. Their souls synced without restraint. For the first time, Dosan's quips brought joy. Xalu's devotion was honored.

They had found their matches.

Uvim would not order these males away from their brides.

Milly had been right. About everything.

Then he must defy Queen Zara and reclaim Milly.

Dosan and Xalu were right.

Milly *was* his bride.

Defying Queen Zara twisted his stomach. But he must confront her.

First, he must make Milly safe and stop the violence against the Sea Festival.

He strode past the couples to Ian's car. "Show me the

attack site. We have a short time to find and defuse the Sea Festival bomb."

The other warriors and brides entered the car, conferencing about how to help him.

They would work together. Mer and human. He would defeat the enemy. Make the Sea Festival safe. Redeem himself.

And then Milly would welcome him.

And then he would challenge Queen Zara once more.

THIRTY

Just as Milly pulled away from the house to begin her journey, Zara called out. "Wait!"

Milly pressed the brake.

Zara approached her sedan with a now serious, frowning Zain balanced against her hip. "You can't take this on yourself, Milly. I forbid it."

"Too bad." Milly rolled down the window so Zara could hear with no glass between them. "I'm reporting this warning to the police. I'm finding Uvim. I'm calling the army. And I'm telling them it was your idea. So if you're going to stop me, you come too."

Zara folded her lips.

"We'll win." Milly raised her fist. "We'll arrive in force, wow the good guys, and show the world we're not afraid."

"Even if we are afraid?" Zara asked.

Her son fussed. "Down. Down. Down."

Zara bounced him, not putting him down, and sighed. "Well, whatever. It's a free country."

"Zara, Portugal is a free country. But Dragao Azul isn't. And you're their queen."

She rubbed her forehead and groaned. "If I'm their queen then why do the elders question everything I say? I can't get Zain to stay in his bed at night. He keeps starting the bathtub at midnight and swimming until he overflows it. I don't feel like a queen."

"But you are. If you tell your warriors to surface, they'll do it. If you tell them to jump on dynamite, they would do that too. If you tell them to take a long walk off a short pier, they will."

"Why do you defend these idiots? Where's the common sense?"

"It's not common sense. It's respect. What you say is law. They're warriors, Zara. Weren't you telling me about warrior culture in your social justice classes? They don't have money. All they have is honor."

"That's why I don't want you involved with them, Milly. I'm their stupid ruler now whether I like it or not. If I say the wrong word, you could get hurt."

Milly waited.

Zara bounced fussing Zain. "You aren't giving up on this, are you?"

"The fate of the mer depends on us."

"You have changed."

Milly had. The old her would have collapsed on her bed, cried her eyes out, and withdrawn.

The new her wasn't standing around.

A sigh pushed out of Zara's lips. "Be safe."

"You too."

Milly left Zara with her mer family in front of their house.

First, she dropped off the warning paper at the police station.

The police confirmed high Sea Festival security. Officers from all islands concentrated on Faial.

"We have made additional arrests," Inspector Periera assured her, clicking his pen. "We will interview all criminals. If there is a bomb, we will uncover it."

Good. Maybe the police could stop the bad guys before they planted the bomb.

But just in case, she wanted answers.

Milly drove to Ian's vacation rental.

No one answered her knocks.

Huh?

She called Ian. His phone went to voice mail. So did Jen's number.

Her stomach dropped.

Could she have missed them? Were they at the beach having a send-off? Ugh. Bad timing! Dutiful jerks.

She drove to the beach.

The lockbox stood strong. Nearby, kids ate an early dinner. An older uncle strolled far down the beach supervising.

Zara had refused to help. But asking for help had secured the lockbox.

Asking for help wasn't always wrong.

Milly removed her clothes, contorting in the car, and wrapped a lavender sarong around her nude body. She took out her contacts and left them in her emergency travel solution case under the front seat. Milly clambered out of the sedan, leaving her phone hidden under her clothes on the passenger's seat, and locked up. Then, holding her keys in one fist, she minced across the gritty parking lot and scrambled over the rocky beach to the crashing shore.

No warriors.

Milly waded into the waves. Rough and strong, they

knocked against her shins and dragged at her sarong. Rocks and seaweed tumbled beneath her feet.

She pushed deeper.

A wave crashed against her waist and rushed back out to sea.

She dove.

Water caressed her with welcome. Releasing her breath, she unwound the sarong and kicked. She zoomed across the shallow rock, deeper and deeper, until the lava cone of the island tilted into the depths. Gorgeous coral, shimmery fish, and haunting eagle rays soared across the active channel. She dragged in a mouthful of warm water. The shift seemed easier this time.

Milly searched the infinite distance.

No warriors.

Okay. One more idea.

Milly followed the spiraling coral down to the small cave Uvim had shown her. A wheezing noise filled the ocean and a small cave guardian popped out.

"Has Uvim been here?" she asked the cave guardian.

He snort-squeaked uncertainly. He didn't understand her question.

"The warriors? Have you seen three warriors today?"

He darted as though seeking the warriors.

So, that was probably a no.

"Do you still have Uvim's daggers and trident?"

The cave guardian jetted into the cave. He returned moments later with the wrapped metal blades.

Uvim's blades.

He dropped them on the ledge and eased into the cave.

"Wait." She gave him back the blades. "It's okay. I don't need them. Oh, actually, I have something for you to guard. If you don't mind."

He danced on his ledge, pretending to walk on his fists. He didn't mind.

She folded her sarong and handed it over along with her car keys.

He clinked the metal in fascination.

"Don't lose it," she said. "I need that back."

He stowed her items inside the cave, buzzing with his duty.

She somersaulted, studying the vast ocean. Where was Uvim? The ocean was dangerous. He wouldn't have left without his blades. She—

Fins!

"Uvim!"

She somersaulted after the disappearing fin tips. He'd snuck up on her. She kicked faster to reach him.

But the faster she paddled, the faster the fin tips disappeared...

Because they followed her.

Oh! They were *her* fins!

Milly stopped, folded over the front way, and stroked the rubbery toes and stretched-tight skin. Her plain fins trembled, ticklish like the skin wanted to snap back into the shape of her human foot.

She stretched wide and kicked.

Great scoops of water propelled her. Like her plastic scuba fins only firmer, more powerful, and better control.

Awesome.

She kicked along the beach for the sheer joy of flying.

And still, Uvim didn't come.

She needed to decide. Climb out of the water to search for him and risk losing her nerve? Or go alone to the echo point and risk losing her life?

Uvim had left his trident and blades...

But she wasn't a warrior. She'd cut herself before any enemy.

She needed help.

Who could help her?

A symphony of terrible noise erupted in the ocean. Punctured bagpipes and un-oiled brakes. A giant shadow rose from the depths.

"Clifford!" she cried. "I'm so glad to see you."

The giant black octopus wrapped Milly in gentle tentacles. She hugged the one closest to her. Clifford stroked Milly in happiness, squealing and buzzing, and held up her injuries. Her stubby tentacles had grown a few feet.

Milly focused on the problem. "We're in real trouble and don't have a moment to waste. Can you escort me to the echo point?"

In answer, Clifford wrapped a tentacle around Milly and dropped into swift water.

This current flowed to the echo point. Not only did Clifford understand; she also heard Milly's panic and helped without hesitation.

They stormed across the ocean. Clifford's size and evasive maneuvers scattered fish and frightened off predators.

Milly spent the time fantasizing about Uvim.

She would hunt him. Catch him. And demand he satisfy their soul connection with his promised five pleasures in one joining — every night for the rest of their lives.

They arrived at the echo point. The still waters engulfed Milly.

It was time

Clifford stayed outside the still water, swerving across brisk currents.

Milly swam through the conversation threads until she

reached one that felt right. The next echo confirmed her feelings.

Dosan, report! Honorable Warrior Xalu, report! Second Lieutenant Uvim, report!

Her stomach dipped.

What if asking for help went wrong? What if she got Uvim in worse trouble? What if no one responded to the call? Or, worse, what if everyone responded and got hurt?

Now or never.

She made her chest vibrate fit to shout.

"I summon the army of Dragao Azul to the surface. By the order of Queen Zara."

The giant octopus squeaked.

Take responsibility. Asking for help is not wrong. Be a queen.

"And Queen Milly!"

THIRTY-ONE

There.

She had done it. Asked for help. Awaited their answer.

Hours later — at least, it felt like hours — the answer from Dragao Azul echoed through the still water.

The army comes.

And then she and Clifford crossed the vast ocean to return to the shore.

Milly radiated power. Together, they were unstoppable! The ocean responded.

Swift blue sharks respected them. The buzzing curtain of jellyfish parted for her. Bottlenose dolphins dove close to get a look. Groupers the size of sheep cast curious eyeballs her way and deep-water fish, like the schools of mammoth tuna, rose from the depths just to watch her pass.

She was the Queen of the Ocean.

And it was awesome.

As Uvim was about to find out.

Back in the shallower water, Milly stopped at the small cave to collect her sarong and car keys. She bid goodbye to

Clifford and then rode a wave to standing-water height and stumbled out of the ocean.

Her fins tangled in her sarong. She landed on her knees on the rough volcanic rock and crawled. Her feet snapped to human.

Air hit the back of her throat and she gagged.

A young woman ran up to her. "*Est ce que ça* ... eh, you okay?"

She accepted the slender woman's help, got her feet under her, and tightened the dripping sarong around her breasts. "*Merci*."

The friendly French-speaking woman rejoined her family.

Crowds thronged the volcanic beach, cars overfilled the parking lot, and a hundred languages passed over her ears as Milly navigated between the tourists snapping photos.

How many days had passed?

The sun seemed higher in the sky as if it were earlier than when she'd left. It was probably a different day.

Milly reached the parking lot.

Chalk lines marked her sedan's tires. But, no tickets. Lucky! Or maybe she had to thank Vaw Vaw's family. She waved at the kids—different kids playing on the beach with their families.

She jammed her still-dripping keys into the driver's door and opened the car. A puff of hot air bathed her in sweat. She moved aside her folded clothes. There, her phone. She hit the power button.

The screen flickered.

Uh oh.

She'd meant to shut it off. But she'd forgotten. It blinked with a red sliver of battery.

The date was four days into the future.

The Sea Festival had already started!

She had six voice messages and a hundred texts.

Only one was from Zara. *Come home.*

The rest were from Brody. She scrolled through without reading them and then dropped the phone on the seat and wriggled into her hot shirt and capris, ignoring her four-days-old, sweaty undergarments.

Her heart flopped in her chest.

Didn't Uvim miss her?

Well, he didn't have a cell phone. He couldn't text.

She wanted to text him. Wasn't he proud? She'd summoned the warriors by herself. The army of Dragao Azul was coming. She'd summoned them as a queen and when they arrived she'd lead them like a queen, too.

She checked her voice messages.

Brody again!

"Call me," he said in his first message and repeated the refrain in the next messages with increasing desperation. "Ty needs those pressure plates! He's constructing the Friendship Float, don't you know? On the stage they signal to blast the flowers. The welcome speech is in two days. I was the one who said you could borrow them. If he doesn't get them back, you'll have to dredge the harbor for my body because he's going to kill me!"

Oops.

Her phone blinked red.

She called Brody. "Sorry! The pressure plates are still in my trunk. Where can I meet you?"

"Just go straight to the dock warehouse." He gave her the directions. "I'll meet you there. But Milly, whatever you do, don't—"

The call ended.

"Brody?" She lifted the phone from her ear. Its screen flashed as the phone shut down.

Out of battery.

She blew air out between her lips.

Uvim. Uvim. Uvim.

She craved to see him. She needed to be with him. She was his bride — his queen — and they were meant to be together. She needed to find him and prove it.

Her doubts had held her back before. She'd let Zara steamroll her. He'd run away to escape the pain.

She would soothe his pain and then jump him.

They would never part again.

She'd go home, grab a shower and change clothes, and then Uvim.

If Zara still stood in her way, Milly would demand she live up to her responsibility. Defend her island and her warriors from the merman-killing cult and anyone else who represented a threat.

That's right. *Her* warriors.

Zara's warriors. And also Milly's.

No vandalizing, dynamite-fishing jerks interfered with her responsibility.

But returning things was responsible, so she drove to the dock warehouse. It was only a few blocks from the main harbor in a rundown lot behind an ancient fort.

Brody's cousin Ty stood outside. He was college-age like her, but in yellow-beige bib overalls and work boots, he didn't fit the college tourist look. He'd worked on a yacht last year and stuck around.

She'd met him a handful of times. Sandy-brown hair, greasy hands, and sky-blue eyes. He had a snub nose and too many freckles to be handsome.

Handsome?

That was unfair to Ty. His girlfriend probably found him handsome. Milly had fallen for a male with olive green skin. She wasn't exactly an expert.

"Thanks for letting me borrow the plates." She opened her trunk. "Where did you want them?"

"This way." He walked off without offering to help.

Huh. She used to like that. But now, she was used to Uvim helping. Ty was rude.

She lifted the heavy plates with her core and staggered after him.

He led her into the warehouse. Cool shadows hid sinister secrets. Dusty boxes tumbled onto rickety carts. Outside the warehouse were a small dock and a boat.

The wooden hull looked too old to float but the sculpture on top was new — two quasi-human people splashing together like waves.

He directed her to put the pressure plates on one cart.

She heaved them in a great sigh. It would have been nicer if they'd brought the cart out to the sedan. But whatever.

Milly waved out the ocean-facing doors. "Is that the Friendship Float?"

Without an answer, he pushed the big hangar doors together, hiding the view, and locked it with a pin.

Okay.

She turned away. "Well, I'll be—"

"Just a minute." He scurried past. "Need to get something out of the office."

She took the extra minutes to inspect the boxes.

Some were open. Big, poufy bags spilled long, white candles. Other boxes held ice. Colorful flower petals trailed across the bare concrete.

Ty brought out a canister of compressed air and a roll of duct tape.

"Almost ready for the parade, huh?" she said.

"Almost." He set the duct tape on a box. A sly smile stole across his thin mouth. "Got some use out of the plates?"

"Did Brody tell you?"

"He doesn't tell me a thing."

"Oh."

Ty brushed off the canister. Not compressed air. It was an air horn.

"And that was the root of my troubles," she said.

He toyed with it, eying her. "I know."

"You know?"

He seemed to stall.

Maybe because she was tired of swimming for days and was suddenly starving. She wanted to finish this. "How do you know?"

His sly smile returned. "I was there."

Wait. "What?"

A rattle of the far doors, closest to her car, shoved one open and Brody pushed in. Alarmed. "Milly! You're inside."

She backed away from Brody's weirdly smiling cousin. "Well, you said Ty needed these or else."

"Yeah, but I thought you'd wait out — Ty, don't!"

Ty held the air horn to her head. "She's one of them."

What?

Was Ty threatening her?

With an *air horn?*

"Uh," she said.

"Ty, stop it!"

One of the boxes was painted with a small triangle logo.

The anti-merman cult!

She gasped. "*You're* one of *them*."

Ty snickered. "Let's see how much you changed."

BWAAAAAAAAAAAAAAAAAAAAAAAAAAAAAAAA.

Pain boxed her ears.

Noise reverberated.

She clapped her hands over her ears. Too late. The sound echoed.

"Milly?" Brody asked, his voice raised over the cottony silence.

"Okay!" she shouted. "Now, I'm obviously deaf."

Ty's smile fled.

She turned her back on him and marched past a shocked Brody. Her heart thumped faster and faster.

Ty and Brody were with the cult.

Brody knew about the dynamite. He'd been so angry on the tour boat and yet he'd known all along.

She had to stay calm, walk out of here, and go straight to the police.

Just stay—

The world shuddered. Weird colors flooded her vision like a film negative exposed to light. The floor wavered in and out of focus.

Had she put in her contacts? Weren't they still in the emergency travel case under the front seat?

The floor lurched.

Earthquake!

Her feet stumbled into molasses.

Milly threw out her hands to break her fall.

But her hands didn't respond. They hung like lead weights at her sides.

She tipped.

The world turned black long before she hit the ground.

Uvim swam the length of Horta's main harbor, weaving between dock pillars and darting beneath docked yachts. His biceps and thighs bristled with daggers. He held his trident snug to his side.

No dynamite.

He reversed and swam in the opposite direction.

No dynamite.

He stowed his weapons in a cave next to a barnacle-coated pillar, surfaced at the end of the dock, and heaved himself onto the wood. Water sloshed out of his lungs. He shifted to human with a shallow cough.

Humans backed out of his way in surprise.

He tossed his towel over his broad shoulders, toed on his flip flops, and pushed sunglasses up his nose. His water-logged shorts drained water.

Now, he looked like one of them.

Uvim crossed the dock to the land and wove through the crowd.

Deep unease chilled his rib cage like icy water. The

unease had seeped in yesterday. Today, his stomach hurt and he had no desire for food.

Was his body punishing him for remaining away from Milly so long? Her absence made his soul sick?

Their souls had connected. So, perhaps.

Xalu stood in the shadow by the stage. Officials fluttered around completing the final arrangements. He watched over the entire harbor from his vantage point.

"No bomb in the boat launch," Uvim reported.

Dosan emerged and scrambled up the rock wall. He wore his human disguise. But the crowd still parted.

He joined them. "No bomb beneath the boats anchored in the middle of the harbor."

Xalu frowned. "I will swim the length of the sea wall to the breakwater." He walked into the crowd.

The crowd parted for him as humans stumbled backward, spilling drinks, to get out of his way.

He dove off the elevated concrete platform into the water. Xalu would make a large loop patrolling the sea wall, ferry terminal, cross the harbor's entrance, and patrol the breakwater wall to his starting point.

Since the dynamite at the octopus colony, they knew the tastes of the plastic, fuse, and explosive powder. It was easy to sense. While swimming the harbor these past five days, they had discovered much human trash but no bomb.

The police inspector neared Uvim. He sweated in a dark suit. "Any dangers?"

"None yet," Uvim confirmed.

The inspector frowned. "I wish that would mean the threat was empty. But we cannot hang our hopes on empty wishes." He clicked his pen, a nervous habit, and waded back into the crowd.

Dosan pulled his T-shirt on. "I wish the threats would be empty. Then we could go to Dragao Azul in peace."

"You must not leave before the welcome speech."

He eyed Uvim. "I will listen with respect."

Dosan feared Uvim would order him once more to give the speech.

But Uvim would not.

He had promised Milly. As the days passed without her, the burning agony in his heart had transformed into a rock-hard will.

He would deliver her speech. He would speak the words the humans needed to hear. It would move her heart. The mer and humans would become friends.

Milly would know his love. She would forgive him for running. And she would once more accept his claim as his bride.

The committee chair stopped in their shade. "It's speech time! Don't leave."

He nodded his understanding.

The committee chair climbed the stage steps.

Milly must come to Dragao Azul and marry him in front of the Life Tree. She must.

His words would woo her.

He swore it.

Dosan's bride, Jen, wove through the crowd. Ian and Bride Sydney trailed behind her. Bride Jen offered her phone. "Uvim, your queen is calling."

His Milly?

He snatched the phone. "Milly?"

"No, I'm not Milly." Queen Zara's imperious voice bit into his ear with a hard edge.

He stiffened.

"Where is she?" Queen Zara demanded.

But Queen Zara had ordered him away from Milly. Why would she ask him Milly's location? Was this a test?

"Hello?" Queen Zara snapped. "Are you there?"

He forced the hard word past his lips. "Yes."

"Then answer me. Where is she?"

Uvim ground his teeth. He had wronged Queen Zara. It justified her anger. "I obeyed your orders and left my bride in your care."

"Days ago."

"Yes."

"Wait." In her surprise, Queen Zara's tone and phrase echoed Milly. "She left that day to talk to you. After our fight. She didn't talk to you?"

The uneasy cold roiled his stomach. "No."

"But you both summoned Dragao Azul's army."

"No."

"Well, the army's here, so somebody did."

Imagining Milly alone, lost in the currents, hunted by predators, congealed his coldness into a sick ball. "She must not cross without protection."

"She obviously did."

The stone beneath his feet lurched.

Nightmare.

Uvim focused on the dark water concealing the harbor. "She summoned the army?"

"They arrived at the beach this morning. Elan's leading them to the harbor."

"Milly is not with them?"

"No, she returned yesterday in the early afternoon. Vaw Vaw's family saw her emerge from the ocean, get in her car, and drive away. But this morning, Nicolette found Milly's car abandoned in front of the dive shop."

"Abandoned?"

"She parked sideways and left her lights on. The battery's dead."

"Milly is careful with her car. She would not make such a mistake."

"Her wallet, cell phone, and contacts were still under the seat. She can't see without them. She couldn't have gotten far." Queen Zara huffed. "Look. I won't be angry. I just need the truth. Are you sure she's not with you?"

Her accusation stabbed deep. "You think I lie?"

"Well, she's your bride, and I know how crazy you mer get about your brides."

Her acknowledgment of their connection only made his anger boil harder. "The only 'crazy' action I took was obeying your order to leave."

She sucked in a breath. "Now, you listen—"

"I entrusted Milly to you, Queen Zara. Enemies have kidnapped Dosan's and Xalu's brides. Yet you allowed Milly to leave without protection."

Queen Zara swallowed.

"I will find Milly," he swore.

"Thank you."

"We," Dosan vowed, quiet. "We will find Milly."

Brides Jen and Sydney nodded earnestly.

"Where are you?" Queen Zara asked, clipped.

"Ocean-side corner of the stage."

"I'll be there in five minutes."

Uvim handed the cell phone back to Bride Jen. She ended the call and linked hands with Dosan. "What do we do?"

"We search," Uvim said grimly.

Xalu leaped out of the water and wove between surprised humans. He arrived out of breath, spraying them with salt water. "The army has arrived. A giant black cave guardian flanks them."

"Milly's friend," Uvim said. "Clifford. Take care."

"I told them."

"Milly is not there?"

Xalu shook his head.

His chest squeezed.

Milly was missing. In a sea of humans, he could not see her. And his enemy's bomb was still undiscovered.

All three warriors and their brides turned outward to search thousands of humans.

Beneath the water, he could pick one fish out of a school. He would know her. But above the surface, resonance faded. The soul lights were washed out, obscured by buildings, faded in the air. He could not see or sense Milly's pure light.

"Uvim!" The committee chair waved him toward the stage. "It's time."

The elevated view would show more.

Uvim climbed the stairs and stood with the other human dignitaries awaiting their turns to speak.

Before him, humans crowded around the stage like grains of sand. They spilled over the docks, onto the many boats bobbing on their tethers, and on the yachts filling the harbor with colorful flags. Humans perched many levels deep on the long sea wall, silhouetted against the breakwater, filled the streets leading away from the harbor, and pressed their hands against shop windows facing the ocean.

The grand platform overlooked the entire harbor.

How many thousands of humans trained their gazes on him?

The first mer warrior?

Stk. Stk. Stk.

The committee chair lofted a black stick. "Welcome to the annual Sea Festival!"

His voice emerged after a delay from other boxes and echoed over the crowds.

Uvim focused.

Milly must be here. This moment meant so much to her. She had cared about it before they had even met. She must not miss it.

Where was she?

"And now, the first remarks by an Azores' native of the sea. Warrior Uvim, a merman!"

The committee chairman offered Uvim the black stick.

Uvim stepped forward and took it. He stared over the upturned faces.

His warriors prowled through the crowds. On one street leading to the harbor, bright Queen Zara forced her way toward the stage. In the center of the harbor, bobbing his head above the water, glowed steady aquamarine First Lieutenant Elan.

Where was Milly?

The crowd murmured.

The committee chairman cleared his throat. Without the black stick, his voice sounded normal. "Uvim?"

Uvim lifted the black stick to his mouth.

He must say words. So the humans would understand. They would all understand. Today was a celebration between mer and humans.

Milly, his love, his bride, his heart, was missing from his side.

He must speak.

THIRTY-THREE

Milly groaned and tried to roll over on the hammock.

It resisted.

Her neck muscles twinged. They bent at an awkward angle, and the hammock was so uncomfortable. It was poky. And made of splintered wood.

Er, splintered wood?

The world rotated and everything made sense.

She collapsed in the belly of a wooden boat. Her cheek smashed the junker hull, her butt rose in the air, and something wrenched her arms behind her. She tugged. Her wrists rubbed on a sticky band. Her ankles were stuck with the same.

Duct tape?

Her fingers tingled, numb, with pins-and-needles.

Around her, piles of plastic bags spilled flowers.

"You're awake."

She forced her million-pound-heavy head off the ground, turned, and collapsed with a groan.

Brody's cousin Ty stood a few feet away in the middle

of the small hull. He checked his wrist watch. "Guess roofies work the same on monsters."

Her mouth and her brain felt like tofu. Memories pounded against her skull. She let some in.

Ty had air horned her. The world had gone funny and she'd passed out.

She'd woken up later in a daze. Someone — it must have been Ty — pressed a cup of lukewarm water to her lips and ordered her to swallow. She had ... and now she was here.

In a small, junker boat.

Ty ripped open a bag of white candles and dumped them onto a big canvas bag.

"What are you doing?" she asked.

The canvas stretched tight. Its four corners were hooked to springs anchored in the ceiling. The center of the bag was hooked to the floor.

Blue sky shone through a huge hole cut in the deck.

She must have passed out with her contacts in. Her vision was so clear. Luckily, her contacts hadn't scratched her eyes like usual when she dozed.

Yeah. Lucky.

Ty organized thin candle strings. He looped the strings over the taut canvas.

Wait. She knew those plastic candles. She knew those strings — as fuses.

"Dynamite," she groaned.

"Yep."

He emptied a bag of flowers on top of the dynamite. Then, he walked to her and knelt, showing her a black box. Inside, a pilot light glowed red.

"They give the welcome speech. Stomp the pressure plates to signal this box. Lights the fuses."

He mounted the pilot light on the wall behind her. Beneath it, a large tank was bolted to the wall. He twisted the aperture. Air hissed. A rotten-eggs smell assaulted her nose.

"After a five-second delay, it releases the pin."

He pointed to the small metal hook securing the canvas bag to the floor. When it was released, the springs would fling the contents of the huge canvas bag — flowers and lit dynamite — out of the boat.

"And they fly like the Fourth of July."

Sprinkling the water in the middle of the welcome ceremony for the Sea Festival. "You're going to kill people," she breathed.

"Monsters. Mostly."

Ugh.

"Not just the mer," she said.

He shrugged. "Sympathizers."

"And the mer are not monsters. They're the same as you and me."

He rose and tested the springs. *Twang.* Ignoring her.

The murderous scope of his atrocity shook her to the core.

He would launch lit dynamite over the whole festival. Kids. Parents. Everyone on the boats and in the water.

She'd called the entire mer army. Had they come? *Please, God, let them not have come.* The army was all warriors capable of raising arms. Most of the population of Dragao Azul. All the warriors who might have come to her aid — summoned by her call — would be dead.

Wait.

If the dynamite flew away from the boat she might survive.

"Why are you telling me this?" she asked.

He formed another sly smile and hunkered down to her level. "For the big finish."

"Huh?"

Ty pointed.

Under a tennis shoe she recognized as belonging to Brody — Brody! — there was a large keg.

A single fuse ran from the pilot light box, coiled around machinery, and snaked across the boat before ending at the keg.

Whether it took five or even ten minutes to burn down, no one would know it was in here.

The dynamite lofted into the air would burn for minutes but they'd catch everyone by surprise and spread out in the water. Impossible to get in time. After the little dynamites killed, the slow fuse would burn to its destination and the entire boat would explode.

The tennis shoe twitched. Somewhere beyond it, a man moaned.

"Brody!" Milly cried.

He groaned louder.

Ty's smile wiped away.

The engine for the tow-boat started. The thin hull vibrated.

Ty stood, tapped the pilot light box, and headed for the ladder.

She thought fast. "They'll know it was you."

"I'll be long gone."

"You stuffed that warning under my door. The police have the paper. They dusted for prints."

He smirked. "They won't find mine."

Of course he hadn't sent it. He'd wanted the mer to attend. This bomb set-up was his grand masterpiece.

"You're killing people, Ty! Killing me."

He shrugged. "You're one of them now."

"Your own cousin?"

He murdered Brody with his gaze. "He betrayed me."

"What? How?"

Ty gripped the rungs.

Milly strained against the tape. "Why are you doing this?"

"With the monsters gone, I'll finally get a girlfriend."

What. The. Heck.

Milly choked. "You're murdering all these people so you can get a girlfriend? Are you insane?"

Ty climbed the ladder.

Of course he was insane. He was murdering all these people. No shock he couldn't get laid.

She shouted after him. "The mer didn't stop you from getting a girlfriend. Your psycho-ness did!"

His shadow disappeared.

She writhed.

The duct tape held.

Could she scream loud enough to alert the pilot in the tow boat? Assuming he or she wasn't in on the plot?

She sucked in a huge lungful and screamed.

Nothing.

The boat chugged toward the inner harbor. Music, talking, and noise grew loud.

The chair of the Sea Festival committee thanked attendees in a tiny, tinny voice.

The welcome speech would soon be starting.

"Brody. Brody!"

He groaned.

"*Brody.*"

"Five more minutes..."

"We don't have five more minutes. We're going to die."

He did a crunch, raising himself up, and groaned. "What's going on? My arms..." He blinked at the open sky. "Am I on the Death Float?"

"So, you knew?"

He blinked hard. "Uh ... Ty was just talking ... it means nothing."

"Oh, no, you're right. This is the Friendship Float and your psycho cousin—"

"Ty's not a psycho. He's confused."

"He's confused?" Fury welled in her chest. "He lucidly explained how he rigged the Friendship Float to deliver flowers with a side of murder. You were in on it. What's your excuse?"

"I wasn't, really. I just went to a couple of meetings."

"Meetings? Psychos hold meetings?

"The 'Sons of Hercules.' Kill monsters, save women, be heroes. Get a girlfriend."

Oh, god. It was true. It was all true.

Brody, her close friend and coworker, attended psychopath meetings to plot how to murder her friends and family.

He noted her horror and shrugged. "They had free beer."

"You sent that warning."

"Warning?"

"About the bomb in the harbor. This bomb. You stuffed it under my door."

"Oh, no way. Not me. I'm never going to your house again."

"Somebody stuffed a warning under my door days ago."

"Probably ... eh, I don't know. Some recruits are more into the 'Be Heroes' part than the 'Kill Monsters' part."

"So dynamiting a helpless octopus colony counts as being a hero?"

"That wasn't me!" He sobered. "The last time I went to a meeting, they were—"

"They?"

"College kids."

"College kids as in more of my friends? In the marine biology department? At our college?"

"Eh ... just some guys." He waved her away like his co-conspirators weren't a big deal. "They wanted to drop a depth charge over a trench and 'hope' it reached a mer city before it blew up."

"There are kids in those cities, Brody. 'Young fry' mer kids."

"It would never work. Real stupid, all of it. Sci fi *Abyss* stuff. Like, how do they find a depth charge? Who's funding them, the military?"

"Well, who funded the free beer?"

Brody shrugged. "Not Ty. He just sent some emails. And his 'recruits' were a bunch of college, er, college-aged kids with nothing better on a Saturday night."

"Nothing better to do than import and sell dynamite to tourists."

"Yeah, I don't know how he did that."

"Your cousin tried to *destroy an octopus colony*, Brody. And they're about to kill us and a lot more people."

"No way."

She re-explained the whole plan Ty had told her.

Brody shook his head from start to finish. "Ty promised he'd stop the dynamite. I threatened to turn him in. And then ... wait. How did I get here?" He tugged on the duct tape securing his arms behind him. "Am I tied up?"

"You lured me to Ty's warehouse."

"Oh, right, the pressure plates. I wanted to keep you away from Ty so he didn't find out about your change-over to mermaid."

Her heart sank. "You knew?"

"Milly." He gave her the "duh" expression. "You were underwater for thirty minutes. Nobody holds their breath for that long."

So, she hadn't been as sneaky as she'd thought.

"Anyway, you weren't outside when I arrived. And after I told you to avoid Ty."

"You didn't tell me!"

"Yes, I did."

"No, you—" Another memory thumped her tofu brain. "My phone died."

"I'd get the pressure plates from you so you'd never run into Ty."

"He was waiting for me outside."

"And then I arrived and he used a sonic ... no. Air horn? And you collapsed. And I told him hurting people was wrong. And he said you were just knocked out and I could take you home after we shared a beer to prove there were no hard feelings..."

"And then he roofied you." She rolled onto her side. "And here we both are."

"Huh. I got roofied?" He twisted at the torso, stretched, and yawned. "I've never been roofied before. Huh. I got roofied. Cool."

"No, not cool! You knew all along your cousin was a mer-hating psycho. A little warning would have been nice!"

Brody shook his head. "Nah, you just have to be careful with Ty. He's always been violence-prone, but he's an all right guy."

She pushed her shoulder into the hull trying to flail upright. "All right guy?"

"Like when I got old enough to beat him at cards and then he lured me to his parents' storage unit and locked me in for sixteen hours. His parents let me out. I thought I was going to die."

"Now you *are* going to die because he will blow you up."

The tugboat engine idled. They were in position. Their time was running out.

She wriggled on her side. "Are you going to hang out and wait? His parents won't show up this time."

Brody stared into the darkness.

"Help me!"

"Okay, give me a minute." He rolled his abdomen into a tight crunch and strained.

"What are you doing?"

"Moving my wrists around to the front. I saw this in a prison movie. You have to dislocate your shoulders."

"What?!"

"I've been practicing yoga…"

She was *not* dislocating her shoulders.

Milly rocked back and forth. She had to rescue her warriors. They were her responsibility.

She was their queen.

Her feet flexed — *fins* — and she rolled to her knees. Her fins flexed to human. She staggered to her feet.

Brody's arm jutted an unnatural angle. "What are you going to do?"

"Put out the pilot light. Then it doesn't matter if the dynamite gets launched. Nothing will blow up."

She hopped across the rolling hull. There was the glowing red flame. She blew.

Her breath fogged the glass.

"Hit the button on the side," Brody suggested, contorting. "Maybe the top. It'll kill the flame."

She looked around. "There's no button."

"Maybe it's behind the box."

The gas hissed out. Slow, concentrated on the fuse, and stinky.

Her head swam. "Ugh."

The glass must protect the pilot light to make the trap work. If she exposed the pilot light now, it would light everything on fire prematurely.

"When this glass drops, I bet there's so much gas here the whole boat explodes," she said.

"Nah, Ty plans for that. He's scary with mechanics. It will go off in a perfect controlled blast."

The committee chair's tinny voice faded away.

Uh oh. Her time had run out.

She tensed.

Whoever spoke next would kill them.

THIRTY-FOUR

Uvim gripped the black speaking stick.

This moment had been important to Milly. He would honor her passion.

"For a thousand years, the warriors of Dragao Azul have lived beneath you, secret."

His voice echoed across the crowd.

"Now we are secret no longer. Our Life Tree has 'healing essence'. Our mating jewels are Sea Opals gemstones. You are curious. So today, our finest warriors surface. They swim here in the water."

Everyone craned.

He did not expect the warriors to emerge. They could not hear his speech beneath the water. But First Lieutenant Elan must have conveyed his words. After a long moment, heads bobbed above the waves.

His city's warriors. Milly had summoned them. They had come.

Now, they too heard him speak.

"We offer our respect. This land is your domain. What

is your answer? Do you welcome us with a friendly greeting? Some humans dislike the mer."

The crowd quieted.

"Yes, some humans hurt, injure, even kill warriors. Some threaten our young fry. Kidnap our brides. They attack us with weapons we do not know. Guns and dynamite.

"But even if we are attacked, even if we are injured, we will protect our brides and our young fry."

His warriors stood tall in the crowds, their lights bright with the vow.

"My bride, Milly, believed this welcome speech was important. I stand before you, a warrior. You see me? We are different. I swim the deepest seas and hunt the wild bream.

"But I, too, search for a bride. And I, too, hope she desires me. I plan for us to marry. I dream for our future young fry.

"Will our young fry enter the world healthy and strong? Will he act with honor? Will he encounter kindness? And will he meet his own bride? I hope he, too, makes a happy young fry. And so on, and so on.

"Are my hopes and my dreams so different?"

The crowd clapped.

This noise had accompanied other speeches. Uvim continued speaking.

"Today, my bride Milly is not here. She is missing. Her car was found but I do not see her light. If you know her, a beautiful female with long brown hair and kind brown eyes and a soul shining as brightly as a sun, please tell me."

Silence.

Uvim waited.

It appeared everyone held their breaths. Waiting for the next part of his speech.

But he had said everything he intended.

The committee chair eased forward. "You are finished? That ends your speech?"

Yes. He had said his piece.

He nodded.

"Step on the plate." The committee chair gestured at the decorative boat floating in the harbor. "Dispense the friendship flowers."

Uvim looked down.

The dull silver plate had not been on stage the day he and Milly had toured here. But he recognized the plate. The last time he stepped on one, an audible weapon had knocked him unconscious.

The committee chair gestured again for him to stomp and dispense the flowers.

He shook his head.

This plate had hurt him once.

No, he would not step on the plate.

———

MILLY STRAINED to hear the new voice after the committee chair.

The next speaker sounded deeper, clearer, surer.

Uvim!

"That's Uvim," she said. "Brody, the cannon is supposed to go off right after he finishes speaking."

Which mean Uvim would be the one to kill them!

"Help me shut off the pilot light," she gasped.

"Find the button!"

"There is no button!"

"Then ... do ... something! Anything!" Brody twisted. "I can't help you, Milly. You've got to — try shutting off the gas!"

She whirled to the gas hose.

A small metal funnel bent to focus the gas on the pilot light. Above it was the pressure gauge and then the valve. Could she turn the valve? It was too high. She poked it with her nose.

It didn't budge.

Hands. She had to reach it with her hands.

Milly backed up and lifted on her tip toes. Her bound-together fingertips brushed the metal body. She'd never reach the valve with her hands. Not by a long shot.

Her elbows clinked the bent metal funnel.

Elbows!

She angled her elbow and pushed. The valve wiggled. Lefty loosey, righty tighty...

It moved.

Great! She pushed harder.

A wave rocked the boat.

Her elbow jammed the valve — in the wrong direction.

Gas whooshed. Rotted egg stink filled her nose and mouth.

She coughed and spat. "Agh!"

"Milly!"

The boat rocked hard.

She lifted onto her toes. The tape bruised her ankles. She lost her balance.

Oh no.

She fell backward onto the edge of the canvas bag. The side folded under her weight. She tipped in head-first. Her feet flew over her head.

Flowers and dynamite buried her.

She wriggled beneath the heavy mass. "Brody!"

"Hey, you did good. You knocked the fuses out of position. They're off to the side now."

"But I increased the gas!"

He was silent for a long moment.

"Brody?"

"Yeah, that's not good. Ty's smart about testing but, uh, this could be bad."

"Like, now the gas could blow up the whole boat?"

"Yeah. That's a distinct possibility. Milly? Get out of the bag."

"I'm trying."

"You're sitting on top of a bag full of dynamite."

"Actually, it's sitting on top of me."

"Seriously, Milly."

"*I know.*" Something else struck her. She stopped wriggling. "I don't hear Uvim's voice anymore."

Brody dropped silent.

The gush of the uncontrolled gas filled the boat.

"I don't either," Brody said uneasily.

Maybe that was okay.

Maybe they would be okay. Maybe Uvim had found her. He had special merman powers, right? Maybe he saw her soul light through the hull.

Maybe someone was coming to rescue them right now...

———

UVIM WOULD NOT STEP on that plate.

The committee chair wiggled his brows. Insistent and impatient. He turned to the person standing next to Uvim in silent appeal and tapped the face of his wrist ornament.

The man next to Uvim shrugged, walked forward, and stomped on the plate.

———

Pop.

The glass fell.

The pilot flame lit the gas.

Whoooosh.

Heat licked Milly's back like the tongue of an angry god. Her T-shirt crackled. She gasped and arched away from the heat. It abated with welcome cool.

"Oh my god," Brody gasped. "The gas exploded, and we didn't die. We didn't die."

Except her shoulder was on fire.

"It's burning," she shouted. A flamethrower raged at her side. "Something is burning!"

"The gas lit the fuses. Milly! It's burning the canvas bag!"

She wormed away from the hot spot.

Dynamite poured over her shoulder toward the melting canvas.

Any second now it would burn through the heavy canvas and ignite.

She would turn into a fine mist of formerly human molecules.

The bag tipped. One corner had burned through. Now the bag hung by three springs.

She fell toward the flamethrower.

Flower blossoms dried up and burned to ash.

"Roll out of the bag, Milly!"

"There's a fire!"

"Roll—"

Twang.

The hook released. The remaining three springs twanged.

They launched Milly into the sky.

With a bag full of flowers and dynamite.

On fire.

SOMEONE in the middle of the harbor screamed.

Everyone turned.

A huge payload launched into the air.

Blackened ash fluttered on the salty breeze.

White, sparkly ropes spattered the water, docks, and neighboring boats around the Friendship Float.

And the screaming came from a female, bound at the wrists and ankles, who popped over the edge of the dual wave sculpture. Her soul light shone like the sun.

"Milly!" he shouted.

The crowds gasped.

She dropped into the water beside the hull. Her scream cut off with a splash.

The sparkly ropes were not flying fish. Some sank beneath the waves. The ones on the boats and docks hissed like dangerous snakes.

This was the dynamite!

The pressure plates once again had caused destruction.

Milly had screamed in fear.

His enemy was on that boat.

He must activate the warriors of Dragao Azul!

Uvim was still holding the speaking stick.

He lifted it to his mouth. "Fight the dynamite! Cut the

burning ropes. Do not ignite the powder! Even one explosion will kill. Dive now. There is no time!"

His warriors shoved through the crowd, clambered across the rock wall, and dove into the harbor.

He dropped the black speaking stick and raced down the steps. He must get to Milly.

Queen Zara was still much too far away.

He jumped into the crowd.

The humans moved back. Parting for him to cross to the docks.

Yet in front of him, a strange thing happened.

A slender male picked up a long stick of dynamite that had landed on the bare wood. His sister produced a short knife from her pocket and sawed off the burning fuse.

He held out the defused stick to Uvim.

Uvim stopped.

Why...?

"*Here!*" An older male called in Portuguese. He gestured to place the inactive stick on cleared stone in front of the marina. "*Dynamite here. You, and you, cut those fuses! Gather the defused dynamite here.*"

Humans cleared the front of the marina. Others jumped off the docks into the water.

They fished for the dynamite!

The humans tumbled in, scores, diving and searching. Some wore the transparent face masks and long breathing snorkels like Milly's tourists. Those humans emerged and handed burning dynamite sticks up to people on the docks who separated the fuses and carried the pieces into the shore.

His orders had been for First Lieutenant Elan's warriors.

But the humans had listened.

To him.

They had heard his words and now they were helping.

Uvim dove into the black water. He shifted as he descended.

Humans and warriors swarmed the hissing dynamite. He squinted to see through them.

Where and how hurt was Milly?

THIRTY-FIVE

Milly hit the ocean like a cannonball.

Water slapped her butt cheeks with a harsh sting. Her tailbone bruised from the impact. Ocean poured over her head, silencing her. She thrashed and choked.

Water lodged in her throat like a fist.

She wasn't shifting. She wasn't breathing. Blackness shrouded her vision. She blubbed her helpless scream.

The temporary elixir had worn off!

A warrior flashed in front of her.

Mer — tattoos — slice, slice — and then her wrists and ankles were free.

She floundered. Her charred T-shirt wafted around her armpits and she could breathe.

She had made it. She was alive.

She had shifted.

Dynamite rained around her and the boat.

Milly ripped off the chunks of tape.

Above, Brody was still trapped with the gas blowtorch and a giant bomb.

Yes, she was alive, but for how long?

"Yank out the fuses!" She reached for a falling, hissing dynamite stick.

A warrior darted in front of her. His trident sliced the burning fuse. The sputtering stub sank. He collected the dynamite as he veered, an expert undersea predator, toward the next live stick.

Huh.

She kicked in a circle. The dynamite hadn't dispersed because her weight had prevented it from launching far. Fifty or a hundred trained males wove beneath the surface in a deadly dance.

Amateur snorkelers collected the dynamite that had floated inland with mild waves. Free-divers, and even sports divers with scuba tanks, launched themselves beneath the waves selflessly endangering their lives to save the mer.

To save her.

Amazing.

"Uvim?" She kicked through the crowds searching for a familiar face.

There, in the distance, swam Elan.

Beside him dove Zara.

"Zara!"

But her sister was busy creating a shield around a mass of dynamite, pushing it to warriors who efficiently tore it apart. She was too far away.

All this effort had deactivated most the dynamite.

Milly could almost relax. If only she could find Uvim...

Sudden knowing filled her with relief.

He was behind her.

Milly turned.

Uvim barreled into her, wrapped her in his arms, and twirled her in the water. His lips sought hers. "Milly."

Relief made her tremble. She yielded to his kiss.

They were whole. Everything would be okay. She had summoned the warriors, and he had commanded them.

His tongue stroked hers. He was real, alive, and whole.

"The dynamite." Her words vibrated in her chest while her mouth was busy with their kiss. "All the dynamite..."

"It is being collected. Humans are assisting. We will survive."

"No!" She jerked back and pointed to the Friendship Float overhead. "There's a huge keg of dynamite on a long fuse inside. Hot gas is flaming like a blow torch. And Brody's trapped inside!"

He ordered his closest warriors. "Cut the hull. We will rescue Brody."

"A hole will let in water. It could float the keg into the flames."

Police boat sirens penetrated the water.

"Can we leave this to human justice?" Uvim asked.

Dosan floated beside them. "The police cannot navigate through the people. Officers are shouting to evacuate. They intend to tow this boat out to sea."

"They'll never clear the harbor," she said grimly. "Everyone in this ocean, mer and human, will die. We have to get inside."

They surfaced.

Black, acrid smoke billowed from the float.

The gas was burning.

Was Brody still alive?

She spat the water, gasping and choking as she shifted back to air-breathing. Through her gasps, she told the males, "Boost me up."

"No." Uvim kicked forward. "I will go."

She took his hand. "Together."

"Never."

"Uvim!"

His solemn vow declared he would never put her into such danger.

She loved him for that so much.

But there was no time to fight. "Just give me a hand ... huh?"

A dangerous black shadow slithered beneath them.

The mer kicked away from the boat with gasps and exclamations.

"Danger!" One warrior shouted as Uvim gathered Milly close. "Beware!"

Huge tentacles crawled up the sides of the boat. A giant black octopus hugged it like a Kraken of the deep.

"Clifford!" she cried.

She emerged. Her big plus-shape eye focused on Milly and Uvim. One tentacle wrapped around the charred friendship statue and plunged into the open section of the hull.

A high-pitched, almost inaudible keen shattered the air.

Clifford jerked her tentacle out. It smoked. She plunged it into the water with a huge splash. Her burned flesh sizzled.

She was screaming.

"The blow torch!" Milly clutched Uvim. The giant octopus's screams stabbed her heart. "She must be in agony."

He turned Milly and pushed her toward the octopus. "Heal her."

"Me?"

"Your touch soothes. Healing is your power, my queen."

My queen?

Her heart swelled in her chest. "I haven't completed the rituals."

His gaze smoldered. His faith filled her with bottomless devotion, a knight swearing fealty, a lover enamored with his one. "You are and have always been a powerful queen."

He was right.

She was a queen.

Milly swam to the giant octopus who had sacrificed one of her few remaining limbs to save them. She placed both hands on the rubbery skin. If Uvim was right — if she did have a power — let her heal now. "Feel better, all right?"

The keening stopped.

Clifford surfaced. Her plus-eyes fixed on Milly. First with gratitude. Then, with determination.

They did not have much time.

Milly lifted her hands. A painful lump formed in her throat. She tried to swallow. "Be careful. Please."

The giant octopus steeled herself. She plunged in the injured tentacle. Then, she lifted yet another tentacle and plunged both into the hull.

She sacrificed herself one piece at a time.

This time, she endured the flames much longer, rummaged around, and pulled out Brody.

He slid through her tentacles and tumbled into the water. His wrists and ankles were still bound. He wiggled like a human-sized worm.

Warriors grabbed him and held him above the water.

"I shut off the gas," he crowed and held up his wrists — which were now in front of his body. "I couldn't let her get hurt again. I just couldn't."

Milly swallowed back her tears. "Thank you!"

A warrior slid a trident through the tape.

Brody jerked back in surprise. Then, he flexed his hands. "And Ty said yoga wasn't manly. It saved my life."

"The dynamite?" Uvim questioned.

He sobered. "Still inside. The fuse has almost reached the bag."

Milly turned back and shouted at Clifford. "Please—"

Her tentacles waved. The hissing keg of dynamite plopped the water right in front of them.

They stared, frozen.

Brody grabbed the hissing fuse.

It was a hair to the main dynamite.

Uvim grabbed Dosan's trident and sliced it.

The deadly blade swished the fuse. The hissing piece floated away.

All the dynamite was inert.

They were safe.

The gas tank landed on top of the bag of dynamite with a dangerous *clunk*. Then the pilot light box with a hiss as it went out. The canvas bag dropped in shreds.

Clifford tossed everything out. Her tentacles waved wildly.

"Okay," Milly called up. "We're saved. Take a breather. We'll get rid of this hunk of junk."

Clifford pushed the boat inland. She smacked it into the rocky sea wall.

On the concrete above, everyone shrieked and backed away.

"Um, you can stop there," Milly cried.

Clifford heaved herself out of the water and walked on her fists onto the land.

People scattered. Her giant tentacles wrapped around the boat and she hauled it onto the middle of the two-lane coastal highway.

Clifford wanted the "death float" out of her harbor.

She pushed the boat across the highway. It tapped the stone wall of an old fort.

She thumped the hull with one tentacle as though saying, "Good riddance!" and slithered into the water, spreading out so her eyes and part of her funnel floated.

Brody climbed up onto the land too. Warriors passed up the dynamite bag, gas tank, pilot light box, and other detritus. He pushed them in a pile.

Their police inspector climbed up onto the boat.

"The bomb is gone!" he shouted. "The octopus is our savior!"

Everyone cheered.

After that, the welcome ceremony descended into semi-organized chaos.

Warriors surged onto land, naked, bristling with weapons — and got happy hugs, requests for photos, free food, T-shirts, and towels.

Clifford floated by the outer sea wall, out of everyone's way. So, festival goers made a point of hauling out crates of frozen fish and took turns standing in line to offer the tidbits to a very willing recipient. She even performed, shooting water out of her funnel so a cool mist rained down, and offered her tentacles so even children braved to touch her rubbery skin.

Milly had hoped the welcome ceremony would go well but turning into a giant party would have stretched her imagination. Yet as the smell of delicious barbecue filled the air, chasing away the last of her nausea, and children ran past with sparkly fuses tied to sticks, she couldn't deny the festive atmosphere.

This was the first mer-human party. And their guest of honor was, correctly, a giant octopus.

Milly let go of Uvim for one moment to walk across the dented highway and hug Brody. "Thank you."

"Whoah." He patted her back. "Glad you're feeling better, Milly."

"Maybe I'll even invite you to my house sometime."

"Don't go all crazy now."

The police arrived to confiscate the dynamite and inspect the boat. Milly let Brody go.

He turned to the police inspector sheepishly. "Time to face the music."

While he was being interrogated by other officers, Milly gave her statement to the inspector. He looked miserable and it was hard to know what he would be charged with. He had known Ty's plan even though he hadn't wanted to believe it. At least now he could help capture Ty — who was, as far as Milly could see, still at large — by telling all he knew.

Who were these Sons of Hercules really? She hoped this was the last time she heard of them. But she was afraid it was only the beginning.

Milly finished her statement and rejoined Uvim.

He drew her against his hard chest. "Are you prepared?"

"For what?"

Beside them, Xalu stood with Sydney and Dosan with Jen. "To return to the city and complete the ritual."

"Yes!"

Their trio of couples wove through the celebration and dove into the harbor. Xalu's bride Sydney had drunk the flower nectar Milly had once coveted for herself. And, during Milly's trip to the echo point, Dosan had taken Jen to drink the elixir beneath Ilha Sagrada. Both women shifted to breathe underwater — the hardest part, even for

Milly — and Milly unfurled her new fins. Everyone celebrated and complimented her. Then, they stuffed their clothes in a convenient cave beneath the harbor.

On Uvim's command, each couple entwined. They flew to the mouth of the harbor.

This was it. She was going to Dragao Azul to marry a merman.

Not any merman.

Uvim.

This was the final turning point of her life.

And she embraced it — him — with her full heart.

They passed the last warriors, who bowed with surprise. The open ocean beckoned. They were home free.

Elan and Zara blocked the harbor entrance.

"Stop," Zara said.

They pulled up short.

Uvim stiffened.

Milly steeled herself.

She would not allow anyone to drive them apart. Not her sister. Not anyone.

No matter what.

THIRTY-SIX

Queen Zara stopped them at the mouth of the harbor.

Her soul glowed with fierce power.

Behind her, First Lieutenant Elan held his trident. His ease belied his deadly ability to wield it.

Xalu and Dosan braced.

Their brides regarded Queen Zara with interest. It was their first time meeting a queen with full control of her powers.

Queen Zara ordered Uvim. "Let her go."

No. His grip tightened. He was never releasing Milly to her care again.

Queen Zara's eyes widened at his insubordination. "You dare hold her against her will? I will—"

"No, wait. Stop this, all of you." Milly disentangled herself. She stroked Uvim's cheek. A confident smile warmed her soul. "It's okay."

He let go because she wished it.

But his heart clenched.

She followed her stroke with a soft kiss. Deepening

their connection. She respected and loved her sister, but Milly would remain with him. Now, and forever.

His fears eased.

Milly pulled back, still smiling, and turned to face Queen Zara.

Queen Zara swooped and tackle-hugged her.

Their twin lights exploded.

Love.

Xalu and Dosan tensed.

Uvim did not.

Milly's light remained calm and happy. The sisters somersaulted in the water.

"I was so worried!" Queen Zara laughed and cried. "Why can't you stay out of trouble? You'll make me crazy!"

"It's payback." Milly rubbed her shoulders, also laugh-crying. "You went to war on a besieged city. I had to watch from the shore."

"Okay, we've got to finish here." Queen Zara pulled back and held Milly's hands. "I'm sure you can't hold off your ceremony until after we get done so you have to delay the wedding feast."

Milly's soul light flared.

Queen Zara approved their wedding.

Shock vibrated in Uvim's chest. *She approved.* Did that mean...?

Milly's chin wrinkled and her eyes reddened. She hugged Queen Zara once more. Her heartbeat stumbled. "Thank you."

And then she returned to Uvim's side and twined her arms around his neck.

Queen Zara rubbed her own reddened eyes and whirled on Uvim.

He stiffened.

Queen Zara's gaze nailed his. "Warrior Uvim. You were one of the three warriors who forced me to the surface against my will."

Her gaze flicked to Dosan. They had made amends long ago.

She refocused on Uvim. "During the battle for Dragao Azul, you were the first warrior to come to my aid. Elan reminded me. I had forgotten."

The First Lieutenant nodded to Uvim, showing him the fairness and clear-sighted respect that had marked his original career.

"So let me tell you this." Queen Zara rested a palm on her chest. "I'm a queen but I'm not infallible. Nobody should rule with life-or-death control. That's not the new way. Don't you ever let anyone — not even me — stand in the way of protecting Milly. Are we clear?"

His greatest wish was now a reality.

Emotions tumbled in his chest. Acceptance, forgiveness, encouragement. Queen Zara bestowed all on him.

Uvim nodded, unable to speak.

"All right, take additional warriors back with you to make sure you're well-protected." She grinned at Dosan and Uvim's brides. "I can't let anything happen to our new residents. Welcome."

"Thanks," Brides Jen and Sydney chorused.

Milly curled her arms around Uvim and laughed at Queen Zara. "You're doing great at this 'queen' stuff, Zara."

"Well, I still can't keep Zain in his travel toddler bed." She bid them farewell.

Elan reached out to her.

Queen Zara reached back without looking and took his hand. They meandered, together, to the dock to rejoin the grand party.

Uvim turned to Dosan, Xalu, and the new warriors who had joined as their escort.

All awaited his command.

He was still Second Lieutenant. Queen Zara had threatened to strip his title but now she supported his promotion.

"Take point." He directed the fastest, most keen-sighted warrior and then pointed his trident to the cautious warrior who had once been his trainee. "And you, guard our retreat."

Both warriors assumed their positions.

He ordered the other warriors to surround the brides and give total protection. Surface predators were a problem in this region. All-Council terrorists rarely trespassed here but three warriors with new brides created an unprecedented target to protect.

When they organized to his satisfaction, Uvim ensured Milly was secure in his protective arms and kicked hard. They flew through the ocean. Dosan and Xalu matched his speed, but they outpaced their guards.

Milly held on tight. "We're leaving everyone behind. Did we hit a fast current?"

He slowed and signaled to the other couples to allow the guard to catch up. "Our resonance fuels our speed."

"My resonance?"

"Yes." He stroked her smooth, unscarred back. "We are more powerful together than apart."

"Of course we are." She pressed her grin into his bulging shoulder. "Resonance is another word for 'synergy,' right? We're unstoppable when we work together for love."

Her words filled him with steady warmth.

On the now relaxed descent to Dragao Azul, the three women chatted.

"This is my second wedding," Jen, Dosan's bride, mentioned. "Ian's sad to miss it. I reminded him he ate the groom's cake by himself, so his waistline will not share his regret."

"His wife said she helped," Sydney, Xalu's bride, interjected.

"Ian's married?" Milly asked.

The women nodded.

"She couldn't get the time off," Jen said. "She wasn't expecting to be invited on my honeymoon. Obviously! She's joining with the kids next week. Boy, are they sorry to have missed the party!"

"So, can I ask?" Milly eyed Jen. "You almost married someone else. Now, on your former honeymoon, you're marrying a total strang— uh, I mean, an extremely honorable warrior. Didn't you have any doubts?"

Uvim focused on Bride Jen's answer. She and Bride Sydney had claimed their warriors overnight. Milly had taken much longer to yield to her soul's desire.

How had they decided so quickly? Did they harbor secret doubts?

"I wasn't worried," Bride Sydney said.

"Yes, I was worried," Bride Jen said.

The males looked at Dosan.

He kicked steadily, firm in his love for his bride.

Bride Jen explained. "My awful ex wouldn't rescue me from a flat tire at night, in the rain, on a highway all alone. Yet Dosan rescued me from thugs while he was still recovering from the dynamite. I couldn't let the ghosts of my past destroy my future. And I couldn't let a guy this heroic go off with any other woman."

"And I could not let a woman with such insight choose any other male," Dosan said.

She laughed and hugged him. Their duo glowed with happy resonance.

"Get a room," Sydney joked, and then gasped. "Can I still say that? Are there rooms in Dragao Azul?"

"There are chambers," Xalu told her, in his deep voice. "And castles."

"Chambers and castles? Oh, my. I could get used to this."

"Good. You will do so."

"Sydney," Milly said, "you said you weren't worried about marrying Xalu?"

"Heck no. I waited for a jerk for 10 years. This huge, muscley, gorgeous guy proposes after one day. And it's not just his looks. Xalu valued *me*. He listens. He's forthright and says what he means. No guesswork. I knew he was what I wanted right away. And he didn't hesitate to put a ring on it, either, if you know what I mean."

"You desire a ring?" he asked.

"See?" She squeezed him. "That's what I'm talking about."

And their resonance also glowed.

Uvim held Milly close. There was no greater satisfaction than her in his arms where she belonged.

"You're being extra quiet," Milly murmured.

"Your conversation is fascinating."

"Oh? Are you learning about human culture?"

Yes, he was doing so. But he had noticed another facet. "Some of your conversations are informational. But some are not."

"Oh, it's all new. We're getting to know each other."

"No." He shook his head. "There are two types of conversation. I have noticed this."

"What? No."

The brides disagreed, but Xalu and Dosan had also noticed two types.

He identified the types for Milly. "One conversation is for information. But the other conversation is for increasing your resonance with each other."

"Oh." She checked with the other brides and they agreed. "That's normal. We don't have the biofeedback to see each other's soul lights so we have to say supportive things and hope for the best."

"Fascinating," he said.

She snuggled him.

While the brides discussed their lives and futures, Uvim conferenced with Xalu and Dosan about the main issue — himself and Dosan wooing a bride out of turn.

"They will not exile our brides," Dosan vowed.

Xalu pledged his agreement. "Not so long as I wield a trident."

That was very generous of the number one warrior.

"I will try to avoid conflict," Uvim promised.

Dosan grinned. "Since it is you, then I am sure the elders will listen with respect."

He swelled with the warmth of his friend's confidence.

"You befriended and commanded thousands of humans." Xalu lifted his chin. "The elders would be fools to ignore your wisdom."

A lump formed in his throat.

He vibrated his thanks. "It is an honor to speak for you."

The most honorable warrior nodded. Dosan grinned.

Uvim used the rest of the journey to prepare for the confrontation.

At the edge of Dragao Azul territory, a patrol of barely trained warriors and one shaky elder met their group.

They exchanged greetings and led the way. Their

brides gasped and spoke with amazement as Dragao Azul emerged from the barren sea bottom.

The first sight of the city always lifted his heart.

In the center, the Life Tree glowed with holy brilliance, its branches stretching up. A thick stem anchored it to the sea floor.

Around the Life Tree, anchored on similar thick green stems, floated the giant orb "castles" of the city.

Summoning the army had been dangerous. It left the already-depleted city a skeleton defense. If invaders killed the Life Tree, the castles would rot and the warriors, who carried the sap of the Life Tree in their blood, would also sicken and die.

But now Uvim's warriors had returned with three powerful queens. They would well-protect the city once more.

They flew to the king's castle. It was the largest bulb growing closest to the Life Tree.

Uvim flew through the long entrance tunnel and emerged into the ancient central courtyard. A great garden flourished on the soil-covered floor, well-tended over the decades. Its walls were thick with inner chambers ever-expanding as the castle itself grew.

In the center of the venerable courtyard, the city's most honorable elders floated around the king. Daggers and tridents at the ready, they prepared for war.

All turned for his greeting. In fact, the elders kicked forward and swarmed them.

The loudest elder did not notice he carried his bride. "Second Lieutenant Uvim, you returned from the surface. You must eject the Newas hunting ... wait, what is all of this?"

Xalu and Dosan floated behind him with their brides, forming a mated trio.

The other warriors — their escorts — moved to the periphery for Uvim's report.

"My king."

Uvim bypassed the elders to greet his king as was proper.

Although the elders had, in their excitement, interrupted his progress, they approved him adhering to proper form.

Dragao Azul's elderly king lowered his head with respect. His gaunt cheeks and weakened, though piercing, soul light was still recovering from the torture of the All-Council's last attack.

"This is my bride," Uvim announced. "Queen Milly."

The elders muttered amongst themselves.

She untangled from Uvim, turned, and bowed to the king. "Nice to meet you."

Her soul light brightened. Sweet and friendly.

Friendliness had been missing from this city for some time.

His king smiled. "Welcome, Queen Milly."

She returned his smile. Their souls shone brighter in shared resonance. A deep, penetrating calm flooded the castle.

Loud elder Veno kicked forth. "Queen? This bride has not performed the ceremony or taken the flower. She is no queen."

Milly smiled at the elder. Unlike Queen Zara, she remained calm after his true observation. "Well, I better get on that."

Elder Veno frowned in confusion and repeated her phrase. "Get ... on ... that?"

Uvim addressed their confusion. "Do not doubt her power. She has made fins. And, from her first swim, she used her healing powers to tame a giant cave guardian."

"Tame!"

The other elders muttered about the revelation.

Elder Veno harrumphed. "As Queen Zara's sister, perhaps, Uvim's bride has a precocious ability."

Milly raised a brow. "Um, 'Uvim's bride' is named Milly, and please speak directly when I'm right in front of you."

The mutters grew more heated.

Dragao Azul had always sequestered sacred brides in the husband's castle. The elders — and warriors — had no experience speaking with females.

Queen Zara had made Milly's same demand. Modern brides would not be shut away, ignored, or silenced.

Dragao Azul's elders struggled with the change.

Uvim growled. "You will speak directly."

The king bowed again. "Many apologies, Queen Milly."

Milly handled it better. "Oh, you're fine. I love Zara. I hope someday you'll find me as impressive."

Veno blinked. The others quieted.

"My apology also, Queen Milly," a quiet elder said. "We have never seen two queens. Change is trying."

"I'm sure we've got lots to learn from each other." She pressed her hands to her glowing chest. "It is nice to meet you. I'm thrilled to be in a mer city. I have so much to discover about my new life. We'll have lots of chances to get things right."

They warmed to her.

"Yes," the quiet elder nodded, and the other elders also glowed with hope. "Many chances."

Already it seemed Milly's transition to Dragao Azul would go more smoothly.

Queen Zara had been hurt badly. She remained abrasive, on guard. The elders struggled to re-forge their relationship. They had made many mistakes.

With Queen Milly they could start from friendship. She was willing to try. The elders must be willing too.

And Uvim would encourage this new start.

He moved aside for Dosan and Xalu to present their brides.

The king and elders were amazed.

"Three queens at once," one elder chortled, ignoring entirely Uvim's worst fear he and Dosan would suffer consequences for taking brides out of turn. "We will have four queens now. More than Atlantis!"

"The army has surfaced," another said. "Who knows how many more queens may return?"

"More queens!"

The king smiled with real warmth. "Congratulations, my warriors. Well done. Welcome, Brides Jen and Si-do-nee." He pronounced her unfamiliar name with three syllables. "Now, you marry."

Xalu corrected him. "My king, my bride's name is pronounced—"

"I don't mind," Bride Sydney blurted. "I like it."

"Shall I—"

"No. You mastered my name. Let's get to the ceremony."

"Sid ... o-nee," the king said, frowning with concentration.

"Sid-nee," Dosan corrected.

"Sydney," Uvim said.

Everyone looked at him in surprise.

Milly elbowed him. "How come you said her name right on the first try?"

"I listen."

Her grin widened. "All right then, good listener, let's make us 'official' queens!"

Uvim flew Milly to the Life Tree.

Around its huge girth, the Life Tree radiated peaceful silence. Bare branches stretched toward the surface. Beads of resin formed at its joints; some rolled off in the rustling currents and piled at the exposed roots on its wide, floating dais. Above the surface, these resin jewels were known as Sea Opals.

Beneath the dais stretched the thick stem anchoring the Life Tree to the sea floor.

Uvim retracted his fins to human feet. He landed on the rim of the dais and bounced.

Milly's face glowed with awe. "This is amazing."

She retracted her fins also and bounced after him across the piles of mating gems.

Dosan and Xalu landed at two other places on the dais so each couple approached the Life Tree from a different direction. Its trunk was so broad they could each marry in privacy. The Dragao Azul Life Tree was a worthy, ancient tree.

It stood because of Queen Zara.

Now, warriors could take queens and embrace a new life.

The city's elders, king, youths, and the escort warriors from the surface spread around to watch the triple wedding ceremonies.

Uvim knelt and bowed his head to the trunk. "I, Uvim of Dragao Azul, present Milly as my chosen bride. Please shower your blessing and healing on our union and bless us with a young fry son."

He kissed the glistening white bark.

Then he turned to Milly.

Milly knelt beside him. "I, Milly of Faial, present Uvim as my chosen husband. Please shower your blessing and healing on our union and bless us with a young fry son. Or daughter. That would also be cool."

She pressed her lips to the trunk.

Tinkle-tinkle-tinkle. The Life Tree chimed in harmony.

Now, they were married. Soon her blossom would grow. She would drink the nectar and be one with this Life Tree.

She was already one with his heart.

The others completed their rituals. The Life Tree tinkled, a shining beacon, and their city had never glowed so brightly.

Milly chose Uvim.

He chose her.

She chose this life as his queen beneath the ocean.

They rose in tandem. He led her away from the Life Tree and introduced her to the one mer who mattered even more than the king.

An old warrior kicked forward. He shared Uvim's same amethyst markings only more faded. After a long absence, Uvim always noticed that detail. "Milly, this is my father."

"I am honored." His father bowed low. "Queen Milly."

"It's very nice to meet you." She returned his bow, startling him, just as she had startled the elders and the king. "Father. Wow. Any other relatives I should meet?"

"Uvim's grandfather is that elder there." He pointed to the quieter elder.

"You didn't say anything!"

"Habit."

She bowed low to his grandfather.

His grandfather straightened and returned her bow as a warrior greeting an equal.

Then, his bloodline approved.

Good.

"We return to the castle," Uvim told his father.

His father nodded in tacit understanding. "I will hunt celebratory meat."

"Hunt! For me? That sounds difficult."

"Less difficult in the king's larder." His father nodded in farewell and swam to Uvim's grandfather. Together, the older males paddled to the king's castle.

Uvim led Milly through the city. With every kick, his excitement grew. He wished to point out familiar sites — his old training grounds, where he had gotten his first fights and his tattoos — but more than that he wanted to join with her. In their private marriage ceremony, in the heart chamber, where they would make their young fry.

"That's your castle," she guessed, picking out the amethyst-tint from the glowing, vibrant green bulbs.

He flew her down the long entrance tunnel into his family's courtyard, past their well-tended crops, and dove through the ancient passages to the innermost chamber.

The heart chamber had never opened for him. He had tried many times. Now, if his ancestors accepted his bride, the entrance would yield.

He placed his palm on the wall. Milly placed her palm beside his.

The green wall flashed with deeper vibrancy and a portal opened, twisting to reveal a chamber sized for two.

Anticipation thrilled him.

He flew Milly through the portal. It sealed them in.

They floated inside the innermost heart of his castle. The safest place in the city.

And she rested nude against him.

His cock flared with heat.

Her chest pulsed with an answering brilliance.

She slid her thumbs across the hard swell of his pectorals. "It's funny we've been naked this whole swim but only now do I feel nervous."

Nervous? But her soul burned a steady light.

He trailed loving hands down her sensuous back, into the slenderness of her waist and over the fertile swell of her feminine hips.

If she was not ready, then—

Milly's lips brushed his, stealing his thoughts.

"I'm ready." Her tongue teased between his lips, seducing his mouth and fueling his hunger with her addictive flavor. Her chest vibrated with her words. "I'm sorry I took so long to commit."

"Do not be sorry."

"I needed more confidence. Faith that loving you wouldn't destroy my self-control but instead give me the satisfaction I need to become my best self."

"You are ready now." He nuzzled her neck. "I did not want you any sooner."

THIRTY-SEVEN

Making love to Uvim was everything Milly had dreamed.

Fantasized.

Whatever.

He kissed the column of her sensitive neck to her throbbing breasts and sucked first one bud into his mouth, rolling it around with exquisite mastery, and then the other.

Pleasure shot to her slick core, making her ache.

She had wanted him from the moment they exchanged their vows in front of the Life Tree. He was her husband now. She was his wife. They were closer than ever before. And this "joining" united them for all time.

And she craved that unity.

She craved a future with her gorgeous, dutiful, olive-amethyst warrior.

Milly craved Uvim.

He pressed hot kisses over her belly button to her trembling mons. His gentle hands quested lower, stroking her sex lips and coating her in her own slickness. He knew what she liked from his careful, dutiful, enthusiastic study at her house. Beneath the water, his focus was even more intense. And her trust for him reached a new peak.

He was hers. She was his. All of her. All of him.

She parted her thighs in welcome, opening herself without hesitation.

He dropped his dark head, tongued her aching channel, and feasted on her tender bud.

Yes.

Floating in the center of his amazing living castle, held by Uvim, bathed in his essence, she felt alive.

And totally in control.

Milly threaded her fingers through his silky hair.

Together, they rotated in the sacred heart chamber.

Uvim's powerful hands massaged her buttocks, shooting her pleasure higher. He sucked on her core and rotated his fingers around her channel, stroking and stretching her from the inside. The warm liquid of the heart chamber flowed in and out, its own current, seducing her.

Here was where she wanted him.

She exploded with pleasure.

Five orgasms. Uvim loved her tirelessly.

Today she wouldn't make him stop.

He continued loving her and a second one built. She exploded. And a third wave crashed over her. He read her mind. No words were necessary. Her only love, her silent warrior, attacked her pleasure with total devotion.

Her third orgasm wracked her pussy in channel-squeezing delight.

She gasped.

At this rate, it would be over before she ever enjoyed the shape of his cock.

And she demanded his cock. Inside. Where he belonged.

"Uvim, I need your help." She pulled away from his head and wrapped her thighs around his torso. "I want to 'join' with you."

His olive-amethyst gaze intensified.

"Will you help me?"

"Of course, my queen."

No hesitation. No asking if she was all right.

She asked. He answered.

Milly had found her place. Here, with him, was where she belonged.

Uvim rubbed the seam of his cock against her slick nub.

Oh, yes.

He studied her, using his cock to tease her.

Her channel clenched as a fourth orgasm fluttered toward the surface.

No, she wanted him inside.

Milly encircled his cock and guided him into her.

Yes.

His thick head lodged against a pressure point. Not painful, but a tight neck requiring care and respect. He bobbed against it, finding his way.

Sweet tendrils of pleasure soothed her inner channel. She relaxed, surrendering to his manhood.

He slid through. Suddenly, he filled her to the brim. Their bodies sealed together into one.

Husband and wife. Male and female. Question and answer.

Eternity in each other's arms began with this infinite moment of tenderness.

They floated together, holding each other the instant everything changed.

She savored his girth.

His fingers dug into her back, massaging her outsides and stroking her insides.

Her thighs flexed to contain his warrior power.

His thick head pressed on her inner button. Her pussy shuddered. She moaned.

He nudged her pleasure spot, guided by her moans. They needed no words. They communicated with bodies. Perfect.

Her silent warrior had overcome his doubts. He'd led an army of human and mer. He'd found his words and his soul.

She filled her palms with his buttocks and squeezed.

Uvim thrust, amplifying her commands.

His cock slid harder and faster into her slick channel.

The orgasm rose like a bubbling tide. Her body contracted for an explosion. She wanted him. Forever. Always.

The orgasm crashed over her. Hot and heavenly and out of control. She flew into pieces and he thrust into her even harder, losing his control and pounding. The fifth orgasm shattered her pieces into shimmering dust.

His own body tensed and his release exploded into her.

They were remade. Her and him. Remade by their ancient dance.

He trembled.

She caressed his broad shoulder blades. "You know, today might be the first day of my new life."

He lifted his head. Strong emotions swept across his face. "First day as a bride? A queen?

"As a mother."

He buried his head in her neck. "We must ensure this with at least two more pleasures."

"At least," she laughed and surrendered herself to her thoughtful, articulate, and convincing new husband.

———

Dear Reader,

Thanks so much for reading.

The next book in the series is *Secrets of the Sea Lord* starring Faier and a new heroine named Harmory.

How will newly crowned Queen Milly deal with the potentially dangerous Newas hunting party? And what is the mysterious after-marriage ceremony that makes all warriors cry? Find out in "Milly's Queenly Life." It's a free exclusive for newsletter subscribers!

Subscribe here:

http://smarturl.it/StarlaNewsletter

BUT FIRST! Enjoy TWO FREE BONUS SHORT STORIES included in this book!

Curious about Dosan + Jen and Xalu + Sydney's lightning-hot courtships? Turn the page and dive in!

See you next time!

Sincerely,

Starla

How did Jen and Sydney become brides? What happened during the dramatic kidnapping? How did Dosan and Xalu "defend their brides" and come to their rescue?

These two bonus love stories — "Her Warrior's Kiss" and "Her Warrior's Vow" — take place during the events of *Surrendering to the Sea Lord*. While Milly and Uvim are busy elsewhere, their new friends are fighting feelings — and more!

It starts the evening Jen nurses heroically injured Dosan back to life at her vacation rental. Honorable yet deadly warrior Xalu stands guard outside.

And yummy warrior-bride sparks begin to fly...

HER WARRIOR'S KISS

"I am not seeing this." Her brother, Ian, stopped in the bedroom doorway with the tray of food and water she'd requested. He made an exasperated noise. "Jen?"

Jen jerked upright, lifting her elbows off the guest bed where she held her vigil. "Um, yes?"

"You are *not* touching the dead man."

Even unconscious, the marine shifter looked deadly. Blunt nose, wide lips, broad forehead. His skin was tinged an olive green that made the sapphire tattoo beneath his lower lip stand out like an iridescent gemstone. Beneath the white bedsheet, his knees and toes stuck up like undersea mountains.

"He's not dead, he's unconscious." Jen stroked the injured warrior's forehead in a way she hoped was soothing. "And look. He likes my touch."

Dosan's closed eyes crinkled and a deep, satisfied sigh rumbled in his badly bruised chest.

"That's not 'like,' that's a growl." Ian left the door open to the courtyard and crossed the vacation rental guest room floor. "His inhuman senses are probably screaming, 'Who is this stranger touching me? Is she one of the humans who threw dynamite in the water and tried to kill me?'"

Ian nudged the bedside lamp with his elbow and eased the tray onto the nightstand. "When in fact, you're a workaholic who can't enjoy a vacation."

"Then he'll wake up and I'll tell him I'm innocent." She put ice chunks into the cold bag and took a quick inventory of the tray. "I asked for three water glasses."

"There's just you and him. Why do you need three?"

She eased the ice pack onto the dark red bruise in the center of his chest, then poured water from the pitcher into the two glasses. "For when Xalu wants to sit with us."

The second warrior poked his head through the door Ian had left ajar. Taller and broader, Xalu's fierce tattoos looked like gray smoke all over his dangerously well-muscled body. "Dosan is awake?"

"Not yet. But I'm sure he will be soon. He responds when I do this." She rested her bare hand on Dosan's forehead.

The sleeping warrior sighed.

Xalu's fierce, hawk-sharp brow darkened. "A mer must only be touched by his bride. No other female. That is the mer way."

Oh. Oops. She jerked her hand away.

Jen was no one's bride. Her heart dropped to her new flip flops. "Sorry. I didn't mean—"

"Well, the 'mer way' is not the American way." Ian reversed his objections, looped his arm around Jen's shoulder and gave her a supportive squeeze in defiance of the intimidating warrior. "Jen opened her home to you and she's sacrificing her vacation to take care of your sick friend. Don't make her apologize."

Ian's criticism made the warrior stiffen and grip his

deadly trident. The blades glinted in the late afternoon sun. He turned and stalked away. The door thudded closed behind him.

"The nerve of some people." Ian dropped her shoulder and headed for the door.

Jen cleared her throat. "Um, Xalu didn't make me apologize. I apologized on my own."

"He has no right to criticize."

"And technically, we're not in America. We're in the Azores."

Ian spun. "You're darned right we're in the Azores. And are you out enjoying the dramatic beaches, volcanic peaks, or homey food? No. You've locked yourself away in a sick room, resisting every effort to get out and enjoy yourself."

"I went snorkeling with you today."

"Which was all well and good — until mermen boarded our boat and you volunteered our rental for their hospital."

"Dosan jumped on the dynamite. He saved us."

"No one's questioning his heroism." Ian rested a fist against the waist of his chinos. "This is your vacation. You're supposed to be drinking margaritas by the pool. Not exiling yourself to a darkened room, shackling yourself to the whims of an unconscious man. Er, male. I mean, look at it from my perspective. How can I have fun when you're stuck in here all alone?"

"I'm sorry," she said. "I volunteered without a thought about you or Sydney. If you want—"

"No, it's not about what I want. This is about you." Ian shook his head. "I know you only agreed to this 'vacation' because you couldn't get back the deposit. But Jen, you've got to stop this pattern."

"Nursing an injured male isn't a pattern."

"The thing with Gary started when you brought him a

pot of chicken soup. He thought the soup came 'with bene-fits'." Ian pointed at the unconscious warrior on her bed. "Just make sure that warrior doesn't think his cheese plate comes with a 'happy ending.' Right?"

"It doesn't," she said. "I know."

Lecture delivered successfully, her accountant brother headed out.

Leaving her alone with the warrior.

Jen rubbed her palms on her dress. The soft, cottony purple fabric of her "wedding trousseau" beach dress felt smooth as silk despite the heat.

She couldn't take Ian's advice.

If she focused on herself, she'd find a heartbroken little girl afraid she'd never be loved again.

Because Ian and Sydney had to be right. Jen was the problem. Loving unselfishly was wrong. The more she gave, the more guys took. She had to guard herself, dole out her love, and lock away her generous heart.

It was too depressing to think about.

"Come back," she murmured near his damp ear. "Come back to us, Dosan."

Another deep sigh moved the thin sheet lower to expose his rippling abdomen. Artful sapphire tattoos swirled across his bulging pectorals, over his arms, and decorated his fierce brow.

It exposed more muscle than a staid insurance processor normally saw. So, Jen tried not to stare as she tugged the sheet up for modesty.

His forehead perspired in the humid island heat despite the fan and air conditioning.

She squeezed her damp wash cloth and rested it across his dark eyebrows.

"Mmhh," he sighed.

His resonant voice sparked little tingles in her lower belly.

She leaned closer and rested her elbows on the bed.

Dosan's face tilted toward hers as if he were as drawn to her as she was fascinated by him.

Ooh, was that a dimple? Hard to tell with the shadows and the tattoos.

Jen teased her finger across Dosan's hard chin.

Yes. Dimple.

Jen knew a secret about the warrior no one else knew.

Her chest tingled.

She withdrew her hand before Ian returned and yelled at her. Or Xalu did.

"Come back," she cajoled, quiet and insistent, and she stroked his high, dominant cheekbones. "Wake up."

Dosan's eyes fluttered open.

She froze.

His piercing sapphire eyes darted over the room and then focused on her.

Her belly dropped.

"You..."

She bolted upright and smoothed her low collar. "Hi! I'm Jen."

"Jen?"

"You don't remember me because we've never met. I was on the tour boat and you saved us from getting blown up."

Dosan squeezed his eyes closed and rubbed his hand across the ice pack on his bruised chest. He winced and moaned.

"Don't." She pulled his hand away. "You're hurt."

His hand tightened reflexively around hers. "Uvim and Xalu?"

"Your leader will be back tomorrow. Xalu is outside."

"Uninjured?"

"Yes, they're both fine."

His fingers were powerful, the skin rough. He'd slashed a stick of dynamite with his trident. These fingers knew how to wield dangerous weapons without hesitation.

A curl of awareness flushed her feminine center with heat.

Down.

"You were the only one hurt saving us."

"Saving?" His eyes opened again. He focused the intense blue irises on her. "Then, everyone was saved?"

His attention made her throat go dry. He was even more compelling awake. Powerfully, radiantly male. And she could no longer pretend she didn't know that he was naked beneath the sheet.

She swallowed. "I think so."

His intense blue eyes gleamed. He dropped his gaze to her chest.

Heat suffused her. Was he checking her out?

His grip tightened. He curled upright.

No, he wasn't checking her out. He was rising.

The ice bag jangled as it rolled off his chest. She caught it and set it beside the bed.

His abdomen tightened and his muscle stood out in sharp relief. He looked like a god. A sculpture. A statue of an ideal male who ate a pure fish-and-seaweed diet and worked out ten hours every day. He was all mouthwatering male fitness.

She, on the other hand, was all soft squishes, dreamy New Years' resolutions and canceled gym memberships.

But she wasn't helpless. Jen put her arm around his

trembling shoulders, helping him to steady himself. "Rest against the headboard."

He obeyed, closing his eyes again with a groan. He released her hand and opened the palm. "Cold."

She handed him the ice bag.

He pressed it to his chest with a pained hiss. "I am not well."

"Sorry."

He cracked one eye to glance at her. "Why do you apologize?"

"Because..."

Wait, why was she sorry? Was she saying it as a reflex? She often apologized when others were upset even if it had nothing to do with her. Sydney and Ian both told her to toughen up. *Don't apologize for no reason.*

"I'm sorry you don't feel better," she compromised.

"No."

"No?"

"I do feel better. Much better." He turned his head to her, careful to keep his chest forward. "Because of you."

Her mouth opened but she couldn't think of how to reply. A thudding heat flushed over her face. The warmth radiated from her chest.

"W-well, uh, I was standing next to the criminals who threw that dynamite. Ian and I even talked to them earlier. I had no idea."

"Do not take blame."

"It's a little my fault. We'd been friendly. That's why I volunteered." She indicated the bedroom. "I, uh, hope you recover quickly. And I'm so sorry I didn't stop those people before they threw the dynamite."

"The most dangerous enemies hide beneath the skin of friends."

"Ah ... yeah, I guess." She tried to laugh. "I'm not a good judge of 'friends' these days."

"You have a bright, pure soul." He glanced at her chest again and nodded as though he could see her aura. "Your kindness is strong. Of course you will share your strength with many less brilliant souls."

Her chest blazed again.

His attention intensified as though he sensed her pleased, embarrassed heat.

Could mermen see auras? An article she'd read said the shifters had a special sense allowing them to visualize "resonance," the strength of a person's affinity for the rare, healing, ocean gemstone Sea Opals, as a light in each person's chest.

So, he definitely was not checking her out no matter how much she arranged the collar on her low-cut, purple beach dress.

She arranged it now, smoothing the hem. "Thank you. But I'm still sorry I couldn't help you when you most needed it."

"You did."

"Did what?"

"Helped when I most needed it." He looked down at the ice bag he held to his chest. "You were the voice in my nightmare."

"That's good?"

He frowned, struggling with the words to explain. "After the explosion, I fell to a dark place. There was agony and danger. But I heard a voice. 'Come back.' And I felt no pain. The darkness went away. I was here. Safe." He focused on her. "With you."

His intense sapphire-threaded gaze reflected the depths of the articulate, honest, fierce warrior's soul.

The world seemed to tilt.

She wanted to slide forward, onto the bed, and taste the lips that had been *her* dream while he'd been sleeping. She wanted to wrap her arms around his neck and tease the dark ducktail at the base of his skull. She wanted to press her tingling breasts against his broad pectorals, release herself from her satin bra, and slide her taut nipples over his sweat-slicked, olive-sapphire skin.

Her channel clenched.

She shook herself free of the daydream.

Dosan was a warrior of a race only recently revealed to the world. And he'd just crawled out of a coma. His chest was bruised badly and his brain had probably gotten scrambled.

And, she'd just ended a two-year relationship. Her heart was cracked. She couldn't jump the next male who complimented her.

"I, uh, thank you. Can I get you something?" She felt the old anxiety creeping in. "Fish? Seawater? Something to eat?"

"Water."

She handed one of the pre-filled glasses to him and gulped the other.

He carefully took it, not touching her fingers. "Thank you, Bride Jen."

She nearly spat her water. "Oh, I'm not married."

"Ian?"

"Is my brother. This is so weird! They thought we were married on the boat, too, even though we — oh. When I booked the tour weeks ago, I probably *did* reserve it was for me and my husband."

Well, that explained the confusion.

Dosan swigged the water as though it were fortifying alcohol. "You are married."

"No."

His gaze focused on her.

"It ended. Embarrassingly."

He tilted his head.

The urge to confess made her words spill out. Excise the memories like they'd happened to someone else.

"A week before my wedding, I spent an extra-long lunch reviewing our flowers. Gary reviewed one of our sales reps naked on the office photocopier."

The embarrassment and hurt of that day rose in her throat like a rising tide.

She swallowed and finished. "And then he accidentally forwarded the copies to the entire office."

Dosan studied her without judgment. "He is a male without honor."

"He really was."

She'd returned in the early afternoon to shocked laughter suddenly cut off, avoided gazes, seeming busyness that slowed as soon as she passed her coworkers' desks.

She'd even stopped by Gary's empty desk to tell him about her progress, not knowing he was then in a meeting with HR about his "future" with his great uncle's insurance company.

But after she'd sat at her desk, opened her email, and discovered what the rest of the company already knew — and once the shocked horror wore away to bitter anger — she'd wondered. Had Gary been callous by accident? Or had he been too lazy to back out and instead used the pictures to break off his engagement?

Either way, she had a problem. She jumped in too deep with guys before knowing their characters.

She was too trusting and set herself up to be taken advantage of.

That had to stop now.

"So I'm not married," she finished. "Not now, and maybe not ever."

Dosan shook his head. The light glinted on his sapphire threads. "Dragao Azul awaits a queen."

"Dragao Azul?"

"My city beneath the ocean." He rested his glass on the nightstand and took her hand, tugging her out of her seat. Her knee pressed his waist.

Setting aside his ice bag, he rested his chilled fingers on the base of her nape. "If you belong to no other warrior then you belong to me."

He bent his head. His mouth swept her away in his possessive kiss.

Hot desire ignited between her thighs. Her oh-so-reasonable voice telling her to wait, be cautious, and not give in dropped silent at the taste of the deliciously masculine warrior.

She melted.

He dominated her lips, sealing hers like a promise, and then his tongue teased her seam. She opened. He plunged in, filling her with heat, with desire, with him.

He tasted of salt and musk and primal spice.

He dominated her mouth, finding where she hid and drawing her into his sapphire light.

Her nipples tightened. Her channel slicked, preparing for his welcome invasion.

She wanted him, hard and plunging into her, with a heat that defied reality. How had she gone all these years without tasting that *this* was the flavor of true love's kiss?

She moaned.

He slipped an arm around her waist and pulled her onto his lap, his biceps bulging. He handled her as if her squishy bulk weighed nothing.

No boyfriend before had been able to do that.

She rested her palm on his hard pectoral for balance.

Dosan sucked in a breath between his clenched teeth.

His bruised chest!

"Oh!" She pulled back. "Sorry. I forgot."

He perspired, clearly pained.

She grabbed the wash cloth and blotted his sweat, equal parts turned on, frustrated, and angry at herself for her frustration.

Dosan had been injured. Nearly dead. Probably his ribs were cracked. And she leaned on him like a section of drywall.

Even though ... even though *he* was the one who had pulled her into his lap...

His face seemed a paler shade of olive. He licked his lips and swallowed. "You are mine."

She shook her head even as she dabbed.

"My bride. Accept my claim."

"I won't."

His frown sharpened his blunt features. "You touch me."

Oops. Xalu had warned her Dosan would misinterpret.

She wiggled free of Dosan's embrace and dropped the wash cloth on the tray. "Not anymore."

"We are destined."

Oh, she wanted to be destined!

She wanted to melt into his arms and surrender to her longing. Lose herself in passion and replace her callous, old fiancé with a mysterious, hotter new one.

This was the problem. Here was her whole problem in a nutshell.

She smoothed her dress over her pulsating body. "Don't think a glass of water — or anything else — entitles you to 'benefits.'"

"Benefits?"

"You can help yourself to anything in this rental, but you can't help yourself to me." She rested her palm over her thudding heart. "I'm worth more than a glass of water or that cheese-and-crackers plate."

He blinked. "Cheese-and-crackers plate?"

"You have to show me respect."

His eyes widened. Stunned. His jaw slacked and his mouth opened. "Respect?"

"Yeah. I, uh, deserve it."

"I did not show you respect?"

"No. I mean, you did. Your words were respectful. But you can't expect that one nice gesture entitles you to take advantage of me."

"I am taking advantage?"

"I brought you food and water and everything. You can't just take. Someday, you'll have to give."

He tipped over. His legs pushed the sheets off the bed and tangled on the sandy wooden floor. He made a choking sound and tried to rise.

She hovered, trying not to touch. "What are you doing?"

"I must ... give ... Provide you ... with food..."

"What? No, no, no. I said 'someday.'"

"In Dragao Azul ... a warrior always ... provides."

"You're not well, Dosan. Rest in the bed."

He rose unsteadily, breathing hard.

She pushed his broad shoulders.

He resisted her like a wall. A deliciously hard wall of masculine power.

And then he tipped, *timber!* and fell into the rental bed with a heavy creak. He rolled to his side and onto his back, legs off one side, pain trembling his face like an earthquake.

"Right now, I'll take care of you." She backed around the bed toward the door. "Rest here."

"I must provide."

"You jumped on dynamite to save my life. That's enough 'provision' for one day."

"But I—"

"Rest."

"But—"

"Stay." She hurried outside.

Dosan's hard gaze lit her on fire.

The door closed, shutting him inside.

She rested her back against the door. Her heart thumped so hard it practically knocked the wood. Her hands shook.

Her soul craved to open the door, hop into his bed, and take from him all the love and comfort and hot sex she'd been missing for her entire lifetime.

He'd give it to her. He wasn't like those other men.

Gary had been easy to resist. She'd wanted to give her love freely and so she'd overlooked his warning flags.

Resisting Dosan was like trying to stand against an incoming tide.

And, given his injures, she couldn't leave Dosan alone in this fragile state.

Jen pushed off the door and crossed the inner courtyard, weaving between the potted plants stationed around the gleaming pool. The sun was going down. It cast deep red shadows on the cloudy sky.

Xalu stood on the other side of the pool. His patrol had been interrupted by Sydney. They stood close and adversarial. Sydney confronted him.

Oh, no.

"Xalu!" Jen strode toward him. "Dosan's awake."

After a miniscule delay, the smoke-tattooed warrior tore his gaze from Sydney and turned to her. "Dosan wakes?"

"He is awake. Go sit with him."

The large warrior hurried to the sick room.

Sydney looked away, flushed, and swirled her empty cup. "That's right. Good riddance."

So Sydney was angry too. "I'm sorry. I didn't think about how you or Ian would feel having foreign men invade our vacation."

"Hmm? Oh, I wasn't talking about ... You know what?" Sydney threw her arm around Jen's shoulders. "Let's get a cup of coffee and chat."

"Coffee? You?"

"I've got something to talk about."

Jen strolled with her to the kitchen.

Like Jen, Sydney was a larger lady who favored Coach and Prada. At work managing the daycare center, her practical jeans were constantly covered in finger-paints and paste. On her vacations, Sydney swathed herself in a Juicy Couture track suit.

She'd recently ended her own decade-long wait on a first class loser and numbed the pain with the same liquid that had prolonged their deadbeat relationship.

Now, she moved around the kitchen tossing ice and margarita mix in the blender.

"Interesting coffee," Jen commented dryly.

"What? Oh, my god." Sydney stared at her blender

contents in dismay, tossed them in the sink, and got out the French press. "Guess I really need this."

She spooned coffee into the press while the water boiled.

"What did you want to tell me?" Jen asked.

"Huh? Oh … I haven't been a very good friend to you, have I? All I've done on this whole vacation is hide in my room and drink."

Considering what they'd both gone through, it made sense. "I understand."

"Well, that changes now. How are you?"

"Me?"

"This is your 'reinvention' vacation and I'm here to support you. So, how are you doing with relaxing and everything?"

Jen rested her elbows on the table. "Dosan kissed me."

Sydney froze, half-push on the press. "He did!"

"But it's not happening again."

She finished pressing and poured the coffee into two mugs. "That bad, huh?"

"It wasn't bad. It was dreamy. Hot. Delicious."

"Yeah." Sydney smiled and then sipped her coffee.

Jen shook herself. "And never happening again."

Sydney carried the mugs to the table. "Why not?"

"Because I'm supposed to be redefining myself. And I can't redefine myself if 'me' is a couple."

"Oh. I see."

"Plus it's a little fast, don't you think?"

Sydney pointed her well-manicured, gold index finger at Jen. "You do not have to mourn Gary. Sister Sydney absolves you."

"I'm not mourning Gary. I'm mourning the person I was when I was with him. The naïve, hopeful idiot who missed he was a jerk and thought we'd be happily married by now."

Sydney folded her hands around her mug. "Okay, then. We'll mourn *her*. And then, Jen, you deserve delicious hot kisses in your life, so we'll do something to make sure you can kiss fearlessly."

"Something?"

"You like checklists. We'll make a checklist. You evaluate your warrior. That way you fall in love with someone who treasures you."

Sydney seemed thrilled with this idea. Her hope was infectious. Jen started to feel a little lift.

They finished their coffees. Jen heaved herself to her feet. It had been a long day, actually.

"Be gentle with yourself," Sydney ordered. "Take a long shower. Get a good night's sleep. We'll tackle this in the morning. You'll be a whole new you."

Well, it was reasonable.

She bypassed the room where Dosan was resting with Xalu and continued around the pool to her bedroom next to Sydney's.

There was no reason for her heart to jump like a squirrel on a trampoline.

There was no reason for her to feel every second they spent apart was wasted. Like, Dosan was her soul mate and if she didn't act now to be with him, always, they might get ripped apart and never have another chance.

Jen closed and locked her own room.

The empty honeymoon suite.

Luxurious furnishings complimented a bucket of chilled wine — now warm and liquid — and a huge box of local chocolate.

She ate a piece from the satin-lined box, rolling the

creamy hazelnut ganache around on her tongue, and sat in the comfy chair looking out over the pool.

The luxury was incredible.

Her responsible savings had paid for it.

When the pictures had landed in her inbox, she had been devastated. But also relieved. Gary had been hiding a lot. Cold feet? The chill had traveled to her toes. An expensive last-minute cancellation was still cheaper than a divorce.

Ian had talked her into going on the honeymoon anyway. "You've been working hard your whole life. You deserve happiness."

Ian's idea of happiness was to lie next to a pool in paradise.

Jen had enjoyed it. But it wasn't her idea of happiness. Her idea was spending time with him and Sydney.

And now Dosan...

She shook herself and headed to the shower Sydney had recommended. In the privacy of her own shower, she could indulge in delicious fantasies...

In the morning she awoke late and dressed casually in a tank top and swimsuit. What were today's plans? If necessary, she'd put a beach dress on later. First thing was to start on breakfast. Wait, no, first was to check on the gorgeous warrior who had filled her with yummy, salty dreams...

Outside her door, on a lounge chair, rested Dosan.

Her heart soared.

Down.

He rose with a wince. Dark hollows shaded his eyes and the bruise on his chest was a deep shade of purple. He wore a new pair of Speedos. His sapphire tattoos gleamed iridescent in the morning sun.

"What are you doing here?" she asked, easing next to him. "You should be in bed."

"Your words were true." He turned his pain-wracked eyes on her. "I must show my respect."

"Sleeping on the lounge chair isn't respecting me," she argued.

"You were unprotected."

"I don't think the bad guys will attack here." She flubbed her lips. "But what if you'd had to defend me? You'd have made your injuries worse."

"I will fight until there is no breath left in my body." Fierce, honest, and decisive. "And then I will dive so the breath is replaced by water and I will continue to fight."

A lump formed in her throat.

"You are sad?" He tried to rise.

"No." She waved her hand at her eyes to dry the threatening tears. "Sorry."

"Again you apologize."

"Let's go to the kitchen. I want to start breakfast."

He groaned to his feet, leaning on her offered shoulder and his wickedly sharp trident, and limped into the kitchen. She eased him into a chair, put on the kettle to boil water for coffee, and served him a jar of yogurt from the fridge while yesterday's bread toasted in the oven. She spread butter and jam for him and he ate. Then, she cut and soaked potatoes for home fries, and cracked eggs for a big omelet.

"Your soul remains sad." He pushed himself to his feet and rested one hand on the counter, hemming her into the corner. "If this sadness is 'nothing,' let me give you happiness."

Temptation heated her.

She traced the deep sapphire tattoo slashing across

Dosan's forearm. "I almost married a guy who was too lazy to rescue me from a flat tire on a rainy highway in the dark."

"He was not worthy of your love."

"Everyone says that." She swallowed. "You're risking your injuries to make sure I'm okay and you don't even know me."

"I know you." He gestured at the boiling water, the toasting bread. "You nurture all under your care. You are tireless." He looked away. "I understand why you hesitate about me."

"You do?"

A shadow of shame crossed his features. "I, too, once allied myself with unworthy males. But that has changed. The queen — *queens* — of Dragao Azul have shown us a better way." He turned to her, again fierce. "You are destined to be a queen. Accept my claim. Join them."

His intense gaze thrilled her soul.

Her heart thudded. Her lips throbbed.

He kissed her.

She let him.

His tongue plumbed her mouth, branding her as his, and she gave in to his masculine hunting and exploring.

He pulled down her tank top, exposing her loose breasts. His gaze feasted on her curves. He marveled.

Had any other man stared at her body with such hunger? She felt beautiful without him saying a word.

He knelt, hanging onto the counters for balance, and kissed her taut nipples. Pulling one in his mouth, he swirled his tongue over her hot skin. Pleasure throbbed in her core. She slicked with readiness for him.

Jen gasped and rolled back her head, opening herself to his delicious onslaught.

He peeled down her swimsuit bottom and kissed her feminine center.

She came alive with pleasure.

He latched on and sucked her, stroking and satisfying even as he left her aching. Above, his hands sculpted her curves and rested on her breasts, pinching the nipples.

She arched against the counter with a shocked gasp. Her orgasm reached a crescendo.

Jen fell back on her elbows, sweaty and trembling.

No one had ever taken her from interested to satisfied in mere seconds. Her sapphire warrior's pleased gaze, as he looked over his conquered territory, made her shivery. She had been his plunder. Please, plunder her again. At least once more!

He knelt before her. His cock was hard and ready in the bulging Speedo. But he didn't interrupt her glow to demand relief.

He rose, captured her hand, and linked their fingers.

"Come with me." He kissed her knuckles tenderly. "To the sacred island. Drink the elixir and transform. We will go to my city and complete our marriage."

Her glow evaporated with the intrusion of real life.

She was doing it again.

Jen grabbed the wooden spoon and held it between them in warning. "Not so fast. A yogurt and a piece of toast don't give you free access to my body."

He blinked. "I do not understand."

"You have to respect me." She swallowed. The harsh words stuck in her throat like splinters of glass. "No more kisses or, uh, anything else until you show that you understand."

He frowned.

Old Jen would smooth his brow, laugh off her words, and embrace him with both arms. She'd cook him breakfast — and later, she'd be left crying at home, alone, while he photocopied himself with some woman who looked cuter in a bikini.

New Jen had to dole out her love, set limits on her generosity, and push away this mouthwatering male.

"How can I prove my devotion to you?" he growled.

Honestly? She had no idea.

"Figure it out." She turned away, straightened her clothes, and washed her hands to start breakfast.

He sat reluctantly at the table and picked up his toast, consuming it with what was starting to look like a permanent frown.

The others wandered in, yawning, and exclaimed at the delicious smells of fresh coffee, crunchy toast slathered in warm butter and sweet jam, and a spicy omelet with chorizo.

Sydney, more awake than Jen had seen her, asked the warriors pointed questions about what life was like for a bride underseas.

Questions Jen ought to be asking, probably. If she wasn't so busy trying not to think about Dosan's mind-bending kisses on her mouth and still throbbing, deliciously satisfied lower places.

"And so would Jen stay home and take care of the kids all day while you go out hunting and exploring? Or do you stay home drinking underwater beer and Jen does everything?"

"What is 'underwater beer'?" Xalu asked.

"Something I just made up." Sydney scooped jam onto her toast. "I'm trying to ask what women 'brides' do underseas."

"You decide." Dosan pledged his attention only to Jen.

"Dragao Azul's queen does not stay in our city. So, if you will stay, then your choices will determine the roles of future queens."

She sucked in a breath.

Wow. She could set the precedent?

Her brother and Sydney stared at the sapphire warrior.

"You want Jen to be royalty?" Ian asked, around a mouthful of egg.

Dosan nodded. "She must use her nurturing powers to rebuild our civilization."

Ian raised a brow at Jen and half-grinned. "No pressure or anything." He scooped another helping of spicy sausages.

After breakfast, they canceled tour plans and settled in for a relaxing day. Dosan rehabilitated in the pool with Xalu. Beneath the surface, he looked so free.

Sydney spent the day with Jen painting nails, exchanging opinions about new designers, and being the funny, vibrant best friend she hadn't realized she'd been missing for the last, oh, decade.

"This day has been so much fun," Jen finally said. "Being single suits you."

Her eyes darted to the left. The pool where Xalu and Dosan both dove beneath the waves. "Yeah ... about that..."

Jen watched as well.

To think, it was possible to transform into a whole other person ideally suited for floating in the pristine ocean and letting go of earthly cares. And there was an entire city waiting for a queen.

Waiting for Jen.

She carried an iced juice to the side of the pool.

Dosan surfaced.

She offered him the drink.

He rested his elbows on the tile. "When I am recovered,

you will receive my castle's finest offerings. I will provide for *you*. I swear it."

"Respect is about more than gifts," she said.

"You are my treasure. How can I show you my respect is more than desire?"

"I'll give you a checklist."

Mer warrior Uvim and his girlfriend, human tour guide Milly, stopped by in the afternoon.

The warriors huddled over Dosan's injuries.

Milly shared the police's efforts to find out who had imported and sold the deadly dynamite.

No one mentioned Dosan's proposal.

Jen didn't know what Milly would say about a recovering warrior seducing her twice. Sydney peppered Milly with questions about being a queen underseas, so Jen didn't have to stress about it.

Milly had barely gotten to enjoy transforming into a mermaid with her mysterious, deadly serious warrior.

"I've always been a diver," Milly said. "Being underwater is so freeing. I'd dive even if it weren't my job. Now I have the power to transform into a mermaid, it's even better."

"But how did you know it was right for you?" Jen pressed. "How did you know Uvim wasn't taking advantage of your generosity?"

"I'm not that generous." The young guide laughed.

Uvim's gaze moved to her. Amethyst tattoos ran in geometric designs like fractures across his olive-colored skin.

Silent communication passed between them.

Milly faded to a soft smile. "I fought my feelings but, in the end, I had to admit the truth. The heart always knows."

"Oh, I think your heart can give you the runaround," Sydney disagreed and sipped her icy virgin drink. "A decade of running around, stuck on the same, stupid guy, refusing to admit defeat."

"That sounds like your head substituting fear for loneliness," Milly disagreed, showing wisdom well beyond her years. "Stop running and listen."

"Yeah, well." Sydney sighed on her new black-tipped nails. "You're not wrong. Most likely."

Jen avoided her sexy warrior that evening, leaving Dosan once more under the care of Xalu. She insisted he spend the night in his own bed. He could surely hear her scream for help if needed.

Sydney was up early for once and she talked Jen into heading into town for an early morning shopping trip. The males needed more than a pair of Speedos apiece, Sydney said, although the gleam in her eye suggested she didn't mind enjoying the warriors in the small, tight fabric that left no bulge to the imagination.

They arrived back at the rental to face two furious males and one amused brother.

"Where did you go?" Xalu demanded of Sydney.

She stroked his forearm, soothing him in a decidedly intimate way. "Wait until you see what I bought you! You're going to flip."

"Flip? Why would I perform a flip?"

"Oh, you'll see. Here." She opened the shopping bags and lofted shirts against his bulk. Again, a little too intimate.

But Jen couldn't concentrate because Dosan drew her into his arms. "I must protect you. Never leave my side."

He was looking healthier. And she loved the strength in his arms and the fearless way he held her despite Ian's side-eye.

"I got you clothes," she said. "So you can go out in public."

"I do not need these things if it puts you in danger."

She needed to dole out her love.

Even though it hurt her.

"So you're saying you don't like the shirts."

"Jen."

She pulled back. "I'm sorry trying to do something nice for you turned into an issue. I'll let you go nude next time."

"Your generosity endangers you."

Pain squeezed her heart. "That's just what Ian and Sydney say. I'm surprised to hear it from you, too."

"We do not need these 'shirts' on the bottom of the ocean." He tried to draw her into his arms again. "You are destined to become Dragao Azul's queen. Our savior. My bride and the mother of our young fry."

It sounded wonderful.

She crossed her arms. "We'll need them when we surface and visit."

"Then we will not surface."

Whoah. "Um, okay, you're right. We won't 'come to the surface' because I'm never going down there with you."

"Do not reject our connection."

"What connection? We've known each other for three days."

"Our souls resonate."

So he also felt they were soul mates.

But she couldn't give up everything. Sydney, Ian, her self-respect. Not this time. She had some pride.

"I refuse to rush into a rebound relationship," she insisted, catching her breath on a sob. "And we will never be happy if you don't appreciate who I am and respect my needs."

"Jen."

"Now, I got you clothes. Here." She thumped the bag at

him and darted away before he could convince her to change her mind.

Sydney found her a short time later wallowing on her bed amid the last wrappers from her chocolate. "Milly's on the phone. She wanted to ask if you had any questions about the 'cultural differences' we might have."

"These are more than cultural differences."

"I know. So why don't you talk to her and then we'll do the girls' spa day we promised? Take care of you, treasure you."

"I could use a little treasuring." She sniffed.

Sydney's smile gentled. "You deserve it."

Jen took the phone. "Have you ever been unsure whether you wanted to strangle a warrior or drag him to the bedroom and do something unmentionable?"

Milly, on the other side of the phone, choked on a laugh. "Why, yes. Yes, I have. What's up and how can I help?"

It was good to talk to Milly. She reinforced what Jen mostly knew: That a warrior devoted himself to one bride for his whole life, and that his honor was his most important possession.

Which meant Dosan believed in everything he'd said.

The only one holding them back was Jen.

Gary had punched her in the heart. Now, she had a chance to open herself to another person and her heart shied away.

"Come on," Sydney urged after the phone call ended. "There's something I want to tell you."

Jen let herself get pulled to the rental car. With Dosan smoldering in the front seat, Jen sat in the back. Sydney, in the middle, pressed against Xalu.

Every time Jen caught his profile, she wanted to tell

him. *Dosan. I'm sorry I said those things. I do think you're respectful. I want to be with you.*

But then she felt giddy — and scared.

What if he was angry? What if he'd changed his mind?

What if he said yes and swept her away in his delicious embrace and everything changed forever?

She kept quiet.

Ian let them off at a hotel day spa; the men were heading to the beach to rehabilitate in the waves.

Dosan caught her eye from the window, his new cream shirt stretched dangerously tight across his broad chest. "Do not leave unprotected."

A part of her thrilled at his protective instincts. He was a male who cared deeply.

"We'll be careful," she promised. "Just like we were the whole vacation before you came."

His jaw flexed.

Did he think she was dismissing him? She wasn't. A dynamite distributor would have to be crazy to attack them in daylight in the center of a large town.

He watched her until the car disappeared.

She joined Sydney inside the day spa. It was gorgeous and European; stained glass shone on their facials and experts plucked, plumped, sanded, and shaped. She lay in bubbles and was massaged next to her best friend, rubbed in sweet-scented lotion and released into the world to enjoy a long, fun, amazing dinner and half a bottle of wine all to herself.

"I really shouldn't," Sydney said, pouring herself a second glass. "Did you know I was numbing myself with alcohol for like a year?"

"Five years," Jen corrected. Not that she was keeping track. "I missed you."

Tears bubbled up in Sydney's eyes. "Well, I'm back now. And I'm here to support you. Or at least support your choice of ordering dessert."

"You've been a great support," Jen laughed, and she ordered a chocolate lava cake to share.

The cab back to the rental let them out across the street.

She faced the artful stucco-white Azores house and turned over the words she'd say to Dosan. Nerves glowed red like spreadsheet irregularities in her belly. She smoothed her emerald dress, sucked in a deep breath, and let it out. The sun was just starting to set.

Okay. Time to do this.

"Jen."

She turned.

Sydney hesitated. "There's something I was supposed to say."

This sounded serious. "Oh?"

"Yeah." Sydney toyed with her tiny braids. "Uh, well, the thing is..."

A clunker van started up down the street. It approached them and the passenger rolled down the window. It was a young college-aged kid in a stained, sleeveless surfer shirt. "Are you two Jen and Sydney?"

He had a west coast accent — American West Coast — but something about him seemed off.

"That's us." Jen hugged her purse tighter to her chest.

"My friend has a question."

The back passenger door opened and another college kid — this one with wonky teeth and uneven glasses — spread out a street map of the Azores.

She backed into Sydney and put up her hands. "Oh, we're not from around here."

"That's okay." The surfer got out and stood too close. His voice darkened. "You can both answer this question."

She clenched her purse. "What?"

The glasses kid reached out and grabbed Jen's forearm. "Hey!"

With surprising strength, he yanked her into the van. She banged her shins on the van door. He hauled her across the dirty floor, smearing crap all over her blissful skin. Sydney collapsed on top.

"Go! Go!"

The van doors closed. The engine clunked again, and the floor vibrated as they careened down the street.

She struggled. "What are you doing?"

"Isn't it obvious?" The surfer stared down at her like she was a worm. "We're kidnapping you."

The kids drove for not a terribly long time and hustled Sydney and Jen into a warehouse in a seemingly abandoned section of town. The kids marched them into the office and locked them in.

They sat on a couch.

"What do you want with us?" Jen demanded.

The surfer kid ignored her. He got a soda out of a mini fridge, turned away, and cracked the top. "Want a drink?"

Her throat was dry. The wine was giving her a headache. If this would put them on friendly terms, then—

"No, thank you," Sydney said loudly.

He shrugged and set it on the low table in front of them. "But—"

Sydney kicked it over.

"Hey! Don't make it worse."

"I can't make it worse." She lowered her voice and pointed her pinkie finger at boxes marked with a busy triangle. "That's the symbol of the bad guy."

"Oh, you saw our symbol." The surfer kid sighed, rummaged in his surf shorts pocket, and pulled a gun. "Now we have to kill you."

Jen's heart stopped.

So, this was the part in the movie where it skipped ahead and two bodies were found by detectives the next morning.

Calm. Think.

"We didn't answer your 'question' yet," she said. Her voice was amazingly steady.

"We don't want anything to do with you," the kid said. "We just want to know about the creatures."

Sydney grabbed Jen. "We'll tell you whatever you want. Nobody touches us."

"Deal."

The kid made them kneel in front of the couch. He confiscated their cell phones and purses. It was like a robbery gone comically wrong.

But it wasn't that funny.

One of them wrapped duct tape around their ankles and wrists.

Jen kept her ankles together to keep from exposing her lacy undergarments.

"You said nobody touches us!" Sydney shouted as they yanked her arms behind her back.

"I'm not touching you," the glasses kid said. "The duct tape is."

Sydney huffed. "Does your mother know where you are?"

"I don't have one."

The kids backed off and left them in the lit office all alone.

"That I believe," Sydney muttered.

Well, this was just great. They were probably going to die on her not-honeymoon.

"This is the last time I let you and Ian talk me into a personal day," Jen said with a long, heavy sigh. "What's wrong with being a workaholic? Nobody was threatening to shoot me back in Atlanta."

Sydney snorted. "We're about to die and that's what you have to say?"

"Shhh. They're saying something."

Snatches of their conversation filtered into the office. An argument about what to do with them while waiting for "their leader" to arrive and start the interrogation.

Jen wanted to plug her ears and sing so she could tell them she hadn't heard anything. But they didn't seem competent enough.

"We can't just let them go," one of them said near the office.

She had to bite her lip.

"Yes!" Sydney called, saying exactly what she'd wanted to say. "Yes, you can! Let us go and we'll forget everything! I swear!"

The kids swore and moved away from the window.

"This is your last warning!"

Silence.

Muffled voices resumed farther away.

"And I told Dosan I didn't need to be protected," Jen sighed. "Apparently when dating otherworldly creatures, otherworldly rules apply. Not that we're dating. Because we're not. Like I said before."

"Jen," Sydney said with a warning in her tone.

"I'm so sorry that I forced you to share your vacation with warriors. Ian was right. I can't relax. And now it's cost you big time."

"Listen."

"I am listening. I'm listening, and I've decided first thing when we get out of here, I'm going to tell Dosan no once and for—"

"Xalu proposed!"

Jen shut her mouth with a click.

"I said yes." Sydney looked embarrassed.

"Oh. Congratulations."

"Yeah. How could I not? Think about it. We get to shape how they run an entire undersea kingdom!"

"You don't care about living deep in the ocean, far beneath the surface?"

"Oh, I am coming to the surface again. I am doing whatever I want. I'm going to be royalty, baby!"

"And Xalu's okay with it?"

"Who cares? I'm his queen! But of course he's fine with it. He wants his future wife to be happy."

"So why'd you keep quiet all this time?" Jen demanded. "I feel like a jerk. You were so supportive and I couldn't be trusted with knowing when my best friend was engaged?"

"No, I'm sorry. You went through so much with Gary and then you were so dead set against Dosan."

"You agreed with Ian," Jen argued. "You said I had to reinvent myself so I wouldn't get hurt."

"I did, but you know what? We were wrong. You're just fine. The problem is them, and you *don't* have to reinvent yourself because you are already fabulous."

Jen let her skepticism show on her face.

Sydney tried to raise her hands in defense. Her shoulders lifted; her hands were still taped behind her back. "It's like Milly said. She'd dive even if she wasn't a mermaid. It's who she is. Jen, you're kind to everyone. Even the people who don't deserve it. It's who you are and there's nothing wrong with it."

She wanted that to be true. "I'm not going to be 'kind' to these kidnappers when we get out of here."

"Well, you're not an idiot."

"Thank you."

Sydney shook her head. "Whatever the case, you were right to demand time to work out what's best for you. You need time to consider Dosan's proposal. Honestly, I was afraid I'd push you in the wrong direction. How could I not get excited at the thought of ruling an undersea kingdom with my best friend?"

That made sense.

"But now," Sydney sucked in a huge breath and wiggled on her knees, "we might not rule anything but a cemetery."

"What are you doing?"

"Trying to get a leg free so my last act can be kicking one of these idiots in the balls."

Despite their situation, Jen laughed. That was so like Sydney. She'd go down swinging.

And maybe there was nothing wrong with Jen. She should have run away from these kids screaming but she couldn't have guessed they were intending to kidnap her. She should have run away from Gary screaming but she couldn't have guessed he was intending to stomp on her heart and publicly humiliate her in her own workplace.

What if the problem wasn't her? What if she didn't want a relationship based on distrust or miserly doling out? What if it was okay for her to love with her whole heart?

Her self-doubts had clarified what she truly did want.

So now she needed to tell him.

Jen did a quick inventory of the warehouse office. Pens,

overflowing ashtray, empty soda cans beneath the beat up couch.

Hmm.

"Pop the tab on that soda can," Jen instructed and shuffled around to put her back to Sydney's. "That will create a sharp edge."

Sydney awkwardly pulled it off the table and did as she asked. Then, she backed up and dropped the tab in Jen's fingers. "You sure about this?"

"No." Jen positioned the tab on the sticky tape binding Sydney's hands and sawed. "But we have to try."

Forever passed.

Sydney wriggled with discomfort. "Any luck?"

"The sticky tape is gumming up the sharp edge. It's still cutting. Slowly."

"Then once I'm free, then what?"

"I'll yell for those guys and you can kick them in the balls."

Sydney perked up. "I like this plan."

Jen worked the tab. It was like cutting through a phone book with a paperclip. Progress was steady but slow.

Sydney strained.

"What are you doing?"

"Something. Anything. I don't want to sit around waiting on others anymore."

"Well, hold tight, because this is going to take..."

Sydney's bonds stretched and she yanked the tape apart.

"...no time at all. Great job!"

Sydney grinned, a new gleam in her eyes. "Your turn."

"Use the pen to puncture the aluminum. You can fashion a makeshift knife from the sharp edge."

Sydney followed her directions, cut the tape off her ankles, and freed Jen.

"I'll call one of the kids in here, make the call, and then, while he's distracted, you clobber him," Jen said.

Sydney draped the tape over her wrists as if she were still tied up and nodded.

Jen's heart thudded in her throat.

Go time.

Jen shouted. "Hey! Give me back my cell phone and I'll call the guys to come on down here!"

The kid with glasses poked his head into the office. "You'll call what guys?"

"The warriors. Dosan and Xalu."

He stared blankly.

"You want to ask us questions about them, right? We'll call them down and they can answer you."

The kid stared at her like he was trying to figure out why in the world he should do that.

"You don't want to talk to them?" Jen prodded. "What's your end goal here?"

"My knees are killing me," Sydney said.

"Mine too. I want everyone to be happy so we can all go home."

"We decide when you go home." The kid puffed out his chest, belligerent. "We already tried it. Your phone's broken."

"You broke it!"

"I didn't break it. It's frozen."

"Let me see."

He shrugged and carried Jen's phone to the small coffee table. Her screen glowed white. A tiny star hid in one corner.

Her *Locate Phone* app was running!

Jen's throat constricted. Pounding sounded in her ears.

Help was coming.

Ian must have remembered her password from when he'd helped her install the app and now he was tracing her location.

"You're right." She eased back on the balls of her feet pretending to be confused and hurt. Adrenaline shivered in her veins. "It's broken."

"Go get mine," Sydney said.

He stood.

"No!" Jen nudged her. "Forget it. Change of plans."

Sydney stared. "Jen, I actually think we should wait to hear their voices before we do anything rash."

"Why should I listen to you? You waited ten years on a guy who was never going to propose."

Sydney's mouth dropped. "How dare you?"

"What I'm saying is sometimes you just have to act. Whether you're prepared or not. *Just act.*"

Sydney's voice broke. She was nervous too. "Fine."

The kid backed away from the table. "You guys are acting weird."

"What are you going to do about it?" Sydney snapped.

He flipped her a rude gesture and turned to leave.

She jumped up and whacked him on the back of the head with the ashtray.

Ashes flew.

He stumbled and closed the door on himself. Hand to the back of his head, he complained. "Ow."

Sydney shoved him down and lodged a knee in his back. He grunted. Sydney grabbed the makeshift knife out of the papers and held it to his throat. "Freeze or I'll cut you."

He froze.

This was going to work. They were going to escape.

Sydney held out her hand. "Jen, tape."

Jen grabbed the roll of duct tape and she bound the kid the same way he'd bound them. Her voice wobbled as she scolded him. "You are in big trouble, mister."

"You can't do this." He wriggled like a worm. "HEY —mph!"

Jen stuck the tape over his mouth.

He grunted.

"I warned you," Sydney said, peering out the office door for the other kidnappers. "So, I assume the guys are on the way?"

"That's right. And Ian has the number for the police."

"We just have to survive." Sydney squinted. Somewhere out there was a gun. "Ooh, there's that surfer kid."

Sydney backed away from the door and lifted the ashtray.

"Hey, G?" The surfer kid pushed open the door. "You oh—"

Sydney brought down the ashtray.

The surfer kid wheeled and threw up his arm. The ashtray bounced off his forearm.

Sydney whacked him again.

He kept his arm up. The ashtray hit his elbow.

"Hey!" He jumped deeper into the office, away from her, and shook out his fingers like they were tingly. He rummaged in his pocket.

Sydney came at him again. This time, with the knife.

He produced the pistol.

Sydney checked. "Uh oh."

He glared at her. "That hurt."

"Well, I'm not sorry."

"You're going to be. Drop that."

She dropped the knife.

It fell like Jen's heart.

"Get over against the wall. Both of you."

Jen and Sydney hurried to comply.

"Ugh." He rubbed his elbow and appealed to the kid still tied up. "Why did we even kidnap you? It's obvious now we have to kill you."

The duct taped kid made a strangled sound.

A knock echoed through the warehouse.

She and Sydney straightened.

The surfer kid started toward the doorway arrogantly, then noticed their reaction. He stopped. His eyes narrowed.

Outside, the rattle of the giant warehouse doors gave way to shouts and fighting.

He trained his gun on the door. "What did you do?"

"Nothing," Jen said.

Wham!

The office door flew open.

One of the lanky kids suspended off the ground by the back of his shirt. He pointed at her and Sydney. "There! The women are there!"

Xalu dropped the lanky kid. He landed on the ground with an "oof" and rolled away.

Dosan's trident gleamed with deadly intent. He and Xalu, also armed with trident and blades, advanced into the office.

The surfer kid backed against the office wall and trained his gun on two growling warriors. "Don't come any closer."

The warriors turned to the women, ignoring him and his threat.

Dosan stroked Jen, checking her wrists and sliding a finger along her jaw for bruising. "You are unharmed?"

"Fine." She touched the tip of the bruise visible between the halves of his dress shirt. Her hands shook again. "You warned me to take more precautions. I'm sorry I didn't listen."

"You know the surface world better than I," he said. "When Ian called, even your police did not believe our attackers intended this stupidity."

He turned on the surfer kid with a snarl. His grip on his trident tightened. "You dared to touch my bride."

The surfer kid held up the gun, shaky. "Stay back."

Jen put her hand on Dosan's forearm to stop him. "Put the gun down."

The surfer kid shook his head.

"Now," Jen insisted. "Your threat is stupid. They're undersea warriors who don't understand guns."

"I'll shoot!"

Dosan placed himself between her and the kid. His hackles rose as he prepared to leap.

If she didn't intervene, Dosan would take a bullet for her.

He was a hero.

Jen told the shaking kid. "And even if you did shoot them, they'd still try to disarm you. And I mean 'dis-arm'. Those tridents are sharp."

The kid swallowed.

In the distance, police sirens sounded.

"It's going to be a lot harder in prison when you're missing an arm," Sydney pointed out.

Xalu growled.

The kid wavered.

"You can't shoot both," Jen pushed. "One of them is going to slice your hand off. Unless you put the gun down now."

He rested the gun on the table and backed up against the wall. "Don't hurt me."

Xalu gestured with the trident for him to exit. "Your human justice is waiting."

He crept out of the office.

Xalu lifted the duct-taped kid and exited.

The police took custody of the kids and searched the warehouse. An inspector collected preliminary reports and made appointments for full statements.

As soon as they were released, Jen threw her arms around Dosan. He had never looked so fierce. "You saved me."

"Jen." Dosan kissed her hands. "I must demonstrate my respect."

"Take me home and I'll share my checklist."

He held her tight.

Ian waited outside the warehouse. He saw them and his worry changed to relief.

Her brother laughed as he helped them into his rental Ford Fiesta sedan. "You just can't help yourself, can you Jen? You can't relax and enjoy a little 'me' time without embroiling us in an international, inter-species war."

Dosan got into the car.

Jen hesitated. "You aren't going to scold me?"

"The other day when Dosan explained how you're literally going to be a queen, and Sydney will be right there with you, I realized this is your life. I love and support you. So, you tell me what's right for you. I'm butting out."

She hugged her brother. "Thank you."

"I will say," he returned her hug, "that visiting you underseas is going to be a heck of a commute."

"We'll figure something out."

"Maybe another vacation," he joked and headed for the driver's seat to take them home.

At the rental, they split off to their rooms like a shot.

Dosan laid her on the honeymoon suite bed, treating her so gently, as if she were the injured one. "How can I prove my devotion?"

She rose to her knees. "You have to treat me like your queen, rescue me if I'm in danger, and promise to love me forever."

His mouth opened and closed. Then, he frowned. "What have I failed to do?"

"Nothing." She threw her arms around him. "I guess you've proved your devotion."

"Then you will drink the elixir and perform the marriage ceremony in my underseas city?"

"First, you have to promise me something."

"Anything."

"This was supposed to be my honeymoon. And you've made it into one after all." She held him tight. "Now, I want my wedding night. Will you give me an unforgettable night of pleasure?"

He grew very solemn. "You have my vow."

She tilted up her lips, teasing. "Let's seal it with a kiss."

His mouth covered hers.

Delicious need seared her. She drank in his masculine flavor. His tongue tangled with hers, darting with skill. He promised tonight would change everything for her.

And she gave in with her whole heart.

He kissed the column of her neck. Heat danced beneath his wet, hungry mouth. She tilted her neck to give him free reign. He kissed to the edge of her emerald dress. She helped him loosen the fastenings and pull it over her head, exposing her bra and panties. His powerful hands delved beneath the lacy silk and scooped her breasts free.

Desire slicked her channel.

She moaned.

His hot palms massaged her pillow breasts. His sapphire gaze enjoyed her bounty. He dipped his head. His tongue laved her pearled nipples.

They contracted with his hot caress and cool night air.

He swept his broad thumbs over the sensitive flesh.

Pleasure shot to her core.

She arched into his masterful touch.

He unhooked her lacy bra, pulled it off, and kissed over her belly button. Reaching the waistband, he pulled off her silky bottoms. He massaged her thighs.

She spread for him.

Her dewy center was exposed to his hungry gaze.

He treasured her feminine folds, latching on and stroking her nub with his tongue.

Heat crashed over her in liquid waves.

He reached up and pinched her sensitive nipples.

Her channel clenched on empty air. She gasped, riding the crest of a beautiful orgasm.

He rose. A satisfied smile teased his usually serious lips.

She reached for him. "Let me love you."

He rested a knee on the bed beside her.

She unbuttoned his shirt and peeled it back. His bruise was much smaller than before as he continued to heal.

He had jumped on dynamite and received a terrible injury.

Mistakenly trusting in Gary had shredded her heart.

But Dosan had rescued her without hesitation. He didn't blame himself for the dynamite or the criminals who kidnapped her. And he had not let the fear of injury stop him from doing what was right.

In the same way, she couldn't let the fear of injuring her heart again stop her from embracing Dosan and living the full, wonderful life she was meant to lead.

Underseas. Wife, mother, and queen.

Pushing down his new shorts, she enjoyed his bulging thighs.

He positioned his thick cock at her ready entrance and plunged into her wet, tight heat.

A deeply satisfying hit of pleasure enraptured her. She wanted this man, this male, for the rest of her life.

She wrapped her legs around his taut buttocks and guided him home.

He plunged deep, stroking her with energy.

Not only would he take a bullet for her or jump on dynamite, he would thrust into her until she was thoroughly sated. Heat exploded in her body. She gasped and arched to take him deeper.

Faster, wetter, hotter he chased her pleasure, hunted it. His cock thrust tirelessly. She tilted her hips and met him thrust for thrust. She opened her heart to him and he returned it to her a hundredfold.

Bliss crashed in her body. Her channel clenched his cock, gripping him in her orgasm.

He grunted. His release filled her with his liquid heat.

Now they were united.

He kissed her brow and her lips. His addictive flavor, masculine and salty, filled her mouth with an echo of their shared promise.

She nuzzled her husband. There was the formality of his ceremony but as far as she was concerned, they were married, and his gently satisfied kiss said the same thing to her.

"You know, when I took that tour with Ian, our guides said we'd spot exotic fish because the waters around the Azores are so deep."

He nodded in acknowledgment. The waters *were* deep;

he'd told her and Sydney during the earlier breakfast that one current led to his city on the bottom of the ocean.

"But I've landed the most exotic fish right in my bed." She giggled.

He stroked her cool belly with his wide, warm palm. "Soon we will marry and you will be the most exotic. Your generous soul glows with brilliance. Your kindness will light up the sea."

"Do you promise? I know warriors are honorable and will never break a promise."

"I promise." And he sealed it with his addictive, masculine kiss.

HER WARRIOR'S VOW

Sydney peered out her bedroom window at the powerful warrior.

Xalu.

He patrolled the courtyard, stalking the pool and weaving between the potted plants of their paradise-like vacation rental. Tattoos the color of iridescent black smoke swirled across his dangerously broad back, mouthwateringly muscled abdomen, massive biceps, and pylon-sized thighs. The black Speedo someone had lent him to cover his thick male prowess left nothing to the imagination.

Lucky her.

A wicked trident was clenched in one hand. His sharp gaze cut the mild summer evening as he searched out evil to become his prey.

Sydney sipped the dregs of her margarita. The ice clinked.

His gaze lasered on her window.

Warm tingles teased her feminine vee and tightened her nipples.

Despite the fact that he could shift into a merman —

and thus wasn't even human, although he certainly looked human right now — she wouldn't mind being his prey.

He stalked in her direction.

Two doors down, the kitchen opened and her best friend's brother, Ian, walked out carrying a tray.

Ian was a nice guy. Paler than he ought to be from his life indoors crunching numbers, and with a gut that had grown these last few years from good home cooking, he had committed. The wedding band on his ring finger was displayed with casual pride. His wife was gorgeous too, and their two kids were adorable.

Because a settled, happy kind of life was possible when a man made a promise and followed through on it.

Xalu changed direction and spoke with Ian. His deep, resonant voice made her tingle. She couldn't hear their exact words from this distance but it was clear that Ian invited him to check on his injured friend, and the well-endowed male followed with high alertness.

His tight butt muscles clenched and released as he walked.

Yum.

Sydney rose unsteadily and hurried to crack her bedroom door.

Xalu leaned in the extra guest bedroom. His broad back was to her.

She squeezed out to the patio and quick-stepped to the kitchen.

It wasn't that she didn't want to meet the hard, dangerous warrior.

She'd been passed out when he'd arrived, and that was absolutely *not* because she'd spend the day sulking in her room, feeling sorry for herself, just because everyone else was out snorkeling and she was stuck at their paradise-like vacation rental with nothing but her regrets and a bucket of frozen margarita mix.

Apparently, terrorists had tried to dynamite the tour boat — or something — and one of the warriors had gotten hurt. Sydney's best friend Jen, terminally unable to relax, had volunteered to forgo her vacation to nurse him back to health.

Xalu was here to protect them against any further terrorism.

Sydney was here to enjoy the view.

She dumped her old ice in the sink and filled the blender with new ice and margarita mix. She set the blender on "high" and blended it into delicious frozen forgetfulness. The drink splashed against the sides. She poured it into her glass with expertise and took a huge sip.

Alcohol burned her throat.

She coughed.

How much had she put in? Actually, she couldn't even remember adding it. But it felt about like what she'd been drinking for the past ... well, two months since she'd kicked The Loser out of her life and approximately ten years she'd increasingly often numbed herself to his lies, false hopes, and misdirections.

I could spend the rest of my life regretting you. He'd said that at their first meeting. *This is my ball and chain.* He'd joked to the waiter on their first date.

She'd picked out color swatches that first month, written her vows by Christmas, and planned the whole ceremony before their first anniversary.

And then a decade had passed.

She'd lost her youth, her hope, and her no-longer-so-little flower girl waiting for The Loser to take a knee.

She'd been maid of honor in five weddings, bridesmaid in six more, and witness in two divorces.

Always a bridesmaid, never a bride. That saying had haunted her night and day. Whoever had said it was particularly cruel. It was like a curse.

Adding enough vodka to a single drink to knock her out was, at this point, muscle memory.

She didn't want to sleep through her life, but Jen probably didn't want to share what was supposed to have been her honeymoon with two third wheels, and Ian probably didn't want to spend his hard-earned vacation cajoling two sad sacks out of their midlife crises.

Nobody got what they wanted. Might as well drink and forget.

"*Salud,*" she told her washed out, exhausted-looking reflection in the kitchen window.

What was "cheers" in Portuguese? She'd ask the next time she convinced Ian to drive her to a bar.

Sydney exited the kitchen.

Xalu stood outside.

She stopped.

The hulking male was even more impressive up close. Well-rounded pectorals from a million bench presses, abdomen so tight she wanted to get on her knees and lick him. The Loser had been no slouch at the gym, but Xalu redefined the word "muscular" with his abs.

And the smoke-gray tattoos drew her lower, a treasure trail, teasing the edge of his Speedo.

"You are Sid-o-nee," the warrior growled.

His deep voice massaged her ears and filled her with powerful longing. Her vee throbbed and her nipples contracted again.

His nostrils flared. His gaze dropped to her comfy

velour lounging suit where her breasts swelled larger-than-life against her plus-sized curves.

"You're Xalu," she said and tried to sip her drink casually.

"Zay-loo," he corrected.

"Zay-loo."

"Zay-loo," he corrected again.

"That's what I said."

He began to correct her a third time.

She put a hand on his chest. "Xalu."

He rumbled, deep within. Pleased? Satisfied? She felt both as his smoky warmth radiated up her forearm and lanced her suddenly thudding heart.

She withdrew her hand. "And, since pronunciation seems to matter, it's 'Sydney.'"

He frowned. "Sid-oh-knee."

"Sydney."

"Siiid-anee."

"Sydney."

"Sid-a-nee."

She rested her hand on his chest again and tapped out the two syllables. "Sydney. Sydney. Sydney."

His dark brows drew together in intense concentration. His chest rose and fell. He approached the pronunciation of her name as a focused warrior attacking a new, unknown, but dangerous prey.

"Sid-nee."

"Good enough." She grinned and let her hand drop.

He caught her hand.

Her breath hitched.

His knuckles were large, bony, and strong enough to crush her glass to powder. He slid his thumb up to her wrist.

Her slippery vee throbbed. He knew how to handle a woman and she hadn't been handled in a long, long time.

"Sid-nee." He took a knee and pressed her hand to his chest.

Her heart thudded. Just because she'd witnessed two dozen proposals did not mean this was one. "Uh ... yes?"

"I am Xalu, honorable warrior of Dragao Azul. Accept my claim and become my bride."

Or maybe it was.

Her fingers started to sweat. "Bride?"

"You will drink the nectar of the Life Tree blossom and transform into a mermaid. And then you will join with me in my city and we will produce a young fry son."

"That, uh, sounds nice."

"It will be very nice."

"Great. Sure. Uh huh."

Her mouth released words that had not passed the filter in her brain. A super hot warrior laid eyes on her and was so overcome with love he wanted to sweep her away to his barbarian castle? Great. Sure. Uh huh.

"So... when do we leave for your city?"

"As soon as Dosan recovers. I hope tomorrow."

"Tomorrow!" She'd waited a decade for The Loser and this Xalu proposed within the first five minutes. "That's sudden."

"We must not wait." He tilted his chin. "My race is dying. Only you, Sid-nee, can make our city bountiful once again."

"Bountiful. Uh huh. I like that."

His brows rose with hope. "You do?"

From this closeness, his features appeared more hawk-ish, with a sharp chin and hooked nose. He looked like a military commander. And deadly serious, as if he had never cracked a smile.

"Sure," she said, moving her weight from one rhinestone-crusted sandal to the other. "I've always been 'ample.' My whole life. I've got a lot of love to give. So, this is a marriage proposal?"

"I offer you this mating jewel." With his other hand, he reached into a darkly colored, woven bag at his chiseled waist and brought out a pearl the size of her fist.

Her stomach dropped. "That's a..."

"You call it a Sea Opal."

The rare gemstone with healing properties. Sea Opals were produced by the Life Tree within each mer city. This size, such a gemstone was worth ... millions?

Suddenly this wasn't funny anymore.

He offered the Sea Opal to her.

She choked. "You're joking."

"Jo-king?"

"Misleading. Saying one thing but meaning another. Lying."

He stiffened. His dark eyes flashed. "I do not lie."

"Yeah, but, if you're serious..."

Perspiration rolled off the margarita glass and sweated across the back of her hand.

"...I must be hallucinating. How much have I had to drink? Too much, clearly."

He frowned, set the Sea Opal in her hand — it was smooth and beautiful and heavy — and took her margarita. He swirled the ice and touched the tip of his tongue to the drink.

"This is poison!"

"Only to my liver." She pressed her chilled fingers to her forehead. Soothing. "I can quit any time."

He stood and overturned the glass. Liquid and ice splattered the tile.

"Hey! I was drinking that."

"You must not drink this poison, Sid-nee. It dulls your soul light."

She teetered on the balls of her feet. "My what?"

He pressed the Sea Opal to her chest. "Your light. The great strength within you. You must let your light shine. You have the soul of a queen."

Her chin wrinkled.

What?

Oh, tears burned at the corners of her eyes and a hard lump filled her throat.

This beautiful, powerful warrior looked beyond the disappointment her life had become and saw the woman she still was deep inside.

She pressed her hand to her mouth to hide the emotion welling up and spilling out, and she tried to laugh. "You don't pull your punches, do you?"

He frowned. "I do not punch."

"Verbally. It means…" Her throat closed. She swallowed. "You know what? Never mind."

"You must not fear violence from me, Sid-nee."

"I don't. It's a figure of speech."

"Hmm."

"You know what?" She clenched the Sea Opal to her chest as though its weight would calm her thudding heart. "Why don't I make a coffee? You have to tell me about this undersea city of yours."

"Dragao Azul."

"And I have to get sober for the first time in … in a few … well, we'll be generous and call it years." She pocketed the gemstone, leaned down, and scooped up her empty glass.

He stopped her. "You have not given your answer."

Oh. Her answer would be the same drunk or sober. "I accept."

He froze. "You accept?"

Sydney believed in love at first sight. The tight band squeezing her heart was that feeling.

She nodded.

Her warrior opened his mouth and closed it again. Like he couldn't believe he'd heard right.

He stepped closer. His warm breath kissed her cheek. An irresistible scent like rum and leather tantalized her nose. Gaze locked on hers, he lowered his head. His lips pressed hers.

Firm. Honest.

Forthright.

He meshed their lips, tilted his head, and pushed for a deeper connection. There was no doubt what he wanted. She was his desire. He prowled at her entrance like a deadly predator hunting his favorite prey.

Heat flared in her belly.

His quest was fierce, relentless, and so welcome.

She parted her lips.

He plumbed her wet depths, probed her hungry mouth and suckled her tongue. Deep, primitive tugs declared his intention to bow her willing body over a lounge chair and thrust his hard, smoke-tattooed cock deep into her hungry channel.

Her feminine sex throbbed.

She moaned.

He ended her kiss with the same decisive movement that had started it. Pulling back, he studied her flushed, breathless face. Analyzing his attack. Learning how to stalk her and pounce.

Her big, strong warrior filled her with the wonder of new experiences. She'd long ago felt like she knew everything about love. But his single-minded kiss said she'd forgotten the most important part.

Honesty.

She caught her breath. "What was that?"

"That was a kiss."

She wiped her mouth and grinned. Her body throbbed for more. "That's right, baby."

"Baby? I am no young fry."

"Huh? Oh. I meant — never mind."

"But—"

"What I'd really like," she snuggled in close and tilted up her chin, "is one more of those delicious kisses."

His confusion cleared to dark-eyed hunger.

He slid both arms around her. "Yes, my Sid-nee."

She melted into his powerful embrace and closed her eyes—

Bam!

The door to the guest bedroom slammed.

Sydney startled and peeked over Xalu's broad shoulder.

Jen rested her back against the door. She looked upset.

Xalu's arms loosened.

Sydney stepped out of his embrace — sadly — and prepared to support her friend.

He drew himself up. "I will announce our union."

Huh? Oh!

"No." She tugged him back. "I'll do it."

"Now?" Xalu pushed.

"Jen just broke up with a jerk. She's in a delicate place right now."

He studied her warily.

"I'll handle it."

"Xalu." Jen strode around the pool toward them. "Dosan's awake."

His expression showed his concern. Then, he tore his gaze from Sydney and turned to Jen. "Dosan wakes?"

"He is awake. Go sit with him."

He strode to the guest bedroom.

Sydney lifted her glass to her lips on a reflex. Oh, it was empty. And she really needed to clear her head. "That's right. Good riddance."

Jen turned back to face her. "I'm sorry. I didn't think about how you or Ian would feel having foreign men invade our vacation."

"Hmm? Oh, I wasn't talking about ... You know what?" Sydney threw her arm around Jen's shoulders. "Let's get a cup of coffee and chat."

"Coffee? You?"

"I've got something to talk about."

She led Jen to the kitchen.

Her insides were dancing. The taste of Xalu's lips lingered on her tongue.

She set out the drink ingredients while she thought about how to broach the subject. Jen collapsed in the kitchen chair and closed her eyes. She looked exhausted.

"Interesting coffee," Jen commented dryly.

"What? Oh, my god." Sydney had accidentally gotten out the blender, ice, vodka, and mix. Was she blacking out now? She tossed them in the sink and got out the French press. "Guess I really need this."

She spooned coffee into the press while water boiled.

"What did you want to tell me?" Jen asked.

"Huh? Oh..."

Jen stared at the darkening brew. A classic purple beach dress clothed her voluptuous figure and complimented her crinkly black hair. But it couldn't disguise the worry wrinkling her face or the dark shadows under her eyes.

Sydney imagined telling her the amazing news. Jen would try to smile. Her honest, happy wishes for Sydney would be given right next to the depressing darkness of her own wrecked engagement.

And it was partly Sydney's fault.

"I haven't been a very good friend to you, have I?"

Jen lifted her head in surprise.

"All I've done on this whole vacation is hide in my room and drink."

A tired smile curved Jen's lips and one shoulder shrugged. "I understand."

"Well, that changes now." Starting with the coffee. "How are you?"

"Me?"

"This is your 'reinvention' vacation and I'm here to support you. So, how are you doing with relaxing and everything?"

Jen rested her elbows on the table. "Dosan kissed me."

"He did!" Well, that made everything so much easier. She took a deep breath to make her happy announcement.

Jen cut her off. "But it's not happening again."

Oh. "That bad, huh?"

"It wasn't bad." The defensive look on Jen's face faded into a starry memory. "It was dreamy. Hot. Delicious."

That's how Sydney had remembered her own kiss minutes ago. "Yeah."

Jen shook herself. "And never happening again."

Hmm.

Sydney poured the coffee and carried the mugs to the table. "Why not?"

"Because I'm supposed to be redefining myself. And I can't redefine myself if 'me' is a couple."

"Oh. I see."

"Plus it's a little fast, don't you think?"

Faster than Sydney accepting a male's proposal minutes after meeting him? But she got it. She'd kicked out the Loser months ago. Jen had left her loser days ago.

Still.

She pointed at Jen's chest. "You do not have to mourn Gary. Sister Sydney absolves you."

"I'm not mourning Gary. I'm mourning the person I was when I was with him. The naïve, hopeful idiot who missed he was a jerk and thought we'd be happily married by now."

Sydney folded her hands around her mug. "Okay, then. We'll mourn her. And then, Jen, you deserve delicious hot kisses in your life, so we'll do something to make sure you can kiss fearlessly."

"Something?"

"You like checklists. We'll make a checklist. You evaluate your warrior. That way you fall in love with someone who treasures you."

Jen nodded uncertainly.

But this was perfect! Sydney tried to contain her excitement. If Jen ended up with Dosan and she ended up with Xalu, then they'd be neighbors *and* queens.

Jen yawned.

"Be gentle with yourself," Sydney ordered. "Take a long shower. Get a good night's sleep. We'll tackle this in the morning. You'll be a whole new you."

Jen headed to her room.

The pool and courtyard were quiet. Empty.

Sydney decided to take her own advice. She lay in bed with the Sea Opal on her chest. Heavy.

This was quite the engagement ring.

Yes! She was engaged!

Sydney hugged the gem and giggled.

She woke at her usual time to the delicious smell of breakfast cooking — sausage, omelets, coffee, and toast — and took a pleasant shower in the guest room bath. Selecting her most sensuous Balencia suit, she styled her dyed henna-and-black hair in a bun with dangling gold clips and slipped on open-toed flats.

Not bad.

She pocketed her massive engagement gemstone, made a kiss at her reflection and, humming, exited her room in search of Xalu.

Sydney did not have to search far.

His dark head emerged above the tile of the guest pool.

"Hey!" Sydney waved and swung her hips. "Good mor—"

The huge male rested his knee on the tile and hauled himself out of the attractive blue liquid. He stood in her path.

"—ning." She swallowed. "Uh…"

Droplets shimmered on his smoky chest tattoos and dripped from his hair. The narrow black Speedo left nothing to the imagination as it hugged his ripped waist. Deep divots of a toned male tantalized her senses and an irresistible scent like rum and leather made her want to bury her nose in his midsection and just breathe in those abs.

The male's fiery gaze burned on Sydney with intensity. "Good morning, my Sid-nee."

"Sydney." She touched her hair ensuring nothing was out of place. "You're a sight to wake up to. How long have you been out here? I would have come out faster."

"Some time." He took her hands in his cool, damp palms. "We must go now to the beach. You will drink the transformation elixir. We will descend to my city and marry."

His words thrilled her. This was what she had wanted for so long. And he just asked! No waiting!

But ... well, she'd waited a decade to become engaged. She could enjoy being a fiancée for more than a day. Right?

She squeezed his fingers. "Give me a little more time."

He frowned. "You are not ready?"

"I'm ready."

"Why must we wait?"

"Because ... because I can't announce my engagement in the middle of someone else's broken honeymoon. It's just selfish."

"Jen is the destined bride of Dosan."

Sydney leaped to her friend's defense. "Jen just went through a huge breakup. This was supposed to be her honeymoon — to someone else. It wouldn't be right to overshadow her recovery with our happiness."

He didn't understand. "Her own happiness will increase when she embraces her resonance with Dosan."

"The heart has its own pace. All right?"

He shook his head. It was not "all right."

She linked their elbows and drew him toward the kitchen. "I'll try to help. I'll ask questions and you make undersea life look good. Then Jen will imagine what she has to look forward to and she'll get more excited about the future than the past. It's a great plan."

In the kitchen, Jen and Dosan glared at each other with tension so taut they snapped apart when Sydney entered. Jen wheeled to the stove and began scraping up an omelet. Dosan stared at her back, smoldering.

Sydney surreptitiously patted Xalu's arm and took a seat. "Wow, that smells delicious. Fresh coffee, crunchy toast slathered in warm butter and sweet jam."

"And a spicy omelet with chorizo." Jen's voice was higher pitched.

"I don't suppose you have all this underwater." She turned the question on Xalu.

"We do not have this," he confirmed.

The kitchen fell silent.

"But ... you have other food that's equally delicious," she pushed.

"It depends on your taste."

"Yeah, but ... what food do you like best?"

"I do not prefer any food. All food is nourishment."

She was going to strangle him. "How about you Dosan?"

The sapphire warrior did not remove his gaze from Jen. "A warrior always provides nourishment for his bride."

"How appetizing," she said flatly and nodded at Ian as he collapsed into an empty seat.

"It is very filling for the appetite," Xalu agreed, throwing back his shoulders in pride.

Her heart tingled. He really *was* trying to help. But he was honest and fair to a fault.

At least he was trying.

The other topics she tried to raise went about as well. There were no beds or furniture under the water, everyone swam naked so there were no designers, no hair styles, no makeup.

Jen served her yummy home-cooked breakfast flavored with Portuguese and Azorean spices. Everything Jen touched was logically organized and well-managed. She was brilliant with management. Sydney had wanted to steal her away to manage the daycare but Jen always refused, partly because of the pay cut, and partly because handling the emotions of their young charges — especially anger or frustration — was her weakness.

That was how the jerks she met controlled her. They threatened to throw a fit and she caved.

It was good to see her stand up to Dosan now.

Even though it was inconvenient.

"And so..." Sydney cast her mind for a new topic. "Would Jen stay home and take care of the kids all day while you go out hunting and exploring? Or do you stay home drinking underwater beer and Jen does everything?"

"What is 'underwater beer'?" Xalu asked.

"Something I just made up." Sydney scooped jam onto her third piece of crunchy toast. "I'm trying to ask what women 'brides' do underseas."

"You decide." Dosan addressed his answer to Jen. "Dragao Azul's queen does not stay in our city. So, if you will stay, then your choices will determine the roles of future queens."

Jen's anger softened.

She *loved* management. She'd be a perfect queen.

"You want Jen to be royalty?" Ian asked, speaking up for the first time, around a mouthful of egg.

Dosan nodded. "She must use her nurturing powers to rebuild our civilization."

Ian raised a brow at Jen and half-grinned. "No pressure or anything."

So, now Ian was on their side.

After breakfast, they settled around the courtyard. Dosan rehabilitated in the pool with Xalu.

Sydney spent the whole day with Jen painting nails, exchanging opinions about new designers, drinking virgin margaritas that Jen made because Sydney was not to be trusted, and *not* bringing up that Xalu had proposed and kissed her.

"This day has been so much fun," Jen said, sighing in her lounge chair as the afternoon faded into evening. "It's like going back in the past a decade before we got bogged down with jerks and losers. You're on fire, Sydney. Being single suits you."

Being single.

Luckily at this exact moment, Xalu and Dosan were both beneath the waves. "Yeah ... about that..."

Jen turned away from her to watch them swim across the pool, lap after lap, never arising to take a breath.

Sydney rubbed the smooth Sea Opal in her pocket.

An entire undersea city was waiting for a queen. Waiting for Sydney and Jen.

Sydney just had to tell her.

She took a breath. "Um, Jen, I—"

Jen rose and carried her iced drink to the side of the pool. Dosan surfaced. She offered him the virgin juice.

He rested his elbows on the tile. As they talked quietly, both couldn't take their eyes off each other.

The difference in this romance was that Dosan listened to every word she said and treasured them like gold pearls. He was enraptured with Jen and she, for once, had the good sense to be interested back.

If he had half a chance, Dosan would spear her a great big fish, leave it at her doorstep like the proudest catfish — dogfish? — and pant for her praise before he swam out and speared her another.

Nothing like the big lunk bobbing in the pool, every movement exact and precise and deadly. He stared at Sydney with the intensity of a hunter. Xalu wouldn't hunt her a giant fish. He would hunt *her*. And when he caught her...

She shivered.

His lips, his teeth, his intensity promised a night she would never forget.

Not that she was putting off his catch because of herself. No way. Sydney was here for Jen. Totally Jen.

Xalu's gaze nailed Sydney.

She looked away.

Mer warrior Uvim and his bride, newly minted mermaid Milly, stopped by in the afternoon.

Uvim was as hunky as Dosan and Xalu. He was their superior officer and he had a steely silence that commanded their respect. Amethyst tattoos ran in geometric designs like fractures across his olive-colored skin.

The trio of warriors had private guy-talk while Milly visited with the humans.

"The police traced the dynamite — in fake-looking 'Merman Repellent' packages — to the tourist stalls," Milly updated them. "They came in with regular shipments of T-shirts and postcards. So our criminal either broke into the shipments after they arrived, or he tricked a government official not to inspect the contents."

"So it's possible the culprit isn't even in the islands," Jen said.

"That's right."

"I have a question." Sydney raised her hand. "It's about being a mermaid."

"Go for it," Milly said.

"You're a queen, right?"

The younger woman hesitated. "I will be after everything's finalized in Dragao Azul."

"But you can transform."

"I drank the elixir," she confirmed.

"You don't get scared going into the water?" Sydney asked. "Knowing there could be sharks, or now, dynamite?"

"It's who I am." Milly pressed her palm to her chest. "I've always been a diver. Being underwater is so freeing. I'd do it even if it weren't my job. Now I have the power to transform into a mermaid, it's even better."

Jen took over, just as curious as Sydney about the perspective of an experienced woman. "But how did you know getting engaged was right for you? How did you know Uvim wasn't taking advantage of your generosity?"

Sydney made a silent "Yes!" to herself.

Milly laughed. "I'm not that generous."

"I'm not that generous." The young guide laughed.

Uvim's gaze moved to her. Silent communication passed between them.

Milly faded to a soft smile. "I fought my feelings but, in the end, I had to admit the truth. The heart always knows."

The heart always knows? Ha.

Milly was at least a decade younger than them. Studying marine biology in college led to the diving tours. She'd only recently gotten engaged to warrior Uvim.

"Oh, I think your heart can give you the runaround." Sydney sipped her icy virgin drink. "A decade of running around, stuck on the same, stupid guy, refusing to admit defeat."

"That sounds like your head substituting fear for loneliness," Milly disagreed, showing her young idealism. "Stop running and listen."

Milly was too young. She didn't know how *shallow* the dating pool was after college. Sydney felt inclined to give her a swim lesson.

Jen read her mind and gave her a quelling look. No need to frighten the kid.

"Yeah, well." Sydney tried to pacify Jen. "You're not wrong. Most likely."

But Jen and Dosan still seemed no closer to resolving their issues that night. They went to bed separately.

Sydney rested on the lounge chair by the pool while Xalu swam beneath the surface. The courtyard gleamed with subtle lights in the sconces.

Xalu emerged from the pool and rested his elbows on the tile near her feet. The shadows sharpened his features. He looked magnificent, a warrior of the gods. "Come into the water."

"Now?"

"You asked many questions today," he stated. "I will show you how you will be safe when we enter the water together."

"That was for Jen's benefit." She took off her suit to reveal her two-piece black and gold tankini.

He admired it, his gaze roving over her curves as she approached the edge of the pool. She sat on the tile and dangled her legs into the warm water. "I'm not afraid of water."

He spanned her waist with his powerful hands and lifted her effortlessly.

She squeaked.

His embrace tightened. She slid down his front to her armpits in the water and hugged his rippling shoulders. The pump of muscle seduced her. Her toes dangled above the bottom of the pool.

He had her totally in his control and she liked it. "Now what?"

"We swim." He slid back and floated her to the shallower end and reversed. "You feel safe?"

The warm water rushed over her in a soothing, relaxing massage. But his thick guns flexed as he held her in a way that made her crave danger.

"I wouldn't call it 'safe,'" she teased.

He stopped mid-way across the pool, worry darkening his dominant brow. "You feel danger?"

"Only for my vow of chastity."

"You have sworn a vow of chastity?"

Their chests touched. Her breasts brushed against his pectorals. Her nipples tightened.

An answering tightness clenched her channel.

She sucked in a breath. "No."

"I do not understand."

"A most decided no. I was teasing you, Xalu. But if I'm honest..." She spread her fingers across his broad pectorals and squeezed. Iron. He rumbled low in his chest. She explored the tight abdomen, his taut belly button, and skirted the flat edge of his Speedos. "...I'd like to tease you in a different way."

His chest rose and fell. His dark brows dominated his face. "You wish for pleasure."

"A little." She grazed his ear and nibbled on the rough jaw.

He captured her lips, dominating her mouth with his tongue. Her pussy throbbed and her channel turned wet and slippery anticipating his possession. She cupped the Speedo containing his erect cock.

He pulled back. A new expression charged his determination. "You do want me."

She licked a drop of moisture from his pectoral. "Could I make it any more clear?"

"Then, my bride, you will receive me."

He disappeared beneath the water. His hands caressed her thighs, her calves, her feet, and then cupped her buttocks.

Her cheeks tingled.

He kneaded her buttocks. The tingles coalesced into heat waves assaulting her with hunger for more. His fingers hooked the bowties of her tankini bottoms.

The Loser hadn't been able to see it but Sydney was desirable. Not only for marriage but for having children, for building a life. And for delicious, hot sex.

Xalu worshiped her.

She rested her elbows on the smooth tile and opened to him.

He pulled the strings, releasing her bottoms. Warm liquid caressed her nethers. It felt exhilarating, freeing.

She sucked in a deep breath.

He rested the backs of her thighs on his ripcord-strong shoulders.

Pool waves obscured her view but what she saw drove her desire hotter.

Xalu's wavery, dark head bobbed near her slick femininity. His lips touched hers. A hot, sweet kiss.

Pleasure shot to her core. Her pussy throbbed with heat.

He was what she'd wanted. What she'd craved. She surrendered herself to Xalu.

His mouth latched onto her bud and sucked. Waves of sweet, hot aches filled her belly. She bit her lip to muffle her satisfied moans.

He kneaded her buttocks, caressing her on two fronts. Dividing and conquering. Her heart thudded faster. Pleasure waves crested higher.

Xalu pleasured her with single-minded focus. Her orgasm was his prey and he hunted it ferociously.

He slid a finger into her channel and stroked her needy center.

Her pussy clenched on his finger. Her orgasm rippled across her body like a bomb thrown into a pond. She bucked and released.

It felt amazing.

A sudden, uncontrollable wave of tears burned the back of her eyes. She sniffed and wiped her eyes. Tender feelings gushed out.

She'd thought she'd never feel this closeness with another male. She'd thought she'd always be alone. She'd thought she'd wasted all of her time and youth and energy, and she'd end up a bitter, hollow shell preserved in alcohol.

Xalu had changed her.

He lifted his head, still under water, and looked up to meet her gaze. Two people from two different worlds, their gazes united and fractured and united once more.

The outlines of his feet were longer and wider, shifted into the scuba diver style of mer fins. Someday soon she would be able to shift like that as well.

He surfaced. Water cascaded off his gorgeous, dark hair and sharp features. His gaze nailed her. "You are mine."

Wordlessly, she nodded and swallowed.

"We go tomorrow to the beach. You will drink the elixir."

Everything would change.

A pang of fear wormed coldness into her heart.

She glanced down in the water. "Where are my bottoms?"

"Do not fear." He focused on her unvoiced doubt. "I will protect you until you are fully transformed."

"I know. Hey, where did my bottoms end up at?"

He collected the submerged swim bottoms and handed her the fabric. "You resist."

"No, I'm thrilled about it. I was just thinking I can't wait to transform."

"But?"

"It's complicated." She focused on tying the knots at her waist. "I still haven't told Jen."

His silence seemed to get more intent.

"I will," she promised, for the umpteenth time. Her fingers fumbled the second knot. She started over, tightening the fabric to modesty. "I need to approach it the right way."

"Why?"

"Because she's my friend, and—"

"Why do you delay in conveying this information?"

"I told you, it's—"

"Do you not wish to become my bride?"

"I do. I do, it's just..." She swallowed, hurt, but unable to dismiss him. "This vacation wasn't the only time I was a jerk. No, I was a jerk to Jen over her whole engagement."

He waited for her explanation.

"I was bitter," she confessed. "So bitter. Jen met this guy, and they got engaged right away. I was still waiting on a loser who'd hinted at marriage a decade ago. It wasn't her fault, but I couldn't stand to see her happy for something I wanted so badly, so intensely, I could barely breathe. I'd waited a decade! And she had it handed to her after a few weeks."

"She is not married now," he intoned.

"I know, and if I'd been there like a good friend, she might have not-married him a lot sooner — on her terms. My withdrawal basically drove them together."

"Now you intend to drive her to Dosan."

"I'm really, really trying not to."

"You dislike Dosan?"

"My worst nightmare is causing her more trauma." She wiped splashes off her cheeks. "I want her to marry Dosan because then we can double date, share childcare, you name it. But I need to focus on what Jen wants. Not what I want."

"You must live your life, Sydney. You must prioritize us."

Bitter anger flared.

"That's so easy for you to say, isn't it?" She stomped up the ladder and wrapped her towel around her body. "You have no idea what it's like when dreams die. How easy it is to give up on everything. Become fat, miserable, and hate humanity. You don't know. But I know."

"I do know."

She paused. "You do?"

"All warriors of the city compete for the honor to surface and meet their brides. After many years of waiting, finally, it was my time. I surfaced. My bride was not there. She had not come. I despaired. This meant I would never have a bride."

"You have me," she said softly.

"The fact that I am speaking to you now is a miracle." He stood in the middle of the pool, half in and half out of the water. Solemn. "The rules of the city changed at the end of a war. My Life Tree flower bloomed a second time. Once more, I journeyed to the surface and found 'my' bride had already joined with another. Once more, I despaired.

"But you, my Sydney, you are my miracle. My final chance. My true bride. And my grief at not finding you earlier is more tolerable.

"Those early nights were dark, painful. Believing I, alone, would never find a bride."

She left her towel on the lounge chair and descended into the water. His gaze followed her. She hugged him, stroking his taut shoulders and caressing his back. "I'm sorry."

"I am not. Because we are here." He stroked her downy hair. "You are my bride."

"I'll tell Jen tomorrow," she promised. "I mean it this time. And then we can go and drink the elixir and move to your city for the official wedding and we'll be together forever. I promise."

The worry lines etched into his mouth and eyes smoothed. "Thank you, my Sydney."

"Yeah. Hey, you can say my name right!"

"Sid-nee."

"Never mind."

He looked confused but let it go.

And then she slept separately because Jen was the early riser. Penance! If she'd only told Jen about her new relationship already, then she and Xalu could laze in bed until the afternoon. And wouldn't that be nice?

So it was a shock when Sydney got up early, determined to tell Jen the truth, and headed into the kitchen and found it … empty.

She sat at the kitchen table and rested her Sea Opal in the center. Brilliant. Beautiful.

The emptiness allowed her to reflect.

On Xalu.

On Jen.

On herself.

All of Jen's phone calls she'd refused, girls' nights she'd blown off, and other ways she'd disconnected with Jen during her long engagement to Gary. Xalu had once been devastated by losing what he thought was his chance at love. Now, Jen was heartbroken and it was Sydney's fault. She—

Jen wandered into kitchen yawning. "You're up early. Did you start coffee?"

Sydney yanked the gemstone off the table and hid it in her pocket. "Huh? Oh. Sure." She filled the kettle and then the French press. Her heart raced as if she'd already drunk ten pots. "So, uh, did you make your checklist yet?"

"Argh. No." She rested her head in her hands. "I'm so over men."

"Good thing Dosan's not a 'man,'" she joked, jittery.

"Males." Her lips twisted and she sighed. "How can I focus on judging his words or his character if he's walking around like a sex advertisement? It should be illegal to be that hot."

"Then, uh, let's go shopping."

Jen lifted her head. "Shopping?"

Yes! There was nothing Jen loved more than taking care of her loved ones. "You're right. He can't prance around in a Speedo all day. Let's go. Right now."

"Now? But the coffee—"

"It'll be here when we get back." She took a deep breath and let it out. "I've got something to tell you."

That clearly intrigued Jen enough that they borrowed Ian's rental car and parked on the main drag for clothes shopping therapy.

And then she lost her nerve.

There was never the right time. She opened her mouth and Jen saw some adorable shirt in a shop so they stopped in. Then she was going to say something and the sales clerk interrupted them. And then a British tourist asked for directions. Jen didn't like to be interrupted when she was driving. And when they got back to the rental, the warriors were pacing outside the house, their tattoos and tridents visible from the street.

Jen drove through the electronic gate, which closed behind her, and parked the Fiesta. They both exited.

"Where did you go?" Xalu demanded of Sydney.

She stroked his forearm, forcing herself not to hug him or draw him into a sensuous welcome kiss. Distract! Distract. "Wait until you see what I bought you! You're going to flip."

"Flip? Why would I perform a flip?"

"Oh, you'll see. Here." She opened the shopping bags and lofted shirts against his chest

"Human clothing?"

Beside them, Dosan drew a resisting Jen into his arms. "I must protect you. Never leave my side."

"I got you clothes," she said, breathless. "So you can go out in public."

"I do not need these things if it puts you in danger."

It was a romantic sentiment, but it came at the wrong time.

Jen hardened.

And then they fought. Quietly but distinctly.

"I'm sorry trying to do something nice for you turned into an issue," Jen snapped. "I'll let you go nude next time."

Dosan tried to appease her with them being soul mates, but she wouldn't have that, either.

"I refuse to rush into a rebound relationship," she insisted, catching her breath on a sob. "And we will never be happy if you don't appreciate who I am and respect my needs."

"Jen."

"Now, I got you some clothes. Here." She thumped the bag at him and raced away.

He stormed after her, the bags forgotten.

Sydney picked them up with a sigh.

"You did not tell her," Xalu realized softly.

"I will." But the words were beginning to sound hollow even in her own mouth. She reassured the both of them. "We'll have a girls' day. I'll tell her before we get back."

Xalu's mouth formed a thin line.

Ian came out of the rental holding the phone for Sydney. "It's Milly."

Sydney dropped Jen's shopping bags and took the phone. She was making a statement. For Xalu.

For her.

"Hi, Milly? This is Sydney. Xalu proposed, and I accepted. We're getting married."

Xalu sharpened on her.

Ian's eyes widened.

"C-congratulations," the young mermaid guide stuttered. "Wow. Just like that! I'm so glad."

"And Dosan's declared his intentions to Jen, but she's in a bad place right now and not ready for a relationship."

"I think I remember something about a broken engagement."

"Right, so, please keep my engagement to yourselves," she emphasized, for both Milly and Ian, "until I can tell her myself."

"Sure," Milly said.

Ian made the zipped-lips gesture. Which he immediately broke when he patted Xalu. "Sydney's like my second sister. Take good care of her."

"She is my future queen," he replied.

Over the phone, Milly grew pensive. "Is there anything I can share that would help?"

"Not for me right now. Let me see if Jen has any questions." Sydney whirled through the rental until she found Jen in her bedroom. Whispering, she reminded Milly, "Not a word."

"Nope."

She pushed open the door. Jen lay in the center of the honeymoon suite king bed. Empty chocolate wrappers spread around her and little smears marked the sheets.

Jen covered her face. "What do you want?"

"About the mermen." Sydney sucked in a breath, knew she couldn't tell Jen right now, and forged ahead. "Milly's on the phone. She wanted to ask if you have any questions about the 'cultural differences' we might have."

"These are more than cultural differences."

"I know. So why don't you talk to her?"

Jen frowned. She didn't have a huge circle of friends. Expanding to take in the young guide was also out of character for her. And it made Sydney feel even more guilty for pushing Jen away at the critical time.

"And after you chat with Milly, you'll relax. We'll do the spa day we promised. Right? Take care of you, treasure you."

"I could use a little treasuring." Jen sniffed.

Of course. "You deserve it."

Jen took the phone. She turned away and her voice muffled as she tentatively revealed things she'd never normally talk about with strangers.

After their conversation, Jen seemed more resolute. They prepared for a spa day. The males were going to the beach for Xalu to acquire Sydney's elixir; he'd apparently stashed it in a submerged cave and had to retrieve it. He clearly intended to be ready for her the instant she and Jen returned from their spa trip.

No pressure.

Dosan smoldered silently in the front seat. Sydney sat in the middle, pressed between Jen and Xalu.

This whole time, she'd chosen Jen. She was still choosing Jen.

But depending on what happened at the spa, on the way home she was most likely going to be prioritizing Xalu.

Ian let them off at the hotel day spa.

Xalu held her gaze from the depths of the car. "I will be waiting."

She wanted to kiss him and she did not. There would be a chance to clear up all the misunderstandings later. In private.

Sydney swallowed. "See you tonight."

His gaze focused on her like a laser of heat.

Tonight would be more than just the confession. She knew, in her heart, that drinking the elixir would be the moment they consummated their love.

Everything would change.

Sydney fingered her empty pocket. She'd left the extremely expensive Sea Opal in her room rather than trust it to a hotel locker. But it made her feel bereft. After she married Xalu, would she still be able to carry it around? Or would she be an old married woman who wouldn't care?

Funny how she'd focused the last decade on becoming a fiancée and spent none of the time imagining what married life would be like...

Sydney stepped back from the window, honoring his promise, and watched the rental Ford Fiesta sedan disappear.

The day spa was a professional European establishment

that knew their Swedish massage from their Thai and their plucking from their shaping. Jen wanted a facial so they ended up on different tracks and her pedicurist was double-booked so Sydney actually finished late. Jen was ahead of her waiting at the restaurant for dinner.

And she'd already gotten into the wine.

Sydney allowed her tightly wound friend to decompress in a way she'd not done this whole vacation. Ian was right. Jen couldn't relax.

Now, Jen let her crinkly black hair all down.

"Have another glass," Jen insisted, pushing the bottle on her friend during a break in the conversation.

"I really shouldn't." But Sydney poured. "Did you know I was numbing myself with alcohol for like a year?"

"Five years." Jen's smile wavered with uncried tears. "I missed you."

Tears bubbled up in Sydney's eyes. How could she be so selfish to interrupt Jen's healing process now? She was going to do it before she got back to the rental — she'd promised herself and Xalu — and knowing that made her guilt triple. "Well, I'm back now. And I'm here to support you. Or at least support your choice of ordering dessert."

"You've been a great support." Jen ordered a chocolate lava cake to share.

Afterward, she reached into her purse to call the guys for a pickup. "I haven't had this much fun in years. Or this much wine."

"Let's not interrupt what might be their dinner." Sydney covered Jen's phone to stop her from dialing. "Let's walk."

"I am *not* walking. I'll get arrested."

"You're not that drunk." But then again, she wasn't so sure. They caught a cab.

And she didn't want to talk in front of the driver, so...

Nerves screamed like over-tired toddlers in her ears. Sydney sucked in a deep breath and let it out. The sun was just starting to set.

The cab let them out across the street.

Jen muttered something to herself about diving.

Sydney faced the artful stucco-white Azores rental house. On the other side of the gate, Ian's rental sedan rested in the driveway.

Now.

"Jen."

Her distracted friend turned.

Sydney hesitated. "There's something I was supposed to say."

"Oh?"

"Yeah. Uh, well, the thing is..."

Growl-chunk-clunk.

Sydney jumped. A clunker van started up down the street. She and Jen both stared at it because it was so loud.

And Sydney was too eager for any delay and hated herself for that.

The van rolled down the street.

Sydney backed against the neighboring house to let it pass, but it slowed. The driver was some lanky college kid who stared at her with unfriendliness.

On the other side, the passenger rolled down the window and asked a muffled question to Jen.

"That's us." Jen hugged her purse.

A low warning pinged in Sydney's chest.

Something about the driver. The van. Everything.

Even though they were standing in front of their rental, a hundred feet from the deadly warriors, the pressure seemed to drop and the street had never looked so isolated.

She needed to get Jen out of here. Now.

Sydney walked around the back of the van because … well, because honestly, she thought the driver might try to run her over if she walked in front — and saw Jen standing way too close to the open window. In the passenger's seat was a cocky young college-aged kid in a stained, sleeveless surfer shirt.

"My friend has a question," the surfer kid said. He was American like them — weird — and sounded vaguely Californian.

The back passenger door opened. Another college-aged kid — this one with wonky teeth and uneven glasses — spread out a street map of the Azores.

Sydney hurried up to Jen to grab her. They had to leave.

Jen stumbled back. "Oh, we're not from around here."

She knocked into Sydney.

Sydney wobbled on the uneven cobblestone.

"That's okay." The surfer kid's door opened and closed. He stood behind Sydney. His voice darkened. "You can both answer this question."

The glasses kid lunged and grabbed Jen.

"What? Hey!"

The surfer shoved Sydney. *Wham.* She fell on one knee, bruising it.

Jen's legs flailed in the van. She shrieked.

Sydney shoved to her feet. Run—

Smack.

She fell into the van on top of Jen. They struggled. The kid grabbed her legs and threw her inside. She hit her thigh.

The door slammed shut, and then the passenger's door. "Go! Go!"

The engine clunked. Jen's elbows jammed into Sydney's gut and boob. The van careened down the street, throwing them against the wall. Her crown smacked into the metal door.

Shock and pain made it hard to think straight.

Jen sounded panicked. "What are you doing?"

"Isn't it obvious?" Surfer kid. "We're kidnapping you."

Kidnapping?

What?

The van parked. The kids manhandled them, dragging Sydney and Jen into an abandoned warehouse. The impenetrable metal doors closed them in with a final warning.

This was not good.

But what could the kids want? They weren't rich. Well, assuming they didn't know about Sydney's Sea Opal. And the Azores weren't poor.

The kids dragged her across the warehouse floor to their office. Stacks of boxes were all marked with a vaguely familiar triangle symbol...

They were forced inside and made to sit on a ratty old couch.

"What do you want with us?" Jen demanded,

The surfer kid opened a mini fridge, got out a soda and poured a plastic bag of white powder inside. He turned and offered the soda to them. "Want a drink?"

Jen seemed to consider it.

What the heck?

"No, thank you," Sydney said loudly.

Jen licked her lips like she was going to ask.

Sydney kicked the soda over. It glugged out on the floor. The surfer kid looked surprised and then irritated.

"Hey," Jen protested. "Don't make it worse."

"I can't make it worse." Sydney nudged her and pointed at boxes. She lowered her voice. "That's the symbol of the bad guy."

"Oh, you saw our symbol." The surfer kid sighed and pulled out a gun. "Now we have to kill you."

Okay.

Things were officially worse.

"Not so fast," Jen said. "We didn't answer your 'question' yet."

Amazingly, the kid lowered his gun. "We don't want anything to do with you. We just want to know about the creatures."

Two other lanky, unwashed kids hemmed them in.

Sydney grabbed Jen. "We'll tell you whatever you want. Nobody touches us."

"Deal."

Except the kid, after making them kneel in front of the couch, had the glasses kid come in and wrap duct tape around their ankles and wrists.

"You said nobody touches us!" Sydney shouted as they yanked her arms behind her back.

"I'm not touching you," the glasses kid whined, demonstrating the level of maturity she often saw in her younger day care charges. "The duct tape is."

Good lord.

Sydney huffed. "Does your mother know where you are?"

"I don't have one," he sneered. Not like he was an orphan, but like he was at college and she couldn't tell him what to do anymore.

The kids backed off and left them in the lit office all alone.

So ... they'd been kidnapped for what? Were they lying that they wanted to know about the warriors? Had the kids just forgotten to ask any questions? Or were they real idiots?

"That, I believe," Sydney muttered.

"This is the last time I let you and Ian talk me into a personal day." Jen sighed. "What's wrong with being a workaholic? Nobody was threatening to shoot me back in Atlanta."

Sydney snorted. "We're about to die and that's what you have to say?"

"Shhh. They're saying something."

"What about the women?" one of them asked. "We kidnapped them like you asked, doofus. Now what?"

"You're the doofus."

"No, you are."

"Look," the more clear-headed surfer guy said, "we can't just let them go."

"Yes!" Sydney shouted, unable to contain herself. "Yes, you can! Let us go and we'll forget everything! I swear!"

The kids swore and moved away from the window.

"This is your last warning!"

Muffled voices resumed farther away.

Ah, jeez.

"And I told Dosan I didn't need to be protected," Jen sighed. "Apparently when dating otherworldly creatures, otherworldly rules apply. Not that we're dating. Because we're not. Like I said before."

Okay, well, if they were going to die then Sydney was going to die with a clear conscious. "Jen."

"I'm so sorry that I forced you to share your vacation with warriors," she babbled. "Ian was right. I can't relax. And now it's cost you big time."

"Listen."

"I am listening," she said, not listening. "I'm listening, and I've decided first thing when we get out of here, I'm going to tell Dosan no once and for—"

"Xalu proposed!"

Jen shut her mouth with a click. Her brows lowered in confusion.

"I said yes." Sydney braced.

"Oh." Her tone was weirdly distracted. "Congratulations."

"Yeah." She couldn't stop the justifications for the accusations that hadn't yet come. "How could I not? Think about it. We get to shape how they run an entire undersea kingdom!"

"You don't care about living deep in the ocean, far beneath the surface?"

"Oh, I am coming to the surface again. I am doing whatever I want. I'm going to be royalty, baby!"

"And Xalu's okay with it?"

"Who cares? I'm his queen! But of course he's fine with it. He wants his future wife to be happy."

Jen's mouth turned down. "So why'd you keep quiet all this time? I feel like a jerk."

Aw. Sydney's chest squeezed. Jen was really hurt by her silence. That wasn't what Sydney had intended at all.

"You were so supportive," Jen continued, "and I couldn't be trusted with finding out that my best friend was engaged?"

Sydney had been supportive? Jen was rewriting history, clearly. "No, I'm sorry. You went through so much with Gary and then you were so dead set against Dosan."

"You agreed with Ian. You said I had to reinvent myself so I wouldn't get hurt."

"I did, but you know what? We were wrong. You're just fine. The problem is them, and you *don't* have to reinvent yourself because you are already completely fabulous."

She felt like she was clutching at straws and Jen looked like she agreed.

Sydney tried to raise her hands in defense. Her shoulders slightly lifted; her hands were still taped behind her back. "It's like Milly said. She'd dive even if she wasn't a mermaid. It's who she is. Jen, you're kind to everyone. Even the people who don't deserve it. It's who you are and there's nothing wrong with it."

"I'm not going to be 'kind' to these kidnappers when we get out of here."

"Well, you're not an idiot."

"Thank you."

Sydney shook her head. "Whatever the case, you were right to demand time to work out what's best for you. If you need to time to consider Dosan's proposal, then that's what I was trying to give you. Honestly, I was afraid I'd push you in the wrong direction. How could I not get excited at the thought of ruling an undersea kingdom with my best friend?"

Jen's brows lifted. Acknowledging her point.

"But now," Sydney sucked in a huge breath and wiggled on her bruised knees, "we might not rule anything but a cemetery."

"What are you doing?"

"Trying to get a leg free so my last act can be kicking one of these idiots in the balls."

Jen laughed.

At least they still had their senses of humor.

She seemed to come out of her introspection and focus on their surroundings. "Pop the tab on that soda can. That will create a sharp edge."

Sydney awkwardly pulled the can off the table and ripped off the tab. It popped. Taking action felt good.

Jen scooted her back to Sydney's and put her palms underneath.

Sydney dropped the tab in her fingers. "You sure about this?"

"No." A subtle sawing motion tugged on Sydney's duct tape. "But we have to try."

It was such a relief to get her big secret out.

On the other hand, it really might be too late. It was angering to think that she'd held back for so long out of concern for Jen and now it was no big deal. Wasn't it more like what Xalu had said? Sydney had been afraid of changing and so she'd put him through the same thing that the Loser had put her through.

At least it hadn't taken her a decade to figure out her mistake.

There was never a perfect time. If Xalu was here, she'd confess her mistake and apologize for what she'd put him through.

There was no excuse for what those kids were putting them through.

Sydney wriggled with discomfort. "Any luck?"

"The sticky tape is gumming up the sharp edge. It's still cutting. Slowly."

Her best friend always had a plan. Sydney could sense she had one now. "Then once I'm free, then what?"

"I'll yell for those guys and you can kick them in the balls."

Now she was talking. "I like this plan."

Jen worked the tab.

Sydney strained.

"What are you doing?"

"Something. Anything. I don't want to sit around waiting on others anymore."

"Well, hold tight, because this is going to take..."

She strained again. The tape parted. Relief gushed into her aching shoulders.

"...no time at all. Great job!"

Yes! Sydney turned to Jen and grabbed the tab. "Your turn."

"Use the pen to puncture the aluminum. You can fashion a makeshift knife from the sharp edge."

Sydney fashioned the knife, cut the tape off her ankles, then freed Jen.

Jen rubbed her sticky wrists. They both had a stretch break, getting limber and preparing. Then, Jen sat again and draped the tape over her ankles and wrists. "I'll call one of the kids in here, make the call. Then, while he's distracted, you clobber him."

Sydney hid the knife under some papers, draped the tape as if she were still tied up, and nodded.

Ash trays were hard. She'd beat the first kid — who shouldn't be smoking — with the ash tray.

Jen shouted. "Hey! Give me back my cell phone and I'll call the guys to come on down here!"

Critical seconds passed.

Sydney's anger warred with her fear. She tried to swallow it down and focus.

The door rattled.

The kid with glasses poked his head into the office. "You'll call what guys?"

"The warriors. Dosan and Xalu."

He stared at her blankly.

"You want to ask us questions about them, right? We'll call them down and they can answer you."

The kid didn't get it.

They were seriously dealing with the stupidest kidnappers in the entire world.

"You don't want to talk to them?" Jen prodded. "What's your end goal here?"

"My knees are killing me," Sydney said.

"Mine too. I want everyone to be happy so we can all go home."

"We decide when you go home." The kid puffed out his chest like he wanted a beat down. "We already tried it. Your phone's broken."

"You broke it!" Jen gasped, her accusing tone not faked.

"I didn't break it. It's frozen."

"Let me see."

He shrugged and carried it to the small coffee table. Her screen glowed white.

"You're right." Jen eased back, shaken. "It's broken."

No. They were not getting derailed because the idiot kids broke Jen's phone. "Go get mine," Sydney said.

He stood.

"No!" Jen nudged her, lifting a brow and squinting weirdly. "Forget it. Change of plans."

Huh? Were they changing plans or was she still supposed to attack? They needed a secret language.

She pushed. "Jen, I actually think we should wait to hear their voices before we do anything rash."

"Why should I listen to you? You waited ten years on a guy who was never going to propose."

Whoah. Fake fighting? Sydney went with it. She raised her voice. "How dare you?"

"What I'm saying is sometimes you *just have to act.* Whether you're prepared or not. *Just act.*"

Okay, that was clear.

Her heart thudded in her throat.

"Yeah?" Her voice broke. "Fine."

The kid backed away from the table. "You guys are acting weird."

Fear slid into anger.

"What are you going to do about it?" Sydney snapped, focusing on the ash tray.

He flipped her a rude gesture that would get a note sent to his parents and turned to leave.

She jumped to her feet, scooped up the ashtray, and whacked him on the back of the head.

Ashes flew.

He stumbled and closed the door on himself.

Hand to the back of his head, he complained. "Ow."

Women's self-defense training leaped to her aid. Sydney shoved him down and put a knee in his back. He grunted.

Sydney grabbed the makeshift knife out of the papers and held it to his throat. "Freeze or I'll cut you."

He froze.

Jen also froze. She stared.

Sydney prodded her. "Jen, tape."

Jen jolted and grabbed the roll of duct tape. She wrapped it around his wrists and ankles, scolding him in a wobbly voice. "You are in big trouble, mister."

"You can't do this." He wriggled like a worm. "HEY —mph!"

Jen stuck the tape over his mouth.

He grunted.

"I warned you." Sydney pushed off his back, rolled him over to the side of the office, and cracked the office door. She peered out. To Jen, she asked the obvious. "So the guys are on the way?"

"That's right. And Ian has the number for the police."

"We just have to survive."

The surfer kid frowned in their direction.

She backed away from the door.

His frown deepened. He started toward them.

She closed the crack. "Ooh, there's that surfer kid." She backed away from the door and lifted the ashtray.

"Hey, G?" The surfer kid pushed open the door. "You oh—"

Sydney brought down the ashtray.

The surfer kid wheeled and threw up his arm.

The ashtray bounced off his forearm.

Uh oh.

Sydney whacked him again.

It hit his elbow.

"Hey!" He jumped deeper into the office, away from her, and rummaged in his pocket. She whacked his elbow again. He yelped.

He would not go down!

Her heart thumped in her throat. She'd never really hurt anyone. But this was life or death.

Sydney lifted the aluminum knife.

The kid produced the pistol.

Sydney checked. "Uh oh."

He glared at her. "That hurt." With a whine.

She swallowed. "Well, I'm not sorry."

"You're going to be. Drop that."

She dropped the knife.

"Get over against the wall. Both of you."

Jen hurried to Sydney's side.

"Ugh." He rubbed his elbow and appealed to the kid still tied up. "Why did we even kidnap them? It's obvious now we have to kill them."

The duct taped kid made a strangled sound.

This was what happened when kids didn't get love and

discipline from their parents. Too entitled. They didn't think things through.

A knock echoed through the warehouse.

It was either their leader or...

She and Jen straightened. Getting ready to counter-attack.

The surfer kid swaggered toward the doorway, then stopped. His eyes narrowed. He toyed with his gun.

Outside, the rattle of the giant warehouse doors gave way to shouts and fighting.

Yes!

He trained his gun on the door. "What did you do?"

"Nothing," Jen said, innocent.

Wham! The office door flew open.

One of the lanky kids suspended off the ground by the back of his shirt. He pointed at her and Sydney. "There! The women are there!"

Behind him loomed their warriors!

Xalu dropped the lanky kid. "Sydney!"

The kid landed on the ground with an "oof" and rolled away.

Dosan's trident gleamed with deadly intent. He and Xalu, also armed with trident and blades, advanced into the office.

The surfer kid backed against the office wall and trained his gun on two growling warriors. "Don't come any closer."

Xalu strode in front of Sydney, his gaze never leaving the kid. He protected her with his whole body. "You are unhurt?"

"Mostly."

His growl deepened.

The kid shivered.

"I told Jen," she told Xalu, sheltering behind his powerful form. "I'm sorry for making you wait."

He nodded slightly, his grip tight on his trident.

Dosan snarled at the surfer kid. "You dared to touch my bride."

The surfer kid held up the gun, shaky. "Stay back."

Dosan advanced. Clearly, he was the blindly heroic type.

"Put the gun down," Jen advised the kid.

The surfer kid shook his head.

"Now," Jen insisted. "Your threat is stupid. They're undersea warriors who don't understand guns."

"I'll shoot!"

"And even if you did shoot them, they'd still try to disarm you. And I mean 'dis-arm'. Those tridents are sharp."

The kid swallowed.

So, he was attached to his arms.

In the distance, police sirens sounded.

"It's going to be a lot harder in prison when you're missing an arm," Sydney pointed out.

The kid looked at her. His gun wavered.

Xalu growled.

"You can't shoot both," Jen pushed. "One of them is going to slice your hand off. Unless you put the gun down now."

He set the gun on the table and backed up against the wall. "Don't hurt me."

Whew.

Xalu gestured with the trident for him to exit. "Your human justice is waiting."

He crept out of the office.

After that, the police took charge. They arrested the kids, searched the warehouse. An inspector collected preliminary reports and made appointments for full statements.

Ian took them back to the rental. They split off right away. She led Xalu to her room.

This bold warrior, who risked his life to save her, deserved to know the truth.

She led him in, closed the door, and seated him on her bed. "I have a confession."

"For me?" He looked grim.

She unzipped her top. "For you."

His gaze riveted on her hands parting the fabric to reveal her seductive black bra.

"I think it's best to confess uncomfortable truths while getting naked. What do you think?"

He followed her hands teasing the zipper of her pants. A large bulge grew in a similar location on his body. "Think?"

She lowered the zipper and slid the pants over her hips, revealing matching lace panties. "I'm sorry I dragged out my confession to Jen."

"Hmm?"

She toed aside her pants and tugged her bra straps off her shoulders. "The truth is, I got comfortable thinking of myself as your fiancée and I didn't want to push to the next step. I told you I wasn't afraid, but I really was afraid of leaving the surface behind."

He fixed on her face. "You were!"

"But I know you'll protect me from any dangers."

He rose and cupped the hands at her central bra clasp, stopping her. "I will, my Sydney. I swear it."

"I believe you. You're saying my name right again, you know."

He swelled with pride. "I listened in my chest." He thumped twice. Two syllables.

"Good. Now I'll listen and you tell me what you think." She twisted the clasp. Her bra released. Her large breasts sprang free and bounced between them, her brown nipples dark against her skin.

He was always freeing her.

Xalu stared. "Beautiful."

This was one reason she'd spent extra time at the spa. It was nice of him to notice.

She unfastened his shirt. "I look good with you."

He sucked in a breath and released it in a hiss. She caressed his pectorals, allowing her voluminous breasts to brush his trembling skin.

Xalu cupped her masses in his warm palms. He buried his face in her, kissing and enjoying, and then dropped to his knees and pressed his face to her lace panties.

Her feminine lips turned slippery.

He nuzzled her. She heated and throbbed, remembering exactly what he'd done under the water, and ready to enjoy it again.

He glared up at her. Fierce. Possessive. "You are my bride."

Yes. He had caught her. She surrendered.

Sydney slipped her newly manicured fingers beneath the lace and pulled it down, stepping out of her panties. "So take me already."

He hesitated for a long moment. Huh. He wasn't going to ask her what she meant and where to take her, was he?

No.

He scooped her up under her knees, rose, and laid her out on the bed. His hands gripped his shorts and ripped them off.

His entire, gorgeous body was laid bare to her eager eyes. Her pussy throbbed. She didn't want kisses right now. She wanted a good, hard man filling her to the brim and making her lose all her inhibitions.

He answered her silent wish.

Kneeling between her thighs, his large cock nudged her pouting feminine lips.

Eagerness made her clench.

She wrapped her legs around his buttocks and drew him in.

He filled her to the hilt. Stretching with his fullness, bliss washed over her. Xalu bobbed against her pleasure spot. Sparkles tingled in her lips, in her fingertips, in her toes. He pumped in and out.

Her body accepted him, writhing up and down on the bouncing bed.

He gripped her hips, perfecting their connection, giving her the most pleasure in one single coupling than she'd had in her entire life. His grip tightened, fingers squeezing her butt cheeks.

She gasped.

Her release rocketed through her and sparkled like a firework. The orgasm shook her so hard she had to clench her teeth on her scream. Tears burned her eyelids.

And he kept pounding into her.

She rocketed into a second volley. A third. Sweat bathed her — dripped from him like he was swimming laps. He treasured her body, claimed her in the most primal way. She orgasmed for him. Her pussy clamped down on his cock, gripping him as she came.

He stiffened. His release blasted heat into her G-spot and she came a fourth and final time.

He tipped over onto the bed beside her. Wiped out.

She stroked the sweat on his brilliant, gleaming pectoral. The tattoos that had mesmerized her. They were so interesting, so unusual. She stroked the male who would become her husband.

He blinked like coming awake and traced the line of salty tears on her cheeks. "You experience sadness."

"I get emotional," she agreed.

"You cry because of my touch."

"A good cry. You were amazing." She tried to put her leg on his and failed with a groan. "I'm wrecked. I'll never sleep with another man again."

"Good. Because you are mine."

She let that sink in. His vow pressed her into the mattress with lovely weight. She could stay here, just like this, with him, for the rest of her life.

Staying here as his fiancée would be comfortable. Safe.

But then she would never grow and enjoy the next phase. That's what she'd learned.

Her long not-engagement was only partly her ex's fault. The Loser had kept her waiting a decade, and she had let him, making it comfortable to stay in their rut, letting the routine grow deeper and harder to escape as every year passed.

Now, she needed to not make the same mistake with Xalu.

She wanted the next step. Marriage. Children. Growing old together, proud of their pride. She wanted all the steps with Xalu.

She forced herself upright with a groan. "The elixir? Do you have it?"

He rose and strode to the courtyard nude, then returned with a glass of water. She closed the door again, glad Jen was busy with Dosan and Ian was ... wherever he was, probably calling his wife and kids, elsewhere.

Inside Xalu's glass nestled a small white flower about the size of a cherry blossom.

He poured just the blossom into his hand, ignoring the drips on the tile, and set the remaining glass on her nightstand. He held the blossom to her lips. "Drink the nectar, my Sydney. Entwine your heart and soul with mine."

She hovered her lips next to his fingers. "Will you swear to love and honor me so long as we both shall live?"

His voice thickened with emotion. "You have my vow."

"Then, I do." She sipped the tiny droplets of nectar clinging to the blossom. They tasted like salt and sweetness. Happy tears from her wedding day.

Now, and forever, they were soul mates.

Xalu's promise burned in his fierce eyes. He loved her. She was his bride. Soon, his wife.

The real wedding was yet to come. It would be filled with just as much happiness as this day.

Xalu set aside the blossom and pulled her into his lap, chasing the nectar with his passion-filled kiss.

His vow was true.

Formerly a bridesmaid, Sydney was now the most radiant bride.

ABOUT THE AUTHOR

USA Today bestselling author Starla Night was born on a hot July at midnight. She hikes, scuba dives, and swims naked in the ocean. She writes about smokin' hot dragons and tattooed mermen at StarlaNight.com.